£12/6/07
Aread
save for
Lydia

Praise for
DONNA ANDERS

"Anders taps the darkest terrors of the human heart."
—Edna Buchanan, Edgar Award-winning
author of *Love Kills*

"When reading an Anders book, make sure you leave the lights on."

—*Romantic Times*

"Donna Anders brings the terror . . . directly into your heart."

—John Saul, *New York Times* bestselling
author of *The Devil's Labrynth*

and her chilling novels of romance and suspense

DEATH WAITS FOR YOU

"With every chapter, the possibility of unthinkable dangers grows. . . . A masterful job. . . . Truly frightening."
—Ann Rule, *New York Times* bestselling
author of *Too Late to Say Goodbye*

"A well-balanced mix of mystery, romance, and creepy horror."

—*Seattle Times*

NIGHT STALKER

"Paranoia, fear, an⬚⬚⬚⬚⬚⬚⬚⬚⬚⬚⬚⬚⬚⬚is thriller, which show⬚⬚⬚⬚⬚⬚⬚⬚⬚⬚⬚⬚⬚⬚n cover up frightenin⬚⬚⬚⬚⬚⬚⬚⬚⬚⬚⬚⬚⬚⬚es

D0681619

Books by Donna Anders

The Flower Man

Another Life

Dead Silence

In All the Wrong Places

Night Stalker

Afraid of the Dark

Death Waits for You

Published by POCKET BOOKS

SKETCHING EVIL

DONNA ANDERS

POCKET BOOKS

New York   London   Toronto   Sydney

POCKET BOOKS
A Division of Simon & Schuster, Inc.
1230 Avenue of the Americas
New York, NY 10020

This book is a work of fiction. Names, characters, places, and incidents either are products of the author's imagination or are used fictitiously. Any resemblance to actual events or locales or persons, living or dead, is entirely coincidental.

First Pocket Books paperback edition December 2007

POCKET and colophon are registered trademarks of Simon & Schuster, Inc.

For information about special discounts for bulk purchases, please contact Simon & Schuster Special Sales at 1-800-456-6798 or business@simonandschuster.com

Cover design by Alan Dingman. Art © Shutterstock

Manufactured in the United States of America

10 9 8 7 6 5 4 3 2 1

ISBN-13: 978-1-4165-1487-9
ISBN-10:   1-4165-1487-2

For my sisters-in-law:
Nancy Crefeld and Fran Sherman on the East Coast,
and Nancy Anderson on the West Coast,
with love and thanks.

Acknowledgments

Words are inadequate to convey how grateful I am to everyone who gave so generously of their time while I was researching this book up on the Hudson River in New York State. I am especially grateful to Fran Sherman, who was my personal guide to all the historical sites, and to Nancy Crefeld, who shot all the photos. A huge thank-you goes to Mary Howell, Columbia County Historian, and to Bob Sister, who gave me a boat tour of the Hudson River. Also thanks to Esther and Jerry Allison for lending me historical photos of this beautiful part of the country.

Again, I'm thankful for my daughters, Tina Holman, Lisa Pearce, and Ruth Aeschliman, who are always there for me. Also, thanks to Ann Rule, Leslie Rule, and Mike Rule for their continued friendship.

Finally, I wish to thank Megan McKeever, my supertalented editor at Pocket Books, and my agent, Sheree Bykofsky.

Prologue

THE SOUND OF GRAVEL CRUNCHING under the tires reminded the driver of the phantom, metal-wheeled carriage that came up the driveway each spring on a moonlit night, a specter from an earlier century. It was said that family ghosts still monitored the comings and goings of their living relatives in the manor house, patiently awaiting each new heir to be born.

A true ghost story.

The driver barked out a laugh, a sound that aroused the sleeping infant who lay wrapped in a blanket on the passenger seat. The baby's cry was a sharp intrusion into the silence of the car, as though the child had not yet recognized the sacred trust of the future that now lay within the grasp of its tiny hands.

"Shush," the driver murmured. "All is well. It's fitting that the moon is full tonight, a sign that I've done the right thing."

"That you've come home."

The infant's response was to cry louder, the high-pitched sound of a terrified animal.

Soothing words only quickened the baby's fright, as though the child sensed the danger—and the tragic loss of loved ones. The driver pressed down on the accelerator, causing the vehicle to surge forward, up the final slope to the side of the immense house—the mansion on the hill above the Hudson River. The car screeched to a rocking stop, gravel flying out from under the back tires. The driver jumped out, opened the passenger door, and reached to pick up the infant.

Holding the baby, the driver comforted the child and the crying subsided into a soft animal mewing deep within its throat. Then they moved forward, past the porch pillars of the side entrance, toward the back door that in pre-Revolutionary War days had been reserved for servants. But the driver kept walking, around the access to the pull-up of the cellar cover and on to the house itself, and pressed a place behind a low fascia board.

There was a pause, then a creaking sound of movement.

The timbered platform in front of the woodpile began to slip open, revealing a crude staircase that led under the house itself. Quickly, the driver, baby in arms, went down the steps and pressed a lever at the bottom, and the opening closed. A dark tunnel loomed ahead.

A scratch of a match brought fire and the driver lifted a torch from its place on the wall and lit it. Instantly, light flooded a dirt-walled tunnel.

The secret passage into the house.

At the end of the passageway the driver climbed steps to the main floor, then rapped on the closed panel that separated the secret place from the main house.

Within seconds a door opened to a woman with

outstretched hands. A moment later the baby was in her arms.

"Thank you—thank you! You will be rewarded."

"When?" the driver asked.

"Soon. I will contact you."

"But—"

"No buts."

"You said when I delivered."

"I know." A pause while the woman fumbled to find something within her bosom. "Here," she said. "Part of what I promised."

The driver took her funds.

"It's only a third."

"I'll get the rest . . . soon."

The driver took a step forward. "But I already paid for the silence of—"

"I know."

"If you don't pay I'll tell all."

The driver was still looking at the woman when the blow to his head struck. Then everything went black.

Chapter 1

GLANCING OVER HER SHOULDER, Abby Carter quickened her pace along Fifth Avenue, aware that the man in the tan overcoat still followed her, had been behind her for the last seven blocks.

Shit! she thought. Maybe he'd been back there the whole fifteen blocks since she'd left her apartment for the early-morning walk to her job at the gallery. How would she know? Her eyes were on where she was going, not on where she'd been. But after initially spotting him she couldn't get him out of her mind: tall, scruffy, and with a mass of thick long hair that obscured his features. He was another street person who'd zeroed in on her, she decided, the third time in the past ten days.

Abby made a quick decision as she waited for the light on the next corner. She flagged down an approaching taxi, its tires squealed to a stop, and she jumped in, leaving her pursuer to stare after the cab as it sped away.

For a moment Abby took deep breaths, realizing that she'd been frightened, that the man had definitely been a threatening presence.

"Miss, where to?" The cabbie spoke with a heavy East European accent. "Uptown, downtown, crosstown?" he asked, his dark eyes meeting hers in the rearview mirror.

"Um," Abby said, momentarily too shaken to remember the gallery address. She pushed back the strand of reddish brown hair that had fallen over her face, then managed to give him the street and building number.

"That's only a few blocks away, yes?"

Abby nodded and ignored the driver's questioning glance. She knew he wondered why she'd bothered to take a taxi for such a short distance. She wasn't about to explain. Instead, she gave him a large tip after he'd pulled in to the curb, even though she was spending more than she could afford. In seconds she was safely inside the gallery. A short time later she forgot all about her random stalker as she began cataloging new art pieces into the gallery. Her fear had been transitory; it was part of living in a city. A slender young woman with long chestnut hair and matching eyes would always be the target of someone on the streets. She smiled wryly. It was just as her aunt Carolina, the woman who'd raised her, had always warned, especially after Abby had decided a few years ago to pursue her art career in New York City. "If you're beautiful you'll be the target of predatory men. You just have to be aware of that fact, Abby."

That thought vanquished Abby's last trace of fear. The incident had been random. No one had followed her for any special reason, only because she'd presented herself on the street at the wrong time—and that everyone she knew said she was beautiful.

*   *   *

Abby stared at Neville Figg, her superior. "Are you saying I'm fired?"

The rail-thin man got up from behind his desk. "Of course not—we hate to let you go but we have to because of our low-volume sales." Abby could almost smell his bad breath as he came around his desk, pushing his glasses up his nose. "The gallery is losing money and we have to cut corners."

"So I'm the one who's expendable?"

There was a silence as he made the final steps to face her. It was right after lunchtime and her summons into his office had been unexpected. She kept her gaze level, knowing that he was right about the sales volume, but she'd believed that revenue would be better once they were into the holiday season.

"We wished not, Abigail, but that is where we find ourselves—you are an asset that we can no longer afford."

"Maybe you should reconsider, Mr. Figg, because you need to employ someone like me to generate income—like I want to do online—sort of like an eBay, even an Amazon-type format, where this gallery can display its inventory."

Mr. Figg's smile was patronizing, his round eyes owlish behind his oversize glasses. "We'll consider that, Abigail, for future reference," he said, evading a direct answer.

Shit, she thought, for a moment longer staring into his opaque gaze. She'd really been let go. She was now an aspiring artist in New York City without a job—or an income to pay the rent—and winter was coming in just a couple of months.

Abby managed a smile but the fear of paying her bills in two weeks was already on the top of her priorities. She'd been saving her money, dollar by dollar, for such a contingency—losing her job—but she hadn't reckoned on the reality of its happening so soon. She didn't have enough set aside for next month's expenses, let alone the rent and the costs of pursuing the possibility of having her own art show.

Damn! she thought. Even though she'd recently started freelancing as a street portrait artist at tourist spots, she hadn't generated much extra income. She'd started at the wrong time. Tourist season was almost over: Sketching in summer attracted many subjects and a steady flow of money; sketching in the wind, rain, even snow, of fall and winter attracted no one. Plain and simple, it was the worst time of the year for her to lose her job. She had few options.

She wondered what her boyfriend Sam would say now. He was a commercial artist, a tall, blondish, wiry man whose brown eyes sometimes twinkled with humor, a man she'd met seven months earlier at a gallery opening, and she'd been impressed by his astute observations about the artists and their work. Captivated by his charm, she'd fallen for him and they'd become a couple shortly thereafter.

It had all seemed like a wish come true. But was that only because she fitted his perfect mold of a woman who praised him?

Of course not, she told herself as she worked to finish up the tasks she'd started that morning. Mr. Figg had told her to finish out the day but not the week, even though the gallery would pay her salary for the week. She was not to return tomorrow.

Abby felt like the proverbial piece of dirt—the lowlife who couldn't hold a job at twenty-eight years old—as she gathered her things at closing time and left the gallery. She wasn't in the mood to walk all twenty-some blocks to her apartment, so she again hailed a cab. Too hell with the cost, she thought, remembering an old English saying: In for a penny, in for a pound. She'd think about financial ramifications later.

The taxi took her uptown to her apartment house, where she paid the driver and then climbed the steps to the front entrance of her building, thinking about checking her mail for a letter from home. Surprisingly, Jacob Sell, her sixtyish landlord, was waiting for her and let her in the door before she could use her key and head to the mailboxes.

Abby stepped into the vestibule and Mr. Sell made sure the outer door closed behind him. He took her arm and steered her to his own apartment on the ground-floor level. His plump wife stood in the open doorway.

"My dear," the woman said, fingering her graying hair nervously. "I'm afraid we have some bad news for you."

"What?" Abby asked, wondering what could be worse than losing her job.

"Just come inside, dear," the older lady said, ushering her into their apartment. "Jacob, make sure the door is shut behind you," she added, her gentle request sounding ominous to Abby. "We don't want to be disturbed."

"It is," her husband replied as the door closed and he stepped into the room.

"What's happened?" Abby asked, glancing between them. She suddenly felt apprehensive, noting the exchanged glances between the older couple. "Please, just tell me what's happened."

The woman took hold of her arm and steered her to the sofa, where Abby had no option but to sit down. "We're so sorry, Abby dear. The call came while you were gone."

"What call? From whom?"

"A Detective Williams from Carterville," Mrs. Sell said.

"Oh my God," Abby said, and tried not to feel alarmed. That was the town in upstate New York where she'd grown up, where her aunt Carolina still lived on the Hudson River.

There was a momentary silence.

"The detective was looking for you, Abby." Another pause. "We didn't have your work number to give him."

"So I took a message," Jacob said. "I have his number for you to call him back."

"But why was he looking for me?"

Another silence.

Mrs. Sell moved closer on the sofa where she'd seated herself next to Abby. She took Abby's clenched hands in hers. "I'm afraid we have bad news."

"What? Just tell me."

A brief silence went by.

"Sweetheart, we're sorry to be the ones to tell you but your aunt Carolina was found dead this morning," Mrs. Sell said, gently. Her voice lowered. "As Jacob said, we have the detective's number."

Stunned, Abby jumped up, unable to stay in their apartment one more second. "Why are you telling me this? It can't be true!"

She ran to the door and yanked it open. After managing to thank the older couple who only meant well, she took the stairs two at a time to the second floor.

With her key in hand she ran to her apartment door. She needed to be alone.

How could her beloved aunt Carolina be dead? It was impossible.

She stumbled into her apartment and slammed the door behind her.

And then she realized that a whole new terror awaited her in the evening darkness.

She wasn't alone.

Chapter 2

THE LOWER HALL WAS EMPTY NOW that the mailman had completed his delivery to the tenants. The man who watched had loitered on the front porch of the apartment building, slumping deeper into his overcoat, knowing that his mass of hair obscured his features. He jingled a ring of keys in his hand, pretending to search for the right one. As the mailman pushed open the door to leave, the man grabbed it, nodded his thanks, and stepped inside. Continuing his role of a person who lived in the place, the man walked to the metal mailboxes on the nearby wall and again pretended to fumble for the correct key.

Satisfied that the man was not an intruder, the mailman hoisted the strap of his mailbag higher on his shoulder and headed down the steps to the sidewalk, his thoughts already having shifted to the next stop on his route.

"Dumb bastard," the trespasser murmured, his lips twisting into a smile. It was always so easy. He could fool anyone, including the two old fools who managed the apartments.

A glance around the entry hall told him it was safe

to take the next step in his plan, which meant the narrow staircase to the second floor. He pulled an envelope from an inside pocket as he started upward, as though he belonged in the building. The first door at the top of the steps was hers.

He sucked air, a half-breath gulp, as he hesitated at her door. No one was in the hallway. He was alone.

He felt sweat under his arms, beading his upper lip, and matting his hair against his forehead. Don't be a wimp, get on with it. You know what you have to do.

He knocked softly with only two knuckles the first time and was met with silence. The second time he used all four and the knock was much louder. He knew she wasn't home from work yet, but just in case someone answered he was ready with an apology: "Isn't this the Thompson residence?" He'd be down the steps and out the front door before anyone realized that he wasn't a resident.

But no one answered his repeated knocks. He was safe.

For the moment.

This time the key he produced from his pocket was real. It fit the lock—as he'd known it would.

A moment later he was inside, the door closed behind him. Instantly, he was struck by the style and artistic flair of the beautifully appointed studio apartment. A faint smell of turpentine blended with an elusive perfume fragrance, both of which seemed enhanced by the smell of baked muffins that she'd left cooling on the counter.

He stood in the middle of the room, contemplating the best place to hide. The tiny kitchen space was tucked into one corner, the bedroom area partitioned off by a standup screen from which she'd hung portrait sketches that he knew she'd drawn. The living room area was small: an apartment-size sofa and chair, an antique trunk used as a coffee table, an end table and a lamp, and a television set. A bookcase against the wall was crammed with books and topped with a huge ivy plant with shiny leaves that cascaded over the books. The walls were filled with framed art and he wondered if they too had been painted by her. The total effect of the place was charming.

But where could he hide?

He quickly assessed his options. There wasn't enough space under the bed, but there were two doors, one to the tiny bathroom and one to a small clothes closet. He chose the closet.

A cliché, he thought, smiling wryly. Wasn't that where all rapists and murderers hid from their unsuspecting prey?

But he didn't fit the typical profile.

He was here for another reason. The rape was only a bonus, if a little ahead of schedule.

The sound of someone in the hall alerted him to action. She was home.

He slipped into the closet, working his way behind the hanging clothes. Then he waited, ready, alert to his next move, as the garments settled back into place.

His excitement mounted.

He was about to experience a perk of the job.

Chapter 3

IT WAS THE SMELL OF SOMETHING male that hit Abby's senses first: shaving cream or deodorant, maybe a man's cologne. It wasn't Sam's; he hated anything that even hinted of perfume.

Had someone been in her apartment?

No, she told herself, reaching for the light switch. It was Mr. Sell, who often used too much cologne. On occasion her landlord had entered her apartment while she was away to check on a plumbing or heating problem.

Oh God, the Sells must have been mistaken, she thought, her mind reverting to their terrible news.

More tears slid down her cheeks and her body seemed to quiver with harmonic tremors; her beloved aunt Carolina could not be dead. She needed to make calls, leave for Carterville up on the Hudson River, do something immediately.

She must clarify what had happened, if what she'd heard was the truth.

Abby found the switch, then stood momentarily uncertain when the light didn't turn on. Had the bulb burned out? She leaned back against the closed door, her eyes scanning the darkness of the studio apartment, suddenly fearful to step farther into the room. She fingered the wetness from her eyes to clear her vision. For a second the words she'd just heard about her aunt faded, replaced by vague apprehension.

Something was different.

Nothing moved, but the smell of male cologne seemed even stronger, as though it originated from someone nearby, not from her landlord or his apartment one floor below hers. The scent was too strong to be secondhand.

Her place suddenly felt alien, like it didn't belong to her. And the smell was almost suffocating. Was it the realization that she no longer had one living relative on the whole planet that magnified her fears? Was that typical of someone who had no one left who loved her? Oh God, she'd never felt so alone. How could she go on without her aunt Carolina, who'd been the only mother she'd known since coming to live with her at age eight—after her parents had died.

Get a grip, she told herself. Focus on the present.

And the present meant facing facts. Get out of the apartment, she told herself. Get the Sells to check out the validity of her current fears, let them ascertain whether she was being paranoid, overreacting to their horrible news.

A silence settled over the room as her hand groped for the doorknob behind her. Once she found it, Abby whirled around and began to yank open the door.

Out of the darkness, arms came around her. The door that she'd begun to open was slammed shut by two hands that suddenly slipped past her to press against the barrier with greater strength. Before she could scream, one hand moved to her mouth, suppressing any sound from her throat.

She was completely incapacitated—unable to cry out for help. But she knew that the person who held down her arms and pulled her back against him was a man, a strong man whose upper arms were muscled and whose body was tall and fit, a man who used a perfumed scent.

Instantly, she was fighting her captor, kicking against his legs, trying to knee his groin, twisting her head to free her mouth from the fingers that were cutting off her air.

"Help! she screamed, momentarily free of the tight clasp of his hand. "Please help me!"

"Bitch!" The word was muttered, deep behind clenched teeth, a voice she'd never heard before. He slapped the side of her head so hard that her knees buckled. Before she could regain her footing he'd stifled her cries once more with a grip that stopped the breath in her throat.

Abby was being dragged farther into the room, unable to release her arms, which were pinned by his against her body. Then he flung her down on the sofa. For a second she was free of his control over her movement. Her hand flew to the lamp, felt for the switch, and turned on the bulb.

He was on top of her, his face only inches above hers, when the light shone directly on his features. He hadn't bothered to disguise his identity under a mask. His dark eyes narrowed to slits and his lips twisted into a snarl, and she knew he had no intention of letting her go.

The frozen moment was shattered by pounding on her door.

"Miss Carter!" Mr. Sell shouted. "Miss Carter, are you all right? Open the door!"

Her attacker jumped up, releasing her. Abby gulped air, filling her lungs so that she was able to speak. The man was already at the door, his hand on the knob, when he glanced back.

"Next time, bitch. I won't be forgetting you."

He flung open the door, surprising Mr. Sell, who was sent sprawling to the floor. Abby heard her attacker's feet on the stairs, then the door to the building open and slam shut.

The man was gone before Mr. Sell had pulled himself back onto his feet.

"What's going on?" he said, catching his breath.

"Jacob! What happened?" Mrs. Sell asked, having come running up the steps after hearing the commotion. "Why are you on the floor?"

"I was pushed," her husband answered. "By the person who just ran out of the building." His gaze shifted to Abby, who'd made it to her door. "Someone you know?"

Abby shook her head. "He's a stranger." She sucked in a ragged breath. "He was in my apartment waiting for me." Her glance darted between them. "How did he get in?" Abby's voice wobbled. "I've never given anyone a key, not even my boyfriend."

"You think he had a key?" Mr. Sell's brows tightened into a frown. "Impossible."

"But true," Abby said. "How else could he have been there? My door was locked when I got here."

The Sells were obviously upset. "We need to report this to the police," Mrs. Sell said. "Not only did the intruder get into your apartment, he also got into the building." She turned and started back down the steps. "I'll call them while Jacob waits for you to get your purse and essentials and brings you down to our place."

Suddenly, Abby remembered her aunt Carolina. "I can't leave here," she said, tears again stinging her eyes. "I have calls to make."

"I understand, my dear," Mrs. Sell said. "But you must come along with Jacob. You can make your calls from our phone. After the police check everything out and Jacob changes the lock on your door you can return to your own apartment." She continued down the steps as Abby stared after her. "We have to make sure the building is secure," she added over her shoulder.

Shattered by all that had happened, Abby had to agree. She retrieved her purse, closed and locked her door, then followed her landlord downstairs to await the police.

She'd just reached the bottom of the steps when a sudden question hit her brain: Hadn't the Sells told her that a homicide detective had called with the news of her aunt's death? She was sure they'd said *homicide.*

Police detectives, particularly homicide detectives, didn't call surviving relatives when there was a death from natural causes.

Had her aunt been murdered?

Chapter 4

ONCE THEY'D RETURNED TO the landlord's apartment, Mrs. Sell led Abby to the telephone table in their tiny entry hall. "The detective's number is on that pad next to the phone," the older woman told her, and indicated that Abby should sit on the wooden chair she'd pulled out from the wall.

"Thank you," Abby said, her voice wobbling with sudden emotion. "I'll pay you for the long-distance costs."

Mrs. Sell nodded. "Don't worry about that, my dear. We'll settle up later." With a pat on Abby's knotted hands, she left her to disappear into the apartment.

For long seconds Abby stared at the pad with the number, knowing that once she called it, the voice at the other end of the wire could change her life forever. Tears welled in her eyes and streamed down her cheeks. Maybe it was a joke; maybe the man who'd called the Sells wasn't a detective at all. Hadn't the caller given himself away by identifying himself as a *homicide detective*? The caller sounded like a novice, someone who didn't realize the difference between homicide detectives and a typical police notification of a death to the nearest of kin.

The more she thought about it the better Abby felt. It was possible that her aunt was perfectly fine—after all, she was only in her sixties, too young to die. The person who'd called might be a fake.

Oh my God! she thought. Too many things were happening all at once. A creep on the street had followed her just this morning, and then she'd been attacked in her own apartment a short time ago.

The thought momentarily caught her breath in her throat. She jerked herself erect, jumpstarting her heart. But her next thoughts threatened to stop her in her tracks. She knew that Mr. Sell had been in her apartment at times while she was gone. What if it had been someone else?—the person who'd followed her on several occasions when she walked to work?

Shit! Why did she have to think of that now?—the paranoia of a small-town girl in the big city imagining all the fears that her aunt Carolina had warned her about.

Her aunt Carolina—that was the person to call first, not a supposed homicide detective. Instantly, her decision released her from her fears. Quickly, she punched in her aunt's number, then waited as the phone rang at the other end. She could just picture her aunt's immaculate little office, the phone and answering machine on her antique desk.

But as the phone rang and rang, Abby felt the apprehension rush back like a tidal wave, drowning her. The answering machine didn't pick up; the phone just kept ringing. Finally she hung up, knowing that something *was* wrong. Oh no, dear God, please don't let Aunt Carolina be dead.

She held the receiver in her hand, focusing on its

shape and length, anything to prolong what she still had to do.

Taking deep breaths, Abby managed to control her feelings, so that her emotions receded while her professional persona took precedence. Then she punched in the number Mrs. Sell had written on the pad. The phone at the other end rang, and was suddenly answered by a deep masculine voice.

"Williams here."

Abby gulped air, momentarily daunted, almost afraid to identify herself.

"Hello?" the man said again.

Still she hesitated, gathering her thoughts.

"Hey," the voice that had been acknowledged as Williams's said. "You may as well answer because you've been on the line long enough to be identified."

Annoyance shot though Abby. Didn't the police in her aunt's jurisdiction have any compassion?

"Okay, Mr. Williams, since you know who I am—I'm Abby Carter, returning your call."

"Carolina Carter's niece?"

"That's right. And I don't understand what's going on." There was a long silence.

"Your aunt is dead, Ms. Carter," he said gently.

She sucked in air as the walls seemed to close in around her. She feared that she was about to faint and fought the sensation. "No, it can't be," she whispered.

Another brief silence.

"I'm afraid it is, Ms. Carter." He paused. "I'm very sorry, and especially so that you had to hear the news over the phone."

"How did she die? She was so healthy."

"We're investigating that."

"What do you mean, investigating? Are you saying that her death might not be from natural causes?"

"Yes, that is the status at the moment. We haven't established an, uh, exact cause of death yet. It appears that she fell down the steps and struck her head on something at the bottom. We know that a blow to the head killed her."

"Fell down the stairs in the house? But my aunt isn't feeble, and even if she were, there are banisters to hold on to." She gulped air. "And there are no obstructions at the bottom except an inlaid wooden floor in the entry hall."

His hesitation sounded louder than words. "Precisely. The fatal blow didn't match the location." His sigh sounded in her ear. "But your aunt Carolina didn't die in her front hall, Ms. Carter. She fell down the steps on the outside of the outbuilding she uses as a garage."

"The barn stairs? But they end on grass."

"Yeah," he agreed, the single word telegraphing his concerns. "The garage was once a barn?"

"Uh-huh, over a hundred years ago. Before that it was the carriage house."

"We'll have lots to discuss when you get here. I'll explain what we know then, okay?"

Reluctantly, she agreed.

She watched the second hand on the wall clock as she processed what he was saying. "Are you really a homicide detective?" she asked finally.

"Yup, I really am."

"Which means you investigate murders?"

Another pause.

"Yeah, that's what I do."

"So you really believe my aunt's death wasn't accidental, I can hear it in everything you're saying." She tried to keep the tremble out of her voice even as a wave a tremors swept through her body. "That's impossible, Detective. Everyone loved my aunt Carolina."

"As I said, we're still in the investigation mode and haven't come to a definite conclusion, Abby—I trust that you don't mind if I call you Abby?"

She switched the phone to her other ear. "No, of course not, uh, Detective Williams."

"As I said moments ago, I'm very sorry that you had to get this news over the phone and not in person, Abby, but we didn't know exactly how to contact you except for the address in your aunt's personal phone book."

All of her limbs—arms, legs, even her torso—quivered with a low steady vibration, a new sensation she'd never felt before. But then she'd never heard such devastating news.

Her beloved aunt was dead.

She was totally alone in the world.

"I understand, Detective Williams," she managed. "I'll take the train home in the morning."

"Good. Please let me know if I can help. If not, I'll see you tomorrow in Carterville. I may have more to tell you by then."

She managed to thank him before they hung up. For long seconds she sat paralyzed as the reality of his words hit her. She couldn't fool herself into thinking that her aunt was still alive. She meant to get up there and find out what had really happened—the circumstances that had led a detective to investigate a possible murder as opposed to natural causes.

It was time to think in real terms, and not to be a victim of magical thinking. She meant to find the truth. If someone had murdered her aunt, she would find the killer.

Or die trying.

Abby sat on the overstuffed chair near the front window with the view of the street. It had started to rain around nightfall and now, only an hour later, the streets were shiny and wet, the scene deserted, as though no one dared to be out in the early evening darkness.

Drops of windblown moisture slid down the outside of the glass, just as a stray tear trickled down her cheek. She'd realized that under the current circumstances she must leave the city, at least until she could settle matters at home. Her foreseeable future was too up in the air to hold on to an apartment when she no longer even had a job. The decision had been necessary but sad.

She shifted position, her mind replaying her interview with the two policemen who'd responded to Mr. Sell's call. She'd told them what had happened, including her belief that she had been followed to work earlier in the day, that her attacker had been waiting for her in the apartment, and that she didn't know how the man had gained access to her place without a key. The officers had taken down her statement, then left with the pat warnings about making sure her door was locked when she left, being aware of who might be following her, and to alert the police to anything suspicious.

During her talk with the officers, Mr. Sell had changed her locks, and had left as they did, letting them out through the front door of the building. Abby thought it was all an exercise in futility. In the first place, none of them could really protect her if someone was after her. She would be in her apartment only until morning, when she'd leave for Carterville, up on the Hudson River. The Sells had agreed to let her out of the rental agreement—because of her circumstances, and the fact that she forfeited a deposit and almost a month's rent, and because they knew they could rent out the place the very day that she left.

Sighing, Abby stared out into the gathering darkness, thinking about her decision to leave the city. It was all so sad. She'd called Sam, her boyfriend, the person she'd hoped would offer to drive her upstate to Carterville in the morning, rather than have her take the train alone. He hadn't picked up his home or cell phone and she'd left a message on both. Once she'd started to talk she'd cried instead. Her messages had been garbled. Finally she'd just blurted out her plea for him to call her as soon as possible.

The sudden knocking on her door startled her. For a moment she froze in the chair. Who would be in the hall? Her landlords? Another tenant? No one else would be allowed through the main entrance to the building. She certainly had not been buzzed on the intercom.

Then she heard Sam's voice: "Abby! Are you in there? It's me—Sam!"

She ran to the door, yanked it open, and flung herself into his arms. "Oh, Sam," she murmured. "I'm so glad you came."

"Mr. Sell let me in," he said, holding her against his chest, smoothing her hair with his hand, her emotions calmed by his words. Then he gently led her into the apartment and closed the door behind them. Back in his arms, he feathered her face with kisses, at first tenderly, then with rising passion as he claimed her lips. "My sweet, it's going to be all right. Believe me, it'll be okay."

"I don't think so, Sam. Aunt Carolina was all I had." She choked back a sob. "I feel so alone."

"You have me, sweetheart." Affection shone in his brown eyes as he looked down at her. "I'm here to help."

Abby smiled faintly, liking what she saw—a tall man who was both handsome and kind, if unbending at times. Somewhere in the back of her mind she wondered if her aunt's death would motivate him to finally make a commitment to her, perhaps insist that they move in together once he heard that she was no longer able to afford living in the city.

They sat down on the sofa and he snuggled her next to him as she explained the day's happenings, from being followed to work, to losing her job, to the news of her aunt's death, to the attack. As her voice faded into silence Sam's breath whistled out of his mouth.

"Jeez, Abby, the whole thing is unbelievable. All that in the space of a few hours." A pause. "I'll help you with anything I can."

She nodded and swallowed hard, again fighting tears. "There's one thing I'd hoped you could do for me."

"Just say."

"Could you drive me to Carterville tomorrow?"

He stiffened. "That's one thing I can't do."

She lowered her lashes, hiding her disappointment. "I understand." She gave a brief smile. "It's okay. I know it was short notice. I figured you probably couldn't, so I planned on taking the train anyway."

He dropped his hands from around her and wiped back his longish brown hair. "At any time I could drive you, but tomorrow I have a meeting at a gallery. They're making the final decision on whether or not they'll display my art. If I cancel I'm afraid they'd drop me."

"Of course you can't sacrifice that opportunity, Sam. That wouldn't bring my aunt back." She hid her disappointment behind a smile. "I'll take the train as I've already planned."

"Thanks, sweetie, I appreciate your support. Being an artist yourself, you realize what's at stake. If my work starts selling I can drop the damn commercial art job."

She stood up. "Can I get you something to drink?"

He got up, too. "Thanks, but I can't stay." He shrugged regretfully. "I have a lot of preparation to get ready for tomorrow." He dropped his hands onto her shoulders and pulled her close again. "You'll be okay tomorrow?"

"Of course," she said, lying. In truth she'd never felt so shattered and alone—and scared. "I'll take a taxi to the train and be met at the station in Carterville, probably by my aunt's best friend, Katherine. I'll make that arrangement in the morning."

"Good. You're a strong woman, Abby." They walked to the door, where he kissed her good-bye. "It's one of many traits I like about you. Your self-reliance is awesome."

She closed the door after him and made sure her new bolt lock was in place. Then she went back to the window and watched Sam head up the street to the corner where he flagged a taxi. She sat on for a long time before getting up to begin packing.

Abby knew what she had to do. It might take all

night but she'd get it done. *Self-reliance* had suddenly become a word she wished weren't in her vocabulary. That and two others: *obligation* and *responsibility.*

She couldn't dodge those. Her obligation and responsibility was to her beloved aunt Carolina—until she resolved what had happened.

Chapter 5

THE TRAIN EASED OUT OF the station into a tunnel, quickly picking up speed. Abby sat back, resting her head against the seat and allowing her lashes to flutter down, for the moment giving in to her fatigue. She hadn't slept in over twenty-four hours, not since she'd gotten up yesterday morning.

Her life had changed forever in that one day: She'd lost her job, her aunt had died, and she'd been attacked in her own apartment. Abby sighed. And she was basically leaving the city and placing her hope to succeed as an artist on hold—because she was the only family member left to take care of her aunt's affairs. She just prayed that her art wouldn't become a fatality, too. She'd make sure that it didn't.

Abruptly, the darkness seemed to brighten; she opened her eyes to see that the train had come out of the tunnel and was headed up the tracks along the Hudson River, and the rain had stopped, even if the sky was still overcast and threatening. But the day was still gloomy, and matched her mood, she thought. She'd never felt so down and alone in her entire life.

Leaning her forehead against the cool window, she

wondered what the future really held for her. Her first task would be to see to her aunt's funeral, her second to settle Carolina's estate. Abby knew she was the sole beneficiary of the will, but that could be a mixed bag. The family home didn't carry a mortgage as far as she knew, yet there were the costs her aunt had incurred in running a bed-and-breakfast business out of her house. Her hope was that she would be up to the task of settling everything in a manner that would have met with Carolina's approval.

And what about her feelings for Sam? She no longer knew what to think about him, aside from profound disappointment. Irrational or not, she couldn't help but feel that he'd let her down, that he'd put his meeting ahead of her loss. All she knew was that she would have placed a loved one first in similar circumstances.

But did he love her? He'd never said so, although in the past couple of months he'd begun to speak about the future they'd share. She'd also realized that he was wary of personal commitment, unable to consider living together, even on an equal, roommate basis. He was totally dedicated to his career.

Whoa, she told herself. First things first, and that means coping with Carolina's death.

The sound of her cell phone was unexpected, jolting her away from the window. Quickly, she rummaged though the handbag that rested on her lap, trying to get to it before the melodious music stopped and she missed the call.

"Hello," she said, even before she pressed the device to her ear.

"Abby?" Sam said. "I can hardly hear you."

"Better now?" she replied, speaking into the receiver and pushing long strands of hair away from her face.

"Yeah. Where are you? No one answered at your apartment."

"On the train to Carterville." A pause. "Remember, I told you that I'd be going in the morning?"

"Uh-huh. I guess I missed the time part."

A brief silence went by while she adjusted the phone. She didn't contradict him. Another piece to their personal puzzle: He didn't pay attention to what was going on around him when he was focused on the important happenings in his own life.

"How did your meeting go?" she asked, changing the subject.

"Super." He transitioned from her situation to his own without missing a beat. "It couldn't have been better."

"Which means?"

"They want to give me a show at some point." He sucked in a quick breath. "I can't quite take it all in yet, Abby. They love my work, told me I have a great career ahead of me."

"That's wonderful, Sam." She hoped she'd managed enough enthusiasm in her response. "It sounds like your career is about to take a giant step forward."

"Yeah, it's what I'm hoping happens."

Another pause between them.

"So, when will you get back from Carterville?" he asked, breaking the brief silence.

"I don't know, Sam." She turned back to watch the passing scenery, and realized that she hadn't told him about giving up her apartment—that when, if, she returned to the city, she'd have to locate another place. "I have to see to my aunt's affairs."

"But that shouldn't take long, Abby." A hesitation. "I know you have no other family up there."

"Which is precisely why settling the estate will take a little time," she replied. "I'm the only one who can do it."

"But it should be simple." A pause. "You're too upset right now to see that."

"See what?"

"That you can see to your aunt's cremation, funeral, whatever—and then take a couple of days to go through her things and then put the house on the market."

She was stunned into silence.

"The house has been in our family for generations. I don't know if I want to sell it."

"Of course you do. The proceeds will pay your way here in New York for several years—the time you need to get your art off the ground."

"And if I did that, what would happen when the money was gone and I, like most artists, hadn't succeeded?"

"You can't think like that, Abby. That's your problem: You think too much."

Annoyance hit her. How would he know what she was talking about?—he had a small trust fund that was just enough to indulge his goal of becoming a successful artist. And he also had wealthy parents who would no doubt step in if he was ever in need—and he had the security of knowing that.

She sat back against the seat cushion as realization struck her: He was one of the privileged people who could not understand those who struggled for success, who worked the hard way. And he did not have a sense of family history like she had, knowing that Carterville had been named for her ancestors. Her aunt Carolina had preserved the family house in the only way she could—by converting it into a bed-and-breakfast that would pay for itself.

He was oblivious to her plight.

He would never understand family tradition.

Or the fact that she was the last descendant, that she had inherited a sacred responsibility—to keep the Carterville home. She knew her aunt Carolina had believed that one day Abby would marry, have children, and carry on in the house and town on the Hudson River that had a history that went back many generations.

Abby couldn't dismiss that responsibility—she didn't want to. The past was everything to her; the past was who she would become in the future.

"I've given up my apartment," she told him, bluntly. "Under the circumstances, the Sells let me out of the rental agreement."

There was a long silence.

"My God! Why would you do such a stupid thing, Abby? You had a sweet deal there—you won't find anything comparable that you can afford in the city."

"That's just it, Sam."

"What?"

"I won't be coming back to the city in the near future."

"Son of a bitch! Why not?"

"First, I have to settle things in Carterville one way or another." She went on quickly before he could interrupt. "And second, I can no longer afford to live in the city without income. Remember, I told you that I'd lost my job?"

"Yeah, but now you have your aunt Carolina's assets."

"Or liabilities."

"What do you mean?"

She told him. She had no idea about the worth of her aunt's estate, although she knew that Carolina had struggled financially. "I might have inherited a bankrupt property, I don't know yet what's involved." A pause. "I only know I was lucky to get out of my lease right now."

"Shit! You make everything sound grim, Abby. Your plight puts a pall on my own success."

"I don't want to do that, Sam."

"But nevertheless, you have."

She drew in a shaky breath, wondering what she could say to make him feel better. Somehow the conversation had turned things around: He was the victim of her sad circumstances. Then she had another thought: Did he really feel bad about her plight?—or was it that she'd put a damper on his feelings of success? Either way, she needed to let him off the hook.

"Sam, don't let me bring you down for even a minute." Her tone was upbeat, just as she'd always reacted to his gloomy outlook on his career in the past. "You're on your way whether I live in the city or not."

There was a silence while he digested her remarks.

"Yeah, you're right, Abby," he replied finally. "You'll be back when you can, right?"

"Right."

But her agreement was only a salve for his position on the issue. She wondered if she'd ever return to the city; the price of doing so might be too much—in money and personal commitment.

"Okay," Sam said. "I'll stay in touch." His sigh sounded in her ear. "But I predict that you'll be fed up with the small-town stuff within the month it takes to settle everything. You'll be back looking for an apartment before you know it."

"You may be right, Sam."

But she knew he was wrong. She had no security but the family house that her aunt had left her. Under no circumstances would she sell the place where her mother had grown up, and her ancestors before that. Not unless she was forced to by law—because of debts too big to overcome. She didn't know what she was up against, but she knew one thing for sure.

She faced it alone.

"I'll stay in close touch," she told him, trying to sound upbeat. But she felt far from happy as she disconnected. He hadn't been there for her, but she would have to think about that later. Maybe she was just being too emotional, even irrational. For now she needed to stay focused on her aunt's death.

She would do her best, keeping the historic significance of the family in mind. For a moment she remembered that she'd been born a twin. She just wished her sister had survived birth.

So she wouldn't feel so alone.

Chapter 6

THE TRIP PASSED IN A BLUR of landscape and Abby gathered her bags and purse as the train slowed for its stop at the Carterville station. She braced herself for what lay ahead.

For the first time in her life, her aunt Carolina wouldn't be there to greet her, wouldn't be scurrying around in the house, attending to her and all the guests. Abby swallowed hard. Dear God, she prayed silently. Please let me be as strong as my aunt would expect. Please allow me the grace to face what must be faced.

You Can't Go Home Again. Of its own volition, her mind flashed on the title of Thomas Wolfe's classic novel. How right the author had been. Even though she was going home to the same town, the same house that had been in her family for generations, the place would never again be as she'd left it. Aunt Carolina was gone forever.

Abby didn't allow her thoughts to drift into dangerous channels, like the dark cloud of murder that had hung over her thoughts ever since she'd heard from the homicide detective. Even as she'd packed her things during the night, hesitating when something seemed out of place, Abby had dismissed the suspicion that her attacker had gone through her possessions. Nothing had been missing, not even the several pieces of good jewelry that had belonged to her mother.

Don't let your imagination go to scary places, she reminded herself for the umpteenth time. Her aunt's death and her assault by an intruder were separate events, if both horrific. There was no reason in the world why they would be connected. It was merely co-incidence that they had happened on the same day.

But was it?

The Sells had promised to keep tabs on the New York Police Department's progress in finding the intruder. "We'll call with updates and let you know either way," Mr. Sell had assured her.

Abby stood up as the train came to a stop at the small Carterville station. Don't think about that now, she told herself again. Once she was home, in her aunt's house, she could begin the process of trying to understand what had happened. She waited her turn as passengers filed toward the door. Then she stepped into the aisle and followed them to the exit. Once on the platform, she hesitated as people moved around her, headed for meeting places or their vehicles in a connecting parking lot. Within the few minutes that she hesitated, considering her transportation options, the hustle and bustle around her dissipated: Passengers had disappeared into the day, and the train had picked up a few more people who were headed north, toward Albany, and was already leaving the station. Seconds later she was alone.

Except for the tall dark-haired man in the tan raincoat who stood watching her. As he noticed that she'd spotted him, he stepped forward, approaching her.

"Abigail Carter?" he asked in a deep, totally masculine voice.

She managed a nod, aware that they were alone on the platform. She measured the distance to the entrance of the small station building, backing away from the man as he advanced, her fears of being attacked surfacing with a terrifying remembrance of last night.

"I spoke to you on the phone," he said, flashing a badge she couldn't make out. "I'm Detective Stanley Williams."

She kept moving backward, her eyes on him, suddenly fearful of trusting his words, even though his voice sounded familiar. He was so tall, so attractive, so sexy. Why would a man who looked like that be a small-town homicide detective? It didn't make sense. More important, she didn't trust that he was who he said he was. Again aware that the platform was deserted, she glanced all over the surrounding area, looking for another person who would come to her aid if necessary.

There was no one.

She turned away and ran, headed for the door to the station, where she knew there was at least one person in a kiosk selling train tickets. Her fingers grasped the door handle just as a hand came down on her shoulder, stopping her cold.

"Abby, take it easy. I'm really Detective Williams. Remember, I said I'd see you in Carterville?" A pause. "Maybe I forgot to mention that I'd be meeting your train."

She turned, facing him as his hand dropped away.

Instantly, her gaze was captured by his, pale gray-blue eyes that were a startling contrast to his black hair and olive skin. A fleeting thought hit her: He was one of the most attractive men she'd ever met, even though he had eyes that reminded her of a wolf.

She immediately controlled her reaction and stepped back, so that a foot of space separated them. In those few seconds Abby composed herself, meeting his stare with her best possible business persona. But she wondered why he was meeting her train. Surely homicide detectives were too busy to meet next of kin as they arrived.

Then another thought surfaced, bringing back her apprehension. She hadn't told him which train she was taking, so how had he known which one to meet? Again her hand was feeling behind her for the door lever.

"I didn't know your arrival time, Abby," he said, guessing her fears, and she glimpsed a flicker of amusement on his face. "This was the third train I met, and I wasn't even sure it was really you when I called your name." A brief grin tilted his lips at the corners. "I was guessing from the picture of you on your aunt's piano in the parlor."

Abby suddenly felt foolish. Oh God, she was a basket case. But she also felt her momentary panic slide away. He'd convinced her that he was the detective she'd spoken to on the phone. About to speak, she closed her mouth as another question struck her: Why was meeting her so important that he'd wait three trains?

"I figured you'd need a ride home," he said, and took her arm to lead her to the parking area behind the small station. "I know you don't have relatives in town."

"I don't have relatives, period," she replied, darting

a glance at him. "I was about to call my aunt's best friend."

They passed a middle-aged couple who had just parked and were getting out of their car. "Hello, Detective," the man said as they passed.

Detective Williams nodded and then indicated that the dark sedan was his. He opened the door for Abby and she slipped onto the front seat. In seconds they were on their way to the bed-and-breakfast, which was only a few blocks up the hill.

As they turned onto the familiar street that overlooked the Hudson River, Abby again braced herself. But she felt better about the detective. The couple in the parking lot had verified his identity. That was the first good thing that had happened to her in days.

She hoped it boded well for her homecoming without her aunt Carolina.

Chapter 7

THE MAN WATCHED FROM BEYOND the waiting area, his eyes on the woman. The crowd of people waiting on the platform surged forward as the sound of the approaching train grew louder. The woman seemed swept up in the movement of bodies when the engine pulling the cars stopped, its metal wheels screeching from the pressure of the brakes. Instantly, the doors slid open, triggering a sudden rush to find seats. Once the crowd was off the platform, the man tightened the belt on his raincoat and stepped forward onto the train. A moment later its wheels were again rolling, heading out of the station to begin the trip out of the city.

He took a seat where he could maintain his vigilance, unfolded the *New York Times* and held it in front of his face, and pretended to read. The perfect commuter: bored, preoccupied, and anonymous.

The words on paper blurred as his mind fixed on other words, other papers, important documents that he needed to find, before someone else did. He fussed with the pages in his hands, enabling him to glance at the other passengers. Satisfied that she was still there, he went back to his pretense of reading, mentally going over his options.

He must not fail or all the years would be in vain. She was the key. She would not get away again.

The journey passed quickly. When the train slowed for Carterville he was surprised. A smile twisted his lips. His thoughts had been busy plotting his next move. He was ready.

This time he was one of the first to disembark, lingering on the edge of the platform near the station, hidden behind a huge planter of summer flowers that had gone spindly and sparse from the cooling temperature of fall. As the people dispersed, the man readied himself.

It was time to get on with things.

Chapter 8

WHEN ABBY STEPPED OUT of the detective's car, she was struck by the heady fragrance of river water, a smell that always lifted her spirits. She paused, glancing down the long, grassy slope to the street below, the city park beyond that, the railroad tracks and the river in the distance. She drew in a long, shaky breath. This place was her roots.

For moments longer she stood, her eyes on the panorama of river and the Catskill Mountains beyond it. For over 250 years her ancestors had enjoyed the same view from the very house her aunt had made into a bed-and-breakfast business. She had that connecting link with them, and with her mother—and now Carolina.

She'd been right in giving up her apartment in the city, Abby told herself. She just hoped she'd be able to keep the property. She'd try her best but only time would tell.

Turning back toward the house, she realized that the detective was standing a few feet behind her, watching, giving her time to adjust to her new circumstances. Then he stepped forward and took her small

bag before taking her arm to lead her through the gate.
In silence they strode up the walk to the wide wooden
steps and across the porch to the front door with its
familiar oval glass window. She produced the key,
unlocked the doors, and stepped into the entry. Detective Williams followed.

"This is no longer a crime scene," he said softly.

She whirled around, facing him. "What do you
mean—*a crime scene*?"

He took a half step backward, as though he was unprepared for her accusing tone. "Only that we processed
the house from the attic to the cellar and found nothing
significant that connected the house with the area
where your aunt died."

"And what does that mean, Detective Williams?"
She hesitated while he seemed to gather his thoughts.
"What are you implying—that my aunt died a natural
death, or that you suspect she was murdered? Surely
you must have a definitive answer by now."

There was a silence as he stepped forward and
dropped his hands onto her shoulders. "I'm implying
nothing, Abby," he said quietly, but with conviction.
"I'm only saying that the house is clear, nothing happened here, and there need be no unhappy memories
attached to the house."

His words almost shattered her control and she
struggled to keep her composure. She saw that he had
momentarily looked upset by her first accusation, that
he had been sympathetic to her feelings.

"I believe I also mentioned that although her death
appears to have been caused by a blunt-force blow to
her head, it doesn't seem consistent with falling down
the stairs in that particular location."

She looked him in the eyes, aware that he had information that he hadn't yet given to her. "You're implying that you know what killed her but not how she came to get the fatal injury, is that correct, Detective Williams?"

A silence fell between them.

"There is still no conclusive determination, Abby," he said finally, and she wondered if he was evading. "To be honest, we are still evaluating the evidence."

She faced him. "What exactly is the evidence, Detective Williams?"

Another pause.

"We know the time of death and the location of her body. We also know that the blow to her head does not match her falling down steps and hitting her head on the grass. Nor does anything account for her being on the barn steps at three A.M."

"In the morning?"

"That's right, Abby. She was in the upstairs room above the garage at three in the morning." He hesitated, as though considering his words. "Why would she have been there? Can you shed some light on her motivation?"

Abby shook her head. "The room above the barn, uh, garage, is only used for storage. I can't imagine why my aunt would have been there in the middle of the night."

He shrugged. "Neither can we but we're still looking into that. If you come up with anything, however obscure, we'd appreciate a call. Although it still isn't official, an accidental death just doesn't fit the circumstances."

Unsettled, Abby moved into the parlor and switched on a lamp, an automatic response to a lifetime in the house. She could hardly believe the words of the detective: Who would have hated her beloved aunt Carolina enough to murder her?

No one, she thought. There'd been a mistake.

It had to be a mistake.

She expressed her feelings: "If someone did cause her death, it couldn't have been anyone who knew her. It had to be random, a transient or someone who just happened to stop in town." She gulped a breath, fighting tears. "My aunt was kind to everyone and was known for economical room rates, excellent breakfasts, and never arguing with guests."

"Look, I promise you, we'll get the person responsible, Abby."

She glanced away, unable to reply. Everything in the house looked exactly as it always had; nothing seemed missing, except for her aunt.

"Thank you, Detective," she said and managed a brief smile. "I'm counting on that."

He studied her face for moments longer, then turned back to the door. "I'll get your larger bag from the car."

He left her standing in the parlor doorway, returning within two minutes with her big suitcase. "Where shall I take it?" he asked. "Your bedroom?"

"Just leave it here in the entry hall. I'll take it upstairs later."

"No way," he replied with a brief smile. "It's too heavy. You lead the way."

She had no option but to do as he said. She realized that he wasn't a man who took no for an answer. They went up the curving staircase to the upper floor, where she led the way to her room. The guest-room doors were shut; the few reservations for the weekend had been canceled. Carolina's room, at the end of the hall near hers, was also closed and for that Abby was grateful. She wasn't up to facing her aunt's private quarters yet. She suspected that the police had already been through everything.

She paused at her own door, staring straight ahead, strengthening her resolve, then she opened the polished mahogany barrier and stepped inside. The detective followed, moving around her to place the suitcase next to the closet. Straightening, he looked around.

"What a charming room," he said. "A young girl's dream come true—canopied bed, antiques and old lace, and a window seat where you can see all the way to the Catskills."

Abby nodded. "This is the way my room has always looked, since my earliest memory." She glanced at the antique desk. "I wrote all my letters sitting at that desk, just as all the little girls in the family before me did." She smiled, remembering. "My aunt always claimed it was the oldest piece of furniture in the house."

"Did she also rent your room to guests once you'd moved to the city?"

"No, only the three other bedrooms that were no longer used. Hers, which is across the hall, and mine stayed ours. My aunt was emphatic about that, said family came first."

"She was right about that, Abby. Family means everything. You were fortunate."

"And you, Detective? Do you have a family?"

"Let's just say I hope to have a family one day." He wiped back a strand of dark hair from his forehead. "But am I married?" Amusement twinkled in his pale blue eyes. "No, I'm not."

Feeling a little foolish, hoping he didn't think she was prying into his personal life, she busied herself by slipping out of her jacket and dropping it on a chair as she changed the subject.

"Can I get you something to drink: coffee, soda?" Abby led the way down the stairs to the lower hall, where the parlor was on one side and the dining room on the other. The door at the back led to the kitchen, a tiny office, and a morning room where guests were served breakfast. The detective declined the offer but hesitated at the front door.

"As you know, Abby, the area where your aunt was found has been processed and there are no restricted places on the property, including the garden area." He hesitated. "One last thing. Your aunt is at the Riverview Funeral Home and they are waiting for—"

"I know," she said, hating the thought. "I'll call them right away and make an appointment for tomorrow morning."

Again he seemed reluctant as he faced her. "You'll be alone tonight. I'm willing to stay in a guest room if none of your friends are available—so you'll have someone in the house for your first night home."

"Thanks, Detective Williams. I appreciate your suggestion but that won't be necessary." She tried to hide the wobble in her voice. "This is my home and I'll be fine."

"Under the circumstances, I want you to feel safe."

"I do, and if I should feel uneasy I'll call one of my old friends—I have lots of them here in town."

"And remember that you can call me at any time, day or night. I left my card on the hall table."

"Is this police procedure?" she asked, wondering.

"Yes and no." A hesitation. "Murder, if it is that, is not a common occurrence in our town. We don't want you to be in jeopardy, that's all."

"You think I am?"

"Not necessarily. We, the department and I, just mean to make sure that you're not, until we get a better handle on the case."

Her gaze locked with his as fear rippled over her skin, raising goose bumps. "I take that to mean you do—that at least you think it's a strong possibility."

The detective held her gaze. "I only believe that there is something here we don't understand, something that might go back to family history."

"What are you saying?"

Detective Williams stepped forward. "Nothing really."

"Except for?"

"It's elusive. To be blunt, your aunt was killed and we don't know why. Now, we want to protect you—until our investigation produces a few more facts."

Abby took a deep breath. "I don't know what was happening in Carterville before my aunt's death. I only know she was a fearless woman who would not have done anything stupid—like being outside on the barn steps in the middle of the night. She would have been afraid of the dark had anything been amiss and called 911 for help."

"Unless she didn't have her cell phone with her."

"Where is her cell phone?"

"That's another missing piece to the puzzle. We never found it, not outside or in the house. Wherever it is, the thing was turned off."

"I'll try to find it," Abby said, her words dropping into the quiet of the hall.

The detective nodded and strode out to the porch, then turned to face her again. "Remember, if you change your mind about tonight just give a call, okay?"

She nodded. "Thanks, Detective Williams. I will."

Abby watched as he went to his car and slowly drove off down the street. Then she closed and locked the doors. After that she made sure the whole house was secure.

Tea, that's what she needed, a steaming hot cup of it. Didn't she and her aunt always drink tea to calm their nerves?

Everything would be all right soon, she told herself. It had to be.

Chapter 9

ABBY LAY STARING AT MOVING maple leaves on the branches outside her windows, her mind a collage of memories, flashes of earlier times when she was growing up and sleeping in this very bed. Back then she'd felt safe. In the darkness of her first night home she felt only fear of her uncertain future. According to the bedside clock she'd retired to her room four hours ago. It was now two A.M. and she still hadn't done anything but doze, only to be awakened by the creaking and groaning of the house, sounds no longer familiar to her.

She sat up, suddenly annoyed with herself, and plumped her pillows before lying back down. But the gesture didn't help. She still stared wide-eyed at the ever-changing shadow patterns on the ceiling. It was as though her mind was too filled with images ever to rest.

Her aunt Carolina's best friend, Katherine Dover, who lived down the street, had dropped by soon after the detective had left, hugging her and offering condolences. Katherine had taken it upon herself to call guests who were booked for the next two weekends and cancel their reservations. She'd also shown Abby the reservations book for the two weeks after that.

"I left it up to you to decide on what you wanted to do," she'd said. "Keep the upcoming reservations or cancel them as well."

Abby had thanked her, then broken down and cried about her aunt Carolina's death. The other woman, tears in her eyes, had been sympathetic, but had also been practical about the future. "You'll need to make up your mind quickly, Abby. Either you continue the bed-and-breakfast business or shut it down, with immediate cancellations for future guests. The ones I canceled are willing to rebook later."

Abby could only nod in agreement, too shaken to think straight. She arranged a meeting in the morning with Katherine to go over financial matters, and then Abby would decide on the future of the bed-and-breakfast.

But what future? Abby wondered. She would either continue the business or she wouldn't. *Wait for your meeting with your aunt's lawyer,* said a voice in her head. *You don't know the status of the estate and have nothing to go on until you know the facts.* She needed to make an appointment with Carolina's attorney.

I'll call him the first thing in the morning, she thought, and for the first time felt relief. Gradually she drifted off to sleep, content for the moment that she had her immediate future in hand.

She slept.

Abby sat up straight in bed. For a moment she was disoriented. What had awakened her? A sound?

She strained to hear anything different from the

wind in the tree branches outside her windows, the normal creaking and groaning of an old house.

Nothing.

Yet she felt on full alert. Something wasn't right; she could sense it.

The sound was vague, as though it came from far away.

What? Was it a bedroom door being closed down the hall? Or had it been a deeper sound, like something heavy being slid across the wooden floorboards?

Neither, she told herself. It was imagination, a manifestation of her fear of the unknown. Her gaze swept the room. She was alone in the shadowy darkness. Quickly, she flung back the covers, swung her legs over the side of her bed, and stood up. She needed to make sure that she was only imagining things in order to take control of her fear—or her mind would never allow her to get back to sleep.

She tiptoed to the door, her long nightgown trailing behind her, and took hold of the antique glass doorknob. It's now or never, she told herself and slowly turned it before pulling the door open just wide enough to let herself into the hall, where she paused to glance around, satisfying herself that no one was there. You need to manage this situation or you'll never feel safe here again, she thought, bolstering herself with self-talk. There is no one in the house; you locked all the doors.

Soundlessly, Abby slipped through the upper passageway, checking each guest room on her way to the staircase. At the top she hesitated, listening, her eyes scanning the steps to the lower floor, wondering again what she had heard.

A ghost? The thought was sudden, paralyzing her. The ghost of her aunt Carolina?

Remembered stories from her childhood surfaced: the town's secrets. Folklore that told of secret caves and tunnels from the river dating back to the Underground Railroad and the exodus of slaves from southern masters before the Civil War. The frightening scenarios told of unsolved murders that resulted in ghosts that hadn't crossed over and still haunted their earthly place of death.

Don't dwell on crazy thoughts, she instructed herself. Her aunt Carolina had never allowed "pagan talk" in her house when she was alive, and now was not the time to start.

What she'd heard were normal sounds, her reasoning brain told her. Yet, she struggled to quell her panicky feelings. The space on the lower floor seemed benign, yet something in her sensed *danger*. What? An extension of the fear-based ghost stories from childhood? After taking a deep breath, she started down the stairs.

And then she knew.

She'd been right to know fear.

A dark shape appeared below her, separating from the wall to flash down the hall to the kitchen, like a shadowy dark cutout against black paper. She blinked and it was gone.

Oh my God! Abby thought, freezing in midstep. What was that? Something? Nothing? A reflection on the wallpaper from outside the oval window in the door?

She stood trembling, uncertain, and unable to move.

As quickly as the fragment of something dark had slipped though, it was now completely gone. The house and the hallway had returned to normal, as though nothing strange had happened.

Had she really seen something?

Abby grasped the banister and pressed back against the paneling above it, shaking as reaction set in. Whatever had happened was beyond her understanding. Maybe her mind was playing tricks on her. Maybe it was the fact of her first night home after her aunt's death. Maybe she was far more traumatized than she'd realized. She'd returned to a house that represented several centuries of ancestors who'd lived and died there, after having lost her aunt, her job, and her apartment, not to mention being assaulted, all within twenty-four hours.

"Get a grip, girl," she whispered into the night around her. "You aren't allowed a pity party."

Still she seemed frozen in place, unable to go back upstairs or continue down to the entry. Call the detective, she thought suddenly. He'd told her to call if anything at all seemed wrong.

Ridiculous! she argued mentally. What would she say? Sorry to disturb you in the middle of the night, Detective Williams, but I think I heard some sounds that woke me up and I saw a shadow on the wall that disappeared in a blink of my eyes? Besides, the house phone was down in the hall and her cell phone was back upstairs on her bedside table.

Stupid! Why hadn't she grabbed her phone when she went to check on the sounds?

Because she'd been consumed by fear and hadn't been thinking right.

Pull yourself together, she told herself again. You must make sure the downstairs is secure or you'll never get back to sleep tonight. Abby reminded herself that she had locked up earlier. No one could possibly be in the house even if that person had a door key. The bolt locks precluded entry as they were secured from the inside and didn't have keys.

So no one could be in here. That knowledge gave Abby the courage to descend the steps and examine the main floor, turning on lights as she went. By the time she reached the kitchen and had checked the walk-in pantry, she knew she was alone in the house, with all the locks still in place. Relieved, she went back upstairs after extinguishing the lights, convinced that it had all been a figment of her imagination. Imagination based on all the changes and traumas to her life in the past two days.

She was settling back between the sheets, her thoughts focusing on the peaceful contemplation of the patchwork quilt on her bed that had been hand-sewn by a grandmother she'd never known, when her cell phone rang.

She jumped up to a sitting position. A glance at the clock told her it was now almost two thirty in the morning.

No one called at that time.

Abby stared at it, uncertain about answering. It had to be a wrong number.

She reached to grab it, then hesitated before flipping it open to answer. Should she or shouldn't she? Impulsively, she did.

"Hello?"

"Abby?" said a familiar man's voice.

"Yes, this is Abby. Who am I speaking to?"

"Bud."

"Bud? I'm sorry I don't know anyone by that name. You must have the wrong number."

"Don't hang up, Abby. This is Detective Williams." A brief silence went by.

"I'm sorry about the Bud reply," he said. "Everyone in Carterville knows me as Detective Bud Williams, even though my real name is Stanley." A pause. "I was just checking in on you, making sure everything was all right."

"I guess I'm puzzled, Detective Williams. Do you always call in the middle of the night?"

"Only when I have a reason, Abby." His tone was low and strangely seductive.

"Which is . . . ?" She hoped she sounded calm and not as irritated as she felt. Who in the hell did he think he was, calling so late? Don Juan?

His sigh came over the airwaves, as though he'd guessed her thoughts. "Why did all the lights in your house suddenly come on, Abby, and then go out just as fast?"

His question took her off guard and she retorted without thinking: "Because something woke me up in the night and I had to check out the upstairs rooms."

"I was talking about the main floor."

"I'd locked everything up, but since I'd heard sounds I couldn't identify, I wanted to make sure the downstairs was okay, too."

"But the sounds were on the second floor?"

"Yeah, but everything was okay there."

"So you went downstairs?"

"Uh-huh, and that's when I thought I saw something."

"What?" The word seemed to shoot into her ear.

She explained, concluding that it must have been a

reflection coming in through the front window and that the downstairs was as she'd left it.

Another pause.

"Why didn't you call me?"

"In the middle of the night when I didn't really know if anything tangible had happened?"

"I believe I told you to call me if you had anything happen, day or night." He inhaled a deep breath. "Do you remember that I said that, Abby? That I also gave you my card with all my numbers on it?"

"Of course, but—"

"But? Sorry, no excuses."

Abby delayed answering while she digested his words. "So why are you calling, Detective? How did you know the lights in the house came on in the middle of the night?"

"The night patrol happened to notice," he said.

But his instant response sent up red flags for Abby. "Are you saying that the patrol just happened to be passing at that precise moment?"

"Yeah, that's what I'm saying."

Why didn't she believe him? What more wasn't he saying? She expressed her feelings.

"Let's talk tomorrow, Abby. You're safe since you checked out the house. You're all locked up and no one could have gone past your security. Right?"

"That's correct, Detective Williams."

"Why not call me Bud like the rest of the people in town."

"Okay, Detective Bud."

"No, just Bud. They all know I'm a detective."

"Okay then, I'll try to remember."

"Good. And remember this: Call me if you hear or

see anything, before you investigate on your own. Promise?"

She switched the phone to her other ear so that she could scan the other half of the room. It was just as it had been—safe and secure. "I'll call before I check out anything again," she promised.

"'Atta girl," he replied. "Keep your cell phone with you at all times."

"I'll do that."

"We'll talk tomorrow," he said, and disconnected.

She was about to replace her phone on the night table and reconsidered. Instead she put it next to her pillow, where it was within easy reach. One thing kept repeating in her mind since the detective had hung up: How had he known about the lights going on downstairs?

Were the police staking out her house?

And if so, why?

Because her aunt had been murdered and they were afraid she was next on the killer's hit list?

Oh God, she hoped that wasn't the case.

Chapter 10

IT WAS LIKE A TIME WARP, Abby thought the next morning as she walked around the grounds of the house. Nothing appeared any different from the day she came at age eight to live with her aunt Carolina twenty years ago. The same rose bushes bloomed in the garden, tall sunflowers still lined the fence along the road, and the 1985 Lincoln Continental sedan in the barn/garage looked as shiny and new as it had back then. The thriving vegetable garden, no longer in its summer prime, still had the last of its tomatoes waiting to be picked and made into Carolina's famous spaghetti sauce, and there were still cucumbers ready to be pickled with the dill weed that grew in the herb garden near the back door. It looked as it always had in early fall.

Except that her beloved aunt was no longer there to see to the house and garden she loved.

Abby swallowed hard and managed to hold back tears. She hadn't been able to resist going outside to see for herself where her aunt Carolina had been found. But first she'd again checked out the whole house, opening blinds and making sure that the doors and windows had remained locked. As the coffee dripped she'd slipped into jeans and a sweater, brushed her hair, and with her first mug of the fragrant brew in hand, she'd ventured out the back door.

She'd already had a call from Detective Williams, making sure she was "doing okay."

"I'm doing just fine," she'd replied. "Everything is just as my aunt left it."

"That's good," he'd said. "And I believe I told you that the yard had been cleared by our investigators, so there is nowhere on the property that is off-limits."

"So I'm free to see where my aunt was found?"

"Yes, you are, Abby."

She'd thanked him for his call and hung up. She was about to leave the kitchen when the phone had rung again and she'd answered it.

"We just wanted to make sure you arrived home safely," Mr. Sell said, kindly.

"Yes, I got here right on schedule." She'd been pleased that the Sells were concerned for her and thanked him.

"You're welcome, Abby." They'd hung up a minute after he'd explained that he hadn't heard from the police yet.

Her third call had been from Katherine, who would be on her way over in a few minutes. Since she lived down the street, Abby had figured that she had time for a quick tour of the grounds and had gone outside.

She felt compelled to see the death scene, but once out there she found herself looking at everything else first. Finally she turned to the staircase that clung to the outside of the barn on the side closest to the house. Although the barn was at the back of the property, the steps ended at the front, where the driveway met the building. It was obvious that the stairs were rarely used, as the grass at the bottom grew as lush and green as the whole lawn.

Abby studied the place where Carolina had been found, scanning the wooden steps that stretched up to the door above the garage area in the former barn. She knew that the huge open-beamed room that had once been a hay loft was now only a storage room with decades of remnants: old furniture, china, and trunks filled with clothing and memorabilia long forgotten. Abby knew that some of the pieces were probably valuable, but neither she nor her aunt had ever felt motivated to go through the items, nor had they wanted to. It was all family stuff and they'd hated to dispose of the treasures of dead ancestors.

Stupid, Abby thought. It was one of the jobs she'd have to undertake in the months ahead.

She bent down on her knees on the grass to examine the ground, even though she was sure that the crime-scene investigators had already gone over the area with their high-tech equipment. What did she hope to find that they had missed? Probably nothing, she thought. But still she was compelled to look. She owed that to her beloved aunt, the woman who'd raised her after the death of her parents.

Oh God, she thought, sudden tears spilling down her face. What had happened that was so bad that a loving old woman had to be killed—murdered?

The hand on her shoulder took her breath away and she dropped her coffee mug, dumping its contents. She braced herself for what was to come.

"Abby, it's just me, Katherine." The hand was withdrawn. "You didn't answer the front door so I came around to the back and saw you here."

Shaken, Abby managed to get up onto her feet. "I'm so sorry, Katherine. I guess I'm still in shock over my aunt's death."

"I know, dear." She embraced Abby against her ample body, her blue eyes filling with tears. "We're all still reeling from what's happened. It's unbelievable."

"I can't figure out what could have gone so wrong, Katherine," Abby said. "It has to be random. Nothing was stolen or disturbed in the house." She sucked in a breath. "It's as though someone targeted her for reasons unknown—that is, if she was murdered." A pause. "Maybe she went to the storage area for something and simply fell down the steps."

"We'll know soon enough, Abby," Katherine said. "But for now, c'mon, let's go have a cup of coffee."

She picked up Abby's spilled mug and then led the way back to the house. In seconds they were headed through the enclosed back porch toward the kitchen. Abruptly, Abby pulled free, stepping back to the door and quickly locking it.

Katherine was momentarily startled but stayed silent. They went on to the kitchen, where Abby poured coffee into regular teacups, having deposited her mug in the sink. They both sat down at the kitchen table. Abby was the first to speak.

"I know I seem upset, Katherine," she began. "But I think I'm very shook up, unable to believe my aunt is dead."

The older woman adjusted her glasses on her nose, her blue eyes behind them glistening with unshed tears.

"I know, Abby. None of us in town can believe this happened. Nor can we understand why. It's unfathomable."

"Had she been upset about anything lately? Worried or seeming concerned?"

Katherine shook her head. "Nothing. She appeared completely normal, and everyone else says the same thing. No one noticed any deviation to any part of her life, including attending church. . . . She wasn't even concerned about any of her customers. As you know, most of the people who stayed at the bed-and-breakfast were regulars. I don't think she usually had strangers staying here. She was overloaded with reservations from all of her returns."

Abby sipped her coffee. "Because her rates were so low?"

"Uh-huh, that's what I thought, Abby." A hesitation. "As you know, I was the one who canceled her reservations for the next couple of weeks. However, there are other bookings for the next several months and your aunt took their deposits."

"Under the circumstances, do I have to return those deposits?"

"Yeah, I believe you do." Katherine got up and poured more coffee. "Unless you want to honor their reservations," she said, sitting back down. "If you decide to do that, please remember that I'll help you. I already do most of the baking for breakfast."

Abby nodded and glanced away. "After I visit the funeral home to make the arrangements later this morning, I intend to go over the books, see where everything stands. I don't think my aunt was a rich woman. I just hope she was financially sound. I'd hate to think she worried over money."

"I don't know the answer to that," Katherine replied. "But I do know Carolina never seemed to have extra money."

"I know." Abby slowly shook her head. "She worked so hard for so little."

There was a brief silence that was suddenly broken by the ringing of the doorbell. The two women exchanged glances. Abby tried to hide her instant alarm; she hadn't mentioned her experience during the night. She put down her cup and moved to the hall, to the oval window, Katherine a couple of steps behind her.

Peeking out through the glass, she saw the man on the porch and the freight truck parked in the street beyond the gate.

"It's okay, Katherine," she told the older woman. "It's my belongings that I shipped home."

She opened the door and then saw the man who stood watching from below the porch.

Detective Williams.

She didn't know whether to be annoyed or relieved at his vigilance. Why was he here this time?

She intended to ask him. And this time she wouldn't let him off the hook until he told her the truth.

Chapter 11

ABBY GLANCED BETWEEN THE MAN who'd rung the bell and the tall, attractive man who stood at the bottom of the porch steps, looking sexy in form-fitting Levi's and a jeans jacket. The truck driver looked puzzled and annoyed.

"You sent your things home by this freight company, I see," Detective Williams said, mounting the steps to hand her the transportation invoice. "Right?" he asked, his pale eyes meeting hers, narrowed and questioning. Again she thought, Wolf eyes.

Suddenly she realized that though she'd showered and washed her hair upon getting up, while the coffee brewed, she hadn't applied makeup or styled her hair. Abby knew she looked about as unattractive as he was virile and handsome.

His expression altered and she wondered what it meant—that he was amused? that he'd read her thoughts? or that he actually thought she was unattractive?

Shit! Abby thought. Was she so transparent that he'd seen through her bravado?

He moved up the last step and handed her the delivery papers that he'd taken from the freight-truck driver. "These seem in order, Abby," he said in a low tone. "You agree?"

Annoyance flashed through her but she controlled her impulse to retort. Instead, she glanced at the invoice and nodded at the delivery man, who descended the porch steps and began to unload Abby's freight with his partner. Then she faced Detective Bud Williams.

"It's exactly right," she said, and tilted her chin, even more irritated with his macho attitude. She appreciated that he was there to make sure she was safe, but she hated his know-it-all attitude.

Was that part of his job? she wondered. Or was he just a self-important small-town detective?

"I'm really only doing my job," he said, his demeanor now devoid of all humor. "We, meaning the department and myself, are trying to protect you, Abby, just in case you might be in danger. I believe I've explained this before."

She nodded. "But I'm not satisfied with the reason for that conclusion."

"We aren't either, which is why we're making sure you're safe while the investigation continues." He paused. "Are you telling me that you don't want our protection because you believe your aunt's death was accidental?"

He took a step closer.

She moved back, slightly intimidated by his question. She needed a definitive answer to why her aunt had died, even if she seemed a little unreasonable.

"If it wasn't accidental, then why don't you just say that?" she retorted. "Why do you keep implying that someone killed her? And then you're present for every significant moment, like my arrival, your call in the middle of the night, now when my belongings are being delivered?" She stepped forward and was pleased when he was the one to move back. "What's really happening here, Detective?" She poked him on his jeans jacket. "I deserve the truth."

"Yes, of course you do," he said, recovering his poise. "And I'll fill you in on anything you're concerned about later."

"Later? When?"

"How about this afternoon, after you return from making the funeral arrangements?"

"Okay, what time?"

He shrugged. "Probably after five."

"When you're off shift?"

"Something like that, Abby," he said, his eyes again reminding her of a painting she once saw of a wolf. "I'll give you a call later about the exact time, okay?"

She nodded.

And then he was gone, headed out of the yard and down the street to his parked car. She was left thinking about her latest encounter with him.

It was disturbing. She also couldn't shake the fact that he was the most attractive man she'd ever met.

It didn't take the delivery men long to bring in Abby's boxes and several small pieces of furniture, and when they left, Katherine followed them out the front door. Carolina's friend had hugged her, and then set the time for her return to accompany Abby to Riverview Funeral Home, where she had the appointment to make her aunt's final arrangements.

"I'll be here well before we need to leave," Katherine told Abby, who only nodded. The reality of where she was going suddenly struck her, and she was unable to answer. It was unbelievable that she was now about to bury Carolina. And she would be making decisions without knowing where she stood financially. All Abby knew was that she'd have to take responsibility, whatever the cost, even if the estate was mortgaged to the hilt. She owed the best to the older woman she'd loved all her life.

Don't think about it now, she instructed herself. You have to be calm enough to get through the next few hours—for Carolina's sake. Her aunt would expect nothing less of her. Hadn't Carolina always demonstrated an iron resolve when it came to coping with adversity—like the death of her only sister and brother-in-law. She'd been Abby's only family since then—Carolina and she against the world.

The thought only added to her feelings of guilt. She'd gone to the city believing that she could make a name for herself in the art world. She'd soon learned otherwise but hadn't returned to help her aunt. Although they'd spoken daily on the phone, she hadn't come home to visit on a regular basis, something she would always regret. And Abby knew why.

Sam.

Once, she'd thought they had a future together. She no longer believed that. For a long time he'd given her mixed messages: He wanted her, yet he backed off when she even came close to suggesting that they might live together.

Abby sighed. She'd wasted important time and now she was home and her aunt was gone. She returned Katherine's final wave and went back inside the house.

Her boxes were stacked in the entry. At least unpacking later, after she'd examined her aunt's financial status, would keep her mind off the present, she thought. The ring of the phone sent her scrambling through the cluttered hall.

"Hello?" she asked, grabbing up the receiver.

"Is this Abby?" The man's crisp voice was vaguely familiar.

"Yes, this is Abby."

"Good," he said. "This is Taylor Jones, your aunt's attorney. Have I caught you at a bad time?"

"No, I'm okay for a few minutes, Mr. Jones," she replied, visualizing the fiftyish, painfully thin man who had drawn up her aunt's will. "But I have to leave in an hour because of an appointment at the funeral home." She hesitated. "I was going to call you after I got home, so we could schedule a meeting."

"Sounds good, Abby. We need to talk."

"I agree, and I—"

"I'm glad I caught you before you left, Abby," he interrupted. "I know your aunt's wishes about—uh, her funeral, and I wanted to relay them to you even though I know we'll meet soon."

"About her will?"

"That's right." He coughed nervously. "As you probably know, there are no other heirs to her estate but you. What you don't know are her wishes concerning burial versus cremation when she passed away."

She sucked in a breath. She'd assumed Carolina had wanted burial because of all the family members in the past. "Are you saying my aunt wanted to be cremated?"

"Oh no," he said. "I've only called before your appointment with the funeral home so that you make the correct choices for Carolina's remains." A pause. "I felt a need to inform you, being I was Carolina's lawyer."

There was a moment of silence.

"Thank you, Mr. Jones," she said finally. "Burial was my plan. I suspected my aunt, who was so totally family oriented, would want to be in the family section of the cemetery, just as everyone has been for several hundred years."

He cleared his throat. "Right," he said. "I was just making sure you knew that."

"Thank you," she said simply.

"Welcome." Another pause. "When do you think you can come into my office to hear the will?"

"Tomorrow? Next week?" Abby said, hating the thought. It seemed so final—so having to accept what she hated to recognize.

"Tomorrow then? Two in the afternoon?"

"I'll be there."

They hung up and Abby went to get ready for the funeral home. Oh God, how could she do that?

Because of Aunt Carolina, the woman who'd loved her and raised her, she reminded herself. Carolina deserved the best.

The memorial service and burial were set for the following Monday. Abby had gotten through the arrangements, with Katherine's help, without breaking down completely. When she got home there were messages waiting for her.

One from Detective Williams.

And one from Sam.

Chapter 12

ABBY SAT ON ONE OF HER packing boxes, staring at the phone on the hall table, the red light blinking to indicate that there were two calls. Her aunt's answering machine was at least ten years old, obsolete in today's world of high-tech electronics, but she appreciated its simplicity. She'd already checked on who'd called and knew that both Detective Williams and Sam had left brief messages saying they'd call back later. She was relieved. At the moment she didn't feel like talking to anyone.

Tomorrow was Saturday and Katherine was bringing her two teenage grandsons over in the morning to help Abby put her things away and do the heavy lifting. All she needed to do beforehand was figure out where to store most of it.

She didn't feel like making one more decision today after her meeting at the funeral home. Abby knew she might have gone overboard financially but at least the details for her aunt were completed. She just hoped there was money to pay for all the choices she'd agreed to, which meant she needed to get to Carolina's personal papers in her office as planned. And that meant forcing herself to get started.

Standing, Abby tried not to feel overwhelmed. She headed for the tiny office off the breakfast room in the back of the house, pausing by her crated paintings. The men had placed all the boxes that were marked as art supplies with the pictures and easel. Resisting the urge to open the boxes, to feel the calm that always came to her as she brushed her inspiration onto canvas, she moved quickly to the ledgers and bank statements and the calendar of future reservations that lay on Carolina's desk.

Abby spent the next hour going through the paperwork, and the preliminary glance told her that there was enough money to pay funeral expenses but not enough for household expenses beyond a couple of months. It appeared that room reservations continued throughout the fall and winter until the first of the year, but it was obvious that Carolina hadn't charged enough and had been falling behind financially each month. She'd even taken a small mortgage out on the house the year before, adding to her expenses.

Leaning back in the chair, Abby realized why Taylor Jones, her aunt's lawyer, had pushed for their appointment. She needed to keep things going and that meant gaining power of attorney over the estate so that she could pay the bills.

She hadn't found a life-insurance policy and suspected there was none. The lawyer would know. She added that to her list of questions for tomorrow's meeting.

Sighing, Abby knew her work was cut out for her. She wasn't sure if she'd be able to pull her aunt's bed-

and-breakfast business out of the red. But she must, or she could lose the house that had been in the family for generations. She either had to honor the reservations, and find another source of income to subsidize the costs, or cancel all reservations, which meant returning the deposits and finding a regular job.

"Oh God," she muttered. "If I cancel all those people I can't send back their money. Damn it! That's all the money I have to pay for the funeral." She added those issues to her list for the lawyer.

The ring of the phone in the quiet room startled her. She grabbed the receiver from the back of the desk. "Hello," she said, expecting another friend of her aunt offering condolence.

"Hey, it's Sam. Did you get my message?"

"I did, Sam, and I wondered why you didn't call me on my cell phone."

"I called that number several times before this one. You never answered."

"Oh, I probably didn't hear it." She picked up the pen and idly doodled on her list sheet. "I've been really busy and my purse with my phone isn't always nearby."

"I figured." His inhaled breath sounded in her ear. "So how are things going?"

"Well, I haven't been here long and everything seems to move at a slow pace, although I've taken care of the burial arrangements."

"When will that be?"

"On Monday."

"Shit," he said. "I'd hoped to come up to be with you for the funeral but Monday is out. I have meetings all day."

"That's okay. I never planned on you being here."

"You sound flat, Abby. You aren't mad that I can't be there for you, are you?"

"Of course not," she retorted, glad that her real feelings weren't apparent. He never seemed to be a person to lean on when she had a crisis. Her last day in the city had been all the evidence she needed to substantiate her feelings.

"I'll drive up as soon as my schedule permits, maybe midweek after the funeral."

"Just let me know and I'll make sure one of the bedrooms is ready for you." She gave a wry laugh. "The B and B has vacancies at the moment."

"Yeah, I can imagine. Are you closing it down, then?"

"No. I'll have to make a decision about what to do after I know the whole scope of my aunt's estate. At the moment it's looking like she was operating in the red." She sighed. "It's a dilemma. I certainly would hate to have to sell the family home."

"But since you're the last of the family it will be your decision. Remember, Abby, if you do sell, you would be able to come back to the city and pursue your art again."

She pushed back a flash of anger. He really didn't appear to understand tradition and the pride of owning a house that her ancestors had lived in back when the founding fathers were designing the future of America. Even her own father had taken the Carter name when he married her mother. Since he'd been an orphan without family roots and tradition, he'd wanted that for his children and believed it was important for the Carter name to continue.

"It's a moot point, Sam. There are weeks, if not

months, of legalities to get through before I'll be in a position for such a decision."

"Understood, darling. You keep working on it and I'll see you soon."

"I'll look forward to that, Sam. Just give me a call when you know for sure."

"Will do." There was a brief pause. "I'll be thinking of you, sending positive thoughts. Remember, I care about you."

Then he was gone, their connection broken. Slowly she replaced her aunt's phone back onto its cradle. His call had not uplifted her. It had had the opposite effect: She felt depressed.

Unsettled, Abby tackled her boxed belongings next, sliding the containers that would be taken up to her bedroom into one group. Her art could be placed in a corner of the office until she decided on an area of the house conducive to setting up her easel and canvases. That left her household items that needed to be stored somewhere.

The second floor of the barn with the outside staircase seemed the logical place but for two considerations. Was there space enough up in that room? More important, was she ready to go up there? Only days ago it had been considered a crime scene.

A glance at the clock told her it was still early enough to go out there. With determination, she grabbed a sweater and the door key and headed out to the barn.

All you need to do, Abby reassured herself, is go up the steps, open the door, turn on the light, walk in, and quickly look around to locate enough space for your boxes. Before she had second thoughts about actually climbing the steps and entering the storage room, she hurried forward. She didn't allow herself to dwell on the place where her aunt had been found on the grass at the bottom of the stairs. But when she reached the second-floor platform, she hesitated, uncertain and suddenly fearful.

It is okay, she told herself, turning to glance around the property and house below her. There is no threat here and no one could have gotten into the storage room when it's locked. You're safe. Get on with it and the boys will take care of your boxes in the morning.

Still she hesitated, her whole body quivering with apprehension, and reminded herself that her aunt's death hadn't as yet been ruled a murder.

Get a grip, she thought. You live here now. There is no one to hurt you. But just as she was gaining courage, her fear of the night before surfaced in her mind.

Dumb. She pushed the image aside and jammed the key into the lock. It was time to be a mature adult.

Taking a deep breath, Abby grabbed the knob with one hand and turned the key in the lock with the other. Before she lost her nerve, she pushed the door open, reached for the light switch, and stepped into the cavernous, open-beamed room. Pausing to look around, she realized that the place was cluttered with old furniture, antique barn equipment, and even a patio table and chairs. It was the accumulation of two and a half centuries and smelled of dust, mold, and dead air. She stepped deeper into the room, glancing everywhere, searching for a space to store her things. She found it back against the far wall after weaving and squeezing between all the obstacles in her path.

This is where I'll have the boys bring my boxes, she told herself, feeling satisfied. She breathed a long sigh of relief. But her gratification was short-lived.

The sense of not being alone was instant, and she whirled around to see . . . nothing. Yet the air currents had shifted somehow, as though she'd seen the movement of a shadow out of the corner of her eye.

Ridiculous! No one was there. No one could be. The upper floor of the barn had only one door and no windows. She was allowing her fears to stimulate her imagination . . . again.

It was time to get out of there.

She ran, bumping into trunks and boxes, furniture and miscellaneous junk, knocking over many items as she went to the open door. She felt a presence behind her but was too frightened to lose precious seconds by pausing to glance. She was breathless when she sprang through the doorway to the upper platform.

The hand on her arm was sudden. Her breath stopped in her chest as her legs folded under her like a puppet without its strings. She would have fallen but for the person holding her captive.

Then he spoke.

Chapter 13

"ABBY! ABBY, TAKE IT EASY. You're okay."

She twisted around and faced Detective Williams. "Why are you here?" She realized that her voice sounded next to hysterical. "Why did you sneak up on me? Were you trying to scare me?"

"I don't understand what you're accusing me of doing." A pause. "Remember, I was coming by around five?"

He released her and she stepped back.

"I was only seeing where I could store my things," she began. "The logical place was where my family stored their belongings—the huge space above the garage, which was once the barn and carriage house."

"Yeah, I understand all that." His word pattern was rapid, like machine-gun chatter. "But you think another person was in the room with you?"

"Uh-huh, that's what I felt."

"Did you see someone?"

She hesitated. "No, but I sensed a presence close to me and I thought I saw a shadow move across the wall."

"I'm sure it was nothing. Wasn't the door locked when you came up here?"

"Yes, but I swear I saw something." His words were calming but Abby wasn't convinced.

"We both know there is no other way in or out of this room." He nudged her to the top of the steps. "You go on into the house. I'll make sure there is no one in the storage area, okay?"

"But, Detective Williams, what if there is? Should I call the police?"

"Not unless I don't show up at the house in the next few minutes." He grinned. "Go on. I'll join you momentarily."

She nodded and started down the steps, but she glanced back and saw that he'd drawn his gun from the shoulder holster under his black leather jacket just before he disappeared into the storage room. She reached the bottom and ran to the back entrance. Once inside, she locked the door behind her, backed up to a kitchen chair, sat down, and waited for the detective.

She couldn't help the niggling feeling that crept into her thoughts: Why was the detective right on the scene of another frightening experience? Was it coincidence?

Or was it deliberate?

And if so, why?

She'd have to ask him.

Ten minutes later he hadn't turned up. She glanced out the kitchen window and saw the storage-room staircase across the yard. The door at the top was now closed.

Her terror returned, sending a trembling numbness into her limbs. She grabbed the tabletop to steady herself, waiting a minute until the feeling passed. Stay calm, she thought. Detective Williams is probably checking the outside of the building before coming inside.

She moved to another window but still saw no sign of the detective. Something was wrong. It was time to call 911.

Her hand was on the phone when he tried the door, found it locked, and then knocked.

"Hey, Abby, it's me," he called. "Open up."

She moved quickly to unbolt the lock. In seconds he'd stepped into the kitchen. "Well?" she asked, happy that her voice didn't wobble. "What did you find?"

He shrugged, spreading his hands. "There was absolutely nothing amiss. I couldn't find anyone hiding anywhere." He stared at her and she realized that he saw how shaken she'd been by the incident.

Her glance was caught by his pale eyes and her first impulse was to look away. She forced herself to hold the gaze, and as earlier in the day, was aware that he was even more masculine and sexy in his Levi's, black T-shirt, and jeans jacket than she remembered him in slacks and sport jacket under a long raincoat.

"Are you thinking I'm only imagining things?"

"Hell no. But I realize how terrible this is for you, Abby." He stepped farther into the room. "Your landlords told me about your traumatic day, being attacked by an intruder in your own home. . . . I think it's only normal for you to be extra sensitive right now."

"So you *do* believe I'm imagining these incidents—today and last night."

"I didn't say that. I'm only saying that you have a valid reason for being fearful, especially since there isn't a definitive determination on your aunt's death yet."

"But you said you'd probably have more information after I returned from the funeral home."

"That's why I stopped by rather than call again." He paused. "The final report has been delayed."

"When can I expect to know now?"

"I anticipate an answer very soon, maybe by the first of the week."

A silence dropped between them.

"What do you think the final determination will be, Detective Williams?"

"How about you calling me Bud," he reminded her. "I think I told you that all my friends in this town do?"

His change of topic disconcerted her. For a moment she didn't know what to say. "Your card doesn't include Bud," she managed, evading.

"True, but then it is a professional card," he said, and the corners of his eyes crinkled slightly, as though he repressed a smile. "As I just said, my friends call me Bud, have since I was a little guy."

"Okay, Bud it is. I won't forget again." Sobering, she went back to her question, wondering if he had tried to sidestep it with the issue of his name, an interchange they'd had before. "So, Bud, I go back to my ongoing question: Do you believe my aunt's death was accidental or murder?"

"Hey, it's against the rules to put a detective on the spot about something he's already answered several times," he said, joking. She wasn't fooled. He was positively avoiding her question. "Do I detect coffee?" He sniffed the air. "If so, I could use a cup."

"Forgive my manners." Abby went to the cupboard and took down two mugs. "Please sit down and I'll pour one for both of us—if you don't mind coffee that's been simmering for two hours."

"Two hours is nothing compared to the all-day brew that we drink at the precinct." He pulled out a chair and sat down at the table. "In answer to your question, Abby, I have to wait until I get the report from the experts in forensics before I can say anything on the record."

"I'm asking what you think off the record."

"And if I tell you my opinion and it doesn't prove to be accurate you might become a very irate citizen, which in turn wouldn't look good for me."

"Okay, I accept that, Detective William, uh, Bud." She sipped her coffee, glancing at him over the mug. "But I think I already know the answer anyway."

"Oh yeah? And what would that be?"

"You can't understand how she got the blow on her head from falling down the steps onto grass. Something doesn't add up for you." Abby knew she was like a dog who wouldn't give up his bone, but she couldn't help repeating the analogy. The real answer was too important to her. "You're leaning away from her death being accidental."

He took a large swallow of coffee. "Remind me to never have a guessing competition with you."

"Which means I guessed correctly?"

"The scientific determination will be the final conclusion, as I've said. That means that I'm not the medical examiner or the forensics expert and therefore I can't make guesses. But that the blow doesn't seem to fit the trajectory of the fall or the obstacles she might have hit on the way down—but that still doesn't mean it wasn't accidental."

"What are you saying?"

"Well," he began slowly. "For example, we know she wasn't accosted by our current rapist, who has been trolling the area for victims in the last year."

"For God's sake, Bud." She shook her head in disbelief. "Surely the police wouldn't think a woman like my aunt was the target of a rapist?"

"Most rapists don't discriminate and go for the easy target. We investigate all possibilities, Abby, regardless of how improbable, until all the facts are in. She could even have suffered a fatal heart attack or stroke."

Abby nodded, digesting his words.

He drained his cup and stood up. "I'd better get going."

She got to feet, still facing him. "I'm sorry to push you, Bud. Really, I do appreciate your position—that all leads must be followed."

"And I yours." He smiled and she was again reminded that he was a seriously handsome man, detective or not.

She led the way to the door and he paused to look down at her before stepping onto the porch.

"I don't have to tell you to take precautions, do I?"

She shook her head. "I always make sure the doors and windows are locked, and as you probably already know, the cellar has no indoor access."

"Uh-huh, I know the layout of the house. It's pretty secure."

A silence went by.

"If my aunt was murdered, do you think I'm in danger, too?"

"Jeez, I hope not." His hands suddenly came down on her shoulders and squeezed gently. "But it was a bit coincidental that you were also attacked in the city on the same day your aunt died."

"You're scaring me again, Bud."

"No need to be frightened, just cautious."

He stared down into her face for another few seconds, as though he were considering something. What? Scolding her?—or kissing her? If Sam had looked at her like that she would have known what the look meant.

A moment later he strode out to the porch, then turned back for his final words. "You have my numbers, call if anything at all doesn't seem right. Backup can be here within minutes."

She nodded. "I will."

"Oh, one last thing. I have a question for you, one I keep forgetting to ask. It's about your last name."

She stared, surprised. "What about it?"

"This town was named after your mother and aunt's ancestors, so how did you come to have the same last name as their maiden name and not that of your father?"

"That's an easy question, Detective Bud. My dad was an orphan without family. He knew how important it was to my mother and aunt to keep the family name going, and since there were no men left to do that, he had his name legally changed to Carter before my mother gave birth to twins, one of course being me."

Now it was his turn to stare. "You're a twin?"

"Was. My sister died at our birth."

"I see," he said slowly, and she wondered what it was that he was seeing. Then he cocked an eyebrow, descended the steps, and was gone.

Once again she was alone in the house. It would

get dark soon so she locked up early. Then she went up to her bedroom to lie on her bed and think about the decisions she needed to make in the next few days.

Abby would not allow the fear to creep into her thoughts. She needed a good night's sleep, deep enough so that she didn't hear all the creaks and groans of the old house—and see imagined shapes on the wall. The solution was obvious.

She got up and went downstairs to the cabinet in the dining room where her aunt kept the brandy she always served her guests as a nightcap. Instead of pouring herself a glass, Abby carried a glass and the whole bottle back upstairs. She might need two hits of the liquor for the desired effect, and no way was she up to going back downstairs later in the dark to refill her glass.

She was in bed a few minutes later, hoping the brandy would allow the sleep she so desperately needed.

Bud poured coffee from his Thermos bottle into a mug, then sat back against his car cushion. He hated stakeouts and this one promised to be a long night.

He was parked down the street in a place where he had a good view of the bed-and-breakfast, but was out of sight from any of the main windows. Abby wouldn't notice him.

Abby. Damn, the woman was special: beautiful, smart, talented, and with enough fire in her temperament to justify the reddish chestnut hair. He meant to keep her safe until he'd figured out what in the hell was happening—if Carolina's death had been deliberate and if Abby might be the next target of the killer.

Until then he'd be losing lots more sleep on his own time. Aside from the case, he had his own agenda after it was all settled, one that included the woman he was trying to protect.

Chapter 14

ABBY ENDED UP DRINKING several shots of brandy before the liquor suddenly hit her with a warm sensation of well-being, reminiscent of the secure feeling she'd always had while growing up in her aunt's house. The last thing she remembered was switching off the bedside lamp and sliding deeper under the quilt.

Sometime later she slowly came awake with a sense that she wasn't alone. A quick glance around the dark, shadowy room told her that she was, and she turned over, snuggled deeper into the pillows, and was again drifting back toward sleep.

Imagination, she told herself, a mental reaction to her current situation. No one had stood at her bedside and fingered her face with a feathery touch. No one could have been in her bedroom; she'd made sure that every exterior door was bolted and each window was locked. She was safe. No one else was in the house.

She'd be damned if she allowed herself to be scared by each sound in the night. I will not dwell on Aunt Carolna's death, she told herself. Once all the facts were known it would be ruled a tragic accident, of that she was positive. It could not have been murder. Everyone loved her aunt. No one would have had a reason to harm her. Carolina had been the keeper of family history, which in turn was Carterville history. From America's founding fathers who'd once lived along the Hudson River, to the American Revolution, to the Underground Railroad, which had saved the slaves who escaped their owners in the South to live in freedom, her aunt knew it all. She'd been truly respected, an icon of the area in her own small way.

Abby's thoughts were comforting and she went right back to sleep.

Bright sunlight shone in through the windows as Abby opened her eyes, then sat up in bed. A beautiful autumn morning, she thought. A good omen. Today she would figure out the course of her immediate future, get started on the rest of her life—just as her aunt would wish her to do.

Energized by a good ten hours of restful sleep, she climbed out of bed, ready to face the day. Katherine and her grandsons would arrive a little later to help move her boxes to storage. But first things first, she reminded herself, grabbing her robe. Everything could wait until she brewed coffee, her daily ritual.

Abby was still tying the belt as she left her room and headed down the hall to the staircase. Everything seemed peaceful, just as it had been the night before. The downstairs entry was splashed with prisms of light that shone in through the front door's oval window. Again, all was as she'd left it before going to bed.

Moving on to the kitchen, Abby soon had the coffee

started, and as it dripped she moved through the house, opening blinds and adjusting the curtains. A few minutes later she took a mug of steaming brew back upstairs to sip while she got ready for the day. There was a lot to do and she was eager to start. The one thing she blocked from her mind was the thought of murder.

That she could be in danger.

Ridiculous, she told herself. The fact that she'd been attacked in her apartment on the day her aunt died didn't mean anything more than coincidence. She had to get past the recent habit of leaping to unfounded opinions—like wondering if someone had been in her room while she slept. It was a crazy. Only a week ago she would never have jumped to such an instant conclusion. It was a bad habit, one she meant to stop immediately.

But you were followed to work along the streets of New York that last day—before someone waited for you in your apartment, her mental voice reminded her.

Shit! Now was not the time to think of random events.

Abby hadn't unpacked her clothing yet but she found a pair of old jeans and a sweatshirt in the closet, discarded garments her aunt had saved. Quickly, she dressed, applied a little makeup, and clipped her hair into a ponytail. By the time she'd made the bed and was headed downstairs she needed a refill of coffee.

She reached the kitchen just as the hall clock chimed nine and she realized that Katherine and her grandsons were due within the next hour. When the phone rang she guessed it was her aunt's friend verifying their arrival time.

"Hello." Abby held the receiver to her ear with one hand and poured coffee into her mug with the other.

"May I speak to Abby Carter please?" The man's voice was vaguely familiar.

"This is Abby."

"Oh, it is you," the man replied. "I didn't recognize your voice."

Abby hesitated. "Mr. Sell?"

"Yes, this is Mr. Sell, your old landlord."

Her surprise was instant. When she'd left the city she hadn't expected to hear from the couple ever again. Now they'd already called twice. "Mr. Sell, I apologize." She put her mug on the counter. "What's up?"

"I have your laptop computer and want to make arrangements to get it back to you."

"You have my laptop? How did that happen? It was in its leather case and I'm sure the taxi driver put it in the taxi." Abby glanced at the hall where her boxes were stacked and realized she couldn't remember seeing it since arriving home. She certainly hadn't used it.

"He did, but somehow it got left in the trunk of the taxi when he gave you your bags at the train station." She recognized his chuckle. "Lucky for you he was an honest cabbie. He found the computer, remembered it was yours, and brought it back to your point of origin. He just left a few minutes ago and then I called you."

"Oh my goodness. I can't believe I forgot my computer. I must have been even more upset than I thought."

"You were pretty upset, Abby. And with good cause."

"Yeah."

"Have things settled down a bit?"

"I'm doing better, Mr. Sell." She sucked in a long breath. "I can't thank you enough for calling and offering to send my laptop. I'll give you my address and repay you for the cost."

"I have a better idea." A pause. "Mrs. Sell and I will be driving up your way tomorrow and we'd be happy to drop the computer off at your house. That is, if you're going to be home."

"I'll be here, Mr. Sell. But I don't expect you to make a special trip because of me."

"No problem, Abby. You probably don't know this but my wife was born and raised up in your area and still has an uncle living in the old family house a little upriver from you. We'd already planned our Sunday visit before the cabbie brought your computer back."

"Are you sure it wouldn't be out of your way?"

"Not at all."

"Then I'll pay for your gas," she offered. "It's the least I can do."

"We can discuss that tomorrow, Abby. Just give me your exact address."

She gave him the information and they settled on a time. After thanking him again she hung up, then slumped onto a chair to sip her coffee. She needed the caffeine.

Damn. She'd really been in a bad way to have forgotten something as important as her computer. She hoped she'd calmed down a little since then.

But Abby knew she hadn't.

"Oh, yes, I've heard of the Sells," Katherine said later as they stood in the hall with the two boys, contemplating the boxes. "Velma Sell is a distant relative of old man Robertson and will likely inherit whatever is left in the estate. I hear she's the last living descendant, even if the relationship is by marriage and not blood. The Robertson family was once powerful and influential, starting back in the late 1600s, and continuing until after the Civil War."

"And no longer?" Abby asked, wondering why she'd never heard of the family.

"Nope, the clan has almost vanished now. Their heyday is long in the past. No one even talks about them, haven't for years. Old man Robertson, who's past ninety and a recluse, was married twice, his first wife died, their child was killed in an accident, and the second wife never produced another heir."

"What a coincidence that the Sells, who were the managers of my apartment building, are also from this part of the country." Abby hesitated. "They are really a sweet couple."

"Uh-huh," Katherine agreed. "But maybe not as much of a coincidence as we might think, since old rumors say that Robertson was once a slumlord, owned quite a few apartment buildings in the city." She shrugged. "It's possible he still has a few left and you happened to live in one."

Abby grinned. "Are you saying that I lived in a tenement owned by a slumlord?"

Katherine looked stricken until she realized that Abby was teasing. Then she sobered. "No, but I know your aunt worried about where you lived, believed it was unsafe." She raised her brows. "How did you come to choose that apartment anyway?"

"Purely random, I assure you. When I first went to

New York I lived with two other women I knew through art school. After they moved on I had to find a place I could afford on my salary from the gallery. Sam, my boyfriend, and I scoured all the places in my price range, found the apartment in the Sells' building—" She spread her hands. "And the rest is history."

"Yep, life can take strange twists and turns, that's for sure," Katherine said.

"Hey, Grandma, can we get started?" Ryan, the taller boy, asked suddenly. "We have to get to practice on time."

"Yeah, if we're late our football coach might bench us," Mike, the younger grandson, added. "He has a short fuse for lateness. Besides, we won't have a practice next weekend because of the jazz concert in the park."

"Oh, I'm so sorry, boys," Abby told them. "It was thoughtless to keep you waiting while we gossiped. The job shouldn't take long. I so appreciate your help."

She showed them the storage area above the garage and where she wanted things placed. All was quiet in the cluttered, cavernous room, as though no one had been there since her frightening visit when the detective had come to her rescue. Within an hour everything was stored away and her personal things had been taken to her bedroom. As the boys left she insisted on giving each of them twenty dollars, above Katherine's objections.

"I insist," Abby said. "Ryan and Mike just did me a huge favor and I'm far more grateful than I can ex-

press." She smiled at Katherine. "Look what you've already done for me."

Tears welled in Katherine's eyes. "I mean to look
out for you, my dear. After all, Carolina was my dearest
friend of a lifetime. I'm already missing her."

They hugged, and Abby watched as they went outside and headed down the sidewalk. Then she closed
and locked the door.

Somehow she felt more settled now that her things
no longer cluttered the hall. She moved toward the office. She had work to do in rescheduling the post-
poned reservations and she needed to get down to the
lawyer's office for her appointment. She would keep
the bed-and-breakfast going through the current reservations and she knew how she might subsidize her
income.

She would set up her easel at public events, like the
jazz concert for the final Music in the Park event of the
season coming up next weekend, and do her quick
pencil portraits of anyone who could pay the small
fee. She'd decide on an exact price later, after she determined what the traffic could bear.

Things will work out, she told herself. They had to.

Abby didn't learn anything new during her meeting
with Taylor Jones. The attorney went over all the legalities of her aunt's estate, reiterating that she was the
sole heir, that the house had a small mortgage, and
that there were no valuable investments and no life-
insurance policy. In plain language, there were no
available funds.

Abby thanked him and went home with a new determination. The only way to save the Carter property was to maintain the bed-and-breakfast, honor the reservations already in place, and then raise the rates.

After the debts were satisfied she would reconsider her options for the future.

Chapter 15

THE MAN WHO STOOD on the bluff between the railroad tracks and the Hudson River suddenly kicked a rock over the edge, watching as it tumbled and bounced down to the moving river. Angrily, he whirled away from the view and headed for the tracks, crossed over them to the path that led to the city park farther up the hill. It was late afternoon and he needed to hurry or he would be late for work.

It would have been so easy to end the whole nasty business last night, or the night before that, he thought. Or better still, the night in her apartment. If he'd succeeded while she still lived in the city, he could have had some fun before killing her—satisfied his growing desire for her. A murder in a run-down walk-up apartment could have been deemed a random risk for living in such a neighborhood.

Now it was a different story. Her death had to be an accident, especially after her aunt's death. The two must not be connected. Anything other than a preliminary police investigation must be avoided.

That meant sex was out of the question. Forensic science had advanced too far. Getting away with a rape or murder was not a sure thing any longer. The police often got their killer these days, especially if that killer was stupid enough to leave traces of himself, like his DNA.

Shit, he thought. The problem was, he was attracted to the bitch now. He'd been watching her for a while: her habits, her style, and even how she slept—like a Grecian goddess with her hair splayed out over the pillow and her soft breasts trembling with each breath.

He'd barely been able to restrain himself after gently fingering her face, a touch that had unexpectedly awakened her. Luckily, he'd been able to reach the hall in the seconds before she'd opened her eyes. There he'd waited, out of sight, ready for action had she had not gone back to sleep. He would not have had time to reach his entrance, the one that had been connected to the house since the days of the Underground Railroad in the mid-1850s.

He wanted her. No, he had to have her, whatever the ruler of the rules said to the contrary. He had to be careful about all that forensics crap, that's all. He could protect his identity by making sure he left nothing of himself behind. He was smart enough to do that.

She would be his before she died.

After he'd found what was needed. After that, the whole world would be his for the taking.

Chapter 16

THE DOORBELL RANG at precisely two o'clock on Sunday afternoon. Abby had awakened early, refreshed, pleased that she'd finally managed to sleep a whole night without interruptions or nightmares. She'd already gone through her aunt's reservations again, this time taking notes on Carolina's procedures on payment and cancellation fees. One truth stood out above all others: She'd made the right decision to continue with the bed-and-breakfast. Later, after the place was showing a profit, she would reassess her options.

Another truth had been confirmed: She needed to subsidize the business income until the reservations had been satisfied and she could raise the room rates. Otherwise she could lose the property.

Although she dreaded the thought of her aunt Carolina's funeral tomorrow, Abby felt upbeat as she opened the front door to see the older couple on the porch. Mr. Sell held her laptop computer while Mrs. Sell smiled and nodded her greetings.

"Please come in," Abby said, stepping back as she opened the door wider. "You're both so nice to have taken the time to deliver my computer. I hope you didn't have to come very far out of your way."

"Not at all, dear," Mrs. Sell said. "We're just pleased that we were able to get it back to you." Her pleased expression was genuine and Abby couldn't help thinking how much more attractive the woman seemed away from the shoddy apartment building. For starters, she was dressed in a stylish pants suit and was wearing makeup.

"And, as I said on the phone, we'd already planned on our trip upstate," Mr. Sell added.

They stepped into the hall and Abby indicated that they should follow her into the sitting room, where she'd prepared a tea tray on the coffee table in front of the fireplace.

"I remembered that you liked a cup of tea in the afternoon," she told Mrs. Sell. "I hoped you'd both join me so I took the liberty of getting it ready. The tea is steeping right now."

"You timed it just right," Mrs. Sell said. "And I'd love a cup after our long drive."

She sat down on the settee across from the over-stuffed chair her husband took and the matching one Abby sat on to face her. For the seconds it took to settle themselves there was silence.

Abby poured the tea into her aunt's bone china cups, handing one to Mrs. Sell and then one to her husband. She poured her own cup last, after which she passed the tea cakes and cookies she'd taken from the freezer, specialties baked by Katherine for her aunt's customers.

"Mmm, good tea, Abby," Mrs. Sell said. "If I'd known you liked tea when you lived in our building I would have invited you for a cup when you were home." She smiled kindly. "I suppose I should have known, since you were from Carterville."

"But then we didn't realize you were one of the original Carters," Mr. Sell added. "Your roots go back as far as the famous Livingston family."

"The Carters were never rich like the Livingstons with a manor estate, were never Colonial landlords, nor were they involved in the formation of our country or signers of the Declaration of Independence," Abby replied. "But they stood with the revolutionaries to free the colonies from England and fought in the Revolutionary War. They were here from the late 1600s, a part of the people who were the foundation of our country."

"And they had a town named for them," Mr. Sell said, taking his first sip. "They weren't born to the manor but were a family of the people."

"That's true." Abby passed the tray of cookies and little cakes. "It was an honor that the settlement where they lived took their name."

Mrs. Sell chose a tea cake. "These are wonderful," she said after taking a bite. As Abby smiled, acknowledging her compliment, the older woman went on. "In light of our conversation, I have a question for Abby."

Abby raised her brows, waiting.

"Your family name is Carter through your mother. So how is it that you have the family name and not your father's?"

"Simple," Abby replied. "My father was an orphan without a real family name so he took my mother's when they married."

"Oh, I see." The woman chewed thoughtfully. "Most unusual."

"So what was his last name before the wedding?" Mr. Sell asked.

Abby shook her head. "You know, I don't recall, as it was never talked about and he died with my mother when I was quite young." She shrugged. "I have the documentation somewhere, in my aunt's papers I suppose."

A brief silence went by.

They finished their tea and the Sells stood up to go.

"Thank you for the delicious refreshments," Mrs. Sell said. "The cookies and cake absolutely melted in my mouth. I'd love to have the recipes."

"You'd have to ask Katherine Dover, my aunt's best friend, for them. She does all the baking for the bed-and-breakfast."

Mrs. Sell started to comment but Mr. Sell cut her off. "Please call us, Abby, if you need anything at all. We're often visiting in the area and we know you're alone up here." He hesitated. "And as I told you on the phone, we'll stay in touch concerning any police updates on your attack."

Abby controlled the urge to cry. After thanking him she quickly changed the subject as they stepped into the entry hall. "Do you have many relatives in the area?"

"Not many, my dear," Mrs. Sell answered. "Only a very elderly man and a grown son. Like you, our son is in the arts."

They'd reached the front door and Abby opened it. "He's an artist?"

"Uh-huh," Mr. Sell said. "A musician, not a painter or singer, although he does write music."

"He plans to cut a record using his own songs, that is, when he has the money to do so." Mrs. Sell laughed nervously. "You know how hard it is to get a break in any of the arts. If you want to be successful you have to fund the program and make it happen."

"You're right about that," Abby agreed. She understood what it took. Hadn't she just left New York, probably forever? Regardless of the circumstances now, she couldn't have afforded to stay without funds.

After final good-byes she watched her former landlords head to their car. Then she went back inside and closed the door, suddenly feeling depressed. It was as though her last friends in the world were leaving her.

Nonsense, she told herself. As her aunt had always told her while she was growing up, "Action cures fear."

Abby shook off her foreboding and did as her aunt had always advised. She went to the office to continue going through the books.

It was an hour later when Abby admitted to herself that she wasn't concentrating on the ledger entries in front of her. She pushed back the desk chair and stood up. She'd go for a walk, clear her head.

She put on her athletic shoes, slipped into a windbreaker, locked the house, and made sure she had her keys zippered into her jacket. After checking the lock from the porch, Abby headed down the path through the trees and foliage, the quickest passageway to the Hudson River beyond the railroad tracks below. It had been her way to the river when she was a child and no one had changed the terrain in all the years since. It was still not zoned to build on due to its steep bank.

As Abby descended she felt her dark mood dissipating, drifting away with the wind that had come up off the river. The day was bright and uplifting, although cool with a hint of days to come later in the fall. She crossed the tracks and kept walking toward the river where she knew there was a bluff overlooking the current, a place where she'd often spent time as a child when she'd felt down and adrift without her parents.

She sat on a familiar outcropping of rock, the place where she'd often processed her fears. She stared out over the water, watching the river traffic, wondering about the people she glimpsed in the pleasure boats. Were they safe? Happy? Were they contented couples on an outing? She hoped so. Somehow she needed to feel that there were successful people, successful relationships.

Why? she asked herself. Because she'd had high hopes for her relationship with Sam—and he'd let her down at a time when she'd needed his strength to lean on?

Unsettled, she stood. It was time to go.

She'd think about her personal feelings later, after the memorial service tomorrow. Abby realized that her upbeat feeling was fragile; she needed to protect it.

After a final glance at the river, she turned away and started back, retracing her steps along the path through the undeveloped gully between the railroad station and the town's park, the place where she would set up her easel to do quick sketches for extra money.

Sighing as she crossed the tracks to the steep path, Abby resigned herself to her decision once again. She'd have to carry on with the bed-and-breakfast. There was no other way to preserve the Carter property. Although she was the last family descendant, she had every intention of marrying one day and having children, heirs to the name and all that it meant.

As she started up the path her mind was elsewhere: her aunt's funeral tomorrow, her course of action after that, and Sam's feelings toward her.

Oh God, she thought. Don't think about the future. All you can do is your best. If you lose the property it isn't your fault.

Then whose fault is it? she wondered.

But she knew she couldn't blame her aunt, who had belonged to a different era, who'd been programmed by her own parents, Abby grandparents who'd died long before Abby's birth, to preserve family history.

Thus, Carolina had broken a scared trust by opening the family home to a bed-and-breakfast, the only way she knew to keep their property.

Deep in thought, Abby was unaware that someone was on the trail behind her. It was only when she stopped to catch her breath that she heard the rustle of the snapping of branches that had overgrown the path.

She whirled around to face the downward path. Behind her the trail seemed undisturbed after her passageway, had settled back into place. Had she heard only her own passing?

Then a snapping twig just beyond her vision below her on the path told her that she'd been right. Someone was behind her—someone who'd stopped after she had.

Oh God! she thought. Someone was following her.

Keep your cool, she instructed herself even as everything in her told her to run. Whoever it was didn't know she was on to their presence. She needed to keep it that way, retain the edge until she reached the top of the bluff, where there might be someone to hear her cry for help.

She started out again, climbing at her former pace, but once above a strategic curve in the path, she began to scramble as fast as possible, glad that she was still in the physical condition she'd been in before leaving Carterville.

The noise behind her told the whole story: Someone was back there who seemed to be chasing her.

Why? Was it someone who simply used the path as she did? Or was it a person with an alternate motive— like catching up with her? And then what?

She pushed herself to go faster, oblivious of overgrown branches that slapped against her and muddy dirt that she splashed through on the path. Behind her she heard someone accelerate his or her uphill climb as well.

Oh God! Someone was trying to catch her in a place where no one could witness her predicament.

Abby sucked air as she sped uphill, hearing the person behind her crashing through the brambles, obviously having realized that she was aware of being followed. She prayed she'd make the top before her pursuer caught up.

She broke into the open space at full speed, and before she could assess her location, she crashed full force into the person who stood at the head of the trail.

"What in the hell's going on?" a voice said as arms came around her.

Abby couldn't answer. Her breath was gone. She was on the verge of hyperventilating.

She'd been rendered helpless. By whom? Friend or foe? She hoped it was the former.

Because she was momentarily helpless in that person's hands.

Chapter 17

"HEY—HEY!" THE MAN SAID. "Take it easy. It's me, Bud Williams, uh, Detective Williams. For God's sake, what propelled you up the hill so fast?"

Abby managed to catch her breath and stepped back so that the detective's arms fell away. "Someone was trying to catch up with me on the path."

"Someone you know?"

She shook her head, glancing over her shoulder at the shadowy foliage of the steep slope. "I never saw who it was."

"Then how do you know there was another person behind you?"

"I could hear them." She took more deep breaths, trying to calm her rapid heartbeat. The sounds from the path below had ceased. "I got scared, and when I started to run, whoever was behind me began to run, too."

His glance moved to the opening in the overgrown brush below the trees. "If someone was following you they should have appeared by now." His gaze shifted back to her. "Are you sure what you heard came from the path? The woodsy part of the bluff is small and sounds can be deceiving."

"Are you implying that I was imagining things?" she retorted.

He cocked one brow as sunlight glinted in his pale blue eyes, again reminding her that the slant and color were similar to a wolf's eyes. "Are you?"

Instantly angry, she turned away and would have run back to her house. He grabbed her arm, restraining her as he took a cell phone from his pocket and made a call. She heard him give brief instructions for a patrol car to check out the street below and the bottom of the path. "Walk the whole trail to the top," he ordered into the phone.

Then he flipped it closed and took her arm, steering her toward the back of her aunt's house. When they reached it he waited as she took out a key and unlocked the door. Then they went into the kitchen.

They stood facing each other before she indicated a chair for him. She still felt shaky as they sat down at the table and he took out a pad and pen from a shirt pocket under his leather jacket.

"I could make coffee. Would you like a cup?"

"No, thanks," he said. "But I think you need something. You still seem pretty upset."

Abby suppressed her annoyance at his suggestion and strived to stay calm. "What in the hell is going on here?"

Her question brought his eyes directly to hers. His gaze was intense but she couldn't read his thoughts.

"That's what I'm trying to figure out," he replied without missing a beat. "And I'm hoping for your help in doing that."

"How can I help if I'm confused," she said, still feeling shaky. "Why is a homicide detective even involved in my aunt's death when the determination hasn't even been made that it was murder?"

His gaze veered away and then returned with such a direct look that she glanced down. "It's the reason I was here today, Abby, to discuss that with you."

"What's that?"

He hesitated, then glanced at the clock. "It's almost six, and I was off duty at five." He raised a thick, dark brow. "Do you have anything alcoholic in the house?"

She nodded. "My aunt serves brandy at night but I think she might have a private stash somewhere for friends. I haven't looked in the liquor cabinet in the office so I don't know what she has, if anything." She didn't mention her own bout with the brandy.

"If she has a bottle of scotch, I'll have one with you, okay?" His gaze was compelling. "And then we can talk about why I'm here."

"Can't we just talk now?"

"No, after a drink," he replied, and she could tell by the look on his face that what he had to say was serious.

She found a half-filled bottle of scotch in the liquor cabinet and brought it back to the kitchen. Taking two glasses from the cupboard, she plopped them on the table.

"Do you take it straight or with water?" she asked.

"With water."

She poured a jigger into each of the two glasses and added cold water and ice cubes.

"You seem like a pro."

"No, only a person with a boyfriend who drank scotch and water."

There was a brief silence.

"So you have a boyfriend." It wasn't a question. Bud sat back in his chair. "May I ask where he is now, when you need him here?"

Another pause.

"Back in New York City." This time she hesitated before continuing her response to his question. "And to be honest, because you're a police detective, I don't really know if he is my boyfriend anymore or not."

She felt tears welling again and looked away. Get a grip, she told herself. Sam has nothing to do with your talk with the detective. When Abby again met his eyes she'd regained her self-control.

"So you're not in a serious relationship with a man," he said. "That means no one has anything to gain by being committed to you."

"My God, what are you saying?"

He gave a noncommittal shrug. "Only that no one connected to you has anything to gain by your aunt's death."

"Detective Williams, isn't that really reaching? What could my personal life have to do with anything?"

He shook his head slowly. "Maybe nothing of significance, I'm not sure yet."

"That's an ambiguous answer. Please clarify, Detective."

He'd dropped the boyfriend issue, but she sensed that he had read between the lines—that Sam had disappointed her. Nonsense, she corrected herself. He wasn't a mind reader, only a detective.

He sipped his drink. "I want you to be okay with what I'm about to say," he said finally. "Even though it's not what I'd hoped to report."

She'd just taken a big drink of the scotch, and now

she met Bud Williams's direct gaze, bracing herself for another jolt of reality.

"Just tell me, Detective."

"Bud."

"Okay, Bud," Abby said. "Tell me what you came here to say."

He emptied his glass and then set it back down on the table, as though he needed to steady his nerves. Abruptly, he met her eyes.

"Your aunt's death wasn't accidental," he said gently. "It's been ruled murder by our criminal science investigation unit."

His words hit her hard.

"Go on." She managed a low whisper, suddenly realizing why he'd wanted her to have the scotch. Somehow she'd never believed that her aunt's death had been murder; she had allowed herself to think that the delay in announcing the cause of death was due to police follow-up procedure.

"At first glance, an accidental cause of death was the obvious conclusion," he said, continuing. "However, there were several indicators that told a different story, so we delayed a final determination until we had the forensic report."

Abby swallowed hard, barely hanging on to her composure. "What did the report say?"

"We know that the cause of death was a blunt-force trauma to her head prior to her plunge down the stairs. She had other injuries that were consistent with the fall but they weren't fatal."

"How can you know this?"

"The forensic-lab guys can prove that she didn't die from an accident. Someone stuck a blow that killed her."

A silence fell between them while she digested his words, willing herself to stay calm, not to cry. Finally she responded: "This is like some crazy dream. Who in this world would kill my aunt? She was loved by everyone since I can remember, from when I came to live with her as a child after my parents died."

"Yeah," he said. "We know about your background, and all the years since." He reached to cover her hand that was resting on the table. "We don't know who did this, Abby. That's what we hope to learn from you, even if it's only a few leads that might give us a starting place."

"I'll help in any way I can. If someone killed my aunt I'd give my own life to get them."

"We don't want you to do that, Abby. We want you to stay safe." His gaze intensified. "And that means you'll have to take precautions, curtail some activities until we can develop our case and catch the killer."

"Maybe it was a random murder, someone who'd stayed at the B and B?" She traced the ring of her glass with a finger. "My aunt treated customers like family while they were here, charging far less fees than other B and Bs, and by keeping her rates low, jeopardized the financial status of the business. She worked hard to save the property that meant so much to her."

"Yeah, we know that, too. And we've checked out everyone connected to the B and B in the past year and they've been cleared. None of those people are suspects."

"Oh my God, then who is?" She quickly drank the balance of her drink and plunked down her glass on the table.

Another silence.

"That's where we need your help, Abby. We want to hear about anything your aunt might have told you."

"Of course I'll do what I can but I don't know anything. . . . How could I? I wasn't here."

He leaned forward, and the look in his pale blue eyes was suddenly warm, not like a predatory animal. "We would like you to give us any background you can, on family, friends, or anyone that your aunt may have had conflicts."

"That's easy, Bud," she said. "She had no family other than me, never had conflicts with anyone I ever knew of, and her relationships with friends were an open book. I'm sure they would answer anything about her that you wish to ask. I know you'll only hear positive evaluations of my aunt."

He nodded and stood up. "You're right about that. I was hoping you could add something that would give us another avenue to follow."

Abby stood, too. "Can I offer you a refill?" She tried to keep her voice steady and was relieved when he declined. That her aunt's death hadn't been accidental frightened her. It was unbelievable and had to be random. She expressed that to the detective again, the only possible answer to the mystery.

"Yeah, that's a possibility, Abby," he said. "It might be so, but in the meantime, as I said before, we want you to exercise caution, especially since you were already targeted by someone before you arrived here."

"What do you mean?"

"Only that we want to make sure the two events weren't connected."

"Is there anything about my life that you don't know, Detective?"

His gaze flickered over her and his eyelids lowered slightly as he answered. "I suspect I don't know everything, Abby. But I intend to make that my job in the immediate future."

Another ambiguous answer, she thought, glancing away. She walked him to the front door, where he turned to face her and she had no option but to meet his eyes.

A silence stretched between them as he stared down at her. He was the first to break it.

"I want you safe, Abby, because it's my job to protect you," he said slowly. "On a personal level, off the record, I'm going to make sure you are. I want you around for a long time."

Then he left, taking the front steps two at a time, headed for his unmarked car parked on the street. She watched him go, wondering about his final statement, feeling her sense of security go with him.

When he was gone she closed the door and locked it.

And then the doubts closed in. Why was he always there when she felt jeopardized? Because he was watching over her?—or because of something else entirely?

She was attracted to him, wanted to believe him. But could she?

She needed to know more about her aunt's life, about what was happening in Carterville, before she could make that assessment.

She hoped he was who he seemed to be.

Chapter 18

ABBY WAS UP AT DAYLIGHT the next morning, feeling too anxious to stay in bed after a restless night of tossing and turning. She'd gone to bed early after checking and double checking that the house was secure—and then she hadn't been able to turn off her mind enough to sleep.

This afternoon was her aunt's funeral.

She made coffee and then straightened up the lower floor, feather dusting the antiques and running the vacuum cleaner over the oriental rugs. Katherine had told her that she and other friends of Carolina's were setting up a buffet at the house for the mourners after the service. They were doing all the work, the setups and cleanup. Although Abby preferred to be alone, she knew that the gathering was important to her aunt's old friends—so they could process their loss.

Abby kept herself busy, trying not to dwell on the upcoming graveyard service so she wouldn't break down. Her final job before going upstairs to bathe and get ready was to gather fall flowers from the yard. Then she arranged them in vases to place in the dining room and parlor.

It was her tribute to her beloved aunt, a remembrance of those golden days when she was a little girl and picked bouquets for Carolina. Dandelions or the first rose of summer, her aunt was always delighted, making Abby feel special, which gave her a happy and secure childhood.

At ten o'clock, her chores completed, she headed toward the steps to go up to her room and start getting ready. As she passed the hall phone it rang, startling her. For long seconds she stared at it. Then she grabbed the receiver.

"Hello."

"Hey, Abby. It's Sam."

She plopped down on the chair next to the phone. "Sam, I guess I'm surprised to hear from you."

"How so?" A flat note crept into his tone. "I thought you'd be happy to hear my voice."

"Of course I am, Sam. It's just that today is my aunt's funeral and I was about to get ready." She hesitated. "Actually I'm pleased to know you were thinking of me."

"Uh-huh, I was." He drew in a breath. "I only wish I could be there to support you."

"I understand," Abby began, "but—" He cut her off before she could add how much that would have meant to her. As it was, she felt totally alone.

"I knew you would, sweetheart." His laugh sounded false. "I am still negotiating for my art exhibit and now there are other interested galleries so you can imagine how busy I am. I have meetings all day today."

"Congratulations." Abby couldn't think of anything else to say. It was like she was talking to a casual friend, not someone she'd believed was her boyfriend who had serious intentions toward her. "It sounds like everything is going well in your life, even more so since we last spoke."

"Yeah, everything's great. I'm really excited about all that's happening in my career."

He went on to explain details but she scarcely listened, wondering why he didn't see how inappropriate his bragging was in the face of her losses—her aunt's funeral and the symbolic death of her own painting career. She waited for him to pause and then broke into his explanation.

"I'm sure it's all wonderful, Sam." Abby realized that her tone sounded contrived and a bit sarcastic. She didn't begrudge him success but she was taken aback by his insensitivity. She guessed he'd forgotten that today her aunt would be buried, that his call was solely because he wanted to talk about himself. "But I must hang up now or I'll be late for my ride," she added.

"Thanks, Abby. I knew you'd be supportive of my—"

"Just as you are for me during my time of need?" she interrupted coldly, unable to hide her disgust.

"What do you mean by that?"

"Just what I said," Abby snapped. "Didn't it ever occur to you that today I may be the one who needed encouragement, a friend who listened to me rather than the other way around?"

"Jeez, you're really upset. What in the hell did I do to you? I only called you on the phone."

"Uh-huh, so you could talk about yourself."

"For God's sake, Abby, that town is really getting to you. I'm looking forward to you moving back to the city, where we can have a normal relationship again."

She didn't bother to respond. Hadn't he heard a

word she'd just said? "Bye for now," she said, and
hung up before he had a chance to say more.

She continued up to her room. In one way she was
glad that he'd called, and in another, hearing from him
had been a downer.

But she'd finally stopped pandering to him and expressed her real feelings—and that was empowering.

Katherine and her husband had come for her precisely
on time, and she was grateful for their consideration.
She'd turned down the offer of the mortuary limo, unable to bear the reality of being the lone relative. The
memorial service at the chapel had been short before
the few people who'd gathered went as a group out to
the grave site. The attending minister had uttered his
words over the casket, words Abby scarcely heard and
could not remember a minute after they'd been uttered. It was as though she were outside of her skin, a
soul looking down on an unreal event.

She came back to the present as the last words were
said, as the people in attendance came to offer condolence. She managed to thank them and wondered how
the whole terrible scene could be happening.

And then she was jolted with reality. *It was true*.

On the edge of the crowd her gaze met pale blue
eyes, the gaze of an alert homicide detective.

Bud Williams.

And beyond him on a knoll was another man, leaning against a tree. A policeman in plainclothes? How
many more surrounded the scene? And why were they
there when her aunt was already dead?

To protect her?

There was no clear answer. And that left her

thoughts spinning. It was all too mysterious. Had she missed something? She'd been living in the city for many months; had something happened while she'd been gone, something her aunt knew that had been dangerous for her to know? Did someone think she knew what her aunt had known?

Magical thinking, she told herself, remembering the term a co-worker had once told her about conclusions drawn by faulty thoughts. At this point she was confused about everything.

She watched as the people moved away to their cars. As Katherine waved and turned away, guided by her son and daughter-in-law, Abby suddenly panicked.

They were leaving her, the people who'd brought her, who were headed back to her house for the gathering of friends. About to call after them, an arm came around her shoulder.

"I'm driving you home, Abby," Bud Williams said. "I told Katherine that you'd be going with me."

Her eyes met his, amber and icy blue.

"But I came with them," she said, protesting.

"And you're going home with me."

She didn't argue. Somehow she felt safer in his hands. Whatever was happening, he would protect her.

Nonsense, she told herself as they walked to his car. He wasn't invincible; he was only a homicide detective.

But that was enough for now.

Chapter 19

THE DAY IS FINALLY OVER, Abby thought as the last person left the house three hours later. Everyone was gone but Katherine, who'd stayed so that they could discuss getting ready for the three guests who had reservations for the weekend, people they hadn't reached to cancel. Mostly, Abby needed to know the routine: who cleaned the rooms, did the laundry, cooked, did the bookkeeping, and paid the bills.

The answer was not surprising: her aunt Carolina.

"Your aunt always said the work kept her young," Katherine explained. "She did have my grandsons do the yard work, I did all the baking, and a girl helped with the cleaning during the summer when she was really busy." The older woman shook her head. "I always told her it was too much for her, that she could hire another person to help."

Abby could guess why Carolina had done so much herself—she couldn't afford not to, a fact that Katherine had not been aware of. The bookkeeping told the whole story. It was obvious that Carolina hadn't understood that when business expenses went up, it was totally acceptable to pass those costs on to her guests.

The room rates would still have been a good deal, less than most comparable places in town. In addition, her aunt had cooked far more food for breakfast than the typical bed-and-breakfast. She prided herself on treating guests like family.

Abby sighed, feeling guilty. She should have been more aware of her aunt's circumstances. She'd assumed that the woman who had always been so capable didn't need her help, that Carolina was financially secure. How wrong she'd been on both counts.

"So you're planning to satisfy the reservations, keep the place going for now," Katherine said over a final cup of tea after they'd completed the cleanup.

"I have to, Katherine. I have to make some money to pay the mortgage, or lose the house."

"Mortgage? Good God, since when?"

Abby explained. "I never knew she was having financial troubles."

"She never let on to me, either." Katherine crinkled her brow, accentuating the deep lines in her face. "She always seemed so upbeat, so healthy." Tears glistened in her eyes. "I don't know what I'll do without her."

"I'm so sorry, Katherine." Abby fought back her own emotional response. "I hope you'll continue assisting me with the B and B as you helped Carolina," she began. "And show me how to get into the routine of running the place."

"Of course I will," Katherine said. "And my grandsons will continue with the yard work, if you want them to." She hesitated. "They don't charge much."

"Oh, please have them stay. The grass should be cut before Friday when the guests arrive."

"I'll make sure they do that on Thursday after school."

"Thanks, Katherine. And will you continue to bake for the Saturday and Sunday breakfast?"

"Of course. Muffins, coffee cake, and a loaf of bread."

"All that for three people?"

"That's the routine. And who knows? You might fill up the third bedroom. I understand you're booked for a double and a single, which leaves one room available. When the word gets out that you're open again I expect you'll be getting calls."

"I suppose that could be true, unless word of how my aunt died gets out."

"Don't worry about that, Abby. Time passes and people forget."

Abby nodded, sipping her tea. "I'll have to make sure that the rooms are ready and the house is clean." A pause. "And that I'm ready for my responsibilities to the guests, like nightcaps of sherry in the parlor."

"I can help you with all that," Katherine said.

"I'll need a menu of breakfast."

"Breakfast was far more than muffins, coffee cake, juice, coffee, and tea."

"I know that, Katherine, even though that might be the menu of most B and Bs. What did my aunt serve?"

"A full breakfast on Sunday. She loved to fix bacon, ham and eggs, hash browns, and all the trimmings, prepared in all variations."

"I'll do that," Abby said. "My aunt taught me to cook and I'll love fixing breakfast." She paused. "I plan to honor all of my aunt's reservations even though they're not going to cover expenses."

"But how can you do that, Abby? You just said Carolina was operating in the red."

"Yeah, that's true." Abby drew in a breath. "But I

have a tentative plan for additional income, until the current reservations run out. Future patrons will pay a higher rate, one that will cover the expenses and leave a little for profit."

"What will you do for outside income, Abby?" Katherine asked. "You're going to be pretty tied down by the work here."

"Sketches."

"Sketches? What do you mean?"

"I do pencil drawings of people in public places, setting up my easel with a tray of pencils. My sketches only take a few minutes and I charge twenty-five dollars. In New York City I made enough money to subsidize my job so that I could afford to pay my rent." She wiped her long hair back from where it had slipped over her face. "I figure I can do the same here at the next event, which is at Riverfront Park, a jazz-group performance where I can possibly make money on quick sketches." She paused. "As long as I can find someone to be here for the time I'm there."

"I'll be here, Abby." She drained her cup and stood up. "After that you can arrange for help to be here for the customers when there is a special event."

"Katherine, how can I thank you, how—"

Her aunt's friend silenced her with a raised hand. "I want to help, Abby. Carolina was my friend all my life. It's what she would have done for me."

Abby had no words. She could only say thank you. After accompanying Katherine to the door, she gave her a long, lingering hug. Then she said good-bye, watched her go out to her car and leave, headed to the store before going home. She closed the door once Katherine's taillights faded away.

Everything will be manageable, Abby thought. She could make it. She had to.

It was an hour later when Abby finished her chores on the main level of the house, including her lockup routine, and went upstairs. It was still daylight, and an anticlimax: She was feeling down, upset, and scared. But she was committed to the one thing she'd been avoiding.

Looking through her aunt's things—in Carolina's bedroom. Someone had killed her aunt. The police had examined the house and her aunt's bedroom, but were there clues she might find that the police hadn't?

It was time for her to face her fears. And whatever it was that had prompted murder. But was it murder? Or was it really only a tragic accident despite what the police forensics unit had indicated? She needed to go through her aunt's things—and the records from the past—before she would be convinced that Detective Bud Williams was right.

But if someone was responsible for the deliberate death of her aunt—the kind, exceptional woman who'd raised her—she wouldn't rest until that person was found. That was her only certainty in her uncertain life right now.

But as she opened the door and stood on the threshold of Carolina's bedroom, smelling the faint fragrance of her aunt's perfume, seeing the antique furniture that had been in the family for generations, tears streamed down her face.

Oh dear God, she thought. Who would kill such a gentle soul? And why?

It had to be a random act, she thought. There was no other logical explanation.

Abby sat down on the patchwork bedspread, trying to calm herself. "Get a hold of your feelings," she whispered aloud. "You can't fall apart now."

Slowly, she composed herself, suppressing the flood of memories that tried to surface each time she looked at Carolina's personal belongings. Abby assumed that all legal documents were down in the office, as she knew that Carolina had not had a safety deposit box at her bank—unless she'd gotten one recently. It had never occurred to her aunt that such important papers could be destroyed by fire or theft. She had continued the family tradition of keeping them safe within the possession of the owner.

Abby shook her head. Faulty thinking in today's world.

Moving from where she sat on the bed, Abby stepped into the center of the room, her gaze traveling over the furniture, some of which dated back over two hundred years. The house was a shrine to the past, one of the reasons why her aunt's bed-and-breakfast had been so successful. Abby realized that some people would pay a higher rate just to step back in history, whether or not the service was as special as her aunt had made it.

Abby tried to separate her memories from the present situation. She needed to stay focused on her current predicament of saving her heritage from foreclosure.

It was her birthright. It was up to her.

Slowly, Abby started to go through her aunt's belongings: her jewelry, which seemed intact; antique pieces that dated back to pre-Civil War days; then her drawers, which produced precisely stacked underwear; and personal effects that ranged from old photo albums and diaries to current calendars of Carterville events. It was a treasure trove of long-ago events.

Abby sank back down on the bed, her mind processing the history that was present in her aunt's bedroom. She stared at the closet, wondering if it was worth an inventory. What could be of historic value in her aunt's closet? Carolina had always dressed in the current fashion, always seeming younger by her slim figure and trendy style.

Going to the closet, Abby flung open the doors, her gaze gliding over the hanging garments. She recognized the clothing, the size 8 dresses, pantsuits, skirts, and blouses. Most of the outfits were old, with a few new pieces each year. Carolina had been a master of looking up-to-date with the expensive clothing she'd bought sparingly over the years.

There was nothing in the closet that was unusual. About to close the doors, Abby hesitated, her gaze on the place where the floor met the back wall. The dark line that marked the connection didn't seem quite right: The crack seemed to be too wide a separation.

She bent down on her knee and pushed at the back wall. Nothing moved. So why did it seem so out-of-sync? she wondered. Because the house had settled?

Still, Abby studied the seam.

It seemed that there was a black line of film at the conjunction of wall and floor, like where carpet met the wall in her apartment in New York—created by air in the walls, her landlord had said. So what would do that in Carolina's closet?

There was nothing Abby could pinpoint as significant. She simply didn't know.

She left her aunt's bedroom and went across the hall to her own room. Tomorrow she would check out the other closets in the other rooms. I'll run it by the police if there is a question, she decided.

Then she directed her thoughts into a different channel. Abby was determined to find the person who'd killed her aunt.

Chapter 20

OH JESUS, HE COULDN'T BEAR IT. How could God expect him to control himself—the woman was too big a temptation, despite other reasons to abstain. Was God with him, or was he supposed to take the high road—allow his natural instincts to be suppressed?

He didn't know.

He could only go by his inner voice. And that voice told him to go for it, that there was a bigger picture that meant his own satisfaction.

The others who demanded his obedience could be damned. They weren't the ones on the line. He was the one taking the chances, the person who took the risks.

Fuck them.

He was important too, the one who could change things for all of them—unless he chose to expose the whole rotten truth, about the people who went to any length to gain their own means.

Shit, he'd followed her up the trail, his desire growing in his groin with each step, and then he'd been thwarted. At the graveyard service he'd been far enough away that the police, the plainsclothesmen who'd tried to blend into the landscape, hadn't spotted him. His desire was growing; he had to have her—soon.

It had to happen despite what the financial ramifications were, what his beloved advisers had entrusted him to do.

It was a bitch! His goal seemed like a conflict, a test of his God-given pledge of commitment to family. He must comply or be kicked to the side, abandoned by his support group.

It wasn't an option. He had the old maps of the secret Underground Railroad routes, and the houses that were on that path for the escape of slaves from their Southern bondage. He knew all the houses on the list even if their owners did not know.

With the secret tunnels and escape routes.

He'd explored all of them.

And he would use them again—when it was safe. Soon.

Chapter 21

THE NEXT FEW DAYS PASSED uneventfully, if crammed with work to get ready for the weekend guests. Abby had examined all the closets and found nothing out of the ordinary. On Thursday, true to Katherine's prediction, Abby received a call from a young university student hoping to make a reservation for Friday and Saturday nights. Momentarily tempted to raise the room rent, Abby decided against doing it. It would be best to stick to her original plan of increasing her fees after all the current reservations had been satisfied. The last thing she needed was for guests to compare prices.

"I'm just grateful to have another two-day reservation," she told Katherine, who was preparing the kitchen for the weekend baking. "I can use the money." Abby would be the lone cook on Saturday and Sunday mornings, and was seated at the kitchen table preparing her menu and making a list of items she'd need at the supermarket.

"Are you nervous about the breakfasts?" Katherine asked. "If you are I could come over and—"

"Strangely, I'm not," Abby said, meeting her eyes. "I

actually love cooking and especially breakfast. While I was growing up my aunt and I had a tradition of me fixing the meal on Sunday mornings before church." She gave a laugh, remembering. "I've cooked it all: eggs Benedict, soufflés, waffles, and pancakes. And according to Carolina, I was good." She glanced down, still smiling. "I guess we'll see."

Katherine pulled off her apron and hung it on a hook behind the panty door. "That does it for me. I'll be back at six o'clock Saturday morning to get my bread and coffee cake in the oven." She hesitated. "But if you need me to help with preparations I'll come over."

"Thanks, Katherine, but everything seems all set except for the arrival of our guests. Your grandsons cut the grass and weeded, you've got the baking under control, and I've readied the rooms and cleaned the house."

"And you know how to check the customers in, like running their credit cards?"

"Yup, I sure do." Abby said. "And I've gone over all my aunt's records and bookkeeping." She blew out a long sigh. "I'm as ready as I can be."

"Good," Katherine said. "Just know that you can call me if you have questions."

"Believe me, I will. Thanks, Katherine. I can't tell you how much I appreciate your help and support."

"I know, sweetie. Just remember that Carolina was like a sister to me. Back in the years when we were growing up, your mom, aunt, and I thought we were the Three Musketeers."

Abby swallowed hard. She'd almost forgotten that story, one of many about her mother, Carolina, and Katherine when they were young. Her aunt had painted a rich tapestry of words so that Abby would remember her mother as she grew up.

"We were all close almost from birth. I too grew up in the house that had been in our family for generations, the one down the street, where I still live." Katherine crossed the space between them and embraced Abby. "We go back so far that our parents and grandparents were friends."

Abby fought tears, a chronic condition lately. She'd known that, but the significance had never sunk in before. She'd been right to come home. Although she was the last Carter descendant, her roots went deep. I'll carry on the lineage, she told herself. She realized the importance of family more than ever before.

As Katherine left, Abby knew that her aunt's friend had no idea how her words had affected her. There was so much at stake, her birthright and that of everyone before her, that she felt a new burden of responsibility.

As Katherine reached the front gate she turned back. "Oh, Abby," she said. "I forgot to mention Jenny who lives down the street and would love a job if you have one."

"What kind of a job?"

"She's seventeen and I thought she might be someone to be here on Saturday or Sunday afternoons to answer phones if you're sketching at special events in town. I know you're hoping to make money with your portrait sketches."

"If you're recommending her, I am interested in Jenny. Is she reliable?"

"Totally. She's saving money for college. Jenny is determined to be a doctor."

"Wow! What's her hourly rate?"

"Eight dollars an hour."

"Thanks, Katherine. Please tell her to come by tomorrow. Everyone checks in on Friday afternoon and I'll guarantee her the hours between one and six for two days, which means eighty dollars to her. The breakfast will be long past and brandy hour will be later. She'll only need to be present and can contact me by cell phone if there's a problem."

"There won't be a problem, Abby. You only have four guests, and they'll be off doing their own thing during the afternoon hours."

"That's my guess."

"Okay, I'll send her by later to meet you." Katherine smiled. "But I did offer to be here for one of those days, too."

"I know, but I want you to be with your family."

Katherine headed to the sidewalk, on her way to her house down the street. Abby went back inside and, as had become her habit, locked the door.

The couple, Laura and Jim Stanton, arrived in early afternoon on Friday. The young man, Harvey Odem, came in with his photo equipment an hour later, announcing that he was a freelance photographer, doing a piece on antiques of the 1700s. Laura Stanton, an antiques buff, was immediately intrigued, and she and Harvey made arrangements to meet on Saturday in town before starting the tour of antiques shops. Jacqui Quinn, a college student, was there to attend the musical festival in the park.

Abby knew she was free to be present at the entrance to the festival to sell pencil sketches, and was

grateful that she'd hired Jenny, a serious and motivated girl, to watch the bed-and-breakfast while she
was away for a few hours.

She'd felt reassured after her four guests had
checked in. They all seemed to like the bed-and-breakfast. The couple and single man had been there before.
She'd already prepared the kitchen before going to
bed and was up, showered, and dressed when Katherine arrived before daybreak.

"You're up already?" Katherine said, smiling. "I had
a key in case you weren't."

"I know, but I wanted to be here to ready the cof-
feemaker and my breakfast stuff. Since I'm practicing
this weekend, I figured I'd add scrambled eggs and
crisp bacon to the menu. It'll help me figure out what
works for a B and B."

Katherine grinned. "You're so much like your aunt. I
know you'll go all out for Sunday."

"Yeah, I expect so. I want to keep up my aunt's reputation as a B and B hostess, even as I have to raise the
rates in the future."

Then she and Katherine went to work, Abby preparing the dining room table, setting it for the four guests,
while Katherine put her bread and coffee cake into the
double ovens. They were ready as first the couple,
then the single man followed by the college girl came
down to eat.

The food was such a success that they all lingered
over coffee even after they were stuffed and couldn't
swallow another bite. When they finally dispersed to
freshen up before they headed out for the day, Abby
cleared the table and cleaned up the kitchen.

Abby changed into Levi's and a green turtleneck,

and, grabbing a windbreaker, left a short time later, after Jenny arrived to be present in case someone needed something. Abby lugged her case of pencils, an easel, her huge sketching tablet, and a folding canvas stool with her. At the last moment before heading out the door she'd grabbed a handful of B and B business cards. Driving her aunt's shiny old Lincoln Continental, she steered along the street, turned downhill toward the river, and upon reaching the street, parked.

She stepped outside and followed the people to the park above the river. Then she set up her easel. Within minutes she'd attracted a small group of people, had given her spiel and begun sketching. When the first portrait was finished to a murmur of praise, her confidence soared, as did her coffers as she quickly sketched one person after another.

For the first time, she felt that she could save the family home.

Chapter 22

WHEN THE CONCERT BEGAN with a loud blending of guitars, piano, drums, and an occasional violin, Abby's line dwindled to one young woman of nineteen or twenty who was inappropriately dressed in a long, hooded raincoat. The male singer's voice blared out over the crowd, who sat on blankets and folding lawn chairs, clapping to the beat of the music. The sound was instantly deafening, even though she was out near the street, some distance from the portable stage.

The young woman waited for a break between songs, then stepped forward. Fortunately, the next number, which began almost immediately, was not as blaring and loud.

"You're so talented," she said with a hesitant smile. "I can't believe how accurate you are with your sketches."

"Thank you." Abby was so glad that she'd remembered to bring the business cards, which had been taken by her impressed audience. Her mind was already jumping to future events in town, wondering if she'd need a business permit to sketch at public places.

"Would you do a sketch of me?" the woman asked. She slipped the hood off her head.

Abby's gaze flickered over the slight woman whose long curly dark hair framed an oval face with perfect features. Her brown eyes were direct as she waited for Abby's answer.

"Of course, I'd love to." She raised her eyebrows in a question. "What's your first name?"

"Maryanne."

"Well, Maryanne, just sit down on my folding stool and we'll get started.

"The sketch costs twenty-five dollars?"

"Yeah, that's right." Abby's tone was kind but firm. At the moment she couldn't afford to do freebies if she intended to pay her bills. "And I'm not set up to take checks or credit cards."

"I know," Maryanne said. "I've watched you handle your customers."

"So you still want a sketch?" Abby asked, sensing something apprehensive about the girl.

"Yes, it's to be a present for my parents on their twenty-fifth wedding anniversary." Maryanne lowered her eyes, as though unable to meet Abby's gaze. "I want them to have a recent portrait just in case."

"In case of what?"

"That I die."

Abby was momentarily taken aback. "Goodness, Maryanne, why would you think you could die?"

"Because of what's happened." Her words wobbled.

"Oh," Abby said, uncertain how to respond. "I'm sorry that you had a bad experience." Her thoughts spun with questions that she sensed shouldn't be asked. Maryanne's darting eyes told the whole story: She was scared to death of something.

"No, I'm the one who should be sorry," Maryanne

said. "I shouldn't have said that. It's just that I can't stop thinking about what happened."

"It's okay," Abby replied, and pretended to look through her pencils, giving the woman time to compose herself. "You obviously have a good reason for saying what you did."

"Yes, I do." The woman hesitated. "Have you heard of the serial rapist who's been attacking women in our area for the past year?"

"Yes, I did hear about him, although I've only been here for less than two weeks. I don't know any details."

Maryanne lowered her lashes again. "I was one of the victims."

"Oh my God." Abby put down the pencil in her hand. "How terrible for you."

A brief silence fell between them as Maryanne composed herself.

"It happened a couple of weeks ago and I've lived in fear ever since," Maryanne said finally. "This is the first day that I was emotionally able to leave my parents' house." She pointed up the hill behind them to a small yellow house. "I watched you from the porch." She licked her lips nervously. "I saw what you were doing through binoculars and waited until the concert was about to start before walking down here."

Abby didn't know how to respond, so she waited as the woman sat down on the stool in front of her. "Before I begin, do you want to loosen the buttons on your coat so that the collar is away from your chin?" she asked instead.

Maryanne nodded and opened the coat, exposing her neck. Abby realized that the young woman was truly traumatized, and in an attempt to help her subject relax for the sketch, she began to chat about the concert.

"Do you like jazz?" Abby asked as the music grew louder. "I have to admit it's not my favorite."

"Mine either. I only came to get a sketch."

Abby kept up light chatter, and by the time she finished the sketch Maryanne was smiling. "Do I really look that good?"

"Absolutely." Abby grinned. "In fact, you're beautiful, Maryanne, and I was wondering if my drawing had done justice to you."

"I love it and I know my parents will, too." She sobered suddenly. "And please forgive my earlier outburst. It wasn't fair of me to burden you with my problems."

"Hey, don't apologize. I understand more than you know." Abby suddenly decided to share her experience, feeling that Maryanne might benefit from hearing it. She dropped her hand onto the other woman's arm, then told her what had happened to her in New York City, although her attacker had been scared off before she was raped.

"I was lucky," Abby said. "You went through a far worse situation than mine."

Maryanne's lashes fluttered, as though she was trying to keep from crying. "Did your assailant threaten you?"

"No. Did yours?"

"Yes. He told me if I identified him he'd come back and kill me." She paused, her gaze direct. "There has been one victim since me and she was murdered. His threats are the reason I haven't been able to leave home. I imagine he's out there, watching. Because I did see him, he might fear that he could be caught, and come back to silence me."

"That's terrible, Maryanne. Did you tell the police that he'd threatened to come back?"

"I did, and I also tried to describe him but I can't seem to remember exactly how he looked. I even looked though mug shots."

"Did they have you describe the rapist to a sketch artist?"

Maryanne nodded. "But I couldn't come up with a viable likeness." She managed a weak smile. "I was too traumatized."

Abby realized that Maryanne hadn't fully grasped the procedure. "Here, let me demonstrate," she said. Quickly, she began to sketch, explaining the steps as she drew. A few minutes later she had the face of an angry man, his long hair obscuring part of his face, his eyes narrowed with determination. "This is how I remember my assailant, even though this isn't too accurate because I didn't get that good of a look at him. He was interrupted by my landlord and didn't stay long." She ripped it free and handed it to Maryanne. "This is just an approximate example of how a police artist works."

She glanced around to make sure no one was nearby before offering to sketch the rapist, if Maryanne was willing to describe him.

Maryanne nodded slowly. "I think I'm up to it."

"Good. Here we go. I start with a circle and you think about him, whether his face should be wider, or more narrow and long." She glanced at Maryanne.

"You tell me and I'll make the alterations. When you're satisfied, I'll continue on until we have your opinion on each of his features, including hair."

With each stoke of Abby's pencil Maryanne described how her attacker was different, pointing out the facial features that needed sharpening or less definition. The drawing was finally finished.

Abby put down her pencil.

"My God," Maryanne whispered. "I can't believe this. It's him. That's the rapist."

"Are you sure?" Abby didn't know if she should be flattered or alarmed. Maryanne was a stranger. Maybe she was also a psychotic mess and had fabricated the whole story. If that was true, she'd played into the delusion with the drawing.

You should have thought of that possibility before the sketch, not after, she reminded herself.

"Can I have the sketch?" Maryanne asked. "I want to give it to the detective who's investigating my case."

"What's the detective's name?" Abby figured Maryanne's answer would give her a sense of the woman's mental state.

"Bud Williams."

Abby was momentarily at a loss for words. She handed the drawing to Maryanne, along with the one of her own attacker. "I'm glad you're taking it to the police and I hope it helps in their investigation."

"Thanks . . . uh, I don't know your name other than Abby."

"It's an old-fashioned name, Abigail Carter. I grew up here too, and—"

"I know who you are, Carolina Carter's niece," Maryanne interrupted, her expression sobering. "I'm so sorry about your aunt. The whole town is upset about her death."

"Thanks, Maryanne." Abby busied herself with packing up her supplies. "I'm trying to keep everything going—thus, my portrait sketches."

"Everyone in town knows about your artistic talents, Abby, because your aunt was always bragging about you."

Abby swallowed back an instant lump in her throat, a precursor to breaking down in tears. She managed a smile. "I intend to find out what happened to my aunt." She took a quick breath. "She was my only living relative."

"Oh, Abby, I'm sorry." Maryanne stepped forward and embraced her. "You can't imagine how much you've helped me." Tears glistened in her eyes. "I'm so glad I made myself come down to the park."

After agreeing to stay in touch, Maryanne took her sketches and headed back to the house on the hill. Abby watched her progress while she packed up. She wanted to make sure the young woman got home safely.

She was about to leave and load her things into the Lincoln when an elderly man, dressed in a black suit and a fedora, stopped her with a stunning question.

"You know that you live in a haunted house, don't you?" His voice seemed to vibrate and his dark eyes held hers in a riveting stare. "It's the site that was on the Underground Railroad. Your house has secret entrances and exits and is occupied by those who were trapped there."

For a moment Abby couldn't come up with a response. She'd heard the legends since childhood, had even searched for the secret places, as had Carolina and her mother before her. No one in recent times had ever found passages in the walls or under the house. If the stories were true, the tunnels would have been closed up by the 1870s, after the Civil War ended.

"That's not true. What a mean thing to say." She swallowed air and, despite his advanced age, continued. "Since you know about my house, you must also know that my aunt was recently murdered." She felt herself losing control.

The old man backed away, seeming intimidated.

"How dare you confront me about where I live," she cried. "Are you trying to scare me?"

In seconds he'd disappeared into the crowd, leaving her shaken and feeling guilty about her outburst. As the band took a break and people circulated among the nearby concessions, Abby adjusted the art supplies in her arms and hands and was about to head to the car. The band members who'd left the stage caught her eye. For a moment she hesitated, watching them from across the park. Then she moved on.

For a moment she'd felt an instant recognition. She'd been wrong.

She didn't know the men in the band.

Chapter 23

RETURNING TO THE BED-AND-BREAKFAST should have been uplifting for Abby, but it wasn't. All the guests had returned for their final night and her focus was on planning breakfast before they checked out. After completing her kitchen preparations, Abby locked up and went to her bedroom. Her thoughts were still on the menu when she finally went to sleep a few minutes before eleven.

Surprisingly, perhaps because the bedrooms in the house were filled with people, Abby slept through the night until the alarm rang at six the next morning. Within a half hour she'd showered, put on hip-riding tan slacks with a wide belt and a brown, long-sleeved, scooped-neck cotton top, and applied makeup and clipped up her hair. After a final glance in the mirror she went downstairs, put on one of her aunt's big aprons, and began to make breakfast. The guests would start coming down to eat at eight and she wanted to be ready for them.

Everyone came into the dining room within five minutes of one another, making Abby's job much easier. Everything she'd prepared could be served straight from the oven and stove: the vegetable omelet, crisp bacon, homemade rolls, French toast, and an oven pancake that was topped with a fresh berry sauce. In addition, she served a platter of fruit—bananas, grapes, oranges, and apples—and coffee, tea, and orange and other juices. Katherine's coffee cake and pastry platter completed the menu.

"It's a feast!" Jacqui Quinn announced.

"We've never had such a great breakfast at a B and B," Laura Stanton said.

"Amen," her husband, Jim, agreed. "This is the best ever."

The consensus of her guests was unanimous: The food was beyond expectations, the rooms were special with the antique furniture that dated back to the Revolutionary War, and the rates were the best in the area. Their affirmation was uplifting and Abby suddenly knew she had a viable business. As the guests checked out, leaving with vows to return even though Abby informed them that the rates were going up soon, she felt even more positive.

"Everything costs so much these days," she explained. "We're forced to raise rates enough to cover the increases, although I'm sure we'll still be reasonable in comparison to other establishments."

Once everyone was gone, Abby cleared the dining room table, putting everything back in order. Then she tackled the kitchen, quickly loading the dishwasher and cleaning up the work areas. When she finished, Abby took off the apron, threw it into the laundry, and headed upstairs to freshen her makeup. Like yesterday, she intended to head down to the concert in the park. Although she would arrive after

the music started, and there would be no point in
setting up her easel, she had another reason for
going to the park. She'd noticed a glass-enclosed information board near the bathrooms posted with upcoming fall events. She wanted to make note of dates
and phone numbers so she could determine if it was
an occasion that might be profitable for her sketches,
and find out if she needed a city permit to set up her
art for pay.

This time she walked down the hill, unencumbered
by her art supplies or the need to find parking for the
old Lincoln. She went the long way around on the
road, rather than her childhood trail. One traumatic
experience on that path was enough for her.

Still a block away, Abby could hear the sound of the
singer, backed by the guitar and drums blaring out over
the riverfront. It wasn't her favorite type of music, but
then she wasn't there to listen; she was there to research her possibilities for income in the future.

As she came up to the park, Abby wondered about
Maryanne, the young woman she'd sketched the day
before.

"Probably moving on," she decided aloud. Maryanne
needed to proceed with her own agenda, being recognized as a victim and then being able to take control of
her life, if only from Abby's sketch. Maryanne would
probably sink into the past with so many other victims
of rape, she thought. It was a textbook case. The victims were too frightened to step forward and pursue
their attackers.

The music was in full swing, and beyond the crowd
of people who sat on blankets and lawn chairs to

watch the concert, clapping, whistling, and shouting at the end of each song, was the band. The gyrating men, dressed in tight jeans and tank tops, their long hair bobbing with each dip and bow, kept up the tempo, and the excitement. It was the type of jazz that Abby found agitating, not fun. She recognized that she might be an anomaly as the fans obviously thought otherwise.

She was at the park for her own reasons.

She moved forward with determination: She needed to read the glass-enclosed bulletin board, make her notes, and be out of the park before the concert was over and the crowd overtook her progress.

She stood in front of the information board and took notes of future events, dates, and phone numbers. She was deep in thought, having just completed her list, when she heard a voice beside her.

"You're Abby, aren't you?"

She turned and faced the man who'd confronted her yesterday as she was about to leave the park. "What do you want?" she asked, surprised.

"I was hoping to see you here, my dear." His voice sounded shaky, not from emotion but from old age. "You're the reason I came to the park."

"Why? What do you want with me?"

He stared at her before spreading his hands in front of him, like a gesture of surrender. "I just needed to look at you again, see if you resembled others I've known."

"That's ambiguous," Abby retorted. "Please explain."

"I'm sorry, but I can't yet."

"Yet? What does that mean? I don't understand what you're saying."

He shrugged, and removed his fedora, revealing a head of thinning gray hair. She suddenly realized that he was much older than she'd first thought. The man before her was probably in his late eighties, maybe even nineties. But old or not, he was somehow intimidating.

"Just that, Abby. I can't explain what I'm not sure of as factual."

"Whatever," she said. "I'm sure I'm not a part of it, factual or fantasy."

"Believe me, Abby, you're not a fantasy." His gaze on her face seemed to intensify. "I'm just trying to determine if you're real or not."

Having turned away and taken a step away from the old man, she whirled around and faced him. "For goodness' sake, what is that supposed to mean?"

"I'll let you know when I know," he said.

"Don't bother," she said, disregarding his age. Somehow, that made him seem even more of a threat. "I don't need to know anything you'd have to say." Abby turned back toward the street and headed out of the park.

"But I will be in touch, Abby. I might have a lot to tell you that's important to your future."

She faced him again. "I doubt that very much, uh, what did you say your name was?"

"I didn't say."

"Well, say now?"

"I'll tell you later, Abby, when it's pertinent."

Abby quickened her step, anxious to leave the kook of an old man behind. He was obviously not all there, probably senile. Whatever, his presence was disturbing.

She headed back up the hill to her house. Taking out

the key, she unlocked the door and went inside, relieved to shut the door against the outside world. But as the silence of the empty house pressed down on her she had another realization: All the guests had gone. No one else would be sleeping in the house tonight.

She was alone.

Chapter 24

A SHORT TIME LATER, after she'd turned on some lights to cast out the shadows, and switched on the radio to soothing FM music, Abby felt more secure in the house. There was lots of work to be done over the next day or two so that she'd be ready for guest arrivals on Thursday.

Where to start? she wondered, taking a visual inventory of the kitchen, parlor, and dining room. The downstairs rooms would require a cleaning and dusting, as would the halls and bedrooms. The bathrooms needed scouring and disinfecting as well as clean towels. Housework was no easy task, but if her Aunt Carolina had done the job each week, so could she.

First things first, Abby thought. Get an organized plan. For this first time in tackling the job she would write down all the tasks, then prioritize by importance and get started.

She went to her aunt's little office—no, my office, she corrected herself. The property and everything it entailed, a generational legacy as well as all the liabilities, now belonged to her.

The realization of what it all meant hit her for the

first time with a feeling she'd never had before. She was now the only person who could keep the family history moving forward, holding that responsibility for future generations.

"Shit!" Abby plunked down on the desk chair, suddenly feeling the weight of her new place in life. At some point it would be up to her to produce heirs to continue the lineage—and she didn't even have a *real* boyfriend, let alone a husband to be the father of her future children. Somehow she knew that person wouldn't be Sam. Then who? A man who was successful but not necessarily in the art world, who was strong, attractive, and protective of the woman he loved, yet wouldn't be domineering and insensitive. A face surfaced in her mind.

Someone like Detective Stanley "Bud" Williams?

"For God's sake, get back to work," she muttered aloud. Why in the hell would she think about the detective? She scarcely knew him, although she admitted that he was one of the most dynamic men she'd ever met—and she did find him to be a totally sexy man.

She grabbed a tablet and pen and focused on the jobs at hand, forcing back unanswerable questions to be considered at a later time. She needed to concentrate on the here and now. She would strip the bedding from the three rooms for washing tomorrow. Then she would make a list of groceries needed for the next round of guests. The cleaning would be done on Monday and Tuesday.

That left Wednesday to pursue her own business: whether she needed a permit to sketch at public events, the possibility of a few hours dedicated to her paintings, and the idea of giving art classes. She needed to supplement the bed-and-breakfast income, at least for now.

Abby stood up and headed upstairs to pull the bedding from the rooms and the towels from the upstairs bathroom. It was still daylight but she turned on the lights because it was cloudy and gray outside. Quickly she went into the rooms, returning to the hall with the soiled linens, leaving them stacked outside each door. Once she completed the task, Abby scooped up the sheets, pillowcases, and towels into one huge plastic garbage sack. The bag was so heavy that she let it bounce down the stairs to the front hall, then she pulled it to the kitchen, where she opened the door to the basement and the laundry room below. Within seconds she had the whole bag of laundry in front of the washer and dryer, ready to be cleaned in the morning.

Abby headed back to the stairs, and heard something behind her.

She whirled around, her senses on full alert. What had she heard? No one was in sight within the bricked walls and floors of the cellar, which went back generations and had been wired and plumbed for a washer and dryer only after her aunt had made the house into a bed-and-breakfast. The sound had to be the creaking and settling of the house, she decided.

Isn't that what her aunt had always said?

Whatever, she was spooked, and of their own volition her legs were moving, headed up the steps. When she reached the kitchen, Abby swung the door shut and flipped the bolt.

And then her knees buckled and she sagged against the locked door. She was a basket case, running scared because of—

What?

Carolina's death that had been ruled a murder?

The words of the old man in the park who'd claimed her house was haunted?

All of the above, Abby decided, plus a few other incidents: odd shadows and noises in the night, her fright in the storage room and on the path, and the attempted assault the night before she'd left the city.

She straightened up, knowing exactly how to get rid of the heebie-jeebies: work. Between cleaning, cooking, scheduling for the bed-and-breakfast, and her freelance sketching, there wouldn't be idle time for her imagination to cloud her common sense. With resolve, Abby made a mug of tea and headed to the hall on her way up to her bedroom. She still had some personal things to unpack and put away. Now was a good time to do that.

Her foot was on the first step when the front doorbell rang behind her. Startled, she splashed a few drops of tea onto the floor as she turned to the oval window. A man dressed in Levi's and a leather jacket stood on the other side of the glass. Then she recognized her visitor, put her mug down on the hall table, and opened the door.

"Detective Williams," she said, her gaze instantly captured by the intensity of his pale eyes.

"Yeah, it's me, Bud." He raised his dark brows. "Remember?"

"Sorry. I guess I can't help but think of you as a detective." Abby glanced away, aware of how he was appraising her, from her form-molding brown top to her hip-riding slacks. She stepped aside and invited him into the house.

"I was just having tea," she said, picking up her mug, hoping to divert his attention. "Would you like a cup?"

He shook his head. "I'm not much of a tea drinker."

"Coffee then?"

"No, thanks. I'm on my way to the office and then on to another appointment and just stopped by to make sure everything is okay here." His gaze was back on her, as though he was doing an inventory of her face. "Is it?"

"What do you mean?"

He shrugged, but his scrutiny of her didn't waver. "You seem jittery."

"You could be right, uh, Bud. I guess I am."

"What happened?" He hadn't asked why but had jumped right to his assumption that something had spooked her.

She gave a nervous laugh. "I'm being oversensitive."

"Hey, I'm not dismissing anything, Abby." He stepped closer. "Just explain why you're on edge."

"It's silly."

He closed the space between them, took her mug and replaced it on the table, then led her into the parlor, where he sat her down in an overstuffed chair near the fireplace. He took the opposite seat, leaning toward her while he waited for her explanation.

"Okay," he said softly. "I'm listening."

Abby's shakiness did not originate from her trip to the cellar; it was due, in good part, to her proximity to Bud, the steely-eyed detective.

The silence stretched between them as she gathered her thoughts. Finally she was able to speak.

"Like I said, Bud, this is dumb. After the guests left,

the rooms needed to be cleaned. I decided to strip the beds after I returned from the park down at the river, then I took the dirty linens down to the laundry room in the cellar to be washed tomorrow." She drew air into her lungs. "I was on my way back up the steps when I heard something. I turned but didn't see anyone. But I felt that someone was there and fled up to the kitchen, slammed and locked the door."

His gaze didn't waver but something altered in his eyes. "That's it?"

"Yes."

He stood up and she followed, forgetting her cooling tea on the nearby table. For long seconds they faced each other before he took her hand and walked her to the kitchen and the door to the cellar.

"I want you to stay here while I go down and check it out, okay?"

"I can tell you there's no one down there. I could see the whole space from where I was on the steps."

"But you're still upset? Still feel that someone was watching you?"

"It's probably just an overactive imagination, Bud."

"Maybe." He unbolted the door. "Just humor me. I need to see that for myself, under the circumstances."

She managed a nod.

He opened the door, flipped the light switch, then glanced back at Abby. "If anything goes wrong close the door and call 911. Got that?"

"But—"

"No buts, Abby." His eyes met hers. "Just do as I tell you."

There was nothing she could say to dissuade him. She could only follow directions.

He went down the steps and she heard him moving around in the cellar. A few minutes later he reappeared, closed and locked the door behind him. Then he faced Abby.

"I found nothing amiss," he said, taking hold of her shoulders. "There is no other way in or out. No one is down there."

"I know," she whispered. "As I told you, I only heard something, I didn't see anyone."

She allowed his arm to slide down hers while he guided her back to the front door.

"I have to go, Abby. I still have to swing by the office before an appointment." He glanced at his watch. "Are you okay here by yourself?"

"I'm fine, Bud." She lowered her lashes to screen her feelings. Abby knew she was being irrational but she still felt like someone was watching her every move. Stupid. Dumb. Paranoid.

She also knew that there was no proof of what she was saying—and she couldn't detain the detective because of her own fears. He needed to go, she understood that. She also realized how much she hated him to leave. But she could never admit that, she had no right to.

"Okay, Abby," he said, after stepping onto the porch. "I want you to lock up as soon as I leave, and I'll call you later, make sure you're still safe and secure."

She nodded.

He stared at her from the porch as she stood in the doorway. Their eyes locked and for once she was unable to look away.

Then, with a quick motion, Bud moved back, took her in his arms, and kissed her soundly on the lips.

After lifting his head so that their eyes met, he declared, "Just call me, Abby, for any reason. I'll be here."

Then he was gone, down the steps, along the walk, and into his car. Moments later he drove away. Abby closed the door, then went to her aunt's small bar. She knew she'd need a drink to help her sleep.

Aside from her aunt's death, her own fears, and her attempt to keep the bed-and-breakfast afloat, she now had another problem.

Her attraction for the detective handling the case.

Chapter 25

BUD WILLIAMS SAT AT his desk going over the forensic report on Carolina Carter's death. She'd definitely been murdered; there was no other way to read the facts, even though the crime scene hadn't produced any evidence that might identify the perpetrator.

Frustrated, he wiped back his hair that had fallen over his forehead, knowing he had to get going soon or he'd be late for his appointment. Still he studied the report, looking for anything he might have missed. Some son of a bitch had killed an innocent woman. Why? Was it a random assault, because she'd caught the person trying to break into her storage area above the barn? Or had someone set out to kill her? Motivation, that's what he needed for a starting place.

And what about Abby's safety? If Carolina's death was a random event, then she wouldn't be the next target of the murdering bastard. The thought didn't calm his suspicions. Something—a gut feeling?—told him he was dealing with a situation far bigger than the death of Abby's aunt. Hence, his nightly stakeouts on

his own time. And his daily sense of being sleep de-
prived.

It was an obscure puzzle.

Some things he knew for sure: Abby had been attacked in her apartment and she'd had a few frightening experiences since arriving in Carterville. He'd
verified that the attempted assault in New York City
had happened. He'd requested a copy of the police report and it was now in Carolina's file that sat on his
desk. But had that incident, combined with her aunt's
death, been so traumatic that Abby had imagined her
scary encounters with ghostly apparitions?

"Jeez," he muttered into the room he shared with
other law enforcement officers. He needed something
more to go on—like tangible evidence.

Abby didn't seem like a lightweight flake, but then
what did he really know about her—aside from the
fact that he was so attracted to her? Damn, who am I
trying to kid, he thought. He was more than attracted.
In fact, of all the women he'd ever known, beautiful
girls he'd ultimately resisted for one reason or another, Abby was the only one who'd affected him so
profoundly upon their first meeting.

It was a pisser, a goddamn mind trip on top of everything else, he told himself. Falling in love at first sight
happened only in the movies, not to a guy like him. He
was a homicide detective, not a freaking schoolboy.

A phone rang behind him and one of the other detectives on weekend duty answered it, then called out
to him.

"Hey, Bud, it's for you. I'm switching the call to your
desk."

"I'm busy here," he replied, again thinking he had to leave soon. "Can't you take a number and I'll return the call later or in the morning?"

"Nope, the woman says it's important, that it has to do with Abby Carter and the serial rape case." The other detective met his gaze from across the room. "Isn't the Carter woman connected to your current murder investigation?"

"Yeah, she is. Thanks, I'll take the call."

Bud picked up the receiver, curious about who was on the other end of the line, and how Abby could have anything to do with the ongoing rapes of the past year or so.

"Detective Williams," he said.

"Detective, I'm sorry to bother you on a Sunday evening but I'm in the building and the person at the receiving desk gave me your number." She drew in a deep breath, as though she was nervous, then went on in a rapid delivery of words. "My name is Maryanne Roberts and I hoped I could see you while I was here. I may have some important information on the rapist at large in our area, and on another criminal investigation."

"Maryanne Roberts?" Bud repeated. "I know that name. Were you one of—"

"Yes. I was one of the victims."

"I'm no longer involved with that case, Maryanne. Detective Fred Harmon is the man you need to see, and I can give you his phone number, which is—"

"Yes, I know it. I've already talked to him and given him the information pertinent to my case. Now I need to talk to you about Abby Carter."

Bud shifted the received to his other ear, intrigued. "What do you know about Abby Carter?"

"I need to show you something concerning her." A pause. "Can I come up and talk to you? It'll only take a few minutes."

"Yeah, sure. Come on up to the second floor and I'll meet you at the elevator."

When the elevator doors opened and Maryanne stepped out onto Bud's floor, he was waiting. They exchanged greetings, then he led her to the conference room. They took seats at the end of the long table.

"I figured we'd have more privacy here," he told her, realizing that she was young, very pretty, and a little shy.

"Thank you, Detective Williams." Momentarily, she glanced away. "I admit that I've been somewhat withdrawn since I was raped. Saturday was my first day out of the house since it happened. That was when Abby Carter did the sketches."

"Sketches?"

She opened the folder she'd placed on the table and pulled out a sheet of paper. "This is a copy of the drawing Abby did as I described the man who attacked me."

"Abby was acting as a forensic artist?"

"Yeah, but not on purpose. She was trying to help me feel better, and I don't think either of us ever thought she would be so accurate."

"How so?"

"The drawing is him, the man who raped me."

Bud shook his head slowly. "How can you be so sure?"

"I am, and that's why I gave the original drawing to

Detective Harmon, who's going to put it in the news-paper."

"Start at the beginning and tell me the whole story of how this happened."

Maryanne nodded, then explained her time with Abby, what they'd both said, and how Abby had pro-ceeded with the sketch. "She also drew the likeness of a man who'd attacked her in the city, which is why I wanted to see you. I know Abby's aunt was murdered and I didn't know if the drawing could have some sig-nificance."

Bud was thoughtful as Maryanne's words sunk in. "Do you have it with you?"

She nodded and handed it over.

"Does Abby know that you're doing this?"

"No, but she told me to take the drawing of the rapist to the police, so I figured she wouldn't care if I also gave this one to you."

"I appreciate that, Maryanne. Was Abby also as sure of this likeness as you were of yours?"

"I don't think so, Detective Williams. But Abby is a far better artist than even she knows." She pursed her lips, thinking. "I suspect she might have some kind of an inner eye that comes out as she sketches, since she was so accurate with mine."

He studied the drawing. "This could be helpful, we'll see." Bud stood up. "Thank you for coming by. I hope the art helps to put your assailant behind bars."

She followed him back to the elevator. "And, Detec-tive William?"

"Yeah?" He faced her. "I hope you catch Abby's at-tacker, too. She seems so sad."

Then Maryanne was gone and Bud was left staring

at the closed doors. The woman was right. Abby was sad, but he meant to remedy that. Somehow I'll make her happy again, he vowed.

Then he ran out to his car. If he didn't hurry, he'd miss his appointment.

Chapter 26

AS PROMISED, BUD CALLED later to check on her after he'd been to the office and kept his appointment. Abby had told him all was fine, that she was in bed and about to turn out the light for the night. The exchange had been brief, as they were both aware that he'd kissed her. But the next afternoon his call was longer and his manner professional when he explained about the meeting with Maryanne. He wanted to hear her version of how she'd sketched Maryanne's attacker, and she explained what had happened.

"And you also gave her a sketch of the man who attacked you in your apartment?"

His question was a surprise. "Well, yes, I did, Bud, but I don't know how accurate it is."

"But you did see the guy?"

"Uh-huh, but only for a few seconds. I was basically demonstrating the drawing technique for Maryanne, who was very upset about her assault." She gave a laugh. "I guess I was trying to help her feel better."

"I believe you did that."

"Yeah, it seemed that way. She recognized the man I

drew right away and said she was taking it to the police. I see that she did."

"And thank God for that. The drawing gives us a lead."

She hesitated, hearing weariness in his voice. "I'm glad to help."

"We haven't had much to go on up until now, and we need to catch this bastard."

"Haven't the other victims been able to come up with a composite drawing?"

"Nope, not until you did your sketch for Maryanne. We had a forensic artist try but he was unsuccessful with all of them."

There was a silence while Abby digested his words.

"Have there been any developments in my aunt Carolina's case?"

"Not much yet but we're working on it, Abby."

"What does that mean, working on it?"

"Following a few leads." He cleared his throat. "As you know we don't have much to go on. The killer didn't leave any evidence behind and no one saw anything."

"Did anyone check out the path?"

"Of course, Abby. We had policemen go over it inch by inch and also the surrounding woods. We found nothing." His sigh sounded in her ear. "It's as though the person who murdered your aunt simply vanished."

She thought about what he'd said. "That's not possible," she said finally. "As you said she was murdered, and that means someone is responsible for her death." She took a quick breath. "Have you looked into the possibility of a disgruntled guest?"

"We're doing that for a second time, but so far

everyone still seems aboveboard. The consensus is that everyone loved your aunt and had no complaints about her B and B."

"How did you know who the guests were? I have the records here in my aunt's office."

"We took copies of the accounts during the initial investigation while the house and grounds were taped off as a crime scene."

"But you didn't know for sure that my aunt had been murdered at that time?"

"True, it wasn't verified until we had the forensic report, but there are certain steps we take automatically."

"I see." Abby had been sitting but stood to pace the kitchen while she talked, suddenly upset. Her aunt's killer had to be caught. If the police couldn't solve the crime, then she would have to find another route to solve the case. Her aunt deserved justice.

"Are you still there, Abby?"

"Of course, but I do have to hang up," she replied, her emotions back under control. "I have work to do that can't wait."

"Understood." A pause. "I'll be in touch real soon, and in the meantime be careful."

"Do you think I'm in danger, Bud?"

"Uh, not necessarily, Abby. But under the circumstances it is always best to err on the side of caution."

"I agree, and I will stay alert."

"Good. And be sure to call me if you're concerned about anything, okay?"

"Okay." His words of caution had become a daily litany.

"And thanks for your help on the rape case. I'll let you know how that goes."

They said their good-byes and Abby hung up. For long minutes she stared at the phone, doing a mental replay of their conversation.

Bud did sound tired. And he seemed genuinely concerned about her safety. As always, though, she wondered what he might know that he wasn't telling her.

Abby sat on her aunt's bed and took a visual inventory of the bedroom: the antique furniture, the lace curtains, and the little oak desk where Carolina had kept her personal letters. Abby had been in the room before, and in the closet, but she still didn't feel up to disturbing anything. She couldn't bring herself to remove Carolina's things, her toiletries, photos, jewelry, and personal treasures that Abby remembered since childhood. It just didn't seem possible that her aunt would never occupy the house again, never sleep in her bed, never come back.

Tears welled in her eyes. For now, Abby decided to leave everything as it was. There would be time enough in the future to pack up Carolina's personal possessions.

Standing, Abby crossed to the desk and sat down on the chair, her gaze on one of the little compartments that held a small bundle of letters. She pulled them out and thumbed through them without untying the pink ribbon. They were all from her, sent to her aunt on special occasions.

Abby swallowed against the growing lump in her throat. She felt terrible. It was obvious that her aunt had treasured the letters.

Oh God, I should have come home more often, she thought. It would have meant so much to Carolina. And now she'd never see her aunt again.

She ran her fingers over the highly polished wood, then put away the letters before she dripped tears on them. The other compartments were filled with odds and ends and she wondered what was in the drawers. Abby pulled one open to see pens, pencils, and paper clips. Closing it, she looked in the other drawer and found note paper and envelopes. As she started to push it shut it got stuck. Trying to fix the problem, her fingers disturbed the ornate strip of oak beneath the open cubbyhole where her letters had been placed. Suddenly the secure strip of wood sprung open on a hidden hinge, revealing a narrow hidden compartment.

Surprised, Abby bent closer for a better look. She squeezed her hand inside to feel around for contents. There was nothing.

The secret space was empty.

She sat back, contemplating what she'd found. Had her aunt Carolina known that the antique desk had such a mysterious place? If so, had she ever stored an important possession—or papers—in it? Abby had no way of knowing.

Carefully, she swung the ornate trim of the desk back into place and heard a slight click. Everything looked like it had when Abby had first sat down . . . nothing ominous, only the little treasures of a woman who had died.

No, she corrected herself. Carolina was a woman who'd been murdered.

Suddenly feeling chilled, Abby noticed that night was quickly encroaching on the daylight outside the windows. It was time to fix something for her dinner, and after that make sure the house was locked before she went upstairs to watch television in bed.

She sighed as she headed out of Carolina's bed-room for the staircase. Once, she would have been ex-cited about finding a hidden compartment in the desk; now, she only felt intrigued, and a little apprehensive.

She had always heard that very old trunks and desks sometimes had secret places—the practice dat-ing back centuries to when there were no safety-deposit boxes or banks. Early settlers hid their valuables back then. It didn't mean anything now. Her aunt might not ever have known that anything was mysterious about her antique piece of furniture.

Or had she? Maybe the space had once held some-thing important, something Carolina had decided to move to a safer place. But what? And why?

I'll probably never know, Abby reminded herself again, knowing that she was being silly to dwell on such a small discovery. But as the silence within the house seemed to press down on her as she began fix-ing something simple to eat, she switched on a little portable radio to fill the quiet with music.

Abby hurried, and as soup heated on the stove and bread toasted in the toaster, she made the rounds in the house, making sure the exterior lights were on and the interior was locked up.

But the back of her neck prickled as she went up the steps with her tray. She had that feeling again.

That someone was watching.

By the time Abby had eaten and watched several of her favorite television programs, reason had re-asserted itself and she'd relaxed. She was beginning to feel silly about how far her imagination had galloped since arriving back at her house.

But then you've never been alone here before, she argued mentally. All the years of growing up, your aunt was with you. To prove that reasoning, she reminded herself that she wasn't apprehensive when other people were in the house, like Katherine and her grandsons or the weekend guests. She was spooked because of the circumstances, she told herself, mostly the fact that her aunt had been murdered.

On that reassuring note Abby turned off the TV and bedside lamp, although she switched on a small nightlight. Then she snuggled under the quilt and began to drift off to sleep.

There was a vague sound somewhere in the house and her eyes popped open. The bedroom was just as she'd left it.

What had she heard? The house settling? Or a car going past on the street? The silence of the house pressed down on her. She held her breath, listening. There was no sound at all except for the distant ticking of the grandfather clock on the landing of the staircase.

It was nothing, she told herself. You're overreacting—being silly yet again.

But the words of the very old man in the park suddenly surfaced in her thoughts. Why had he even mentioned secret passages, caves, and tunnels used by the Underground Railroad to free fleeing slaves from the South before the Civil War? Why would he tell her that Carolina's house had been one of the drop-off places on the route to freedom? Had he been trying to scare her? Or warn her?

Crazy thinking when I'm trying to sleep, she thought. But she knew that rest was out of the question now. Instead, she concentrated on a plan of action. She couldn't continue to live in constant fear.

The historical society in town would be her starting point. She could research the Underground Railroad, its importance to Carterville and her own house in particular.

That would be her priority for tomorrow.

Somehow Abby needed to find out what in the hell was going on. Because something was, of that she no longer had any doubts.

Chapter 27

"YOU'LL WANT TO GO DOWNSTAIRS to the history room," the young woman told Abby from behind the book-checkout desk in the library. "The history volumes go back generations and we have an impressive number of old newspaper accounts on microfiche."

"Thank you," Abby said, smiling as she hoisted her backpack that contained her purse, tablet, and pens. "It sounds like I could be down there for a while."

The pretty blond glanced at her watch and grinned. "You've got plenty of time because it's only noon. We're open until eight tonight."

Abby's spirits had risen once she stepped into the library after her walk across town, knowing she might be able to quell a few fears once and for all. She did not really believe in ghosts and had never experienced strange happenings in her house during her years of living there. Indeed, as children, she and her girlfriends had searched everywhere for secret passages, having heard the tales of hauntings and ghosts. They'd had summer slumber parties in a backyard tent and dressed up like ghosts from the Underground Railroad at Halloween to scare trick-or-treaters. She'd never been frightened or felt threatened during all the years she'd grown up with her aunt; it was only lately, after Carolina's murder.

Now, in light of her recent experiences, she needed find to out if the bed-and-breakfast had once been connected to the Underground Railroad, or if the odd old man in the park had simply been repeating an urban legend.

Once, the creaks and groans of her home wouldn't have given her imagination such a hit of adrenaline, and frightened her so badly that she couldn't sleep. In the past, the place had been a safe haven and there had never been even a mention of any dangers. Ghost stories had been a joke.

Abby headed down the wooden staircase to the basement of the three-story building, hoping she remembered enough of her college research skills to find the information she needed. Pausing at the bottom, a glance told her that the windowless room was much smaller than the upper floor and that it was crowded with book racks, and the air smelled stale with the dust of decades. Behind a scuffed desk in the back of the room a lone woman bent over her work in front of a bank of filing cabinets. All of it looked old and mostly untouched by human hands.

Odd thought, Abby told herself with a wry smile. Who did she think touched the books? Ghostly hands?

As she moved forward, the woman glanced up, saw Abby, and lifted her wire-rimmed glasses up and onto the top of her head, where they caught in her permed gray hair.

"Do you need assistance?" she asked.

"Yes, I would sure appreciate it." Abby smiled. "But I might have a few strange requests."

The sixtyish woman grinned, and her narrow face creased into a maze of fine lines. "Good, I could use a few interesting requests. In this department the few I get are pretty predictable and dull, although I have to admit my love of history."

"Even questions about ghosts?"

The woman's grin broadened, relaxing her expression even more, momentarily taking years from her age. "All the time. Most people coming in here ask about possible hauntings. There are those who say this part of the historical building has its own ghosts."

"Then I guess I won't be disappointing you," Abby said. "My questions have to do with that very topic."

The woman shrugged, her blue gaze examining Abby. "I think I know you."

"How so?"

"You're Carolina's niece? Aren't you Abby Carter?"

"I am, but how did you know that?"

"Your aunt and I both belong—uh, she belonged to the County Historical Society, although she wasn't able to attend many meetings because of her B and B business."

Abby was momentarily disconcerted. There were parts of her aunt's life that she didn't know about even though they'd talked on the phone almost daily.

What else didn't she know?

Had her aunt Carolina been involved in a situation that had culminated in her death? Once again, Abby wished that she'd visited more often than special occasions and holidays.

"I'm sorry but I don't know your name," Abby said. "I can't remember my aunt ever telling me about you, but then I've lived away from Carterville for a number of years now."

"Laura Himes," she replied. "I suspect she wouldn't have, since you had already graduated from college when she joined our organization." She gave a brief laugh. "But we knew about you through her updates." She paused, her face wrinkling into a sad expression. "I'm so sorry for your loss, Abby. Carolina's death was tragic for us in the historical society. Although she didn't come to meetings, she was an invaluable resource, given her family genealogy and her knowledge of Carterville."

Abby nodded, momentarily too sad to speak. "Now I'm researching the history of her house," she said finally.

Neither spoke as Abby's gaze met hers.

"It's a long history," the woman replied.

"I only want to know about certain things, like its connections to the Underground Railroad, if any."

Laura Himes stood up. "I'll show you the section with the books you'll want to read."

"Thank you," Abby said. "I appreciate your help."

"You do know that the Underground Railroad wasn't a train that went underground?"

"Of course, I learned that in grade school. It was the symbolic name for the route of fugitive slaves who'd fled their owners for freedom in the North."

"Very true, but you'd be surprised to know there are many people who take the story literally, believe there was such a railroad."

Abby nodded as Laura Himes came out from behind

her desk. "It was really only a secret way the slaves traveled, sometimes in a horse-drawn buckboard or cart, or even a fancy carriage, or on a real railroad, even by boat, horseback, or walking. They were helped by sympathetic people who hid them on their long journey."

"Uh-huh," the older woman agreed. "Those people were called railroad workers and they made sure they got to the next safe hiding place, which was referred to as a station."

Following Laura Himes to a back corner where the brick walls indicated that it was part of the original structure, Abby continued. "The station part is one of my questions."

"Which is?"

"Was my aunt Carolina's house one of those stations, a place where my ancestors hid slaves?"

"That has always been a part of the folklore around here but no one knew for sure, including your aunt." Laura grinned. "In any case, she wouldn't have wanted to scare you since those safe houses for slaves usually had secret entrances and hiding places—the things that frighten children in the night."

And adults, too, Abby said to herself. Laura Himes's explanation did not provide the comforting information she'd hoped to find. Reserve judgment, she instructed herself. Maybe the old accounts would prove otherwise.

The librarian left her after pulling down books and showing her how to access the microfiche information and print a copy of anything pertinent to her needs. Abby spread out her tablet and pens and then opened the first volume. She anticipated a long afternoon ahead of her.

* * *

Her stunning discovery was buried in an old newspaper. Abby found the article right after Laura Himes had gone upstairs. It was only two paragraphs long and she reread it several times, digesting several pieces of her own history that she'd never known.

She sat back in the chair, suddenly fatigued. Her restless night coupled with several hours of reading were catching up to her. She pushed the Print button and retrieved the page, then stared at it again. It was a brief account of her parents' fatal accident, explaining that they were survived by her and Carolina, that Abby's twin had died at birth, and that her father had been a foundling and grew up in an orphanage.

The mention that his parentage was surrounded by mystery was something Abby had never heard before. The final sentence stated that rumors had connected her father to one of the most influential families in upstate New York, that he might have been the illegitimate child of a prostitute.

After her initial surprise, Abby felt outrage. How dare someone dredge up a scandalous past that her father had nothing to do with—after he died in such a tragic accident. But the alleged information whetted her appetite: She'd just found another issue to research, something that might be vital to her background. She didn't give a damn about the supposed influential family or the prostitute. What angered her most was that any family would give up their own flesh and blood, however scandalous the birth.

She stacked the books so that the librarian could put them away, then put all her notes, copies, and pens into her backpack. As she stood up, a movement caught the corner of her eye. Instantly, she turned her gaze in that direction.

There were only empty aisles lined with six-foot bookshelves. No one was there, but she felt spooked. It was time to go, before she came to believe she'd glimpsed a resident ghost.

Weaving her way among the rows of books, Abby headed for the stairs. She was almost there when she heard the whisper of a sound behind her, like muffled footsteps on the rough wood-plank floor. She whirled around and again there was no one in sight.

The realization that her line of vision was limited, that someone might be only a couple of feet away, hidden from view by the crowded shelving, prompted her to bolt forward. Her backpack bounced with each step as she ran up to the main floor, slowing to a sedate walk when saw the checkout desk with the young woman behind it.

Abby said good-bye and asked that she pass on her thanks to Laura Himes. Then she went out though the front door to the street, still feeling uneasy. Glancing back at the ancient building, the blank windows seemed to stare in return.

For God's sake, straighten up, she told herself. You're acting like a person who's losing it.

But as she began walking home Abby was again plagued by the feeling of being watched. Darting quick glances over her shoulder, she never spotted anyone who looked suspicious. But she was glad of the traffic along the street and the people hurrying along the sidewalk. Glancing at her watch, she saw that it was almost five, and she suddenly worried about the last few blocks to her house. There wouldn't be people or traffic there.

She would be vulnerable.

She was about to try to find one of the few taxis in town when a car pulled to the curb and the window slid down. Surprised to see Bud Williams, Abby was grateful to hear his voice.

"Need a ride home?" he asked, his eyes crinkling at the corners as he grinned. "You still have quite a walk, and in case you haven't noticed, the weather has changed and it's going to rain."

Abby's relief was equal to her acute awareness of how sexy he looked in his off-duty jeans and casual shirt. Even his dark hair was ruffled in a way that only made him more attractive, and she remembered his kiss.

"Thanks, Bud, I'd love a ride," she replied finally, pushing that memory away. Now was not the time to ponder what it meant.

He reached across the passenger seat to open the door. She climbed in and sat down, tossing her backpack onto the seat behind her.

"Hey, are you okay?" he asked, sobering.

"Yeah, I'm fine now."

"What happened?"

"I'll tell you over a glass of wine when we get to my house. I assume you're off duty?"

He nodded, and then steered the car back into traffic. "It's a deal."

Chapter 28

BY THE TIME BUD STOPPED his car in front of her house, Abby felt calmer and a bit silly. If her reactions to vague sounds and shadows continued, she might need to talk to a psychologist. Maybe the murder of her aunt had traumatized her far more than she'd realized, triggering a response that the killer was now after her. Although she hoped that the police would solve the case, Abby wondered if that was possible, especially if it had been a random crime committed by a stranger.

"Looks like we're here," Bud said. "You invited me in for wine and conversation?"

"Yeah, at least the wine part," Abby replied as they got out of the car. "Maybe not the part about being upset—I think I may have overreacted to a perfectly innocent situation."

"Let me decide that after I hear what happened, okay?"

Abby led the way up to the porch and inserted her key in the lock. As she pushed open the door she asked him the question that had been on her mind during the drive home.

"How did you happen to see me walking on the sidewalk? Were you in the area?"

"I was." He grinned. "My office is a block away."

His answer silenced her. She'd begun to wonder if he was following her because he often appeared when she least expected him. It's a small town, she reminded herself. It wasn't unusual to run into people.

"I didn't realize that," she replied inanely.

One eyebrow shot up over discerning eyes. "So you thought I was following you?"

Instant heat touched her cheeks as she glanced away. "I only wondered at the coincidence of running into you," she said, evading. "I didn't know that the homicide unit was that close to the library."

"Hmmm." Bud seemed to control a grin. "I'll take my turn explaining over that wine you promised."

She stopped short, facing him. "So there was a reason you were there to offer me a ride."

They'd stepped into the entry with the door still open. He reached beyond her and closed it. "No, but I admit I was on my way to your house."

Her eyes widened with the question still forming on her lips. But instead of speaking she shrugged off her jacket before taking his and placing both on the chair next to the entry table. Then he followed her down the hall and into the kitchen, where she motioned him to a chair at the table.

"I'll pour," she told him, "and then we can talk."

"Right," he said, taking his seat.

"Chardonnay or Merlot?" she asked.

"Merlot." His brows shot up. "You've expanded your choices of liquor."

Abby inclined her head before pulling two wineglasses from the cupboard and retrieving a bottle of Merlot from a lower shelf. As she searched for a corkscrew, Bud asked another question.

"How are your portrait drawings doing? Are you getting customers?"

"Just the ones from the concert in the park," she replied. "But I plan to pursue that possibility for income and I've inquired about possible licensing for public events."

"And?"

"I don't need a license for most events if I'm not on the actual premises. Therefore, I'll be right outside at the few future park performances this fall, weather permitting."

"Right. So what else have you got scheduled?"

"At the moment only the grade-school carnival in two weeks."

"At the school gym?"

"Uh-huh."

"And you don't need special permission to do that?"

"Nope."

"I'm surprised."

"I'm to be a part of the carnival, although the school and I have struck a deal: We share equally in the profits I make from my pencil portraits, after my actual expenses for materials."

He shook his head. "You're amazing, Abby. I admire your enterprising spirit."

"Thanks." She placed his wine glass in front of him and then her own on the table where she sat down. "Because of the mortgage on the house, taxes, and running expenses, I'm just hoping that no one cancels their reservation once they hear my aunt was murdered right here on the premises. If there were a rash of cancellations and I couldn't make all the payments, I could lose the property that has been in my family for centuries." She sipped her wine. "I have to avoid that possibility in any way I can."

"God, Abby. I didn't know your financial future was in jeopardy." He'd also sipped the wine and now he placed the glass down on the table. "Do you still have reservations for this weekend?"

"Yeah, I do. All three rooms are reserved, starting tomorrow. I have two out-of-town couples for two of the rooms through Saturday night and a widow who's here for the antiques tour this weekend in the third room. The first couple arrives before five tomorrow evening."

"And you fix the breakfast?" he asked, his expression seemingly sincere but uncertain, as though he'd presumed that she was not a good cook.

"I do," she said primly, then sipped her wine again. "In fact, I'd venture to say the people who have sampled my menu think I'm an excellent cook."

Their eyes locked, chestnut brown and pale blue.

"I see," he said finally. "Hopefully I'll be invited for breakfast one of these weekends."

"Perhaps," she said. "So long as you don't tell my customers that you're investigating a murder."

A momentary lull in conversation dropped between them.

"It's your turn to explain," he said finally. "You were almost running along the street before I picked you up, Abby. Was someone chasing you?"

"I never saw anyone."

"But you thought someone was behind you? Why?"

She considered her answer. "I'm getting sick and tired of sounding paranoid."

He reached to cover her hand with his. "Listen, Abby. I'm investigating your aunt's murder. If there's anything unusual happening in your life, I need to know about it."

She explained that she'd gone to the history room in the basement to research her house and had brought home copies of old newspaper articles about her family that she would read later. Then she told him about the movement in the library, her sense of not being alone. And later the feeling of being watched, and followed. She spread her hands and admitted that it was all perceptions, that she could prove nothing.

He didn't reply for long seconds.

"I'm not discounting your perceptions, Abby, although it may well have been nothing. Your sketch of Maryanne's attacker proves to me that your awareness and insights are valid." He sipped his wine. "Your drawing of the rapist has given us a pretty reliable suspect."

"You've arrested someone?"

He shook his head. "Not yet, and I need to tell you that what I've just said is confidential information at this place in our investigation. I need your word that you won't mention anything I've said to anyone."

"Of course I won't," she replied at once. "I'm just pleased that I might have helped you catch a monster."

He finished his wine and stood up. "You'll be the first to know when we do," he said, "right after the victims who were involved in his numerous attacks."

"God, I hope you get him," she said as they walked back to the front hall.

"We will."

They'd reached the door, and before she could open it, he faced her, putting his hands on her shoulders, causing her to take a step closer to him.

"Thank you for the drawing, Abby. I owe you."

"What? You don't owe me anything."

"We'll see about that later."

"Later?

"Yeah, I'll explain what I mean then—after you're ready to hear it." His eyelids lowered and the light from the lamp she'd just switched on seemed to glow in his pale eyes. "In the meantime be damn careful, Abby," he said, still sounding ambiguous. "I want you to pay attention to all of your senses whether or not they seem paranoid."

She managed a nod, still mesmerized by the intensity of his gaze.

Then, as he'd done once before, Bud pulled her into his arms, lowered his face, and kissed her. This time the kiss lingered and deepened, until Abby found herself responding, her arms going around him.

Abruptly, he stepped back, but she sensed his reluctance to do so, which was matched by her sudden need for him to kiss her again.

"I'm not sorry about that even if I should be," he said huskily. "But it isn't exactly procedure for a detective in a murder investigation to be kissing the victim's niece."

"Nor is it proper for the niece to kiss the detective back."

Unspoken words seemed to stretch between them. He was the first to speak.

"I want you to promise again that you'll call me if

there's any disturbance at all here." He'd changed the subject completely as his hand went to the knob. "Do I have your promise?"

She managed a nod, confused about his romantic intentions toward her—and hers toward him.

One minute later he'd opened the door, had traversed the porch to the steps, and had reached his car, where he turned and gave a good-bye salute. Then he drove off down the street.

She closed and locked the door and went back to the kitchen to finish her wine. Who knew, she might even need a refill to consider what had just happened.

Or else she needed to dump the glass and stay completely sober to understand the actions of the detective, a man who was more sexually attractive to her than any man she'd ever met, including Sam.

She needed to put that aspect out of her mind . . . for now.

Chapter 29

ABBY WENT OVER HER NOTES from the library after she'd dumped her wine and made herself a pot of coffee. As she sipped and tried to piece together the significance of what had happened in the past, she realized that there was still no proof that her house had been a station on the Underground Railroad route.

Sitting back, Abby mulled over what she had learned: Most safe houses had remained anonymous, there were 250-year-old estates in the county that were said to be haunted, and there were underground tunnels in those houses that had secret entrances. Especially noteworthy was the Robertson Manor, which dated back to the early 1700s. The Robertson family had once helped shape the American republic and was now a dynasty that had been reduced to history books. The lineage had come down to the last descendant, an old man who'd become a recluse in his mansion.

Sad, Abby thought. She wondered why such a vital and important family was almost extinct, but that was none of her concern. She still needed to answer the question at hand: Who had killed her aunt and did that have anything to do with the history of the Carter family? At this point it didn't seem to be the case. She was glad that she hadn't gone into detail about that theory with Bud. Abby already felt a little overreactive.

The lack of substantial information only added credence to her theory that Carolina's murder had been a random incident. Or someone with a grudge that her aunt had been unaware of?

Sighing, Abby gathered her notes into a pile to put away. Then she went to the refrigerator to pull out salad fixings for supper. She planned to have another early night. Katherine would start work at eight to prepare her baked goods for the weekend, and Abby would make her last-minute preparations. The guests would arrive by five tomorrow afternoon.

"You can't think of anything at all that my aunt might have been concerned about?" Abby asked Katherine as they worked in the kitchen the next morning. Abby had just confided her worry that Carolina's killer might never be arrested and the crime remain unsolved.

Katherine stopped kneading bread dough as she considered the question. "To be honest, Abby, she didn't tell me about anyone threatening her or that she was afraid of something." Her eyes met Abby's. "But several times I felt she had something on her mind that she wasn't sharing."

"Like what?"

"I don't know." Katherine sprinkled flour on the dough and began kneading again. "I asked her if she was troubled by something, even if you were okay in the city, and she assured me on every front that all was just fine. But—"

Abby leaned forward. "But what?"

"That's just it, Abby. I have no idea, but in the light of

her murder, I now believe I wasn't mistaken that she was worried. I just wish that I'd insisted she come clean." She drew in a ragged breath. "If I had, she might still be alive."

"Oh, Katherine," Abby said, going around the table to hug her aunt's friend. "You're not responsible for her death. No one knows what happened yet. I'm praying that the police turn up something that will lead to the killer."

"Me too," Katherine said.

There was a silence as each continued her own work. Several minutes later Abby left the kitchen to do a final check of the house, to make sure everything was ready for the guests. As she walked through the hall she remembered that the morning newspaper was still on the porch. Quickly she retrieved it and stepped into the parlor. It was her aunt's practice to subscribe to several magazines in addition to the local paper, reading material should anyone wish to look at the news. About to place it on a side table, Abby's glance was caught by the drawing on the front page.

The drawing she'd sketched of Maryanne's attacker.

The headline read: POLICE CATCH RAPIST.

Quickly, she read the article under the caption, then plopped down on the closest chair, staring at the paper in her hands. "Oh my God," she murmured.

"What's wrong?" Katherine said from the doorway. "Are you all right?"

"Uh-huh, I think so," Abby said. "They caught the rapist, a sex offender named Cliff Blancher, from Florida, who'd come here after skipping bail a year ago. He was hiding out with family members who live in Carterville." She indicated that Katherine look at the paper. "It's on the front page."

"What a relief that they caught the creep." Katherine stepped forward to take the newspaper, her gaze sharpening on Abby's face. "Is something about the article upsetting you?" she asked.

"They identified me as the sketch artist," Abby replied, feeling shaky. "And they also mentioned that Aunt Carolina was murdered and found in the backyard of her bed-and-breakfast, although there were no guests staying here at that time."

"Oh no."

Katherine sat down to read the piece as Abby waited, trying not to show how horrified she felt. She didn't blame Maryanne for taking the drawing to the police; she was glad that the monster had been identified and arrested. Nor was she upset that Maryanne had given her credit for the drawing; but she was angry that the reporter had been so irresponsible as to connect the artist to a murder victim and the bed-and-breakfast. She just hoped that her guests' reservations wouldn't be canceled because of it.

In silence, Katherine put the newspaper down on the lamp table, sighed, and stood up. She put her arms around Abby. "I'm so sorry, dear. I'm going to call the paper and tell them a thing or two. You've gone through too much without this notoriety."

"No, please don't do that, Katherine. I don't want to stir things up. Right now the focus is on the rapist, not the B and B and Carolina's murder. I'm praying that the police catch her killer but I just want my connection to this story to fade away."

Katherine hugged her again, then they both went back to work. The guests would soon be arriving.

*   *   *

The first couple rang the doorbell right on time. Katherine had left several hours earlier, and Abby, dressed in black slacks and a scoop-neck white blouse, looked relaxed and welcoming. Having stayed at the bed-and-breakfast several times before, they offered condolences, then took their key and went up to their room to freshen up.

Abby had just reached her little office to check off her first arrivals when the phone rang. She picked it up and sat down on the desk chair.

"Hello? This is the Carter Bed-and-Breakfast."

"This is Ms. Fleming. I have a reservation for the weekend."

"Yes, Ms. Fleming. You're scheduled to arrive tomorrow midmorning."

"Uh, that's why I'm calling. I've had a change of plans, an emergency in my family, and I'm afraid I must cancel."

"Oh, I'm so sorry. We were looking forward to having you with us."

"Yes, well, thank you." She cleared her throat. "Of course, I expect you to keep the deposit."

"I'm sorry about that, but that is the established rule of the house," Abby said, realizing that she'd just had her first cancellation because of the article. In a way, she couldn't blame the single woman. A single woman had been murdered on the premises.

And now, on top of all the loss and worry, Abby feared she had another problem. What if everyone canceled? Even though the canceling guests would forfeit their deposits, she'd lose room rents. She'd be bankrupt.

And lose everything.

Chapter 30

"SON OF A BITCH," the man murmured, feeling frustration and anger suffuse his body. His eyes fastened on the sketch that had been reproduced on the front page of the newspaper. It had been drawn by Abby Carter, an artist who'd been born in Carterville, the town named for a founding father, Abby's ancestor.

He crushed the pages of newsprint in his hand, grinding them into a twisted coil of paper. Then he tossed it into a nearby trash can.

Shit! She'd identified the rapist by sketching the description given by the victim. What more could she do to identify him? Create his portrait to be circulated among law-enforcement agencies in New York State?

No, he decided. She would have done that if she'd remembered seeing him. Nevertheless, she was a formidable enemy.

And that meant he was right about killing her to preserve his lineage.

And the rights of his loved ones to their heritage, even if it didn't go back to the beginning.

The beginning? What was that?

Alpha and omega, the beginning and the end.

Not his. He was the new beginning.

Hers. She would be the last in the ending of her family.

He picked up the other drawing in his possession, which had nothing to do with the earlier sketch by Abby that was in the newspaper. How many people had a copy of what was in his hand at that moment? Probably no one, because it was a primitive drawing of the Underground Railroad route, showing the "stations" along the way that weren't a part of contemporary information.

He grinned, looking down at the old map that lay open in front of him. He would prevail in all things.

Like his haunting of the Carter Bed-and-Breakfast.

A haunting of death.

Because that's how it had to be—in the end—for the beginning.

Chapter 31

"HEY, THESE THINGS HAPPEN, sad as it is." Jim, who was one of her guests, had paused at the front door as he and his wife were leaving for the day. "We just feel very bad that your aunt met with this type of an end. She was a special woman."

His wife nodded agreement. "We wouldn't have canceled because of her death, even though it might not have been an accident. We were just happy that you're taking over and keeping the B and B open."

"Thanks," Abby said. "I appreciate your support." She hesitated, struggling to keep her composure. "My aunt's death was tragic, but accident or not, I'm sure it was a random thing. My aunt didn't have an enemy in the world, no one who'd want to harm her."

"Yeah," Jim said, agreeing. "She was just in the wrong place at the wrong time."

Jim's wife stepped forward and gave Abby a quick hug. "We love this B and B and I know the other couple who are staying for the weekend feel the same way."

"That's what they said at breakfast," Jim added.

"And we're sorry about your other reservation being canceled," his wife said. "I doubt you'll see much of that happening in the future. People understand."

Abby thanked them again, watching as they headed out the door. She just hoped they were right, especially when word got out that the killer was still out there, maybe still in Carterville.

She went back into the house to finish cleaning the kitchen. Both couples were gone until late afternoon and she welcomed the chance to fill her mental well with a little solitude. As she worked, Abby listened to FM radio music and found herself daydreaming of Bud and his kisses. Was he as attracted to her as she was to him? Although he'd been the one to break off their embrace, she'd sensed that he hadn't wanted to, that he was a passionate man who would be an exciting lover. He was the opposite of Sam.

Sam. The image of him was like cold water on her warm thoughts of Bud. But at least her earlier stress had slipped away, and she anticipated having a shower now that the guests were out of the house for a few hours.

Maybe Jim and his wife were right. Everything would settle down.

And she would make it after all. Maybe she would even find love.

The doorbell sounded above the music just as Abby stepped out of the shower a half hour later. She wondered how many times it had rung and quickly dried herself before winding the towel like a turban around her wet hair. Then she slipped into her green satin robe and headed for the stairs as she was still tying the belt around her waist. She sped down the steps to the front entry. At the bottom she hesitated, her eyes on the door.

Through the oval window she could see the tall form of a man although his identity was obscured.

Slowly, cautiously, Abby stepped forward, her bare feet silent on the wooden floor, her eyes on the person who stood on the porch. As she approached the door Abby realized who the person was.

Detective Bud Williams.

"Oh shit," Abby muttered, adrenaline rushing through her limbs, her cheeks suddenly hot as she remembered their last meeting. It was as though she'd conjured him out of her daydream a short time ago, and she wished she could ignore the doorbell. But she knew he must have glimpsed movement in the entry.

As she grabbed the knob and turned it, she suddenly realized that her satin robe clung to her damp skin. She hoped to talk to Bud while keeping her body behind the barrier of the door, because she suddenly felt naked. It didn't work. As it began to open, he pushed it enough to reveal her full length in robe and turban.

His gaze slid down her figure, from her head, over her shiny covering that clung to her damp skin, and back up to lock with her eyes. She realized that he'd noticed that her breasts were outlined by the fabric— that she was naked under her robe. More heat flushed her cheeks as his brows raised in a question. With iron resolve, Abby didn't lower her eyes, determined to keep her poise.

"Did I interrupt your bath?" he drawled in a way that made her know that he was completely aware of her body under the material. "If you like, I can come in and wait while you finish dressing," he suggested.

She nodded and stepped aside. "Wait in the parlor and I'll only be a few minutes."

Abby felt his gaze as she hurried back up the steps to her room. In only a few minutes she'd dressed in jeans and a T-shirt, clipped her damp hair behind her head, and was on her way back downstairs. To hell with the makeup, she thought. He'd already seen her looking her worst.

She hesitated in the doorway to the parlor as he replaced the magazine he'd been reading on the coffee table and stood up to face her. Stepping into the room, she was aware that he'd taken in every aspect of her appearance, that his evaluation was one of admiration.

"You're a woman after my own heart," he said in a low tone.

"How so?"

He shrugged.

"C'mon, Bud. What?"

His smile was slow, starting in the creases at the corners of his eyes. "What else? You're a woman who doesn't keep a man waiting."

"How do you know that?" she asked inanely, uncertain of the dynamics that seemed to throb between them, wondering if he'd sidestepped her question. "You don't really know me, Bud."

There was a momentary silence as he considered.

"I know all I need to about who you are."

His reply was ambiguous and she chose to disregard it. Abby stepped into the room and seated herself on the sofa opposite the chair in which Bud sat back down.

"So what can I do for you, Bud? Do you have news about Aunt Carolina's murder case?" The question had become her mantra. She always seemed to be asking it.

He shook his head, his expression abruptly serious. "I'm afraid there's nothing new, but we're still working hard to follow up on even the smallest lead." His gaze intensified. "I came about another matter."

"The newspaper article about the rapist and my drawing?"

"Yeah. I wanted to explain what happened. Although we might not have caught this Cliff Blancher without your sketch, it wasn't our intention to disclose the artist, or the fact that your aunt was murdered."

She glanced down. "I'm glad my drawing led to the creep's capture, and relieved that he's been arrested. But because of the publicity I've had my first cancellation."

He leaned forward. "Jeez, Abby, I'm so sorry."

"I am, too. I only hope that it doesn't start a domino effect." Her voice quavered despite her effort to control it. "The two couples who are staying this weekend say they understand that it was just a tragic event and they wouldn't cancel because of it."

"Thank God for that. I have two more issues to mention and one of them might not be significant but I felt you needed to know."

"That sounds ominous."

Bud's eyes narrowed slightly, as though he was more concerned than he'd expressed. "It seems that your other sketch, the one you drew of your own attacker, was given to the same reporter. Maryanne was so impressed by the accuracy of your sketch for her that she told the man about the other one. He asked to see it and she lent it to him, silly as that sounds."

"You've got to be kidding, Detective. Surely Maryanne realized that the drawing was only a vague glimpse of the person." She leaned forward. "I need to get it back."

"Yeah, I agree, and the guy is bringing it into the station tomorrow."

"He won't print it in the paper?"

"He said he wouldn't." He spread his hands in a gesture of frustration. "But I can't guarantee that. His article with your drawing cracked the serial-rape case, culminating with an arrest and a huge career boost for him. He might think a follow-up piece with the second drawing would add to his moment of fame."

"Damn it to hell!" Abby jumped up. "That's all I'd need if he did. More bad publicity could kill my aunt's B and B business for good."

"Hey, that's not going to happen, believe me, Abby. Even if your business slows down for fall and winter, people will forget the whole episode by spring and you'll have more reservations than you can handle."

"If my art can make enough money to see me through until then," she retorted.

He stood too, facing her across the antique coffee table. "That brings me to the second reason I'm here."

"My art? Or making money?"

"Both."

His eyelids lowered slightly but his gaze was locked to hers and didn't waver. Again Abby resisted the urge to lower her own and kept her eyes steady, waiting for him to explain.

"The department is way more than impressed by your ability as a forensic artist. I was asked to request a favor from you, one that requires art and pays money."

Her surprise was instant. "But I'm not a forensic artist."

"Maybe you're not technically trained for it, Abby, but believe me, you succeeded where the police artist failed completely." He shook his head. "You seem to have a natural affinity with the victim. You made Maryanne feel safe enough to relax and she was then able to recall enough detail for you to create a credible likeness of her attacker. Your ability to accurately portray the perpetrator might in part be because you—" He broke off, as though he suddenly realized he'd almost said too much.

"Are you implying that I can identify with the victim because of having been attacked myself?" She hesitated. "You do realize that I wasn't raped, don't you?"

Something flicked momentarily in his eyes. "I know that, Abby. But I do believe you have a certain sense of identity with victims, along with being a fantastic artist."

His compliment was unexpected and for long seconds she was at a loss to respond.

"Our local police department wants to hire you on a part-time basis to be a sketch artist for victims of crimes. Although murders and serial rapists aren't a common occurrence in Carterville, we have our share of robberies, burglaries, and lesser crimes where the victims have glimpsed their attackers."

"But as I said, I'm not trained in forensics. I got lucky once but that doesn't mean I will again."

He shook his head. "Doesn't matter, Abby. You succeeded where the hired professionals failed. The department wants you—hopes you'll accept our offer." Again he spread his hands, this time in supplication. "Because we could sure as hell use your talents."

"What does the job pay?"

He shrugged. "I don't really know. The going rate I'm sure, whatever that is." He spread his hands. "If you're interested, they'll lay out the job description and its compensation."

She considered his offer.

"Can I think about it?"

"Of course."

"When do you need my answer?"

"In a day or so? We have a couple of cases where we could use some help. The victims are pretty scattered in their impressions and your way of dealing with them would be greatly appreciated, especially if you came up with a valid drawing."

She nodded. "I'll get back to you soon."

"Great."

"Can I offer you coffee or something?" she asked, changing the subject.

He shook his head. "Thanks, but I'll take a rain check. I'm on duty."

She led the way back to the front door, where Bud moved around her.

Abruptly, as she took a step forward, Bud stopped and turned, and she bumped into him, her breasts crushed against his chest. His hands came out to take hold of her upper arms, so that he held her in place against his body.

Their eyes locked.

At that moment the phone rang but somehow she was still frozen in place. The answering machine could take a message.

"Thanks for coming," Abby managed to say.

Still he held her, as though he was hesitant about

his next action—was he contemplating pulling her into his arms and kissing her? she wondered.

"You're so welcome," he said in a controlled tone. "Please consider how you can help us get these offenders who prey on innocent people, Abby. We'd appreciate your help, and you'd be monetarily rewarded." He raised his eyebrows. "This would be a symbiotic situation—we'd help you just as you're helping us."

"You'll still continue to investigate my aunt's case?"

Bud moved so that he held her tighter against his chest. "I promise you that your aunt's murder will be solved," he said softly, his mouth next to her ear, his breath ruffling her hair.

Finally he released her and stepped back. "Again I need your word that you'll call me if anything comes up."

"You have it," she said, grinning because he was so predictable about his warnings each time he left her.

Before she could add anything else he was gone, headed for his car. As she closed the door she wondered what was happening between them.

He was damn sexy and her attraction to him was getting stronger with each encounter. Did he feel the same sexual tension that she experienced whenever they were together? Or was it all just police procedure.

She closed the door.

There was a lot to consider—her fears, her worries, and her feelings about the detective who was in charge of her aunt's murder investigation.

Abby forced thoughts of the detective aside, because she felt so drawn to him and knew that she needed to stay focused. Her feelings toward him were not relevant to the case.

Abby was about to go upstairs when she remembered the phone call. A quick check told her the message was from Sam, her so-called boyfriend. Screw him, she thought. He'd never been emotionally supportive of her and was probably still annoyed about their last phone conversation. She'd listen to his message later.

And then she went up to fix her hair and apply makeup so that she was presentable when the two couples returned. She'd think about the sexy homicide detective later.

Chapter 32

ABBY WAS ABOUT TO lock up for the night when she remembered Sam's message. She went back to the office and pressed the Play button on the answering machine. The guests were already in their rooms for the night but nevertheless she turned the volume on low.

"I'm worried about you." Sam's voice sounded in the tiny room. "I saw the article about the rapist. Call me, Abby. I really am concerned."

She stared at the phone. How had Sam seen the local newspaper? she wondered. To her knowledge, he'd never even read the *New York Times,* let alone a paper from a small town. Abby picked up the phone. It was eleven o'clock but she decided to call Sam anyway. He never went to bed before midnight.

After punching in his number she sat back, listening to the ringing on the other end of the line. After four rings his answering service clicked in, asking the caller to leave a message.

"It's Abby," she said. "I'm returning your call and I look forward to talking with you soon."

Again she sat back, marveling at how distant they'd become; once, she'd believed that he was her future.

Now she realized that their relationship had been one-sided, that his career ambition left no place for a permanent commitment to her.

Abby sighed and stood up. The ball was in his court now. It was up to him to call back if he wanted to talk with her. She headed for the stairs, turning out lights as she went, leaving a few small lamps on for the guests. Upstairs, all was quiet, except for the low sound of a television in one of the rooms. Using the key to access her bedroom—her practice for both her and her aunt's private quarters when there were guests in the house—she went inside and locked the door behind her. Then she sat down on the bed, mentally replaying all that had happened during the day. She'd be glad when the two couples checked out after the Sunday breakfast.

It's a catch-22, Abby thought. On one hand, she felt more secure with others in the house; on the other, she liked her privacy, and felt a need to grieve for her aunt. It had all happened so fast, and there'd been no time to gain some perspective.

And she was becoming more and more frustrated that her aunt's murder investigation seemed stalled. She was beginning to think it would never be solved, but she didn't blame Bud or the police investigation. Even she could see that they didn't have much to go on.

It's time for me to ask questions myself, she thought, as she changed into her nightgown. Her aunt had been loved, had belonged to the historical society and to her church, had shopped at certain stores, had lifelong friends: Someone had to know something. I'm the best one to find out what might have been going on, she told herself. No one knew Carolina better than she did, even though she hadn't lived with her aunt for years. But Abby had also begun to realize that her childhood perception might not be the same as her adult view of her aunt. Carolina might indeed have kept secrets from her.

As she climbed into bed her thoughts flashed on her time in the library researching the Underground Railroad and whether the Carter house had been one of the stations. Surprisingly, she'd learned that her father had a mystery surrounding his birth—that an old rumor connected him to an important family. Could that be significant? she wondered. And who was the family?

Stop it, she thought. Now she was pulling imaginary possibilities out of the air. God, don't let me lose perspective on top of everything else, just because all is not what I once believed. My poor dad was an orphan and if anyone had wanted to claim him they would have by now.

Abby plumped up her pillows, placed her cell phone on the night table, then turned out the lamp. She snuggled down under her sheet and down quilt, hoping to fall asleep immediately. A half hour later she knew it was one of those nights: too many thoughts and mental images to allow her to drift off.

"Damn it!" she muttered into the dark room. "I need my sleep. I have breakfast to prepare in the morning."

She resisted an urge to head downstairs for a jigger of her aunt's brandy. Instead, she turned on her bedside lamp and reached for a magazine to read. Whatever it took, she needed to get sleepy.

The ring of her cell phone startled her. For a moment she stared at it in disbelief, then grabbed it, re-membering that the bed-and-breakfast had guests right down the hall.

"Hello?"

"Abby? Why are you still up?"

"Why are you calling so late, Bud? It's almost mid-night. Is something wrong?"

For long seconds he didn't answer.

"No, I was just checking to make sure all was well. I guess I didn't realize it was this late. Did I wake you?"

"No. Unfortunately, I wasn't asleep," Abby replied. "May I ask how you knew my cell phone number?"

His chuckle sounded in her ear. "You forget that I'm a homicide detective. I have my ways."

"I see."

"So what's giving you insomnia, Abby?"

"I couldn't seem to shut off my mind, Bud. My aunt's murder, the information I learned at the library, any number of worries kept me awake."

"Yeah, you told me about researching the old records of your family and property and that you were going to reread the printouts." He paused. "Something you read is worrying you?"

She told him about the article that speculated on her father's birth.

"So your father's orphan background is a mystery—because of a possible birthright to an old, rich family?" He hesitated. "Why would learning about that rumor bother you now? Is there some reason why you might connect that to your aunt's death?"

Abby shifted on the bed. "Not really, unless there *was* a connection to my aunt's murder, and I can't see how that could be the case. I think reading about my dad left me feeling even less grounded and more alone, especially after losing my aunt."

"Yeah, connecting the two events is a bit of a stretch."

"But since I was never told anything about my father's past, what I read intrigued me. I've decided to do a bit of investigating on my own, Bud. Carolina's murder was probably a random event but I need to satisfy myself that I've explored all possibilities, so I'm going to check out a few things."

"That's our job, Abby. I want you to promise you won't do that."

She switched the phone to her other ear. "I can't do that. I'm the only person who'd recognize anything that might have worried my aunt."

"You're really grabbing at straws."

"Yeah, you're probably right. And while I'm poking into the past I'm going to find the old newspaper articles about my parents' accident and even the death certificate of my twin. I've never seen those documents, either."

"Your aunt doesn't have those papers?"

"Nope, not that I've been able to find anywhere in the house, although they could be in the storage room above the garage or in the attic."

"Why would any of that ancient history have concerned your aunt this many years later?"

"Probably didn't. I might be spinning my wheels."

"I can't change your mind?" His tone had hardened.

"Nope."

"Then you'll keep me in the loop?"

"Of course. You're the detective on the case, aren't you?"

"I'm serious here, Abby."

"You have my word."

"Good. In the meantime, I'll let you get to sleep."

"Thanks, I just hope I can."

They hung up and Abby turned out the lamp for the second time. As she stared into the darkness a lethargy stole over her and she felt herself dozing off.

Her last thought was one of relief.

Chapter 33

BUD FOLDED HIS CELL PHONE and slipped it back into his pocket. Then he pulled away from the curb where he'd stopped down the street from the bed-and-breakfast and headed for home. He'd worked late at the office, catching up on paperwork, and had decided to swing past Abby's house before taking the highway out of town to his place five miles into the country. Although he knew she had overnight guests and wasn't alone, he'd still been worried about her.

His apprehension about Abby's safety was growing. He couldn't help but feel that something was going on behind the scenes, something he couldn't pinpoint.

But what? There was no tangible evidence in Carolina Carter's death or in the phantom presence that Abby sometimes reported seeing, hearing, or sensing around her. Could the answer lie in the past?

A farfetched assumption, he told himself. And yet if that was true, and something had surfaced that Carolina had discovered, then might Abby not be in imminent danger as well.

"It's crazy," he said aloud in the quiet of his car as he sped along the blacktop, leaving Carterville behind.

Slowing the car, Bud turned off the main road onto a narrow lane that led to his driveway a few hundred yards farther up the slope. His two-story log home was right at the top of the hill, overlooking his five acres of grassy slopes that were dotted with blue spruce, pine and soft maple trees, and oaks with leaves that were beginning to turn color. The land had been his inheritance from his parents, as had his sister's parcel, where she lived with her husband and two sons. Their property was separated by a miniature pine forest that guaranteed both of them privacy. Their parents had been deceased for a decade.

The place was his sanctuary, had been since he'd built it after his fiancée had left him for an acting career in California. Since then he'd dedicated himself to his job and improving his property. Gradually he'd gotten over being jilted, and when his old girlfriend ultimately moved back to town, he'd quickly known that she'd never been the woman for him anyway. Now he'd met Abby and realized that he was more attracted to her than he'd ever been to the woman he'd almost married.

Bud left his car in the driveway and headed for the back door to the house, his thoughts lingering on Abby and what she'd told him about her father. Surely she was wrong about the past being connected to her aunt's death.

Yet, the case was going cold for lack of leads and evidence. And he was getting more frustrated all the time, sensing that Abby could become the next victim.

"Jeez," he said, switching on a light as he stepped through the door and tossed his keys and briefcase onto the kitchen table. After he placed his jacket over the back of an oak chair, he poured himself a whiskey. It had been a long day and he was bone tired.

The idea hit him after two swallows of his drink. He could at least do a little research of his own on Abby's family, beat her to it.

Just in case her woman's intuition was onto something.

Something deadly.

"Pam? This is your brother." Bud held the cell phone in his left hand and manipulated the driveway with his right, on his way to work the next morning.

"For goodness' sake, Bud, I recognize your voice, having known you all of your life. What's up this early in the morning?"

"I know the boys are getting ready for school and I wanted to talk with George because I might have a little job for him."

"Oh God, Bud, that's great. George is trying to save for college next year."

"I need someone for a day or two to do some research into the old archives at the library."

Momentarily, conversation stalled.

"There's no danger to George if he did this, is there, Bud?"

"Absolutely not, Pam. I would never suggest it if there was."

"Does it have to do with one of your homicide cases?"

"I won't lie to you, Pam. I don't think it does but I'm covering all of my bases, just in case there's a remote connection to a murder case I'm investigating."

"Your bases? What do you mean?"

For the next several minutes he explained, ending

with his conclusion to research the Carter background, even though he had no probable cause to do it on police time.

"So you'll be paying George yourself?"

"Yeah, I'll be the one to pay him."

"And the department, or anyone else, won't even know my son is doing this research for you?"

"Uh-huh, that's about it. It's off the record."

"Then I'll hand you over to George, Bud. You can talk to him about the job, okay?"

"Thanks, Pam. I will. But first I want you to know what I'll be expecting from him."

He explained, then talked to George. They hung up after Bud had arranged a time to meet his nephew later with his information and what he needed from the library research.

His nephew wouldn't be in jeopardy, Bud told himself as he drove back to Carterville. No one would ever know the research was being done, because it was off the record.

But I need to know, Bud thought. There are no leads in the case. Past family history had to be ruled out, even if there was no probable cause to pursue it.

Abby Carter needed to be protected, even if his motivation had become more personal than professional.

Chapter 34

"OH SHIT!" ABBY MUTTERED as she picked up the Sunday newspaper that had been delivered on her porch. She continued to read as she went back into the house and closed the front door. The two couples had not come down for breakfast yet, so Abby decided to put the newspaper away, keep it out of sight of her guests.

Shaken by what she'd scanned on the front page, Abby forced herself to concentrate on her food preparations in the kitchen. She would read the article later, once she was alone in the house. She just needed to hold herself together until then.

The dining room table was set, Katherine's cinnamon rolls had just come out of one oven, the breakfast rolls and muffins out of the other, and the cheese soufflé would be ready within a few minutes, as would the coffee. Her bacon was in the warming oven, her freshly squeezed orange juice was in the refrigerator, and her batter was ready to pour into the waffle iron. Abby stood back, surveying the condiments she'd placed on the table: butter, syrup, jam, salt, pepper, and ketchup. She was ready for the guests.

They came down a short time later and Abby

served breakfast. Once the meal was over, they went back to their rooms, got their things, and checked out by noon. As Abby watched the last couple drive away she was relieved. But still she didn't allow herself to look at the newspaper. She wanted to get the kitchen cleaned before becoming upset by the article.

When the doorbell rang Abby was startled. She stepped into the hall, her eyes on the oval window, trying to see who stood on the porch.

"Bud," she said, opening the door.

"Yeah, it's me again." His pale eyes fixed onto her face, not allowing her to glance away. "I figured you might need some support, given today's paper and what was said about you."

"I saw the front page but I haven't read it yet."

"Where is it?"

She indicated the parlor. "I placed it under the wood in the basket by the fireplace." She glanced away. "I thought it best that my guests not see it. I'm in a crisis control mode, hopefully to preserve the business. I don't need this kind of publicity."

"Yeah, I agree." He went to basket and retrieved the paper. "Why don't you sit down and read it now. Then we can talk about it, okay?"

She nodded. "But I'll read it in the kitchen, after I give you a cup of coffee."

"That's perfect." He followed her, sniffing the air as they headed for the back of the house. "It smells like you just served a wonderful breakfast."

She shot him a glance. "That was the consensus of my guests." She grinned at him. "I have lots of left-overs. Have you eaten, Bud?"

"I had coffee and a roll earlier."

"I'll fix you a plate." She grinned as he sat down at the kitchen table. "You can tell me what you think about my cooking. I'm certainly not as good as my aunt Carolina but I'm learning, with Katherine's help."

"I won't refuse the offer of home-cooked food." His brows shot up. "Even more tantalizing is that everything looks delicious."

"Good." She dished up his plate, heated it in the microwave, then placed it on the table in front of him. She added a tray with cinnamon rolls, muffins, and breakfast buns, poured a glass of freshly squeezed orange juice, filled his coffee cup along with her own, then sat down with the newspaper. "You eat and I'll read."

"Jeez, Abby, is this an example of what you serve on Sundays?"

She nodded, absently, already having started to read the article about her—which included the drawing of the man who'd attacked her the night before she'd returned to Carterville because of her aunt's murder.

"This is an incredible breakfast," Bud went on. "No wonder your aunt's regular guests keep coming back. I can't imagine how she even made a profit."

"Thanks," she said, and concentrated on the words, becoming more and more upset as she took in the content of the article. When she finished, Abby looked up.

The room went still as Bud seemed to examine her face.

"Are you okay, Abby?"

She managed to nod, straining to control her emotions. "I think so, but I admit to being upset."

He shoved back his plate and stood up. "Hey, Abby, the piece is very positive toward you and I think that's what you need to focus on right now. You're being touted as an artistic genius, rightly or wrongly, but the media isn't coming down on you."

"But they're playing up who I am, where I live, that my aunt was murdered and identifying the bed-and-breakfast." She drew in a deep breath. "They're even going into my background—that I was raised by my aunt after my parents had their fatal accident."

He came around the table, pulled her upright so that she was against his chest. "You're forgetting one thing."

"What's that?" she asked, trying not to think about the past sadness in her life or what the publicity might mean for her to stay afloat financially. Instead, she tried to control herself, so that she could at least retain her personal power.

Bud wrapped his arms around her, so that she was totally entrapped against him, so that she had no option but to look up into his face,

"I want you to know that you're going to be okay, Abby. You will be safe, the B and B will come out of this publicity, and you will make it."

She pulled away. "How can you know that, Bud? You don't know who killed my aunt." She swallowed back an urge to cry. "You don't know why or what happened. You—we—don't even know if we'll ever learn who killed her." Her voice faltered and she felt tears gather in her eyes and slide down her cheeks.

"Hey," Bud said, fingering her tears away. "It's going to be all right, believe me, Abby."

"I hope so, Bud, because all of what has happened is such a mystery."

"So what you need, Abby, is a change of scene."

"Yeah, you're probably right." She turned away.

"But in the meantime I need to clean the kitchen, wash the dishes, and put things away."

"I'll help," Bud said. "Just tell me what to do."

"Why would you want to do that?"

"Why not?" Bud quirked a brow as he grinned. "We need to get done as quickly as possible so we can go out on our special jaunt to get past stress."

"Do I seem stressed?"

"Yeah, but we can take care of that. I have a plan."

"Which is?"

"A surprise," he told her. "Believe me, off the record, you'll be feeling more balanced once we take the day off. Sort of a time-out between all the heavy feelings of what has happened."

For the next fifteen minutes Abby cleaned up the kitchen and gave instructions to Bud, who wiped down the table and put things away.

"Now I'm in charge," Bud said. "Get your things and I'll wait," he told Abby as she went upstairs to change. When she came back down he told her, "We're off the record now. I'm not a homicide detective and you're not a part of my investigation. Okay?"

"Yeah, that's fine with me." She hesitated. "But will it be all right with your superior?"

"Like I said, we're off the record for a few hours."

They locked up and then went out to his car at the curb. She entrusted herself to him and his opinion that she should get away to relax.

She wondered what he had in mind, where they were going.

Chapter 35

"HEY, WHERE ARE WE? I've never been outside of town in this part of the county," Abby said, as Bud turned off a main road onto a lane that led up to a house on the top of a grassy hill. She liked what she saw: a large, rustic log home with a huge wraparound porch that faced the view, shrubs and trees and a vegetable garden in the back that was fenced with chicken wire to keep out the deer.

"Do you like it?" The sun glinted in his eyes, silvering them so that she was again reminded of wolf eyes. The impression was gone the next moment as he turned his car toward the open garage behind the house.

"This is lovely," she said, realizing that down the long, sloping hill, across the forest of trees that were beginning to turn into their fall colors, was the distant Hudson River, beyond which were the soaring Catskill Mountains. "I had no idea that such a view existed."

"Really—that's hard to believe." Bud stopped the car and turned to her as he switched off the engine. "But you grew up in Carterville. Surely you explored the countryside. This area is only a few miles outside the city limits."

"I know. My aunt was overly protective. I didn't real-ize how much so until after I'd grown up and gone away to college."

"How so? Surely you had friends who lived in rural areas?"

"Oh yeah, I did, but they mostly came to my house, and my aunt made our giggling slumber parties such fun that everyone always opted for my place rather than theirs, although I did visit a few girlfriends, but never for overnight. My aunt always picked me up by eight or nine in her Lincoln Continental, the same car that's still in our garage." She shook her head, smiling. "But none of my friends lived out like this, on property with such a fantastic view."

"Yeah, I lucked out when I inherited these few acres from my parents."

"Inherited?"

"Uh-huh. My parents passed away some time ago, leaving their land to me and my older sister." He ges-tured toward a patch of woods at the side of his prop-erty. "She and her husband and two boys live beyond the trees in the house where we grew up. I built my own place—to fit all of my interests."

"Like gardening?"

"Among quite a few other things."

Her smile broadened. He was a man of surprises. "You have a family compound here. How nice."

"Well, it works for us, especially since we all have our privacy, given the trees and property size." He hes-itated. "As I said, it's astounding that in all your years living in town you never ventured into the countryside beyond the main roads."

"I know it does sound odd, but remember, my aunt

was a spinster. She took the responsibility of caring for me seriously."

"I can understand that. She'd never been around kids."

"So basically, once I came to live with Aunt Carolina after my parents died, I did have a pretty sheltered life. I went to school, participated in academic and church functions, but we didn't venture out of town except on our annual two-week summer vacation to the Jersey Shore. My aunt had friends who owned a place there." She shrugged. "There never seemed a need; our life was already full. My aunt had her lifelong friends and I had lots of friends, too."

She had his full attention.

"So why were you allowed to go away to college?"

She pursed her lips, considering. "I always wondered that myself, although I never thought of it in terms of being allowed. I figured it was because I was in another controlled environment, the small university that both my mother and Carolina had once attended." She shook her head. "My family, all those ancestors I never knew, believed in higher education."

"Didn't your aunt object when you went from the university straight into New York City and got a job with an art gallery? Surely that's a contradiction— sheltered upbringing versus the evils of a big city."

"I know it seems that way but I think she just wanted me to spread my wings. She helped me financially, giving me the boost to get started."

"So once you went to college your aunt wasn't as protective as she was before that, as you were growing up here in Carterville?"

Abby grinned, meeting his eyes. "Are you saying

that she was only guarding me while I lived in Carter-ville?"

For a moment he didn't reply. "Of course not. Why would I?"

She shook off her momentary impression. "I'm just sorry that I didn't come home more often, that I wasn't aware if something bad might have been going on in my aunt's life."

"What makes you think that, Abby?" he asked, look-ing genuinely interested in her answer.

"I don't know, Bud, I just do. I keep wondering if she was worried, even afraid of something and didn't tell me."

"What?" He leaned closer, intrigued.

Again she shrugged. "I can't say. It's just a feeling I have, especially at night when I'm home alone and imagine that someone is in the house. I know that's crazy, because no one is ever there, couldn't be be-cause all the doors and windows are always locked up each night." She managed a laugh, realizing that she was sounding weird. "I believe I'm still trying to get over my aunt's death, and because it was a murder I allow my imagination to be carried away."

He reached in front of her and opened the car door. "Hey, we've been sitting here for five minutes and I wanted to show you my place."

By the time she'd stepped onto the driveway he was already out, standing on the passenger side, ready to close the door behind her. For a second their gazes locked, giving her a jolt of sensation that fluttered into her chest. She was the first to look away.

"Thanks," she said, suddenly too aware of his close proximity. "It isn't often someone closes car doors for me," she added, trying to keep a light mood, the opposite of how she felt.

"Hey, it's called hospitality to welcome a guest."

"And I'm the guest?"

His eyelids lowered ever so slightly and his smile seemed momentarily frozen. "For now you are, Abby."

She shook off the sensation of intimacy, that he was implying a deeper meaning, and replied in a joking manner, "So you're saying that I have to pass muster?"

A slow smile spread from the crinkling corners of his eyes to the curve of his lips. "You already have, Abby."

"And that's the reason you even brought me here?" she asked, deliberately playing ignorant—because she was uncertain about his motives.

"You could say that." His expression changed to amusement as he took her arm, leading her up the steps to the deck and the back door. "Just remember that only valued friends come in this way; strangers come to the front."

"I think you just paid me a compliment, Bud." She shot him a glance, grinning. "I'm honored."

"Good."

"I'm trying to think of the right words to tell you how impressed I am by your place—it's like a scenic postcard. I feel honored that you've shown me where you live."

There was a momentary silence between them.

He broke it with a laugh that blew away all trace of his flirtatious words, as though he suddenly remembered that their relationship was professional, not personal. "Seriously, Abby, I just wanted you to have a diversion and my first thought was of a drive in the country." He shrugged. "I ended up bringing you here."

He'd opened the door to the house and stepped inside. "Believe me, I have no ulterior motives."

"Of course not," she said, sounding stilted. "Why would you?"

Then she stepped right into a modern but rustic kitchen with high, open-beamed ceilings, wall paneling, and a wooden board floor. Even the furniture was rustic; the dining-room table was made of heavy planking, as were the benches on both sides and the sideboard on the back wall that held the china, which was obviously not the fragile type for an afternoon tea. The whole place, from the hanging pots and pans near the stove to the pictures on the walls, denoted a male occupant. The place was almost totally masculine, from the handwoven rugs scattered on the floor to the dark brown leather sofa and chairs she glimpsed in the living room beyond the front entry.

"Hey, your place is really unique, Bud—I love it!"

His expression reflected his pleasure. "Thanks. It's basically a representation of me, is what my sis always tells me. She claims that a person can be characterized by their home."

She turned back to him. "Then, as suspected, you're a good person," she said simply. "No pretense, just straightforward."

Their eyes met and locked.

"So, let me show you around," he said, breaking into the sudden awkwardness between them. "I was going to give you the tour, and then introduce you to my sister and family—if they're home—and then take you down to a restaurant on the river."

"Wow, Bud. That sounds wonderful, but . . ." Her words drifted off.

"But what?"

"Can you do that? I mean can we have a meal together when you're investigating my aunt's case? Is that, uh, appropriate police procedure?"

They'd been standing in the middle of the combination kitchen and dining area, separated by several feet because of an eating bar between them, and now he strode around it to face her.

"Hey, hey, remember? This is a day off." His hands came down on her shoulders, gently holding her in place. "I'm not being a homicide detective and you're not worried about an article in the newspaper for the next few hours. We're simply Bud and Abby, two friends who are having a day away from personal stress. Okay?"

She managed a nod.

He held her for a second longer, his eyes examining her face. Then he stepped back, his hands dropping to his sides. "C'mon, let's get started with our time-out, a day without worries."

"Agreed," she said. "I'd love a tour of your house."

"Good." He led the way through the entry area, past the staircase to the second floor, and into a living room large enough to handle the oversize furniture and a massive stone fireplace. Through the front windows she could see the porch with wicker chairs that faced the view. "Just remember that the place is a work in progress," he added. "I still have lots to do."

"I can't see what that would be," she said, following him though a doorway to a small back hall with three doors: one to a TV room, another to a bathroom, and a third to the basement steps. The final opening was an archway that opened back into the kitchen. The house had a circular floor plan, she realized. "Everything looks perfect."

"Thanks, but you'll see what I mean when you get to the basement." He hesitated in the first doorway. "This is where I spend a lot of time when I'm home," he said, meaning the TV room. "My computer station is in the corner, the music system is next to the television set, and the sofa is where I often eat my supper."

She nodded, uncertain how to reply. She felt a bit uncomfortable and wondered why he was giving her such a tour. Was it really to give her a few hours' diversion from her worries, because she was alone in the world, or was there something more?

Nonsense, Abby told herself. She needed to guard against always suspecting ulterior motives. Maybe Sam had been right—she should sell out and make a new start, if not in the city, then somewhere else.

He took her upstairs next, where she viewed the master bedroom with bath, two other bedrooms, and a bathroom from the doorways, then on down to the basement, which was unfinished except for the laundry area. "Someday, if I have a family, I plan to make two more bedrooms down here."

"Sounds like you hope for lots of kids," she said as they went back up to the first floor.

"Three or four would be perfect." His tone was serious but the corners of his eyes crinkled slightly, as though he was amused.

"How does the proposed mother feel about that large of a family?" she asked, pretending innocence.

"We haven't discussed the issue in any depth yet." They'd returned to the kitchen and he motioned her to a stool at the counter. "The truth is, I haven't even popped the question."

"Popped what question?" The female voice brought them both around to face the woman who'd just stepped in through the back door. "Am I missing something?"

"Not that I know of, Sis." Bud motioned her into the room. "I'd like you to meet Abby. And, Abby, this is my big sister, Pam."

"I'm so happy to meet you, Abby," Pam said, and Abby could see that Bud's sister had long, dark hair, silvery blue eyes, and looked like an older, feminine version of her brother. "You're the artist, right?"

"Yeah, I'm an artist. I just hope I'm not an infamous artist." Abby was half laughing as she spoke. "I think you've been reading the Sunday paper."

Pam's smile was wide, revealing perfect teeth; she was around forty and wore faded jeans and a T-shirt, and Abby wondered if she'd ever seen a more beautiful woman. No wonder Bud was tall, dark, and sexy. It was in his gene pool.

"I confess, I have been following the rape case," Pam went on. "But I'm sorry that your identity was revealed on top of what happened to your aunt." She'd sobered and her expression was genuine. "I'm so sorry about your loss and I hope Bud and his homicide guys nail the bastard."

Abby nodded. "That's my hope, too."

Bud had watched the exchange with interest, and when he spoke, both women turned their eyes on him. "I was about to make fresh coffee, Pam. You're welcome to join us."

"Thanks, little brother, but I came over here to invite you to Sunday dinner." Her gaze shifted to Abby. "We'd like you to join us, too."

"Uh, I was planning on taking Abby out for dinner," Bud said. He turned to Abby. "What would you like to do?"

"We'd love you to come, Abby," Pam said. "I'm having pot roast and it's really delicious. Plus, we serve a good red wine before dinner."

Abby couldn't control her grin. "You know, I think I'd love dinner at your house. It sounds wonderful."

"Okay, I've been upstaged. We'll come over under one condition," Bud told his sister.

"What's that?" Pam asked.

"That Abby agrees to a rain check."

"I do agree," she told him. "It isn't every day that I get to have a Sunday family dinner with a real family." As soon as she spoke her thoughts, Abby realized how odd her statement must have sounded. Bud's thoughtful expression confirmed her realization. She felt silly.

"It's settled then," Pam said. "Come on over in a bit. We eat in an hour or so."

She turned back from the door, her eyes on Abby. "We're looking forward to having you." Then the door closed behind her.

"Sorry about my little outburst," she said. "I think my envy of people who have a real family unit overtook my sense of proprieties." She grimaced. "It was also very sweet of your sister to include me."

He stepped next to her and circled her waist in a gentle grasp. "I'm just sorry that you grew up without your parents, Abby." He dropped a kiss on her forehead. Then he made coffee while they chatted about everything but her aunt's murder case and the fact that her name, the drawing of her New York City attacker, and her connection to her aunt's bed-and-breakfast were in the morning newspaper.

A short time later they headed next door to the house where Bud had grown up.

"Thank you so much for the most enjoyable day I've had in a long time. I like your sister, and the boys are great teenagers." She grinned, her hand on the door latch, her gaze meeting Bud's as he stopped the car in front of the bed-and-breakfast. "You were right. Getting away for a few hours really lifted my spirits."

He inclined his head, his expression unreadable, then opened his door and came around to the passenger side. "I'll see you inside, Abby, make sure everything is secure before I leave."

"No need for you to do that. It's still daylight and everything looks just as I left it."

"No problem. I insist." Although his tone was casual she sensed that she couldn't dissuade him. She led the way up to the porch and he waited as she unlocked the door, then followed her inside. He made a cursory examination of the lower floor, was satisfied that all was fine and would have checked out the second floor but she stopped him.

"If no one has been down here they certainly couldn't be up there," she reminded him.

He took her hands in his and pulled her close. "Now I'm being protective like your aunt was," he said. "The condition seems to be contagious."

A moment later his arms had come around her and she was pressed against his body. Then his lips claimed hers, igniting a sharp emotional response within her, so that she was straining against him as the kiss deepened. Abby found herself kissing him back, until he finally lifted his head, breaking the tension between them.

"Abby, remember when you asked if spending the day together was proper protocol and I said it was?" His voice was low and husky and she knew that what he was about to say wasn't what he wanted to do—make love to her.

She managed to nod.

"Well—uh, yeah, at this moment it isn't." He tilted his head, his eyes glowing in a shaft of setting sunlight. "We'll have to take another rain check for later."

"You're right, Bud," she whispered.

"There are times I hate to be right." He stepped back, his hand on the doorknob.

Impulsively, he stepped forward and kissed her again. Then he was gone, the door firmly closed behind him. She watched from the oval window as he drove off before she headed up to her bedroom to shower and get ready for bed early.

She was walking down the hall when she heard the faint shuffling noise, as though someone had moved in one of the bedrooms. Abby stopped short, paralyzed to the spot, straining to listen. She had no idea where the sound had originated, or what had caused it.

Oh shit. She was alone. God help her if there really was someone else in the house.

Bud drove home, but he sure as hell didn't feel like it. He wanted to turn around. But he knew better.

Gradually, he was able to cool it and think a little

more logically. His thoughts went over the facts he'd learned from Abby today during their small talk. She had revealed a few things she probably wasn't aware of—like her aunt's overprotectiveness during the years Abby had been with her. Something didn't jell. It was as though Carolina had been fearful about something. What? . . . Or whom? And if so, had that had anything to do with her death?

Bud pressed down on the accelerator as he made a mental inventory of what needed to be checked on, starting with the accidental death of her parents, anything on the mystery surrounding her father's birth, and the history of the Carter family. In particular, he needed a follow-up on the historical research Abby had begun at the library.

He'd get his nephew started on that as soon as possible. Something was terribly wrong, and, if his hunch was correct, time was of the essence. Abby could be in danger once the predator was ready to strike.

He wiped his hair back from his forehead with the flat of his hand. He needed to find some evidence. Without it he didn't have a suspect. He had only a phantom.

Chapter 36

"DAMN IT ALL TO HELL!" he muttered under his breath. He'd been right out in the open when she came into the house and he'd had to scramble.

He'd almost fallen but had caught himself. Still, he'd made a noise and she'd heard it, stopping to listen. Watching her, he'd wondered if she would bolt, or scream, or do something where he'd have to end the whole business right then. The anticipation of that happening almost overwhelmed his good sense.

Patience, he told himself. It will happen soon. Savor the anticipation. Don't blow it now for a quick hit of perversion, sex, and death, which always restored him.

So he'd waited too, listening for her next move. He'd heard her start forward, open the doors to all the bedrooms, including Carolina's. She'd found nothing and gone on to her bedroom. After a while he'd been able to move as well, making sure he was safe. He'd decided to stay and keep an eye on what she did. Maybe he'd even find what he needed, so the whole bullshit game could end.

Now, as he watched her begin to undress, he became aroused, again, his fantasy quickly taking over his reality. For a moment she stood naked before pulling her skimpy nightgown over her head to fall over her flesh.

He forced himself to control his breathing—or she might hear it. He almost hoped she would, so that he could take her now, feel her skin under him, her squirming body, which would finally be stilled forever when he took her life.

She would be the fuckin' best yet.

Finally she was in bed and sometime later she turned out the light. He stayed put, waiting for the right moment for his move.

He had to take the risk. He was owed. The wait for the ultimate needed a special perk, so he could hang in there for the duration—until it was time.

She was asleep, he was sure of it. She'd been still and breathing quietly for a long time now.

He stepped out of the shadows, softly, carefully, alert to any movement of the air currents.

Slowly he glided over the carpet to the foot of the bed. He peered through the darkness, fastening on the long hair that was splayed against the white pillowcase.

He forced deep breaths.

She was an exquisite prize, one he deserved.

He slipped forward once more to the side of her bed; she lay sleeping, unaware of his presence. He savored the moment, allowing himself the erection that held the promise for later. He allowed his passion to build, knowing what he had to do to appease it.

Touch her.

For a long time he held his hand inches above her chest where the sheet had slid away to expose part of her breast. He stroked the air, gradually lowering his fingers to her skin, gently skimming it with barely a tickle. Then his fingers traced a path up to her neck, and on to her mouth, where they lingered, absolutely still.

His climax was intense and he couldn't help the soft moan that escaped his lips.

She stirred and her hand came up to wipe her face, barely avoiding his fingers.

Quickly, he stepped back, knowing she could awaken at any moment. He slipped into the shadows at the same time as she turned over onto her side. Seconds later she reached for the lamp.

Before the light flooded the room he was gone. He was okay now. He could last for a while longer. Until the time when he wouldn't have to leave her.

Chapter 37

ABBY SAT UP IN BED after switching on the lamp, her mental antenna emitting warning signals. Had someone been in her room? Touching her?

She peered into the familiar space that had contained her personal things since childhood, examining the shadowy corners, making sure the door to the hall was still closed. Everything seemed serene, just as it had been when she'd turned out the light for the night.

She wiped a hand over her mouth, trying to stop the tickling sensation, a feeling reminiscent of a feather stroking her lips.

Had Bud's kisses, her response, and their mutual sexual attraction prompted such a vivid dream? Was she manifesting her desire for him in sleep fantasies so real that they woke her up?

She tossed back her covers and got out of bed. Now wide awake, Abby doubted she'd get back to dreamland anytime soon. She headed to the connecting bathroom. Three minutes later she returned to her bedroom, feeling back on track, ready to snuggle under the covers and get to sleep.

About to climb into bed, she stopped in midstride.

There was another vague sound somewhere deep in the walls and timbers of the house. Abby backed away, until she was against the wall next to the headboard, too frightened to get into bed. She was frozen in place, listening, waiting to identify the direction of the sound.

What had she heard?

Was it the natural settling of the house? she wondered for the umpteenth time.

No, she answered herself. It was different from any of the sounds she remembered hearing while she was growing up—the normal creaking, groaning, and settling of such an old house. The recent disturbances, vague, unidentifiable noises, had been something she'd heard only since returning after her aunt's murder.

Like the other times when she'd heard scratching and shuffling at odd moments of the day or night, it was a scary sound, as though history had been released into the present. She was reminded of the ghosts of fleeing slaves who'd come North on the Underground Railroad, and the sympathetic people who'd sheltered them so long ago.

Jeez, Abby thought, trying to calm the frightening scenarios that were leaping to mind—because she was so frightened by the unknown sounds and the unsubstantiated history of her house. Get real, she told herself. There are no such things as ghosts and apparitions from the past. If there were, she reasoned, they would have surfaced years earlier when she, as a vulnerable child, was in this very room, frightened and suffering from the devastating loss of her parents.

One thing she did know: There was no way she could go back to sleep now.

She had no explanation for what she'd heard. Common sense told her that there was a reason for every sound. She just hadn't found out what that was yet. She sat down on the bed, took a historical novel from the nightstand, propped the pillows behind her back, and began to read.

After a few pages Abby knew it was hopeless. Putting down the book, she got out of bed and strode to the door. Taking a deep breath, she opened it, glanced in both directions along the empty hall, then tiptoed to the staircase, careful not to make a sound. Once on the lower floor, she went to the kitchen, reminding herself that the house had been in the Carter family for generations, that it now belonged to her and not to some creepy phantom who quite possibly was only a figment of her imagination.

Sacred or not, she refused to be intimidated.

She heated water in the teakettle, made a cup of tea, then headed back upstairs. She felt empowered by her actions: No one, real or imagined, had stopped her.

Back in her room, she made herself comfortable on the bed, took up the book, and, sipping her tea, kept reading *Sun of the Morning,* a historical romance saga that had belonged to Carolina. When the sky behind the windows began to lighten, she finally put the story down, too tired to continue.

The night had been uneventful after she'd awakened with her frightening thoughts. She leaned back, hoping to rest, if not sleep, so that she could get up refreshed enough to do her daily work.

Abby came out of her sleep with a start, looked around, and felt glad that she'd had a few hours of rest after all.

Getting up, she dressed quickly in jeans and a sweatshirt, knowing she had lots of housework: cleaning the rooms where her guests had stayed, changing the bedding, and making sure that everything was perfect for the people who had reservations for the upcoming weekend. She was glad that there were usually no weekday guests.

She had no excuses to postpone getting started, despite her lingering fears. She was in the lower hall when the phone rang.

"Hello?" she said.

"Hi, Abby, this is Velma Sell."

"Mrs. Sell?" Abby was surprised. She'd just seen her former landlords several days ago.

"I won't keep you, my dear. I know you're probably busy, but Jacob wanted me to let you know that he'd heard from the police department about the intruder who attacked you." She gave a nervous laugh. "You'll recall that Jacob said he would keep you informed of any progress."

"Yes, I remember. Did they arrest someone?"

"I'm afraid not. The officer just said that the case would be kept on file but wouldn't be actively pursued."

"Why?"

"They have no real evidence, is what he told us."

"I see," Abby replied. "I'm not surprised. It's a big city with much more important criminal cases."

"I'm sure you're right, Abby." Her sigh came over the wires. "But nevertheless we wanted you to have the update."

"Thank you, Mrs. Sell. I appreciate the kindness both you and your husband have shown me."

After another minute of conversation they hung up. But as Abby began her work, vacuuming and dusting, while the bedding was in the washer, thoughts of all that had happened since the attack whirled in her mind. She prayed she wouldn't get any more cancellations.

It was still early afternoon, and even though it was only Monday, and the guests wouldn't arrive until Friday, Abby wanted the bedrooms cleaned and readied by the day after checkout, a practice her aunt had established when she first opened the bed-and-breakfast.

"A business must always be ready for spur-of-the-moment guests," her aunt had always stated. "We need to be prepared."

Abby sighed. Her aunt had been hardworking and wise, traits Abby had always tried to emulate. She hoped Carolina's dedication to keeping the family property hadn't been in vain. It was up to her to make sure she didn't lose it. She straightened her shoulders and kept working, and a short time later she put her cleaning supplies away, satisfied that the house was back in order.

As she went upstairs, her arms loaded with bedding from the dryer, Abby heard another strange sound. She stopped to listen, but everything was still. Again Abby wondered if she was imagining things.

It was nothing.

After making up all the beds she'd completed the jobs she'd intended for the day. Downstairs, she made fresh coffee, straightened a few things in the kitchen while it dripped, then took a mug into the little office, where she wanted to take a look at the ledger. It had suddenly occurred to her that she hadn't paid Katherine for her services and she wanted to write her a check. But she couldn't figure out how much she owed her.

Abby picked up the phone and punched in the numbers.

Katherine answered up on the second ring. "Hello."

"It's Abby. Do you have a minute?"

"Of course I do. In fact, I was going to call you about stopping in tomorrow. I need to take inventory on the supplies I'll need for my baking on Thursday."

"That'd be perfect, because I owe you some money and I want to give you a check."

"Please don't worry about that now," Katherine said. "You have more important considerations."

"No, I insist, Katherine. I couldn't run this place without your help and I know my aunt would want me to pay you." Abby drew in a long breath. "We'll talk about it tomorrow, okay?"

"Sure, that'll be fine." Katherine hesitated. "There's one more thing, Abby. Your aunt was letting me borrow a crib that's stored in your attic because my daughter and her husband are coming from Denver for a visit. Would you mind if I had my grandsons move it tomorrow?"

"I certainly wouldn't. But is it still in good enough shape for a baby?"

"It is. Carolina and I examined it about a week before her death. I've borrowed a little mattress from another friend."

They decided that Katherine would be over around ten in the morning before they hung up. Abby finished her coffee and took the mug back to the kitchen. The phone rang and she grabbed the extension in the kitchen, thinking it might be Katherine calling back.

"Hello."

"Ms. Carter?"

"Speaking."

"I'm a reporter with the *New York Daily News* and I'd like to ask you a few questions concerning your drawing that resulted in the arrest of the rapist in your area." His words shot into her ear like the rapid fire of an automatic gun.

For a moment Abby was shocked into silence.

"Ms. Carter, are you there?"

"I can't talk now. You'll have to excuse me but I have guests," she lied.

"Can you just give me a brief statement?"

"Not now. I have to go."

She hung up quickly, then leaned against the counter until she'd regained her equilibrium. For God's sake, what did the call mean? That the story was being picked up by newspapers beyond Carterville? Was that why Sam had mentioned it, too? She couldn't think about that now. She needed to occupy her mind with a diversion.

The crib, she thought. She hadn't been in the attic since coming home and now would be a good time to do that. Quickly, she headed upstairs to the bolted door beyond Carolina's bedroom. A minute later she'd opened it, switched on the light, and climbed the narrow wooden steps to the small room under the peak of the house.

Once at the top it took a few seconds for the scene before her to sink into her consciousness. Dust hung in the air as though it needed to settle back onto the open trunks with the contents on the floor, antique furniture with the drawers hanging open, and boxes ripped open. The place was trashed.

Realization took her breath. She clasped a hand over her mouth to stop the scream that threatened to burst forth from her throat. As she took deep breaths of stale air, Abby whirled around and bounded back down the stairs, tripping and sliding until she reached the bottom. Then she slammed and bolted the door.

Someone had searched the attic. What had they been looking for? Had they found it?

Maybe the police had done it after Carolina's death? No, she told herself. Bud would have mentioned it.

Terrified, believing that she was alone in the house yet having a crawly sensation of being watched, she continued running down to the entry hall and flung open the front door. Once it stood wide, she inched back into the hall, far enough to grab the phone and pull it to the end of the cord. She stood in the doorway and punched in Bud's number.

"Bud Williams," he said crisply, sounding like a homicide detective.

Her relief was so intense that for a moment she couldn't answer.

"Hello?"

"It's me, Bud," she whispered. "Something's happened."

"Are you all right, Abby?"

"Yeah, I think so." The words wobbled off her tongue. "I'm just scared."

"Where are you?"

She told him.

"Hang up and get clear of the house. I'm two minutes away. Wait on the sidewalk."

The phone went dead and she put it down. Closing the door, a barrier between her and the rooms inside her house, she went out to the gate and waited for Bud's arrival.

What was happening? She leaned against the fence, trying to control her trembling limbs. Why would anyone have gone through old memorabilia in a dusty attic? The Carter keepsakes had no value to anyone but her family.

The only thing Abby knew for sure was that she was scared to death.

Chapter 38

ABBY KNEES SAGGED with relief when Bud's unmarked sedan came to a jolting stop at the curb. A moment later he'd jumped out, come around his car, and approached Abby.

"Jeez, Abby, you look like you've seen a ghost."

She shook her head. "I didn't see anyone, but I have heard unexplainable sounds." She tried to calm down. "Oh God, Bud. Someone was in the attic and tore though everything—trunks were dumped over, drawers in old furniture were yanked out, and packing boxes were ripped open. It's a terrible mess."

"But you say that no one is in there?" His gaze moved beyond her to the house.

"I don't know." Her words still quivered. "I just finished cleaning most of the rooms. I went up to the attic because Katherine wants to borrow a crib that was stored up there." Her voice wobbled again. "I didn't see a crib. I only saw chaos, everything in disorder."

"Wait here, Abby. I'll check it out."

"Wait!"

He turned back to her and Abby suddenly realized that he was dressed in his work clothes: shirt and

tie, black slacks, and a suit jacket. Even in her frightened state she was aware that he was devastatingly
attractive.

"I have a question."

"Shoot."

"I know this was a possible crime scene even before
it was determined that Carolina was murdered. I know
the property, including the house, was examined by
forensic experts."

He nodded.

"Did they also check out the attic, a place no one
went because the door was always kept locked?"

"Yeah, it was inspected, too."

"And did your investigators turn everything upside
down?"

"No, nothing was disturbed. They were only making
sure they didn't overlook possible evidence."

"So this has happened since then?"

He didn't answer. Instead, he took her arm and led
her back to his car, opened the passenger door, and
helped her slide onto the front seat. "I'm going to
check out the house," he said, "and I want you to wait
here—with the doors locked until I come back."

"You're going in by yourself?"

His expression altered, as though he was amused
by her question. But a moment later his manner was in
keeping with that of a homicide detective about to investigate a crime scene.

"Just stay in the car. I'll be back shortly."

"But what if someone is in the house?"

His eyes narrowed slightly, as though he was probing for information behind her words. "You said you
were alone, didn't you?"

"Yeah, but there have been little sounds I couldn't identify. I never saw anyone but I heard things."

"Okay, I believe you, but first things first. I'll make sure no one is hiding anywhere and then we'll discuss the noises."

Abby nodded and tried to reassure herself about his safety. He was a trained cop who knew how to take care of himself in any situation. She also knew that cops carried guns. Just because she'd been so frightened didn't mean that he was, too.

He closed her door, watched while she locked it, then strode up the walkway to the porch and disappeared into the entry hall. He left the front door open and her eyes were glued to it.

It seemed like an eternity but it was less than ten minutes when he reappeared. She opened the car door and stepped out, facing him, waiting for his report on what he'd found. His expression told her nothing.

"You were right, Abby. No one's in the house now, but the attic is completely trashed." He shook his head, perplexed. "It would seem that someone was searching for something."

"That was my impression as well," Abby replied, feeling calmer. "But for the life of me I can't figure out what that might be. There's nothing of value stored in the attic. The only valuables my aunt owned were the antiques scattered throughout the house, and the property itself."

"Yeah, I know. All of that information is in the ongoing investigation, even the fact that your aunt Carolina took out the mortgage to keep everything going, including the B and B."

"Damn, so I discovered once I went through her business records," Abby said, sighing.

He put an arm around her shoulders. "C'mon, let's go in the house where we can sit down and talk about all this, including these strange sounds you mentioned."

They went inside to the kitchen. "Can I offer you coffee or a soda?" she asked as he took a chair at the table.

He glanced at his watch, then raised his eyes to hers. "Just off three minutes ago. But before I answer let me make a call."

She nodded and sat down while he punched numbers on his cell phone. "This is Williams. I'm at the Carter B and B responding to Abby Carter's call about an incident here in her house. She discovered that someone had been in the attic and completely turned it upside down."

There was a long pause while he listened.

"Yeah, it does appear that someone might have been looking for something."

Another pause.

"You're right. The crime-scene guys need to check it out again. It may not be connected to the investigation but we must make sure. So when will they be here? . . . That'll work. Tomorrow morning will be fine. In the meantime I'll make sure that no one goes up there." He snapped his phone shut, his gaze shifting back to Abby. "Something alcoholic will be good for both of us." His eyes crinkled slightly at the corners in what she'd come to recognize as the precursor to a smile. "What are our choices?"

"My aunt's bar or a bottle of pinot grigio imported from Italy that's in the refrigerator."

"Let's go with the pinot grigio."

Bud opened the bottle while she found the goblets in the cupboard, and after the wine was poured they sat back down at the kitchen table.

"So someone went into the attic after my aunt's death," Abby began. "Do you think it was before I returned home?"

"No, I don't, because we'd only cleared the crime scene a few hours before your arrival." He sipped his wine, his eyes abruptly level. "I'm guessing it was after you were here but not while you had guests."

She swallowed hard. "But I would have heard them. There's no way the attic could look like that without the person creating a lot of noise."

"You probably weren't home when it happened."

"But I always locked up when I left. And the only access to the attic is through the house."

His eyelids lowered as he considered her words. "Then someone had a key." He took another drink. "Do you know who that would be?"

"I think Carolina's best friend, Katherine, has a key."

"Is that because she comes in early some mornings to do her weekly baking?"

"Bud, Katherine is completely trustworthy."

"But she has teenage grandsons who might have access to that key." His voice had taken on a professional tone. "The destruction in the attic is typical of when kids vandalize looking for items of value."

"I don't know the boys very well but they seem like nice kids. I can't believe Katherine's grandsons would try to rob me."

"You never know, Abby. We'll see what comes up in

the morning when the forensic people go over it." He smiled suddenly, as though trying to put her mind at ease. "In the meantime, tell me more about these noises, your unsettling feelings in the house, when and where they happen."

She told him everything she remembered, the feeling that she was being watched, shadows that seemed to move, and the vague sounds she couldn't identify. "And I woke up in the middle of last night believing someone had touched my face," she ended, skipping her evaluation that she might have been dreaming of him.

He was silent, considering her narration, and she wondered if he thought she was delusional, even paranoid. Finally, he spoke.

"Aside from your experience in the storage area above the garage, it sounds like most of these things happen when you're in your bedroom."

She nodded. "Are you thinking I'm crazy, Bud?"

"Hell no I'm not. I'm just trying to make heads or tails of the whole weird scenario." He got up and got the wine, refilled their glasses, and placed the bottle on the table. "One thing I know for sure is that I want you to have your locks changed tomorrow."

"I agree."

"So what's for supper?" His abrupt change of subject surprised her. He grinned. "I guess I forgot to mention that I'm staying, for supper and for the night."

She was momentarily caught off balance. "Of course I'm happy to fix us something to eat." She swallowed hard. "But you don't have to stay. I'm not that terrified since you made sure no one else was in the house."

His grin widened into his devastating full-tooth smile. "I just told my boss that I would make sure the crime scene wasn't disturbed until the experts arrive in the morning to process it." He cocked one brow at her. "That means I'll be staying, in the house, until then."

A wave of emotions washed over Abby even as she seemed outwardly calm: relief, uncertainty, and—oh God—desire.

Get hold of yourself, she thought. No more wine. You're out of control.

She got up quickly and went to the refrigerator. "How about a vegetable and chicken stir-fry?" she asked, glancing at him. Immediately, as their eyes met, hesitant brown and knowing light blue, she wished she hadn't. Somehow she managed to keep her cool and proceed with her cooking preparations.

"I need to lock up my car," he told her a few minutes later. "And get my duffel bag."

"Duffel bag?"

"Uh-huh. I always keep a change of casual clothes in my car. In my business, I never know if I'll need them."

She had all the ingredients in the wok, cooking the vegetables and chicken. She felt like she could take a deep breath once he'd left the room. The man affected her whole nervous system; she was too aware of his presence.

When he returned to the kitchen a few minutes later he'd changed out of his more formal clothes into jeans and a light blue turtleneck pullover. She had the table set and was waiting to dish up their food. Surprisingly, they had a nice meal, reminiscing about the day they'd spent together, families, and work. She felt that he avoided quizzing her more about why he was there, and she was grateful.

Later, she opted for an early night and he agreed. But when she offered him one of the guest bedrooms he shook his head.

"But you have to sleep somewhere, Bud," she protested.

"I am."

"Where?"

"In your bedroom."

She stared, words escaping her for an instant. "But I only have one bed," she replied inanely.

"But you have an overstuffed chair?"

She nodded.

"Good. That'll be fine."

"But—"

"No buts. Didn't you tell me that most of the sounds were heard from your bedroom?"

"Yes, but you—"

"Shhh. Remember, no buts about it. That's where I'm staying tonight." He grinned suddenly. "Don't worry, Abby, I'm not going to seduce you. I'm here on official business."

She couldn't think of anything to say, and in a strange way she felt reassured by his presence. After changing in the bathroom she came out with her robe on and headed for her bed.

"My face is turned." She heard the humor in his tone. "You can take off your robe and get into bed."

"Thanks," she said, very aware of his presence. She tried not to react like a Victorian virgin.

He turned to face her just as she pulled the covers up to her chin. His expression was suddenly unreadable, as though he'd guessed her thoughts. Then he made himself comfortable in the overstuffed chair, pulled the footstool close, and stretched out, the quilt Abby had given him draped over his long body.

"Night-night, Abby. You can turn out the lamp."

"Good night." She switched off the light. With the cover of darkness as a shield, she added, "And thanks, Bud. I feel much safer because you're here."

For long seconds he didn't respond.

"You're welcome. My goal is to keep you safe."

Sometime later, Abby was jolted awake and sat up suddenly in bed. For a moment uncertain, she switched on the light, then she saw Bud straighten up in his chair.

"What's wrong, Abby?" He got up, the quilt dropping to the floor, and stepped to the bed, where he sat down next to her. Watching as she glanced around the room, he pulled her into his arms, much as a father would comfort a child. "Were you having a dream?"

She shook her head. "No—that is, I don't think so. I'm just unsettled, I think, and it woke me up."

"Just lie back down, sweetheart. There were no sounds, shadows, or intrusions of any sort. I've been keeping watch and you're safe."

Still drowsy, she lay back on the pillow as he suggested, and he lay down with her, still holding her in his arms.

"It's okay, Abby," he whispered next to her ear. "Go back to sleep and know I'll keep you safe."

Abby believed him and cuddled closer, loving the feeling of his protective arms around her. With her head against his chest, she drifted off, listening to his soothing words that tickled her ear.

She gave a soft moan of contentment and drifted off to sleep.

Chapter 39

ABBY AWOKE TO THE SUN streaming through the windows. She sat up just as Bud came into the room with two steaming mugs of coffee on a tray. He still wore the jeans and turtleneck that he'd changed into last night.

"You're spoiling me," Abby said, sitting up higher against the pillows. She made sure that the sheet covered her chest, suddenly feeling self-conscious, remembering that she'd gone to sleep in his arms.

"So?" he said in his deep, masculine voice. "Everyone needs a little spoiling once in a while." He sat down on the bed and, when she'd settled herself, handed over one of the mugs. "I noticed before that you drink it black, as I do." He grinned, his pale eyes strikingly dramatic under his black lashes as he held her gaze.

She glanced away, suddenly vulnerable in a way she'd never felt before. He was so devastatingly male—and she was so aware of his magnetic personality. Damn, she thought, and realized that her feelings for Sam were lukewarm compared to the emotions Bud evoked by simply stepping into the room. She hadn't known what real physical attraction meant—until now.

And you must remember that he's the homicide detective investigating your aunt's murder, she reminded herself. He's here because of following up on all the leads, not because he's interested in you as a woman. But she knew that wasn't completely true.

Whatever, the thought was sobering, just what she needed at that moment. She had to remember that he was there because of his murder case, and anything connected to it, including her, was relevant. He was trying to catch a killer.

Abby sipped her coffee and they talked of the night they'd just spent, when nothing extraordinary had happened, of her upcoming presence at the grade-school carnival where she was scheduled to sketch quick portraits, the charge she was sharing equally with the school, and the fact that forensic investigators would be arriving soon to check out the attic.

She finished her coffee.

"How about having another cup?" Bud asked as he drained his mug. "I've got a whole pot down in the kitchen."

She grinned. "So you took over my kitchen?" She tilted her head. "Maybe I should hire you for Sunday breakfasts."

"I don't think so. I can make coffee but you're the gourmet cook around here, not me."

"Gourmet?" She laughed. "I hardly think so. I simply follow my aunt's recipes and Katherine does all the baking." She handed him her mug. "Katherine! Oh my God. She's arriving at ten to start baking. Maybe I should postpone her coming since the forensics people are getting here at that time."

He shook his head and stood up. "Katherine is okay

as she'll just be in the kitchen kneading dough." He held her gaze a moment longer. "I gather we won't be having a refill of coffee up here, right?"

She nodded. "I have to get dressed and be ready for everyone." Her fears resurfaced, threatening to overwhelm her. "Thanks for the coffee, Bud, and for—everything." She couldn't bring herself to remind him that she'd slept in his arms. "But I need to get showered and dressed and then . . ." Her thoughts drifted off as she contemplated the morning, its contradictions of bed-and-breakfast preparations versus a murder investigation.

"And then what?"

Their eyes locked. "Oh God, Bud. Don't ask me. I don't know—figure things out, I guess."

He put his mug on the tray and set it down on the end of the bed. Then he moved closer and took her hands in his. "You do know one thing for sure, Abby."

"What's that?"

There was a long silence as his eyes continued to lock hers to his. "I'm here, on your side. Nothing is going to happen to you." Although he didn't change expression, his gaze intensified. "I intend to keep you safe."

Before she could reply he'd moved closer and pulled her into his arms again, his face mere inches away. "Whether we've talked about it or not, Abby, we both know that something has happened between us—something that is important." He waited for her response.

She managed a nod.

"Say it out loud." He tightened his grip so that she was even closer, her breasts against his chest.

"Yes," she whispered finally. "Something is between us."

"What?" His eyelids had lowered, masking the sudden fire in his eyes.

"I can't explain," she said in a low voice. "I'm still trying to process everything."

"That's fair enough, Abby."

A moment later he'd lowered his head and was kissing her, a long, deepening kiss that had her clinging to him, holding him as much as he held her. Her body cried out for more than just the touch of their mouths; she needed him in a way she'd never needed anyone else before in her life.

He broke the connection, moving back until he held her at arm's length. "Just remember that, Abby. We need each other, maybe even belong to each other, but now is not the time to figure everything out." He let go of her and stood up. "Others will be arriving soon and we need to be ready." He hesitated. "But I want you to always know that I'm in your corner, that you will stay safe." His expression seemed to tighten as he looked down at her. "I promise you that I will make sure nothing bad happens to you, and that I intend to solve this case."

"You don't think I was imagining noises because there were none last night?"

"No, I don't. I have another thought on all of that and it has nothing to do with whether or not you're imagining things."

She leaned forward, oblivious that the sheet had dropped away from her low-cut nightgown. "Can you tell me?"

"Nope, I can't." Bud stepped back. "But I can advise you to cover yourself or I might not be able to stay honorable."

Heat flooded her face. Abby glanced down and realized that her breasts were almost fully exposed. She yanked up the sheet, her gaze flying back to meet Bud's.

"Don't worry, Abby." He moved away to the door. "Now is still not the time for us." His brows elevated over his wolf eyes. "When it is, I want it to be perfect, so that we'll remember that precious time when we're old and in our rocking chairs, holding hands in front of the fireplace."

She had no words, and just watched as he left the room so that she could get ready for the day. Then she got up and went to the bathroom to shower. Much later, as she applied her final bit of makeup, she was still thinking about what Bud had said. He'd expressed her very dream: marrying the man she loved, having a family, and growing old together.

Katherine arrived first, just as Bud was leaving, and, after insisting, Abby wrote her a check for her previous work since Carolina's death. Then Katherine made her inventory of what she needed for Thursday, when she'd get everything ready to bake, some on that day and some for later in the weekend.

"Do you still have the key to the house in case I'm not here?" Abby asked, bringing up the subject of the key in a casual way.

"Yup, I do." Katherine rattled her key chain. "It's with my other important keys that stay in my handbag." She hesitated. "Why do you ask, Abby?"

"Just making sure you have it," Abby said, evading. "If I shouldn't be here it would be a disaster if the rolls and cinnamon buns weren't available to be baked."

"No problem," she replied, grinning. "If I ever lost that key you'd be the first to know."

"Thanks, Katherine. I appreciate knowing that, and I count on your baking skills." She grinned at the older woman. "Where would I be without you?"

"Fine, I'm sure."

They'd moved from the kitchen to the front entry as they talked. Now Katherine glanced up toward the sounds coming from the attic. "You know, I think I'd better find another crib to borrow." She paused. "I'm so sorry that someone trashed your keepsakes, but in light of Carolina's death, I'll just find another crib."

"I'm so sorry, Katherine," Abby replied. "My aunt would have loved you to have it." She controlled a sudden impulse to cry. "I can't imagine why anyone would want to tear the Carter memorabilia to pieces like this. We have nothing of value."

Katherine stepped forward and gave her a hug. "I know, Abby. It's beyond our understanding."

They said their good-byes and Katherine promised to return on Thursday, her baking day. Then Abby turned back into the house, hearing footsteps on the stairs, knowing that the attic investigation was probably at an end.

The two men who had gone over the attic with all their high-tech equipment left with polite good-byes but did not explain anything that they might have determined from their investigation. She closed the front door behind them and was greeted with absolute silence.

A stillness that was unsettling.

When the phone rang she jumped and picked it up on the second ring.

"Hello?"

"Is that you, Abby?"

The woman's voice was familiar but Abby couldn't place it.

"Yes, this is Abby."

"It's Velma Sell, calling you again. But this time I have a different reason."

Abby relaxed. "It's always nice to hear from you, Mrs. Sell. What can I do for you?"

"Well, I need to ask a favor."

"A favor—I'll certainly see what I can do."

"We called you first, praying you could, and hoping we'd be helping you in the process."

"What do you need?"

"We'd like to book a room at your B and B for the weekend, if you have a vacancy." Mrs. Sell took a deep breath. "My elderly uncle is having a birthday party and all of his few habitable bedrooms will be occupied." She gave a laugh. "He has other bedrooms in the closed part of the mansion, but they're not fit to house a rodent."

"Of course, I'll fit you in," Abby said, unable to refuse the kindly couple. Even though the three bedrooms were booked, she'd make a place for the Sells. They could stay in her room and she would use Carolina's bedroom. She couldn't turn them away.

They set the room rate and time and hung up. She'd barely returned the phone to its cradle when it rang again, this time with a cancellation for that very weekend. As Abby completed the call she couldn't help but wonder if the couple had been influenced by the newspaper coverage. They hadn't said so, so she'd never know for sure.

One thing she was grateful for: The Sells would take up the slack and she wouldn't need to give up her bedroom. When the phone rang again she was resigned that it would be another cancellation. It took her by surprise when she recognized the caller.

It was Sam.

"For Christ sake, what in the hell is happening up there?" were his first words after they'd exchanged greetings. "The wire service is full of your artwork."

"What are you talking about, Sam?"

"I'll tell you when I see you, Abby." He paused. "I can only say I'm terribly concerned. I'll be up there in time to take you out for dinner, okay?"

"That would be nice, Sam, but you need to tell—"

The interruption was met by a dial tone.

For God's sake, what next? she wondered. But the one thing she did know was that Sam always did what he said he would. He'd arrive before suppertime.

But why would he? she asked herself. What could be so drastic that he'd put himself out?

Chapter 40

BUD CALLED LATE in the afternoon with the forensic report. "They found no evidence that would connect the attic event with your aunt's death," he told Abby. "The conclusion was that if it had been a part of the crime scene, it would have been trashed at the time of the murder."

"Then what are they calling it?"

"They concluded that it was random vandalism probably committed by teenagers looking for items to sell, maybe for drugs."

"But why wouldn't they have stolen something from the house itself?" Abby retorted, pacing the hall as she talked on the phone. "And how did they get in the house in the first place?"

"Possibly because they figured no one would notice the attic for a while, and how they got into the house is obvious. Someone had a key." His drawn-in breath sounded in her ear. "Hence, to come full circle on the issue, the vandal didn't want to call attention to the intrusion, figuring no one would look in the attic for some time—and that person was correct. It's taken you a few weeks to get up there."

"But I just asked Katherine about her key. It's still on her key chain." She switched the phone to her other ear. "Bud, this just doesn't make any sense at all."

"Not on the face of it," he said, agreeing. "On the other hand, we don't know if your aunt had an extra key or two and who might have been given one."

"You're right about that. I don't know."

"Look, we can talk about this later in more detail," Bud said. "How about I pick you up around six and take you to the Italian restaurant down on the river that we missed on Sunday?"

"Oh, Bud, thanks, I'd love to, but I can't. Can we discuss this at another time real soon?"

"Uh, sure we can." His words seemed to vibrate over the line that connected them. "May I ask why you can't?" His professional tone was abrupt. "Is this because of a reservation at the B and B, or because of something else?"

There was a silence as Abby gathered her thoughts.

"A friend of mine from the city called, concerned about the write-up in the *Daily News,* and is on his way to see me to make sure I'm really okay."

"So your friend is a man?"

"Yeah."

"He must be pretty special to be so worried about you." He cleared his throat. "Will he be spending the night?"

"I don't know, but he could, since I have empty bedrooms." She licked her lips, anxious that he wouldn't misunderstand. "You sound like you don't approve. He's not anyone I'm committed to, he's only a friend."

"That wasn't my main concern, Abby. I was only

thinking about you not being there alone—until you have your locks changed. I know you've been apprehensive about strange noises and now the fact that someone was in the attic."

"I appreciate that, Bud, and my locks are scheduled to be changed tomorrow morning."

"Good." His tone sounded professional. "Under the current circumstances, I need to ask you his name."

"That's no problem, Bud. It's Sam Mathews, a man I met at an art exhibit shortly after I moved to New York City, and yes, at one time I did think we might have a future together."

"And now?"

She gave a laugh. "No way."

"What exactly does that mean, Abby?"

"Oh, Bud, it's really not important."

"Tell me anyway."

Abby sighed, wondering if his interest was professionally or personally motivated. "Sam is a committed artist; his career comes first with him," she began. "That's okay, but it also makes him a little self-centered, not really tuned in to anyone else's feelings. I'm not up for a casual relationship so he's just my friend."

"But you did care for him?"

"Let me put it this way, Bud. I've hardly missed him since returning to Carterville."

"Oh, but does he often call you?"

"Occasionally, but then I haven't been gone long."

"I see."

He didn't elaborate and she wondered what it was that he saw. Then he clarified: "So he didn't accompany you on your trip home, the day after you were attacked in your own apartment."

"No; as you know, I came alone. He had appointments he couldn't break."

"And he didn't come later to be with you for the funeral."

"He didn't because of the same reason—meetings."

"So what was it about this newspaper article that prompted him to come now?"

"It was about my drawing that helped identify the serial rapist, probably written by that reporter who called me yesterday."

"A reporter called?" he asked surprised. "Jeez, I need to look into that article, see what it said, where the guy got his information unless he picked it up from the wire service. The last thing you need is more publicity."

"You're right about that. I don't need another cancellation."

"You had a cancellation?"

"Uh-huh, but fortunately I rented the room to someone else. Luckily, my old landlords needed a room for Saturday night and that saved me."

"The New York couple?"

"Yeah, their uncle who lives in the area is having a birthday party and has too many guests and too few bedrooms."

"Okay then, Abby. You have a nice time with your, uh, friend, and don't forget to call if you have a problem."

"Thanks."

They hung up and she went upstairs to get ready for Sam. She suddenly looked forward to seeing him.

A short time later, dressed in hip-riding black slacks and a white lace pullover with a low-scooped neckline, Abby headed downstairs to await Sam's arrival. A glance in the hall mirror assured her that she looked her best: Her hair was left long and casual, her makeup highlighted her features, and her clothing looked sexy in an understated way.

"What are you trying to prove?" she asked her image. "That Sam has blown his chance for my love?"

She grinned and turned away, knowing he had, just as the phone rang on the hall table under the mirror. She grabbed it.

"Hello?"

"Is this Ms. Carter?"

"Yes it is." She didn't recognize the man's voice and guessed that the caller was interested in a reservation. "May I ask who is calling?"

"Roger Blest, a reporter with the *Investigator*. I would like to schedule an interview to discuss your amazing ability as a novice forensic artist. We'd like to run the piece in next week's edition."

"Are you talking about the weekly tabloid?"

"We're a tabloid, yes, but we only publish facts, Ms. Carter."

"And what does this have to do with me since I'm not a forensic artist?"

"Perhaps not a professional police forensic artist, but you did what they were unable to do, draw a sketch from the description of the victim."

"That's old news, Mr. Blest." She was ready to hang up. "The rapist has already been arrested."

"Yeah, I know that, Ms. Carter. That's not the focus of my article."

"What is then?"

"The drawing of your own attacker before you left New York City."

"What?" She sank down on a chair. "You're not serious."

"I am. Due to the success of your drawing that culminated in the arrest of a serial rapist, we're hoping your own attacker can be identified, too—if we give it the media coverage it deserves."

"Please, Mr. Blest, don't publicize that drawing—it's probably not accurate."

"It's news, Ms. Carter. I'm afraid it's on the schedule."

"Take it off. That drawing belongs to me and is not for publication."

"Sorry, you gave it away, and now we have the rights," he replied, his tone final. "We'd like to report your side."

"Please don't publish it. You don't have my permission."

"Like I said, sorry."

She hung up on him before he could say more.

Then she slumped over herself on the chair, horrified by the ramifications of the phone call. *She could be in the* Investigator. And that could be the end of the bed-and-breakfast, which was her income at the moment.

The doorbell rang, bringing her upright on the chair.

It rang again.

She got up and strode to the door, knowing it was Sam. Swinging open the door, she stared into a crowd of men and women, some with cameras flashing lights in her face. Sam was nowhere in sight. The people before her were from the media, each one trying to talk to her.

"Oh my God," she muttered, as the cameras continued flashing their lights in front of her and people rushed forward. Questions came from all directions. She slammed the door and locked it.

Then she called Bud.

Chapter 41

BUD'S ANSWERING SERVICE CAME ON. She waited for his message to end, then explained what had happened outside her front door. "It's a circus, Bud. Evidently the media has advanced their interest from catching the rapist in this area to the attempted-assault case on me before I came home—because of the sample sketch I gave Maryanne."

She hung up the phone and crept to the oval door window and peeked out, making sure she stayed hidden. The gathered crowd had moved off the porch but there was still a group of photographers between the yard and the street.

Oh dear God, what had she done in trying to help Maryanne? She'd placed herself in jeopardy, and the bed-and-breakfast, her heritage.

She'd been too successful with her drawing of the rapist—and then he'd been caught. Now she seemed to have become an instant expert of some sort and had attracted the interest of the media.

It was ludicrous, attention from the media, which seemed like a left-field assumption, all based on the whim when she'd drawn the profile from Maryanne's instructions.

The phone rang again and she ran to answer it, then hesitated, wishing her aunt had caller ID.

As she stood over it, Abby realized that she had to answer. It could be Sam or Bud. If it was a reporter, she'd pretend to be a housekeeper. She grabbed the receiver.

"Carter Bed and Breakfast," she said in her most professional tone.

"I'd like to speak to Ms. Abby Carter please," a woman said.

"She's not available," Abby replied. "May I take a message?"

"Are you Abby Carter?" the woman asked curtly.

"I'm only the housekeeper," Abby said, equally curt. "May I ask who's calling?"

"Never mind, I'll call back."

The line went dead and Abby replaced the receiver in its cradle. For a moment she felt a rush of pleasure. She was in control, not they.

The phone scenario went on for the next half hour, and she answered in the same way. When a knock sounded on the door, Abby was hesitant and again peeked from the edge of the oval window.

Quickly, she opened it just wide enough for Bud to step into the entry, then closed it right behind him.

They stood in the entry facing each other, his eyes hooded as he took in her appearance. He was the first to speak.

"You're looking especially lovely, Abby."

For a moment his compliment disconcerted her; she'd expected a comment about the crowd. "Thank you, Bud." She lowered her eyes, unable to hold his discerning gaze. "I'm looking much as I always do when expecting to go out to dinner with someone."

"Your date with Sam?"

She nodded. "With my friend Sam," she corrected him.

He tilted his head, as though waiting for her to continue.

"I believe Sam wanted to warn me of the media swarm that was about to happen, because of what he'd read in the newspaper." She shook her head. "I don't think he realized that it would be on my doorstep this fast."

Bud held her eyes, as though he pondered her evaluation of Sam. Or was he considering something entirely different? she thought suddenly. Was he thinking that Sam's sudden appearance on the scene had something to do with the investigation?

Silly thought, Abby thought. Why would he think that? He wouldn't, she corrected herself. She was putting thoughts into the detective's head that had nothing to do with anything. There was no reason why he would believe that Sam had an involvement with her aunt's murder.

"But he isn't here yet?"

She shook her head. "I'm expecting him at any time. He didn't give a definite hour, just that he'd be here in time to take me out to dinner.

He inclined his head. "I see. Then he must be planning to stay overnight."

"I don't know that, Bud, but as I said on the phone, if he does, he'll sleep in one of my guest bedrooms."

He held her gaze.

"Just in case you're interested, Bud, I don't have casual sex."

"I'd be disappointed if you did, Abby."

A silence stretched between them and she realized that their conversation was not typical of that of a homicide detective speaking to a victim's family member. But then their relationship was not typical either; they were attracted to each other on a whole other level, that of man and woman.

Oh God, she thought. That was her version of it, but was it his? Was he as drawn to her as she was to him? She had no way of knowing. Someone had once told her: Without the words actually being said, you can never know for sure about the feelings of another person. And there was no way she could ask him to clarify his feelings for her.

"Thank you. I appreciate that you're looking out for me."

"As I've said numerous times, I intend to keep you safe, Abby."

She was gathering her response when someone knocked on the door. Both of them turned to face the barrier between where they stood and the crowd of reporters. Then Bud stepped forward and opened the door. Sam came into the hall.

For a few seconds the men stood silently, then Abby stepped forward and introduced them.

"You're the homicide detective on this case?" Sam asked Bud.

"Yeah, that's right. And you're Abby's friend from the city." A pause. "You're new to this area?"

"That's right," Sam replied. "It's why I'm late."

"Which is?" Bud replied, his professional manner totally in place.

"I got lost."

The two men, equally tall and lean, one with light hair and brown eyes, one with black hair and pale blue eyes took the measure of each other. Then Bud stepped back to the door and, with his hand on the knob, spoke to the couple behind him. "I'll make sure the crowd goes away." His eyes shifted to Abby. "And you make sure you call me if anything comes up that I should know about."

She nodded.

Quickly, Bud opened the door, stepped onto the porch, and closed it behind him, leaving Abby and Sam alone in the hall.

"Jeez, that guy has an awesome presence. I wouldn't want him to be investigating me," Sam said, as he slipped an arm around Abby.

"Yes, he is thorough." She allowed his hug and then took a step back, so that his arm was no longer around her. "I've come to see that he's relentless when it comes to solving his cases."

He inclined his head, as though digesting her evaluation of the man who'd just left. "I see that you already know about your story hitting the wire service," he said, changing the subject. "I bet it's in newspapers all across the country—the talented artist who was gifted beyond her own realization."

"Oh my God, Sam, I hope not."

He turned her to him. "Hey, don't worry, Abby. I'm here to help you make decisions."

"What decisions?"

He looked down into her face for several seconds and then stepped back, shrugging. "You know, what is best for your career and your future. Whatever keeps you safe."

"But I am safe here, Sam. This is the house I grew up in, the place where my ancestors have lived since the town was only a settlement." She hesitated, wanting him to understand. "This house is my roots."

"Yeah, I understand that, Abby. But your aunt was also murdered here."

She shook her head, trying to shake off his words. "Yes, she was, but it was a random thing that had nothing to do with this property. No one in the world had anything against my aunt. It's entirely possible that someone killed her because she was in the wrong place at the wrong time. It was probably a stranger."

He pulled her back into his arms. "I hope you're right, Abby, and we'll talk about it later." He kissed her lightly on the lips and then stepped back. "In the meantime, if your homicide detective has gotten rid of the reporters, I'll get my suitcase from my car." He peered out through the oval window. "Yup, it looks like they've cleared out, so I'll get my stuff before they decide the coast is clear to come back."

With those words he stepped onto the porch and ran out to his Lexus at the curb while she watched, realizing that he'd come prepared to spend the night. He retrieved his suitcase, locked the car, and ran back to the house, and she closed the door behind him. Once inside, he turned to her again.

"This is a nice place," he told Abby. "I didn't know the old homestead was a museum filled with antiques. I see priceless furniture and picture frames every where I look." He glanced around. "I'd love to see the rest of the house."

"C'mon then, I'll show you," she said, then faced

him with a question. "What are your plans for tonight, Sam? Will you be driving back into the city?"

"Hell no. This is a B and B, isn't it?"

"You know it is, Sam."

"Well then, I'm hoping to stay the night."

She grinned. "Okay then, I'll show you your room so you can deposit your suitcase and freshen up."

"The words of a proprietress welcoming a guest?"

"Uh-huh, that's exactly what I say."

She led the way up the stairs to the second floor, showed him into a room next to the hall bathroom, then gave him a tour of the upstairs, ending up in Carolina's bedroom.

"This is a beautiful room," Sam said. "And the antiques could be priceless."

"A few are valuable," Abby replied. "But priceless, I don't think so."

He shrugged. "I guess I wouldn't know." He stepped to the fireplace. "This goes back to our forefathers. They always heated with fireplaces; some houses had them in every room."

"I know, but my ancestors were never rich, even though this house is bigger than many were back then."

"And look at that desk." He strode across the room to it and ran his finger over the smooth wooden surface. "This piece has to be as old as the house."

"I think it is, Sam, and my aunt loved it. In fact, she wrote all her letters sitting at that desk."

He glanced at her. "You know, many of these old desks had secret compartments, just as old trunks had them."

She moved to him. "This one does, too." She slid

open the hidden drawer. "But as you can see, there are no treasures—the space is empty."

"That's too bad. It would be fun to discover something that hadn't been touched by human hands for many decades."

"Yeah, it would be." Abby went back to the hallway and he followed. "Why don't you freshen up while I go downstairs and pour us a glass of wine."

"Sounds like a deal. I'll be down in a few minutes." He disappeared into the room she'd given him. Before heading back downstairs, Abby detoured into her room to grab her purse and jacket. Her eyes fell on the desk in the corner, one of the same vintage as her aunt's, although it was smaller and had no secret compartments. At least none that she'd ever detected over all the years it had resided in her room.

Smiling, she closed the door behind her as she stepped back into the hall to head downstairs. As she reached the entry, her eyes rested on the front door. She stopped short, as something occurred to her for the first time.

The vandalized attic and the attack on her in her New York apartment had a common thread.

Both times, someone had had a key.

Chapter 42

BUD STRODE INTO THE police station. It was past quitting time for many of the staff, who'd gone home for the day, but the night shift had already begun their work. He passed the front desk, waved at the officer who was on the phone, and continued to his office in the back.

He tossed his jacket over a chair and then sat down behind his desk. Grabbing the phone, he called Pam.

"Hey, how you doing, Sis?"

"Cooking dinner. You're welcome to join us."

"Thanks, it's a tempting offer, but I have to work here in the office."

"Good Lord, Bud, you work too much."

"Yeah, yeah, I know. It's just the way it is with my kind of job."

"Okay then. What can I do for you, aside from giving you supper?"

"Can I talk to George about the historical research he's doing for me?"

"Sure, I'll call him."

A few moments later, his nephew picked up the phone.

"Hi, Uncle Bud."

"So what have you got for me?" Bud replied.

"The Carter family has an interesting background—and surprising."

"Tell me what you turned up."

George gave a brief history of the generations behind Abby, but it was when it came to her parents that it got interesting. Her dad had been an orphan but there were newspaper articles that speculated on his real family, even though they never claimed him.

"Did the articles name that family?"

"Yup, and the last descendant still lives in this county."

"Who?"

George told him.

Bud whistled into the phone. "You've got to be shitting me."

George's chuckle sounded in Bud's ear. "Nope, I made copies for you." Bud heard him shuffling through papers. "There's one or two more things I found, although the quotes by a reporter back then weren't expanded on, and so far I haven't found anything else."

"What's that?"

"That there was a suspicion that the deaths of Abby Carter's parents may not have been accidental. Also I found copies of birth certificates for twin daughters of the dead couple, and one death certificate. There was a final statement that the mother, due to problems at birth, would never bear more children."

"Good work, George." Bud was already grabbing his jacket from the chair. "And tell your mom that I'll stop by for dinner after all—and pay you for your time."

"Will do, Uncle Bud. And thanks, I can use a little extra money."

"Want to make some more?"

"Yeah, you bet I do."

"Okay, I'll explain what I need when I get there. It'll involve more research, this time in the newspaper archives. The library's history section is too limited for what I'll need next."

"See you soon, Uncle Bud. And by the way, Mom has fixed her famous roast chicken. It smells delicious."

"In that case I'll be there even sooner."

They hung up and Bud hurried back out to his car. Fuckin'-A, he thought. He might be on the verge of hitting the jackpot. The case was finally starting to make sense.

Chapter 43

"I'M SERIOUS, ABBY. I believe you should close the B and B," Sam said. "There's someone out there who attacked you in your own apartment, you drew a sketch of him and now your story and his face are being printed in newspapers across America, not to mention they're on even more television newscasts. For God's sake, your life is in danger."

"I can't think that way, Sam. If I'm to keep the property I have to make sure my aunt's commitments and debts are satisfied." She glanced down. "Besides, the sketch of my attacker wasn't all that accurate, since I only glimpsed him. I drew it to make another woman realize her own power—and consequently the victim relaxed and was able to describe the rapist."

"But, Abby, that's precisely what I'm saying. Despite why you did it, the rapist was arrested. The writing is on the wall. You need to sell this place and get out of this town. The legacy of the Carter family will always be a part of upstate New York history, and you'll be safe."

Abby stared at him across the table where they were having dinner at a local riverfront restaurant, having driven down the several blocks in his Lexus. He looked genuinely upset about her safety, but she couldn't help but think it was a contradiction. Wouldn't a man who cared that deeply for a woman, who'd come to visit because he was so worried, want to commit to his feelings? Somehow, his words, however valid to the situation, fell flat.

So what was his reason for being there? she wondered.

"I know the Carter family will stay a historical fact, Sam—after all, the town was named for them. That isn't my consideration in keeping the house. I'm sorry that you can't see why I'm hanging on, the last descendant of the family." She picked up her goblet and sipped her wine. "It's a matter of roots; I can't explain it in words you'll understand if you don't feel the same way about your own heritage."

He refilled their wineglasses as they waited for their salmon entrees.

"No, I guess I don't," he replied finally. "My first priority is to keep you safe regardless of history." He took a sip. "I thought you would realize your jeopardy in the face of what's happened."

"The rapist was arrested, Sam. As I said before, I don't think my quick drawing of my own attacker is all that accurate."

"But what if it is?"

She shrugged, unconvinced. "Then I'd be vulnerable."

"Touché."

They finished the meal with small talk, catching up on what was happening in Sam's life and career, and he mentioned a studio apartment that had become available in his building.

"I'd love to have you as a neighbor, Abby."

"Yeah, that would be fun—if I had a job in the city to pay the rent."

"You would, believe me," he said. "After this publicity, everyone will want to hire you. You've become an expert in the portrait-art world."

Abby sat back, wondering. Was he impressed with her current celebrity status, or was he being sincere? She honestly didn't know.

"But right now I can't afford an apartment, regardless of the cost of rent."

"Yes, I understand that, but you can if you sell your property and move on," Sam said. "You'd be very solid if you did, able to pay your way in the city so that you can promote your artistic career. With the current publicity, you could make it big."

She glanced down, for the moment at a loss for words.

"Maybe I could and maybe I couldn't," she said. "Haven't you ever heard the cliché about the fifteen minutes of fame?"

"Yeah, but I don't think that applies here."

Again she couldn't come up with a way to convince him.

"Hey, here's the salmon," Abby said, relieved by the intrusion of the waiter with their food. "I hear it's flown in directly from Alaska and is the best."

"Great, let's dig in," Sam said.

Their conversation went back to casual topics, and when the waiter came with the check, Sam put down his credit card. A short time later they were on their way to the car. And a few minutes after that they were driving back up the hill to the bed-and-breakfast. As they parked on the street out in front, Sam seemed congenial, as though he realized that he could continue his argument about selling out and moving back to the city tomorrow morning.

The street was clear; there were no reporters in sight. Once inside the house, Abby offered Sam a nightcap or tea. He declined both, kissed her, and optioned for an early night.

"I was up most of last night because of a gallery opening, then went home, slept a couple of hours before driving up here," he told her.

She was relieved. Abby had realized, almost from when he'd first stepped into her house, that their relationship was a thing of the past. She was honoring their former feelings for each other only out of respect for him. Now she was free of her earlier conviction about his motives—dumb assumptions, she told herself.

"Let me get you a bottle of water," she said, sounding like a bed-and-breakfast proprietor, as they hesitated in the entry.

He nodded, waited as she went to the kitchen to grab a bottle from the refrigerator, then they went upstairs together.

"Hey, this was a great evening," he told her at his assigned bedroom door.

"Thanks for dinner," she said, smiling. "I really appreciate your concern, Sam, that you drove way out here to give me advice, because you're my friend."

He kissed her again, and she felt it was an automatic response. Then he stepped into his room and closed the door. And she was left with a final revelation about their relationship: He was not committed because he wasn't in love with her. Then why was he there?

*   *   *

Abby watched television in her room for a short time after getting into bed, disturbed by her time with Sam, then switched it off.

She couldn't change Sam's opinion of what she should do. But what was his motivation? she wondered. Because of his feelings for her? She had no other explanation; she accepted that he was concerned about her, that he might be withholding his feelings because he didn't want to complicate the situation.

He must care about me in some way or he wouldn't be here, Abby thought.

Feeling safe with Sam in the house, she drifted off to sleep. Sometime later she awoke with a start—a frequent occurrence since arriving back in Carterville.

Slowly, she sat up, wondering what had awakened her. Straining to hear, the silence seemed to roar in her ears.

There was nothing.

It's operant conditioning, she thought. Awakening didn't have to mean that there was a threat.

And then she heard a subtle sound, as though someone was moving down the hall beyond her bedroom door.

Listening, she hoped to identify the noise, place it in a normal perspective. But her heart rate had accelerated alarmingly. It was as though her fear had brought a ghost from an ancient setting into the present.

Shit, she thought. Ghosts be damned. She could not accept ghosts in her very own house.

But she had to recognize the possibilities: that the sounds were real, or that it was actually something she'd conjured out of her imagination—because she was now conditioned to fear.

Stupid, she thought, and got out of bed to tiptoe to the door, straining to listen.

There was nothing.

Then she heard another sound in the hall and made a sudden decision. She swung open her bedroom door to reveal the hall.

And found Sam.

Startled, he faced her.

"For God's sake, Abby, you just scared me to death."

She stepped into the hall and faced him. "Why are you out here, Sam?"

"I heard a noise and opened my door to make sure everything was okay." He looked unsettled. "I didn't think it was, so I investigated."

"The house has odd sounds, Sam, especially at night when the temperature changes. It was probably nothing." Even as she said the words she felt strangely justified: He'd heard the unexplainable disturbances that she'd heard many times.

"Yeah, that's probably the reason."

She went back to her room, just as he did. He was as upset as she was—but were they on opposite sides?

Chapter 44

ABBY WAS RESTLESS after returning to her room, still awake several hours later. She wondered how Sam was doing—sleeping, she hoped. She'd never told him about the Carter house allegedly being a stop on the Underground Railroad route, that there were even stories of her house being haunted. Nor had she mentioned all her frightening experiences since taking over the bed-and-breakfast. He would only have used that as another argument for her to sell.

She lay under the covers, staring out the windows at high-flying clouds drifting across the sky, which foreshadowed the wind and rain forecast by last night's weather report. She sighed, knowing that dawn was only an hour or so away.

The soft shuffling outside her closed bedroom door was subtle at first, almost indecipherable from the night sounds beyond the walls of the house. Instantly, Abby was on full alert, straining to identify what she'd heard.

The disturbance seemed to be coming from the hall again—or across it, in Carolina's room.

She got out of bed and crept to her door, where she pressed her ear to the wooden panel. Everything was so quiet that her own breathing seemed overly loud. Had she only imagined something for a second time that night?

You must check it out, she told herself. It was her house, where she'd grown up, where the Carters had lived for generations. She could not allow herself to be scared or she'd soon be too frightened to live in her own home.

She opened the door a crack, so that she could peek into the hall. No one was out there, not even Sam this time.

Slowly she pulled it wide, looked both ways to make sure that no one was in sight, then stepped from the safety of her room to move quietly along the hall. She examined all the guest-room doors to make certain they were firmly closed—including the bolted door to the attic—then she stood at the top of the staircase and peered into the shadowy entry below. Everything seemed as she'd left it.

As Abby returned to her bedroom another vague sound came from behind her and she froze. It was as though something moved in her aunt Carolina's bedroom. She whirled around and saw no one.

She fought sudden panic, her gaze fixed on the closed door, telling herself that it couldn't be an intruder. Then what? Rats? Maybe squirrels? She'd heard that rodents came into buildings in the fall when the weather was colder. Had they found a way into her house and that's what she'd been hearing at night?

You have to make sure, she told herself. If someone is there you can scream for help because Sam is sleeping down the hall. It would be a relief to find squirrels. Calling an exterminator would be a quick fix for all the phantom noises in the weeks since Carolina's death, and would allow her to finally relax at night.

After giving herself a pep talk, she stepped over to Carolina's door and slowly opened it just wide enough to glance inside. Everything was still, but as she reached to find the light switch the shadows seemed to move on the other side of the room. Startled, she jumped back, her eyes darting into the darkness.

Outside the windows, the tree branches swayed in a slight breeze, casting moving images on the wall. Is that what she saw? she wondered. One thing Abby knew for sure: She was spooked.

Determined to exorcise yet another imagined ghost, she stepped forward and flipped the switch, flooding the room with light.

Everything was in its rightful place. No one was there. Abby's breath whistled out of her mouth in a sigh of relief. She turned, flipped off the light, and went back to her room. At least Sam hadn't been awakened by her second venture into the hall.

Snuggling back under her covers, she stared out her windows and realized that not only was the wind blowing but it had started to rain. That's what she'd heard, she decided. It had only been the wind.

Abby was up shortly after daybreak, showered, dressed and was sitting at the kitchen table sipping coffee while reading the newspaper when Sam came downstairs.

"Jeez, Abby, do you always get up with the birds?"

She grinned. "Usually, even earlier on weekends when I have guests." She stood up. "I bet you could use a cup of coffee?"

"You got that right. I'm never fully awake before my hit of caffeine."

She poured Sam's coffee, then sat back down, facing him across the table. "I'll even fix you a nice breakfast." She set the newspaper aside. "I know you're driving back today, so I expect you'll be leaving before the rush hour traffic this afternoon."

"Unfortunately, I have to leave soon. Seems I always have meetings and today is no exception, so I must be back for it by three." He raised his brows. "I will have time for one of your famous breakfasts. I understand you're a fabulous cook."

Surprised, Abby put down her cup. "Thanks for the compliment, Sam. But how would you know that? I don't think I ever did very much cooking for you when we were dating in the city."

"Your reputation preceded you, Abby. When I was lost yesterday I asked directions from a local resident. The woman told me how to get here, and then added her personal opinion about how great the food was at the B and B." He shrugged. "I figured that meant you."

"She probably meant my aunt, who was known for the best breakfast in town."

He shrugged and sipped his coffee.

"I want to apologize for scaring you in the night. I thought I heard something and went to investigate, hoping it was nothing," Sam said, putting down his cup. "I probably overreacted because I'm so concerned about you and your location being identified in the media."

"I'm upset, too. I still can't believe that the story hit the wire service."

"Yeah, and as I said yesterday, I saw a few short clips on the national television news. All of the reporting included your aunt's murder, your drawing that was instrumental in catching a rapist, and the sketch of your attacker, which is the latest focus of their coverage."

"This might be the end of running this B and B. No one wants to stay where someone has been murdered and another person might be the target of a lunatic."

"I believe that's an accurate assumption." He nodded. "But the important issue here is you staying safe."

"I know that, Sam. Believe me, I don't want to be killed either." Suddenly too antsy to stay seated, she got up to get more coffee. "I'm just trying to sort things out, grieve for my aunt, and in the meantime keep the bills paid."

He stood and came around the table, taking her into his arms and preventing her from grabbing the coffee carafe. "I think the writing is on the wall, that you need to sell the property and get the hell out of this fucking town." He pulled her closer. "Damn it, Abby. Face it. You're in danger."

"I don't know that for sure, Sam. It's all so intangible. And it takes time to sell, even if that's what I decide to do. My aunt's financial matters aren't even settled yet."

"That shouldn't take long, especially if all the legal documents are in place."

"Which they aren't."

"Why not?"

"It just takes time. My aunt's lawyer is verifying some things." She stepped back, and explained that she was making sure everything moved forward but didn't want to waste their visit by discussing it.

"Please understand, Sam. It's distressing to talk

about it but I really appreciate that you cared enough to come." She took in a shaky breath. "So in the meantime, until the estate is settled, I have to keep on with my aunt's business. I have no income other than what's generated from the B and B—and some freelance drawing."

"Tell me you're not considering doing more forensic sketches!" He blew out a quick breath. "Abby, that would be suicidal."

"Please—I'm not crazy. I'm talking about harmless drawings, like the ones I'll do at the school carnival on Friday night. You know the type I used to do at park concerts and tourist places." She went on to explain her agreement with the school. "I could make enough to pay this month's house payment."

"Okay, I guess that's safe enough. I understand that you can't sell yet, and can't make a move without money." He looked thoughtful. "But couldn't you consider getting a temporary job to pay the bills and thus be able to close the B and B? For God's sake, Abby, you have no idea who your guests are. One of them could be the murderer."

She shook her head. "They're all reservations my aunt made before her death, mostly people who've stayed here before." She hesitated, hating to explain all her financial woes, which he couldn't seem to understand, never having experienced being poor. "If I canceled the reservations I'd have to pay back all the deposits—and I don't have them. My aunt was not managing her finances very well and she'd even taken out a mortgage, the first one ever on our house."

"Hey, look, Abby. I'm not trying to make you feel

worse." His expression creased into worry lines. "I simply care about you."

"Thank you." She managed a smile.

Another lapse in conversation fell between them.

He inclined his head, his gaze steady, holding hers. "Can you guess what I'd like at this point?"

"I know you want me to be safe."

He embraced her again. "I want you to move back to the city—when you can," he amended, conscious of her fragile feelings. "Then I'd like us to start over with our relationship." He kissed her lightly on the mouth. "I've missed you, Abby, and I want you back in my life."

Pulling herself together, she kissed him back, then turned away to start breakfast. As she worked, she questioned him about what was happening with his work and his life in the city. Within a half hour they were seated at the table, having freshly squeezed orange juice, scrambled eggs, crisp bacon, and Katherine's leftover homemade biscuits that she'd frozen from last week and reheated.

"You know, I believe that woman was talking about you when she bragged about the B and B's food," Sam said as he polished off the last of a cinnamon roll with fresh coffee. "That was the best breakfast I've had in years."

Their small talk continued while they had a final cup of coffee and after he'd gone upstairs to get his suitcase and was standing in the entry hall, ready to leave.

"I've had a nice visit," he told her after a long kiss. "Keep me in the loop of what's going on and think about what I said about starting over, okay?"

"I'll do that, Sam, and thanks again for caring and coming all this way to check on me."

Momentarily, he stared down into her face with an odd expression flickering over his features. Then he kissed her again and went out to his Lexus. After a final wave, the car moved down the street and soon disappeared. She closed the door and locked it—and then remembered that the locksmith would soon be arriving to change the locks.

In the meantime, she would clean the kitchen before she changed the bedding and freshened up the room Sam had used. She appreciated his concern, and that he wanted her back in the city so that they could resume their relationship. But what did that really mean? If he was serious, why hadn't he offered her the option of moving in with him?

Abby smiled wryly as she loaded the dishwasher. She was relieved that he hadn't. That was no longer something she would consider. The time when she might have agreed to such an arrangement had passed.

She sighed. Sam might be a good catch for someone. But that someone was no longer her.

Chapter 45

WHILE THE LOCKSMITH WORKED, Abby took the bedding from Sam's room to launder in the cellar, glad that someone was in the house while she did it. She remembered how scared she'd been down there in the past.

The day also brought more phone calls from the media and reporters to her door, all wanting an interview. She avoided everything she could, and when Bud came by around five she welcomed seeing him stride up the walk to the front porch, glad he was there to shoo away the last of the reporters.

She'd already recleaned the kitchen and spent time in the office doing bookwork and was ready for a break. Besides, she had more questions for him, like how safe he considered her to be now that she'd become the focus of national news.

She opened the door to his knock and Bud stepped into the entry. For long seconds they only held each other's gaze. Bud was the first to speak.

"Your friend Sam is gone?"

She nodded. "He left right after breakfast."

"Hmmm." Bud's eyelids lowered slightly as he contemplated her answer. "I'm surprised his visit was so short," he said finally.

"His concern for my safety prompted him to drive out here to make sure I was okay."

"Because . . . ? Did he explain why he was that alarmed?" Bud inclined his head. "Something doesn't sound quite right."

"What do you mean?"

Bud shrugged. "Why don't you explain, since he's your friend and I don't know him."

Abby gave him a brief account of Sam's fears over the media coverage. She shook her head. "I admit I was surprised by his reaction, since he didn't seem all that upset about my attack at the time. He was more worried about me leaving the city and tried to convince me that I should sell the house."

The hall went quiet as he contemplated her words.

"Hey," he said, and abruptly changed the subject. "I'm just off duty and could use a glass of that wine. You still have some available?"

She grinned, relaxing. "I sure do, and a whole new bottle. If you'd like to sit down in the parlor I'll get us each a glass."

"How about just sitting in the kitchen?"

"That would be even better," she said. "I always did think the parlor was too formal, not conducive to a friendly conversation."

"Good," he said, and followed her down the hall to the kitchen.

She took the goblets from the cupboard, placed them on the counter, then took a bottle of Pinot Grigio from the refrigerator. As she pulled the corkscrew out of the drawer, Bud took it from her.

"I'll do the honors." He raised one eyebrow in a question. "That okay with you?"

She nodded and lowered her eyes. He was so damned attractive that he almost took her breath away when he was this close and concentrated on her.

He uncorked the bottle, then poured wine into both glasses. He handed her one and picked up his own.

"Shall we have a toast?" he asked, suddenly serious.

She nodded. "Go ahead, Bud."

He raised his glass. "To us."

"To our friendship," she added, clinking hers against his.

They both sipped, and she felt that his eyes never left her, although she pretended ignorance of his scrutiny. They each took a chair and sat down at the table across from each other.

"So tell me more about Sam. What is his motivation in all of this?" He put his glass down and his next question was direct. "Is it you—or something else?"

Her gaze flew to his. "What do you mean by that, Bud? Of course it's me—what else would it be, for God's sake?" She gave a laugh. "Do you think he has an ulterior motive?"

He shrugged. "I was only asking your opinion." His tone was casual but his pale eyes had narrowed ever so slightly. "You believe Sam's only interest in the media fallout was that a felon would think you could identify him." He sipped his wine. "Do you agree?"

"Of course. I can't understand why you'd think he wasn't up front, unless there's something that I don't know." She put her glass down. "Is there?"

"Not that I know of," Bud replied with a casualness

that seemed contrived to Abby. "I guess I'm only questioning the motives of everyone who knows you." He suddenly grinned. "It's hard to shed the homicide-detective persona. No insult intended toward your friend."

"Okay, I accept that," she replied, and smiled. "So let's start over." She got up, retrieved the wine bottle, and brought it back to the table. Once she'd added to their glasses Abby sat down again. "I'm glad you're here, Bud. Thanks for checking up on me."

For a second he was sober before tilting his head and returning her smile. "Another toast?" he asked.

She nodded and raised her glass.

"To us," he said, repeating what he'd said the first time. "And future happiness," he added.

They both sipped, and Abby wondered what he'd meant. Had he implied that their future would be together? The toast was ambiguous, exactly like the detective who'd offered it. She was the first to look away.

"How about a snack to go with our wine?" she asked, changing the subject. "I have cheese and crackers, potato chips, and mixed nuts."

"Mixed nuts sound good." He raised his brows. "It never hurts to have a little food with alcohol."

She stepped into the pantry and found a small can of nuts, opened it, and poured them into one of her aunt's antique glass serving bowls from the sideboard. She smiled when she placed it and napkins on the table, suspecting that Detective Bud Williams would never overindulge.

He grabbed a few nuts and popped them into his

mouth as she sat down again. "Would you mind if I ask you a few personal questions, Abby? They've come up in my investigation into your aunt's death."

"No, go ahead. I'll gladly answer anything that might help solve this case."

He nodded. "I've done a little research on your family, and I'll say up front that I haven't found any connection of past to present, but I want to clarify some facts anyway."

She took a sip of wine. "Go ahead, ask away."

"What do you know about your father's background?"

"Only that he was an orphan who never knew his parents, his family name, or any possible siblings or other relatives." She glanced down. "He grew up in a foundling home but managed to work his way through college, where he met my mom. They were married a year after they graduated."

"Did you ever hear a rumor that your dad's biological family might be prominent people who live in this area?"

"I, uh, did my own research at the library, as you know. In one of the articles about the accident that killed my parents there was a reference to that, but that's all. That same piece also mentioned that I was their only child, my twin having died as an infant."

"Didn't your aunt ever talk about any of the details?"

She shook her head. "Although she spoke fondly of my parents, relating little stories about their lives, she didn't dwell on their deaths. I guess she was protecting me so that I had as normal a childhood as possible. I always felt there was time to talk about past events later—that is, if there was anything more to tell me." She hesitated, tears welling in her eyes. "Then, without warning, my aunt Carolina was gone."

He reached to cover her clasped hands with his. "I'm sorry, Abby. I know it's hard to talk about this and I apologize." He scooted his chair closer to hers. "I want you to know that my questions pertain to following another lead in the investigation. It might not go anywhere, but in a case where there are no suspects I look into any possibility, however remote."

"I understand. I want you to do that." She dabbed her eyes with a napkin. "I want you to arrest the monster who killed my aunt."

"I have just one more thing to ask you."

"Please go ahead, Bud. I'm okay now."

He inclined his head, gave her hands a final squeeze, and continued. "Do you have their legal papers?"

"Such as?"

"Birth and death certificates, their marriage license, university diplomas, anything like that."

Abby glanced toward her aunt's little office, her thoughts whirling. He'd asked the very question that had surfaced in her mind many times lately. She'd already looked through the desk and drawers in her aunt's bedroom and all the files in the office. She'd found no important papers or evidence that Carolina had had a safety-deposit box at the bank. Taking a ragged breath, she explained to Bud.

"I was going to look in the attic but—" She shrugged. "You know what happened with that. I haven't been up there since your guys checked it out for possible evidence."

"You say she didn't have a safety-deposit box. Could she have entrusted those papers with someone else, like with her friend Katherine?"

"I'll ask her."

"Good, and in the meantime, I'm still doing more research. It just strikes me as odd that those records
aren't readily available where they should be."

He waited while she composed herself.

"By the way, you did have the locks changed, right?"

"Yeah, this morning."

"Good girl." He took a drink of wine and replaced
his glass on the table. "Just so you know, I've beefed
up security for you and your property."

"What does that mean?"

"A police cruiser coming by periodically during the
night, even a stakeout if it becomes necessary."

"You mean a stakeout like in the movies?"

"Something like that."

"Who does it?"

"Someone in the department," he replied. "Whoever
draws the duty."

The conversation moved into a more casual channel with talk of Bud's sister and her family, who would
be at the carnival on Friday night, along with much of
the town.

"It's an annual event," Bud explained. "Lots of people
support it because the money goes to school causes." A
pause. "And you'll be there, too? Right?"

She nodded. "Doing quick portrait sketches, as I explained before."

One of Bud's eyebrows slanted up in a question.
"Have you decided about trying another composite
sketch or two for the department? I don't know what
they'll offer to pay but I suspect it would be fair."

"I need to know what type of cases before I make
that decision." Her gaze was direct. "I certainly don't
want to be involved in a murder or rape investigation

even though I could use the work. Also, I wouldn't want to be publicly identified as the artist. I don't need more notoriety."

"I understand. One of these sketches would be of a man who habitually shoplifts and the other would be of a teenager who breaks into cars at the mall parking area."

"Can I think about it overnight?"

"Yep, that'll work." He drained his glass and stood up. "I gotta get going."

She walked him to the front door, and after his usual words to be careful and call him if anything came up, he headed out to his car. She watched him leave, then closed and locked up.

Abby ate a light supper, then went into the office to look through the desk more carefully, hoping she could find where her aunt had kept the legal documents. Tomorrow she intended to call the bank to verify whether or not Carolina had had a safety-deposit box. As she worked, night came down over the bed-and-breakfast. She got up to make her rounds, closing all the blinds and rechecking the doors. Then she went back to the office and called Katherine down the street.

"Hello?" Katherine's familiar voice sounded in her ear.

"Hi, Katherine. It's Abby."

They exchanged small talk for a minute before establishing a time for Katherine to come over and bake for the weekend guests.

"I have another reason for calling and I hope you can help clarify something for me, Katherine."

"I will if I can. What is it you need?"

"I can't find any legal papers like birth certificates, and no documents concerning my parents. I've looked everywhere and can't find them. I was wondering if Aunt Carolina might have given them to you for safekeeping of if you might know where she put them."

"My goodness, Abby, I have no idea. Didn't she have a safety-deposit box?"

"Not that I know of so far but I'm checking further." Abby paused. "It's kind of strange that they aren't in the files."

"Huh, yeah, it is." Katherine sounded puzzled. "Have you asked Taylor Jones, Carolina's lawyer? Maybe he has them."

"I asked him about a safety-deposit box and he didn't know. He only had a copy of her will."

"They're around there somewhere, Abby. You'll find them eventually."

"Well, thanks for your help anyway, Katherine, and I'll see you when you come over to bake."

"You bet, honey."

Abby was taking the receiver from her ear to hang up when she heard Katherine again.

"Abby? Are you still there?"

"Uh-huh. Did you remember something?"

"Nope, but I noticed that detective fellow is parked down the street from me. You probably wouldn't be able to see him from inside your house." She gave a laugh. "Whattaya think he's up to?"

"I have no idea," Abby said, lying, not wanting to alarm the older woman. "Probably talking on his cell phone or something. I imagine he'll be gone soon. You have a good night," Abby said.

"You too."

They hung up and Abby went to get a jacket. She knew exactly why Bud was up the street. He was the stakeout—on his own time.

She went out to the front porch and locked the door behind her. She was on her own mission.

Chapter 46

THE NIGHT WAS EXCEPTIONALLY dark because of the low cloud cover and steady drizzle of rain. If Abby hadn't known Bud was right down the block in his car she would have felt apprehensive about being alone on the deserted sidewalk where houses were widely spaced and set back from the street. Bud was parked parallel to a high hedge that concealed him from the scrutiny of people who lived close-by.

As Abby approached, the driver's door of the vehicle suddenly opened and Bud stepped out into the rain. She stopped, uncertain, facing him from the other side of the car. Although she couldn't discern his expression, she felt his alarm, that he wasn't pleased.

"For God's sake, Abby, what in the hell are you doing outside in the rain?"

"Looking for you."

"Jeez, how did you know I was here?"

The rain fell between them, a soft whispery sound in the sudden silence.

Abby pointed to the two-hundred-year-old house

that was almost hidden behind the high hedge. "That's Katherine's house and she told me on the phone that you were parked on the street. She was concerned."

"What did you tell her?"

"Not to worry, that you'd probably stopped to use your cell phone."

He laughed, shaking his head. "You know, Abby, if you ever change your mind about being an artist, you might consider public relations. You're a natural."

He came around the car and opened the passenger-side door, took her arm, and led her to the front seat. Once she was closed inside, he slipped behind the wheel and drove down the street to park at the curb in front of the bed-and-breakfast.

"We need to talk," he said as they got out of the car. He locked it by remote, then they headed up the walk to the porch, where she got out her key, let them into the entry, and secured the door again.

"C'mon, let's have something to drink while we have a conversation in the kitchen."

She nodded, and realized that he was serious and saw no humor at all in her action. "Wine?" she asked.

"Ice water," he replied.

"Coming right up," she said in an attempt to lighten the mood. Then she took two glasses from the cupboard, filled them with ice cubes and water. She placed them on the table and sat down to face him.

They sat in silence. She realized he'd changed his clothes since leaving her earlier and was now dressed in Levi's and a dark turtleneck top under a jeans jacket. Undercover garb? she wondered.

"Uh-huh," he said, his pale blue eyes screened by black lashes. "We always wear dark clothing on a stakeout."

"How did you—"

"Know what you were thinking?" His smile was slow and seemed what?—sexy?

She managed a nod.

"I'll only say that your expressions sometimes reveal your thoughts." He lifted one shoulder, almost nonchalantly. "But then again, I've been schooled to read people."

"I'll work on controlling my expressions," she said tartly, then took a drink of her water.

He leaned back and laughed. "Abby, don't be mad at me. I was only reacting to your unexpected appearance next to my car."

"I'm sorry about that, Bud. When I heard you were down there I went out to tell you something."

"Which was?" His gaze narrowed with intensity.

She glanced down. "Only that I'd realized it was you who was the one staking out my house—on your own time." A pause. "I was going to tell you that you could stake it out from the inside, where you would be comfortable, rather than outside." She spread her hands. "I guess I shouldn't have done that, even though I want you to know how much I appreciate your efforts."

"Hey, I know you do, Abby." He looked pleased. "But the definition of a stakeout is that no one, especially the perpetrator, should know anyone is out there watching for him." He tilted his head, abruptly serious. "Think of it as setting a trap for an unsuspecting rodent and then catching it. At least that's what a law-enforcement person hopes will happen."

"So that usually doesn't happen unless you're watching from outside?"

"That's right. We want to grab them in the act but before they gain entry."

"I'm sorry I screwed it up."

"We're okay, Abby. There's a long night ahead, but I think I'll have to choose another parking location."

His explanation had raised many questions for her. She took a deep breath and asked the first one.

"Is the police department paying for someone on duty to watch my house all night?"

"I believe I told you that there are extra patrols that check your house all during the night," he replied, evading.

"But not to actually sit at the location, am I right?"

"Shit, Abby, suffice it to say that I feel this type of surveillance is necessary."

"Please explain why it's so important that you'd stay up all night in your car—to protect me. Do you suspect that the person who murdered my aunt plans to kill me, too?" She managed a ragged breath. "I must admit that all of this is really starting to scare me."

He got up and pulled Abby to her feet so that they faced each other just inches apart. "No one is going to hurt you, Abby." His voice was low and deliberate. "Remember, I've told you that I intend to make sure you stay safe."

She forced herself to hold his eyes, which looked more silver than blue from the reflection of the ceiling light. "You haven't explained why you believe I'm in danger." When he didn't reply, she rushed on. "And don't say I'm imagining things, because you really were down the street in your car watching this house on your own time. Not you or anyone else is being paid to do that. What do you know that you're not telling me?"

"You got me there." He shook his head. "I'm gonna be honest. You deserve that, Abby." His hold tightened on her ever so slightly. "Your aunt's murder is fast becoming one for the cold-case files. We've got nothing: no suspect, no clues, and no leads." He stared down into her face, so close that she could see her image in his eyes. "But I have a hinky feeling about it, that it's not what it seems on the surface of known facts."

"Hinky? What does that mean?"

He tilted his head closer. "Hard to explain, Abby."

"Try. I need to hear."

He nodded. "I call it my personal antenna, an invisible aerial that comes up automatically to alert me of a threat, even if that threat isn't apparent. It's what motivates an investigation above the defined guidelines."

"In other words, you feel that there's more to Carolina's death than it being a random event."

"Yeah, that's it in a nutshell."

"And because you don't know what this hinky feeling means, you have to consider that I could be next on a killer's hit list?"

"At the moment I'm afraid so."

She looked away, struggling to keep her poise. "Thank you for being honest, Bud." Her lashes fluttered as she raised her gaze. Instantly, her eyes were again caught by his: a wolf's hypnotic stare that would not release its prey? Oh dear God, she was becoming paranoid. He was not a wolf and she was not prey. She gave herself a mental shake and continued. "I hope your hinky feeling is wrong but I thank you for acting upon it. It's certainly above and beyond your call of duty."

"I hope it's wrong as well."

"One last question."

He raised his brows, waiting.

"Why would you do all this for me?"

She regretted the question a moment after she asked it, suspecting the answer. When his arms tightened and he pulled her against him, her suspicion was verified. His next words confirmed it.

"Because I want to stake a claim on your future," he said, and his voice was husky with meaning. Then his face lowered and his mouth came down on her lips, sealing that claim on her.

His touch was like an electric current that shocked her whole body. Somewhere in the back of her mind she knew she should pull away, but as his kiss deepened, and her mouth opened under his of its own volition, her resistance slipped away. She found herself pressing even closer to his body, giving back kiss for kiss.

He edged her backward, until they were in the hall, then at the base of the staircase, caressing her, his mouth against her lips murmuring endearments that only excited her more. At the top of the steps they moved toward her bedroom, and as his gentle yet aggressive lovemaking grew more intense, Abby gave in to the moment.

"Bud, what are you doing?" she murmured against his lips once they were in her bedroom.

"It's what we're doing, Abby," he said, kissing her with a passion that was both tender and demanding. While he held her close to his body, Bud managed to caress her with a gentle touch, stroking her face, smoothing her hair, crooning soft words against her mouth, lulling her and creating new sensations within her. He communicated through her flesh the words that were yet to be spoken.

"Wait," she whispered.

His body stilled momentarily. "I know what you're thinking, sweetheart." His breath was a soft ripple against her cheek. "It's against the rules when your aunt's case is still open." He lifted his face so that their eyes locked. "Do you want me to stop?"

Slowly, Abby shook her head.

"You know that I'm going to make love to you, don't you, Abby?" he whispered next to her ear.

She swayed against him, her eyes closed. When she finally met his gaze, which burned into hers, she nodded. Everything went quiet around them, except for the sound of rain against the windows, a gentle background of nature that became a part of their passion.

"Yes," she agreed softly, and the word seemed to soar into their mutual desire. All Abby thought of at that moment was her need for the man holding her in his arms.

His gaze unwavering, he helped her undress and then reclaimed her mouth, his probing tongue inspiring her response over and over again as he shed his clothing. Moments later they were on the bed. Briefly she thought of Sam, who'd spent last night in the guest room, a man she no longer desired, for whom she had never felt the passion that she now knew with Bud. Sam's attractiveness had paled into insignificance.

Sam was banished from her mind completely as she

lay naked next to Bud. His touch was liquid fire on her skin; his mouth left a trail of tingling flesh as he nibbled and kissed his way over body. It was as though they couldn't get enough of each other.

Her low moans swelled into the room, her desire growing until she could scarcely bear it, knowing he felt the same, and his hardness confirmed this. Still he hesitated to explore the soft mounds of her breasts, tasting and gently sucking her nipples. He'd sent her to a place she'd never been before, a place that was ecstasy even while the anticipation was an exquisite agony.

"Bud," she whispered, the word torn from her throat of its own volition. "Please—now."

He lifted his head, and even though his eyelids were lowered she could see that her plea had a profound effect on him. The room was dimly lit but he searched her face, satisfying himself that her words were true. There was no mistaking her slightly parted lips that seemed swollen from his kisses and her slumberous eyes that were alight with anticipation.

Then he positioned himself over her, and her thoughts were wiped away as she ascended into perfect bliss. Sensation after sensation flooded her senses and her total focus was on him as they soared together into the still waters of absolute contentment. Spent, they collapsed side by side, their bodies still touching, as their passion gradually subsided.

He turned to her, taking her back into his arms, holding her against him, flesh against flesh. Neither spoke as they savored the time left to be together. "You're my woman now," he told her, his arms tightening as though he couldn't hold her close enough.

"Mmm," she said softly, too sated to add anything to what he'd said, or to question his meaning. She snuggled to him and a short time later felt him becoming aroused once more.

It wasn't long before they began their lovemaking all over again.

Chapter 47

"STUPID BITCH! FUCKIN' SLUT!"

He'd watched her after the detective left the first time, been patient while she spent time in the office, and had finally been rewarded by vitally needed information when she spoke on the phone to the old biddy down the street. He'd learned what she knew about important matters: nothing.

The secret was still hidden. Carolina had not told her. The old lady had died just in time to prevent that.

Her mistake, he thought, and his lips twisted into a brief smile. There was still a little time. The weekend had to solve the problem once and for all.

And if not? His hand went to his pocket, where he fingered his cigarette lighter. Everything burns in the cleansing heat of fire, he reminded himself. Even bitches. Laughter rose in his throat but he managed to hold it back.

Patience, that's what he needed now. Everything in its own time, and that moment of reckoning hadn't arrived yet. He must still wait or blow his whole future.

He'd almost done just that after she'd rushed out of the house and brought the detective back a few minutes later. He'd watched everything—except what had happened in her bedroom. He hadn't dared go there while the damn cop was present for fear of being heard. But he'd remained in the house, hidden, straining to hear.

It had been agony. He'd imagined what was happening and his frustration and anger had exploded and he found himself jacking off. The bitch belonged to him, not the fuckin' cop.

Now the guy was gone again but that didn't change anything at the moment. He still had to wait.

Sloppy seconds, that's what he'd settle for. He could do that, just before he killed her.

Chapter 48

ABBY CLOSED THE DOOR after Bud's long good-bye kiss three hours after he'd driven her home. "Sweet dreams," he'd whispered against her ear, and she'd wished he could stay. It was still raining and she watched though the window as he ran out to his car. He planned to resume his stakeout but from a location where Katherine wouldn't spot him.

She went back upstairs to her room, amazed by her feelings. She had no regrets about her total response to Bud's lovemaking. In a strange way, it had been an affirmation for her loss of feelings toward Sam, a final closure of their former relationship. She realized now that he had never been right for her. Aside from their very different values, they'd lacked the spontaneous passion that was a must for a successful future together.

But as she showered and then climbed back into bed, savoring the lingering smell of Bud on the sheets, Abby recognized that she had fallen for him in a way she'd never believed was possible. She wondered how he felt about her. Was he thinking of her just as she was of him—at this precise moment?

She hoped so.

She switched off the light, turned over, and snuggled deeper into the pillows. She'd see Bud in a few hours, when he drove her to police headquarters, where she'd agreed to do the forensic sketches. When she heard a slight sound from somewhere deep in the house, she only sighed.

She was safe.

Bud was making sure of that.

"Hey, Bud just drove up, so I'll be going!" Abby called from the front hall to Katherine, who was baking in the kitchen the next morning.

"Okay," Katherine answered. "I'll lock up when I'm finished. When the boys are done with the yard work they'll leave the equipment in the garage."

"Great!" Abby replied. "I might even be home before you leave."

"Whatever—we'll be fine on our end," Katherine said, coming to the doorway at the back of the hall. "Call me when you get home if I'm not still here."

"Checking on me?"

"Yup, you could say that. I just want to make sure you get home safely."

Grinning, Abby waved her hand in a farewell salute, picked up her supply case, and went out to Bud's car. But she was glad that Katherine was looking out for her. It made her feel safer.

Bud was waiting at the curb, standing next to the passenger door, which he'd opened for her. She hesitated in front of him before stepping into the vehicle, taking in the fact that he'd changed back into his homicide-detective garb: slacks, sport jacket, and tie. Her breath caught in her throat, for a moment robbing her of words. He was so sexy in anything he wore and Abby's thoughts flashed on being in his arms a few hours ago.

"Hey, Abby, are you all right?"

She nodded and met his eyes. He looked concerned, as though he was worried that she was having second thoughts about last night. Realization hit her hard. He was as uncertain about her as she was about him.

"Sure I am," she said, gaining confidence. "In fact, I'm feeling better than I have in a long time, thanks to you." Abby smiled, watching him break into a grin. "And you?"

"I couldn't be better, with or without sleep." His eyelids suddenly hooded his eyes, giving him an expression that left no doubt in her mind that he was remembering their lovemaking—just as she was.

"I'll make it up to you," she said simply.

"How so?"

"As I said before, if you're committed to stakeouts, you can always do them right on site rather than down the street."

"Are you inviting me to spend the night, Abby?"

"Yes," she said honestly.

"I could make love to you right now, you know that, don't you?"

She nodded, holding his gaze.

"But I'll take a rain check—for the very near future. We've got work to do."

Then he drove them to police headquarters.

Once in the police station, Bud introduced her around before leaving her with Maggie, a large, fortyish woman who was in charge of the forensic-art unit. After a short conversation, Maggie led Abby to a small room and introduced her to her first subject, Beatrice Wooley, a grandmother who had seen a teenage boy break into her car at the mall.

"He ran before he could steal anything but I saw his face," Beatrice said after Maggie had left them to get started on the drawing.

"That's good," Abby replied. She took out her supplies and set up her drawing tablet on the table where they sat across from each other. She explained the process she'd be using to come up with a composite of the thief, listening carefully to the woman's feedback on the incident, which was interspersed with comments about her own life. "We'll take it step by step," Abby told her. "And feature by feature."

Beatrice nodded, and although she was obviously nervous, she was intrigued by what Abby was doing.

"If something I sketch doesn't seem quite right to you, just point it out and I'll adjust the drawing." Abby smiled, trying to put the woman at ease. "For example, if the young man you remember had a wider nose than what I come up with, I'll narrow it." She hesitated, allowing Beatrice to digest her instructions. "That goes for eyes and brows, hair, shape of face, anything you can remember. I can keep changing until you're satisfied, okay?"

"I'll try my best, Ms. Carter."

"Call me Abby and I'll call you Beatrice—that is, if you don't mind a first-name basis."

"Of course not, Abby," she replied, visibly relaxing.

By the time Abby started her drawing, following the same procedure she'd used with Maryanne, her subject was no longer ill at ease, and the whole session took less than two hours. When Maggie came back to check on them she was surprised to see the completed composite.

"Wow, that sure looks like the kid," Beatrice said, standing to gather her purse and coat. "I hope I was helpful because there are lots of cars that get broken into at the mall."

"We do, too," Maggie told the woman as she led her out of the room. At the doorway she turned back to face Abby. "We have one more case for you."

Abby gave a nod, smiling. "I know. Detective Williams told me." She hesitated. "Shall I wait here?"

"Yeah, that'd be perfect. Can I bring you anything—more water or coffee?"

"Black coffee would be great." Abby shrugged. "A hit of caffeine might help sharpen my perceptions."

A short time later Maggie reappeared with the coffee, accompanied by a short, balding man. "This is Gustaf, who owns a small neighborhood grocery store that was robbed at gunpoint last week," she told Abby, making the introductions. "His establishment doesn't have cameras but he believes he can describe the thug."

"Excellent," Abby said, shaking his hand.

"Call me Gus," he said with a European accent. "The robber emptied my cash register and I want him caught."

Maggie left them and Abby was soon into her routine, drawing as Gus talked. "I never thought I would be a target for a thief," he explained, shrugging. "But then I find that most people are just like me—they don't recognize that crime can happen to any of us, that we could be in jeopardy."

Abby nodded, still drawing, but her thoughts went to her own situation. Was that what she was doing— denying that she could be in danger? Dear God, she hoped that was not the case. Maybe she needed to be more realistic, really evaluate the facts, even if that meant closing the bed-and-breakfast and getting a regular job to pay the bills. She forced herself to forget her concerns and concentrate on the job at hand. She worked for another hour and then sat back, allowing Gus to consider the finished sketch.

"It looks kind of like him." He waved a hand at the drawing. "I may not have gotten as good a look at the guy as I first thought." He peered harder at the face on Abby's drawing paper. "I can't tell you what to change to make him look more like the guy who robbed me."

"So we don't have a positive match here," Maggie said from the doorway, where she'd heard Gus's comment. She stepped into the room. "But you think there's a resemblance, Gus?"

"Uh-huh, I do. But I can't be sure if this face is the one behind the gun."

"It'll do for now," Maggie told Gus. "We'll run it just in case someone else sees that resemblance and we come up with the right person." She glanced at Abby, indicated that she'd be right back, then accompanied Gus from the room. A few minutes later she returned, just as Abby had finished packing up her supplies.

"Thanks, Abby. You did great."

"I don't know, Maggie. Gus wasn't sure about an identification of his armed robber."

Maggie gave her a brief hug. "Like I said, you did a

good job. Most artists don't get your results. Beatrice Wooley claims you drew accurately and Gus isn't sure. I'd say that's a pretty good percentage."

"Thanks, Maggie. I sincerely hope I helped."

"We'll see." She met Abby's gaze. "Your composite of the mall marauder, as Beatrice's composite has been dubbed, is already in the hands of our patrolmen out in the field."

Startled, Abby stared at her. "You're kidding."

"No, I'm not." Maggie tilted her head. "Your accuracy on the drawing of the rapist has given you more credibility than you can imagine, Abby."

Oh my God! What had she done? That kind of publicity, like all she'd gotten lately, was dangerous. At least she knew that her drawings today would not be connected to her earlier one of the rapist. Bud had assured her of complete anonymity.

"Thanks, Maggie. I appreciate the compliment but I'm only doing these drawings with the assurance that no one will know I'm the artist."

Maggie glanced away. "I'm sure that will be the case. We here in the department are just glad to use your talents in such a positive way."

Before Abby could say more, Bud appeared in the doorway, grinning, pointing at his watch. "Time to go, Abby. It's already six."

"You're kidding." She glanced between Maggie and Bud, astounded by how late it was, how the afternoon had melted away. One good thing, she told herself. She'd made extra income in the process.

After more compliments from the people on duty, Bud drove her home. They were on the front porch when she asked her question.

"Tell me you're not the one to stake out my place tonight, Bud. Even you have to sleep sometime."

He glanced away. "Of course I have to sleep sometime. Doesn't everyone?"

"You're evading a direct question."

He shrugged. "Hey, I'm off duty. Why don't we finish off that bottle of wine?"

She unlocked and opened the front door. "That sounds good to me. I even have a spare bottle in case we need it." She stepped through the doorway, then stopped, turned, and faced him so fast that he bumped into her, a hard chest against her breasts. "But I'll still be waiting for an honest answer to my question," she said, glancing up to meet the shuttered pale eyes that seemed to see into her thoughts, her very soul.

"Wine first," he replied, "and then we'll see about the question."

"Damn well said." She turned away, but not before she saw amusement crinkle at the corners of his eyes.

"Oh," she said, glancing at the blinking red light. "Please excuse me while I check my phone messages."

He nodded and closed and locked the door, then stood waiting while she listened to her messages, which soared into the silence of the entry hall from her aunt's old-fashioned answering machine.

"Damn, another cancellation for the weekend," she told him as the first message ended. The next three messages were from newspaper reporters wanting to interview her, leaving names and numbers to call back. The final voice was chilling and seemed to wail into the quiet house like a Halloween ghost. But the threat was not imaginary. It was real.

"Now I know how to get into your house—I know that." A long pause. "And when I do, you will die, Abby Carter."

"End of messages," said the synthesized voice of the machine.

Abby stood in a paralyzed silence, broken by Bud's voice calling for backup on his cell phone. Then he was by her side, holding her close against him.

"It'll be all right, my darling. No one is going to touch a hair on your head. Help is on the way."

"Now we can have our wine," he told her an hour later.

"And you're spending the night in the house?"

"That's the plan," Bud said, his eyes hooded by lowered black lashes. "And in answer to your earlier question, no, I won't be the person on the outside stakeout tonight."

Abby nodded and went to get the glasses in the cupboard while Bud retrieved the wine bottle from the refrigerator. Everything had happened fast after her phone messages. Two patrolmen had arrived within minutes, taken down a report, and searched the house and property, although Bud, gun in hand, had made sure the rooms were secure before the police were at the door. Police procedure indicated that further safety measures were needed in light of the threat and the circumstances of Carolina's murder. Hence, the decision for surveillance was made for both in and out of the house.

She fixed them supper after they'd had the wine and exchanged light conversation that was relaxing for Abby. They ate and then cleaned the kitchen together. Too soon it was time for bed.

"I'll need a pillow and blanket for the parlor sofa," Bud said.

"You're sleeping downstairs?"

"Uh-huh, because it's the best place to make sure the house stays secure."

"But I'll be upstairs."

"I know that." The smile started at the corners of his eyes and spread to his lips. "And I plan to tuck you in, make sure you're so relaxed that you'll sleep all night, free to dream of a wonderful future with the man you love."

"And who is that?" Her voice was scarcely above a whisper.

"You don't know?"

She swallowed, fluttering her lashes nervously. "Yes," she said softly. "I do know."

Silence swelled between them.

He'd stepped closer and taken her into the circle of his arms, his lips only inches above her mouth. "Is it me?" he asked, his breath a warm tickle on her face.

Her words seemed paralyzed in her throat, unable to soar from her mouth. Her gaze glued to his, she could manage only a weak nod.

But it was enough. His lips claimed hers in a passionate kiss that rocked her whole body, robbing her limbs of strength.

With one quick motion he picked her up in his arms, climbed the stairs to her bedroom, and gently put her down on the bed. And then he proceeded to tuck her in as he'd promised. The relaxing procedure took much longer. For the next couple of hours he made sure she was sated by his lovemaking, and when he finally went downstairs to the parlor sofa, Abby was daydreaming of their future together.

A few minutes later she drifted off to sleep in a real dreamland, and her last waking thought was of her lover.

The lean, handsome face of Detective Bud Williams.

Chapter 49

ABBY CAME DOWNSTAIRS early the next morning but Bud was already sitting at the kitchen table, reading the newspaper and sipping coffee. She glanced at the wall clock. It was six thirty.

"Hey, that's the second time you've made the coffee. Didn't you know guests aren't expected to do that," she said, grinning and trying not to look self-conscious. "That's my job."

"Really?" His gaze swept over her, admiring, respectful, and with knowing eyes. He pushed back his chair and stood up, then took her into his arms. "Anyone ever told you how gorgeous you are first thing in the morning?" he asked softly.

His mouth stopped her response, coming down on her lips in a heart-stopping kiss. Of its own volition, her body swayed into his.

They jumped apart when the doorbell rang, announcing someone on the front porch. Heading into the front hall, a glance told them it was the officer who'd been on the stakeout, and Bud quickly opened the door and stepped outside. The two men talked, the cop turned to go, and Bud came back into the house.

"I have to get going," he told her in a low tone. "Even though I'd like to take you back upstairs and close the door on the world."

She breathed deeply, her gaze never wavering from the hypnotic intensity of his pale eyes under the long black lashes. "I understand, Bud. It's a workday for you."

"And you?"

"Just last-minute preparations for the weekend guests." She spread her hands in a gesture of disappointment. "I've had two cancellations, which mean four people. Fortunately my former landlord and wife from New York are still checking in before noon tomorrow." She lowered her eyes. "It's a good thing that I had that job for the police yesterday and the carnival tonight. That, with the one room reservation this weekend, will keep me financially afloat for the moment."

"Jeez, Abby. This sounds dire from a business point of view."

"Only at the moment," Abby replied. "I intend to get past all the bad publicity." She managed a smile. "I have to or lose everything."

"I've said before that you aren't going to lose anything, Abby." Bud's hand was on the doorknob and she knew he had to go. "We'll discuss this later. In the meantime, keep the doors locked, and I'll call you later, okay?"

She nodded.

He gave her a quick kiss before turning to go. Once through the doorway, he stopped to face her again. "What time do you have to be at the school?"

"Four, an hour ahead of when the doors open for the carnival. I want to be all set up before the crowd arrives."

"How are you getting there?"

"Driving myself."

"It'll still be daylight when you leave, so you should be safe." He stared, considering. "The security will continue around your house today, and I'll see you at the carnival and make sure you get home after it's over."

She nodded and he continued out to his car. She closed the door and went back to the kitchen. It was her turn for a cup of coffee.

She drove down to the school in her aunt's old Continental, unable to stop the memories that flashed though her mind about all the times her aunt had driven her there in that car. Those had been golden days that she'd never forget, just as she'd always remember how much she loved her aunt Carolina.

Shifting her thoughts from the past, Abby parked, gathered up her supplies, and went into the school gym, where the carnival booths had been set up. Her spot was near the door, for which she was glad. She hoped to catch customers before they spent all their money on games and food.

Several hours seemed to fly by and she was continuously busy pencil-sketching the portraits, averaging six an hour. Vaguely, she was aware of the elderly man in an old-style fedora and overcoat. He stood leaning on a cane at the edge of her waiting customers, watching as she sketched. At a lull when she'd finally caught up and could take a breather to straighten out her money tray, the man stepped forward slowly, keeping his balance with the cane. She suddenly remembered where she'd seen him before. It had been at the park, where she'd been sketching people on their way to the outdoor concert. She'd thought he was a little crazy then; now, he seemed like a lonely old man.

"You're a very talented young lady," he said, his voice crackling with age. Then he swept off his hat with a flourish that was reminiscent of a bygone era. "You are also an ambitious woman, I see."

She met his eyes, still bright and alert for his advanced years. "Thank you for the compliment," she said, and extended her hand, a little embarrassed by how she'd treated him at the park. "My name is Abby Carter." She hesitated. "And yours?"

"You don't know who I am?"

"No, I don't."

"Henry Robertson," he said, and after replacing his hat on his white hair, he finally took her hand.

"William Henry Robertson?" she asked, surprised. If he was a member of that family, then he was one of the most influential men in the state, with roots that went further back in America's history than hers. The difference between the Robertsons' background and that of the Carters was that his was prestigious, rich, and instrumental in the early formation of the American republic. Hers numbered among the working class. Both families fought in the Revolutionary War for independence.

"Yes, that is my full name," he replied. Instead of shaking her hand he examined it, tracing her fingers with his thumb. "You definitely have the hands of an artist, my dear," he said in a low tone, almost to himself. Abruptly, his brown eyes shifted to her face. "I once knew a young artist and she was very much like you."

She pulled her hand back, wondering, as she had that other time, if he was a little senile. He was certainly old enough, and she wondered why he was there, and if he'd come alone or if someone had brought him.

"Did your artist friend become well known?" she asked. "Perhaps I knew of her, since I'm pretty well versed about artists and their work."

His glance shifted beyond her, as though he was seeing again the artist he'd mentioned, as though he'd slipped into a momentary time warp—and she glimpsed a profound sadness in his expression. Her perception was gone the next second when his eyes again met hers.

"Her paintings only hang in my house," he said. "She died young, long before she had a chance to make her mark in the artistic community."

"I'm so very sorry, Mr. Robertson." This time she took his frail, arthritic hand and patted it gently, a spontaneous gesture. "She was obviously someone you loved."

His eyes brightened with unshed tears. "She was my wife, my first love." He hesitated. "She gave me a son but didn't live to raise him."

A silence went by as they seemed suspended in his old grief.

Then, abandoning inhabitations, she moved from behind her easel, still holding his hand, and gave him a gentle hug, careful not to upset his balance. "Someday I would love to see her paintings, Mr. Robertson. She was fortunate to have been so loved." Abby stepped back. "I suspect her son adores her memory, too."

A slow smile touched his lips. "He too died, killed at age eighteen in an automobile accident."

"Oh my God!" she retorted. "And he was your only child?"

He nodded. "My second wife and I were never blessed with more children. My only son and his girlfriend were killed on their way to elope—against my wishes."

Abby was at a loss for words. "How sad," she said after a hesitation, and tried to remember where she'd heard that story before. "What a terrible loss for you."

"You're very sensitive, Abby, and I have to say I'm pleased." He shook his head as though he couldn't believe that she was so open to his sad narration. "You're a throwback, Abby Carter, strange as that is to me so many decades later."

"A throwback, Mr. Robertson? To what?"

"Carolina Carter, I'm sure," a female voice said, and both Abby and the elderly man turned to face the speaker. "Carolina was also sensitive and supportive of this town that was named after her family."

"Thank you, Ms. Himes," Abby said, recognizing the drab woman who worked in the historical archives at the library. "Yes, my aunt loved this town."

"I suspect you do as well, Abby," she said.

At that moment a middle-aged man stopped next to Mr. Robertson. "Are you ready to go, sir?" he asked.

"Yes, I am tired, Barney." His gaze switched from his caregiver to Abby. "I enjoyed our conversation," he told her, then allowed his escort to guide him to the door. Seconds later he'd disappeared into the night, leaving Abby staring after him.

"How very odd to see him here," Laura Himes said. "He has to be past ninety years old and it's a rare day for him to be out and about, let alone at a school carnival. Did you do a drawing for him?" she asked.

Abby shook her head. "I noticed him watching me

as I drew, and at a break we had a brief conversation. He seemed interested in my skill as an artist, said I reminded him of his first wife, who was also an artist."

"Goodness. That was long ago." Laura said. "She died shortly after the birth of their only child; he remarried several years later but never had more children. His son was killed in an accident when still a teenager."

"That's what he said."

"Interesting that he would be talkative like that. He must be getting senile."

"I wondered about that, although he seemed lucid while he was talking to me."

"What's really sad is that a great American family that played such a role in the formation of our country is gone forever when he dies," Laura said. "There is no one to continue the Robertson bloodline."

"I suspect my aunt worried about my family, too."

"She did talk about the historic value of your property and mentioned one option she meant to discuss with you." Her gaze was suddenly direct. "Carolina believed she still had a few years to consider a course of action for her estate once she was gone and in the event you had your own life and career in another part of the country."

Surprised, Abby's hands stilled on her supplies, which she'd begun to reorganize in preparation for new customers. "What was that?"

"You knew that your aunt belonged to the historical society?"

"Yes, you told me that when we first met."

"Well, she was thinking the Carter property could be preserved if it was declared a historical site by the state and became a museum with the focus on it having been a station on the Underground Railroad. Our local society would manage the undertaking, and the fees it generated would cover expenses." She frowned, thoughtfully. "That was only a possibility if the last Carter descendant—you—had no plans to ever live in the house."

"I had no idea," Abby said.

"It was only in the talking stage," Laura replied. "A backup option. Like I said, your aunt's preference would have been for you to live there, have a family, and carry on the Carter name for more generations." She sighed. "I'm going to get a cup of punch." Laura raised her brows. "Can I bring you one?"

Abby thanked her and declined, then watched her move away toward the food booths. Then she got busy again with more sketches. Sometime later the crowd thinned, the carnival wound down, and Abby packed up her supplies. Just before she was about to leave, Bud came into the gym to follow her home.

"All set?" he asked.

She nodded, closing up her cashbox and giving it to the person in charge. "I'll settle up with the school tomorrow." She smiled. "I haven't counted the money yet but I think I made quite a tidy sum."

Bud's eyes narrowed, studying her face. "Are you okay, Abby?"

"Uh-huh. However, I did have a couple of interesting conversations that were also a bit depressing."

"May I ask with whom?"

"Are you coming back to the house?"

"Yup, I'm still on stakeout status."

"Good. I'll tell you then."

He carried her supplies as they walked out to her car, then he followed her all the way up the hill to the bed-and-breakfast. She pulled into the garage and he parked on the street, then they went into the house.

She'd been feeling a little down, but now she felt her spirits lifting—because of Bud.

Chapter 50

"SO WHAT WERE THESE INTERESTING but depressing conversations, Abby?" Bud asked, as they sat in the parlor and sipped wine, their stocking feet resting next to each other's on a footstool. "And who were the people involved?"

Abby stared into the fireplace, where she'd switched on the instant gas flames under the fake logs, one of the few upgrades her aunt had made when converting the house into a bed-and-breakfast. Tonight she was grateful for the comfort it gave her, and for contributing to the cozy, intimate feelings she had for Bud, who sat next to her on the settee.

"Mr. Robertson wasn't the depressing one, although I found him a bit puzzling."

"Mr. Robertson?" Bud asked. "What's his first name?"

"That's the strange part. He is none other than William Henry Robertson."

"Jeez, Abby. You don't mean the old guy who's past ninety?"

She nodded. "According to Laura Himes, a librarian at the historical society who substantiated his identity, his history goes back to the country's forefathers."

"If it's him, it does."

"It was him, Bud."

He leaned forward, his feet falling from the footstool as he placed his glass on a side table. "He wanted you to draw a portrait of him?"

"No, we just talked." She explained that he'd been watching her do quick sketches, then she repeated the conversation between them. "I wondered at first, as I had the first time he watched me work, if he was senile."

"What do you mean—*the first time*?"

She explained her first encounter with the old man when she was sketching outside near the concert in the park.

"So this old man has sought you out several times now?"

"For God's sake, Bud, I never said he sought me out. I just happened to run into him."

"Bullshit."

"What do you mean?" She too leaned forward, dropping her feet and facing him. "That he was there because of me?"

A silence went by.

"I can't answer that for sure, Abby. All I can say is that it looks that way—and I don't know why."

She stood up and glanced back down at him. "Do you think I should refill our glasses?"

He nodded.

She went out to the kitchen, grabbed the wine bottle, then returned to the parlor and refilled the glasses. Then she sat back down next to Bud.

Neither of them spoke.

Bud was the first to make a move, reaching to clasp Abby's knotted hands in her lap.

"I'm on your side, sweetheart," he said softly. "I'm only trying to figure things out that pertain to your safety."

She managed a smile. "I know that, Bud."

"What was the second conversation that was upsetting?"

"Laura Himes, from the library, told me that my aunt was considering donating this property so that it would become a historical site, and any proceeds be donated to the local historical society."

He frowned. "Why is this upsetting?"

She took a sip of wine and repeated the conversation. "I can understand my aunt expressing such sentiments because her heritage meant so much to her, but I can't understand why she never talked to me about it."

"I can understand her feelings," Bud said gently.

"What?"

"Just what Laura Himes said," he replied. "She wanted to preserve family history but didn't want to control your future happiness."

Abby glanced down. "I realize that, Bud, and I honor her feelings. She was always there for me and I know she didn't want to stand in the way of my happiness." She shook her head slowly. "If only she hadn't died, we could have come up with a mutual plan, one that would have suited us both."

He took her in his arms. "Whatever happens, my love, you'll be all right." He fluttered her face with kisses. "I promise."

She believed him.

A long time later, Abby was alone in her room. Bud had seen her upstairs, made love to her, and then gone back down to his post in the parlor for the night. Outside, a police stakeout was still in progress as Carterville tried to protect her from a threat that no one could identify.

She lay in bed, staring at the shadow patterns on the ceiling, her thoughts going over the conversations at the carnival. She wished she'd thought to ask the old man why he'd attended the carnival. Something about him was sad, as though he was reaching out to her.

But why her?

Abby turned over, plumped the pillows, and tried to get comfortable under the covers. There was no answer, just as there were no clues to anything that had happened since her return to Carterville.

Abby threw back the sheet and comforter and got out of bed, straining her ears to hear anything that might sound strange. There was absolute silence.

She felt secure. Bud was asleep in the parlor and a policeman was on a stakeout, guarding her house.

She wandered the room, settling for a moment on the window seat in an alcove where she could look outside. Nothing moved. There was not even a flicker of a breeze, let alone any person in sight. Abby sat down at the little antique desk that rested against the wall under a side window, remembering all the times she'd sat there as a child doing her homework, daydreaming. She ran her fingers over the worn wooden surface, stopping on a faint groove in the trim under the long drawer that held her pens and pencils.

The inlaid panel moved.

Abby stooped for a closer look. The piece of polished wood that had always seemed part of a solid section of the desk was ajar, as though something was stuck in the crease so it was no longer seamless.

Remembering that the small desk was a replica of the larger one in her aunt's bedroom, Abby searched for the place that could open a secret drawer—if there really was one.

The panel moved, she grabbed it and gently pulled, and a drawer slid open.

She stared. Unlike the concealed place in her aunt's desk, this space was filled with documents that were folded and banded together.

What did it mean? Should she turn on a light and read the paperwork now?

No, Abby told herself, remembering all the times when she'd heard sounds, seen shadows, and felt eyes on her in this very room. Crazy as it seemed, she felt a need for caution. Quelling an almost over-powering curiosity, she decided to remove the papers and put them in a safe place, see what they were later. She might be paranoid, but she wanted to be away from the house where she knew no one was watching. She suspected that her aunt had also tried to hide the papers.

They were important.

Although it was dark in the room and no one could make out exactly what she was doing, Abby retrieved her handbag from a chair and took it back to the desk. She pretended to search through it and then took out her makeup case. When she replaced it in her purse, her hand also held the banded documents. Once safely inside and the clasp of her bag closed, she took it back to her bed and placed it on the floor.

You're totally paranoid, she told herself again as she got back under the covers. Who do you think was watching—ghosts from the past?

Or the person behind the noises in the night? She hoped not, because she didn't want to think someone also watched when Bud was in her room.

Chapter 51

DAMN IT! THE PIECE OF SHIT detective was in the house for another night. There was no hope to pursue the quest. Something drastic had to be done—and soon.

Again he hadn't dared get close to Abby's bedroom, although he could guess what was going on in there. It made him hot to think about it—and it made him mad as hell.

The weekend was coming—zero hour. There would be house guests, making things even more difficult. But not impossible if the detective was eliminated from the equation. He meant to do that.

He had a plan.

Now, as he was finally able to look over the house after the detective was safely down in the parlor, he was satisfied that all was ready for the next move. The bitch had been restless, had gotten up to look out the window, then had gone through her purse to check out her makeup.

Why? To make sure her war paint would impress the fuckin' detective? Was she preparing herself to see him in the morning—after she'd applied her makeup?

He suppressed his laugh. Later, he told himself. His

elation would come later—after he'd made sure that his future was secure and he could celebrate everything all at once.

After she was dead.

After the Carters had been wiped from the face of the earth.

It was years past when that should have happened. By this time next week it would be done.

There was no turning back now.

Chapter 52

BUD LAY IN THE SHADOWY parlor on the firm surface of the sofa, which in reality was the prim settee of a bygone era. Even with a pillow and blanket it was the most uncomfortable surface he'd ever slept on, including his boyhood outings in a sleeping bag on the hard ground. He smiled wryly, and reminded himself that it was a labor of love.

Yeah, he thought. Love was the operative word. He'd fallen in love with Abby and meant to protect her—so that one day in the not-distant future they could start a life together. His personal preference was to take her out of the bed-and-breakfast to somewhere safe, but three things barred that from happening. First, she'd never go, because preserving her family history meant so much to her; second, there was no tangible threat, no real evidence that connected her personal safety to her aunt's murder; and third, she meant to carry on until the killer was apprehended. The case was weird, illogical, and without credible leads in any direction.

Except that he had that hinky feeling that the motivation behind the horrific and seemingly senseless murder of Aunt Carolina was fast surfacing, coming to a climax that meant harm to Abby, too. But damned if he could figure out what that was. There was nothing in Carolina's life that indicated a threat, nor was there in Abby's, aside from the strange little incidents that had begun when her aunt died. So, if there wasn't an indicator in investigating the present, could that mean there might be something from the past?

Bud suddenly sat upright on his hard, makeshift bed, his thoughts shifting from the "what is" to the "what if."

Was it possible that something vital from the past had something to do with the violence being played out in the present—something that might alter the course of the future? What if that was true? Would someone out there kill to protect his interests?

You're reaching, Bud's inner voice told him.

Yet, one piece of his earlier conversation with Abby niggled at the back of his mind. Why had William Henry Robertson, a ninety-something-year-old recluse whom even he, a law-enforcement officer in Carterville, had never laid eyes on, turned up to watch her sketch—and for a second time? The last descendant of a historic family hadn't been seen in public for years.

Bud's mind raced with questions and possible answers. And then he fastened on several facts that his nephew had turned up in the research on the Carter family.

"Jesus Christ Almighty, thank you," he whispered into the silent room.

He finally had the best lead in the whole case and could hardly wait to get down to headquarters to check out the computer databases.

He lay awake for the darkest hours of the night, his

thoughts churning. Shortly before dawn he dozed off, but was awake and up before Abby came downstairs at six thirty the next morning, tossed her handbag onto a chair, then faced him, pleased. It was he who offered her fresh coffee that had just stopped dripping.

She smiled and gave him a fond peck on the cheek. "You know that most women would tell a thoughtful man who had the coffee ready that he was a keeper."

"I don't need most women to tell me that," he replied, suavely, trying to hide his humor—and his rising desire. "I only need to hear those words from one woman." Then he pulled her into his arms and kissed her with a passion that made him wish it were last night again and not the morning when they had to part.

"Wow," she said as he released her.

Her large eyes fastened on his face, her long hair shimmering in a shaft of sunlight that had slanted in through a kitchen window, and he realized again how beautiful she was, that the color of her hair and eyes was a perfect match. Jeez, he was a goner as far as Abby was concerned. He'd never felt so attracted to anyone before. No, you're a besotted mess about your feelings for her, he told himself.

He forced himself to straighten up, to stay professional. Now was not the time to indulge his feelings.

They shared the next five minutes together, drinking coffee. Then he stood to go with a promise to call later.

He knew she watched until he was out of sight.

Chapter 53

ABOUT TO CLOSE THE DOOR after Bud left, Abby noticed that the Friday newspaper was at the edge of the porch. She stepped out, retrieved it, then went inside and locked the door behind her.

She went to the kitchen, looking forward to her second cup of coffee while she read the paper, a habit she once enjoyed before she'd landed on the front page. A minute later she took her mug to the table and opened the newspaper—and froze, her eyes on the headlines.

FORENSIC ARTIST DOES IT AGAIN. ANOTHER CRIMINAL CAUGHT.

She sank onto the chair, her eyes scanning the article that explained how the drawing based on the victim's description had caught the teenager who broke into cars at the mall.

Shit! she thought. It was the Maryanne scenario again, naming Abby and recounting her aunt's murder. She reached for the phone and punched in Bud's number at the station. He hadn't arrived yet but she left a terse message, explaining that she'd been deceived by the police—and by him, who'd promised that her privacy would be protected. "Don't ever ask for my help again," she'd said and ended the call.

Ten minutes later he called her back.

"Jeez, Abby, I just read the article and I can't believe this happened," he said, sounding genuinely upset.

"I can't either, Bud. I'm beginning to understand why the street people in the city don't trust the police."

His sigh of frustration sounded in her ear. "This isn't typical, Abby. We always honor our source's privacy." His frustration was echoed in his voice. "I guarantee you that I'll get to the bottom of who leaked the information."

She switched the phone to her other ear. "I'm sure you will, but I'm afraid it's too late for this bed-and-breakfast. I expect the notoriety will motivate more cancellations, just as they have for this weekend. All three reservations were terminated, and had it not been for my former landlords, who are staying tonight, the bedrooms would be empty." She drew in a ragged breath. "This is a terrible blow."

"Damn but I'm sorry, Abby."

"Yeah, I know. As I've learned the hard way over the course of my life, that's the way it is."

He didn't reply at once.

"Jeez, life can be shitty at times, sweetheart, but it'll get better, I promise." He sounded upset. "Your old landlords? They've come by your place before, right?"

"Yes, they were kind enough to bring my laptop computer by after I forgot it when I moved."

"How does a person forget their computer?" he asked, softening the question with a brief laugh. "When I take mine anywhere it always seems attached to my hip."

"I'm protective of mine too, Bud, but in all the clamor of leaving that morning, the taxi driver left it in his car trunk when he unloaded my luggage at the train station. After finding it, he took it back to the Sells."

"What brings them to this area?"

"Family. The Sells have an elderly relative and a son living nearby."

"What are the relatives' names?"

"I've never heard a name, although the son is a musician and must be a Sell."

"I think you mentioned that they'd reserved a room, but tell me again. Why are they staying with you and not with the relatives?"

"Mrs. Sell said it was a party event and I guess they ran out of beds, so they're renting one of mine, thank goodness. They're really nice people who have also called me several times with updates from the police about my attacker."

"Is that so? Guess I should give the NYPD a call."

She gave a wry laugh. "Not surprisingly, that case has gone cold, too."

There was a brief silence while he digested her words.

"Okay then, you get on with your day and I'll do the same," he said, sounding distracted. "And let me know if anything comes up. I imagine you'll have more calls from the media once the new story gets out. As I said, I'll find out who told the reporter. It's always possible it was one of the victims who opted for their five minutes of fame."

"I'm hoping its old news by now and the media has moved on to more interesting cases."

"Yeah, we'll hope for that." She heard him expel a deep breath. "In any event, I'll come by this evening."

She smiled, knowing he couldn't see her over the phone line. "Before dark?"

"That, too. Definitely after the Sells are gone and you're alone."

"What does that mean?"

"A couple of things. For starters, I want to make sure you're safe, that no one finds a way in to ransack your house as they did the attic."

"You think someone was looking for something, don't you?"

"I don't know anything for sure, Abby. But all indicators point to that."

Her mind suddenly flashed on getting up in the dark, finding the secret drawer in her childhood desk. She'd brought her handbag downstairs with her but then had forgotten about the small bundle of documents—because she'd been distracted by seeing Bud and remembering their lovemaking. After that, she'd been upset by the newspaper article.

How could she have been so sidetracked? No, stupid. After searching for the documents she'd finally found them—and then forgotten to mention such an important fact to Bud.

Now, as she glanced around the silent house, her paranoia from the middle of the night surfaced again, and she resisted the urge to tell him over the phone. She was alone and helpless if a phantom stepped from the shadows, someone who could be watching from a hidden place—the person who'd trashed the attic searching for something? Oh God, was the pot of gold resting in her purse right now?

"We need to have a little talk about your options on leaving the house until we get more of a handle on what's going on," he continued, unaware of her sudden dilemma.

"You're right about having the talk about options," she said in a controlled tone. "But probably not correct if you're thinking I should move out of my own house."

"So, as I said, we'll discuss the matter later."

She was momentarily silent.

"Abby, are you still there?"

"Uh-huh, just thinking."

"About what?"

"If you have another reasons for coming by later," she replied, evading.

"I'll leave that to your imagination. It'll give you something positive to think about today."

She hung up grinning despite her fears. He was right. Abby glanced at the clock, already counting the hours until he returned—and she could again feel safe.

This isn't a house of horrors where eyes move behind the eyes in portraits, Abby told herself as she took her handbag with her from room to room. It's simply a very old place that has creaks and groans and you're just spooked because of what happened to Aunt Carolina and all the myths about the Underground Railroad stations. Still, she resisted the urge to pull the documents from her purse and look them over. She'd save that until she was in a place where her fears didn't kick in to scare her.

Although she'd resisted Bud's words about leaving the house temporarily, until the mystery surrounding it was cleared up, she recognized the wisdom of his suggestion. But it was still a matter of where to go and whether she could afford it. Sighing, she set such an important decision aside, at least until after the Sells left tomorrow. She was committed to stay until then.

They arrived a short time later, the two kindly people she remembered. Velma brought her a box of stationery as a hostess gift, even though they were not houseguests but paying customers. Typical, Abby thought. They're simply nice people—about the age my parents would have been, she thought. She immediately shifted her thoughts away from sad memories. Life was what it was.

Abby saw them getting settled into her best bedroom, the one with the connecting bathroom to Carolina's room, which was now locked from that side. After she made sure that everything suited them, from the ample stack of towels, to the freshly cut flowers in several vases, to the excellent view of the distant Hudson River, Abby left them to settle in. "I'll have refreshments downstairs if you'd like," she told them.

"Tea would hit the spot," Velma said, then turned to Jacob. "Will we have time?" she asked.

"You know, I don't think so." He smiled at Abby. "We got stuck in that danged traffic and I'm afraid we're running late. Our son is coming by to fetch us in about fifteen minutes."

"We'll have it another time," Abby replied, smiling, liking the idea of their staying for the night.

She went downstairs to the office. She needed to check on reservations, and the financial ledger. Would it be feasible to shut down the bed-and-breakfast? Would she have the money for the refunds if she did? Maybe she could reschedule some of the people for several months from now.

She sat down behind the desk and stared at the paperwork. Right now it seemed hopeless.

Abby knocked on the Sells' door. "Your son is here."

The older couple came out of their room, thanked Abby, then followed her downstairs.

"Your keys will let you in the front door," she told them, then watched as they went down the walkway to the street, where their son sat behind the wheel of his black SUV, which was parked in front of his parents' gray Honda. All she could see was the back of his head and a brief glimpse of his face as he watched his dad get into the front seat and his mother slide into the back. Then the vehicle pulled away and she closed the door, feeling puzzled.

Where had she seen the son before? Then she remembered. He'd been with the band that performed at the Music in the Park concert while she'd been sketching portraits. She shrugged. It was a small town after all. That's when she'd first seen William Henry Robertson, the very old man from last night at the carnival.

Her gaze landed on the hall clock. Good, she thought. Bud wouldn't be returning for several hours. That gave her time for what she needed to do next—finally have a look at the documents in her handbag.

And that meant going somewhere private.

She grabbed the keys to the Continental. She knew just the place.

Chapter 54

"I SAID I WANT A BACKGROUND check on Velma and Jacob Sell and their son—I don't know his name. All I know is that their kid is a musician and plays with a local band."

Bud sat at his desk, the phone held to his ear, and gave instructions to a Jeff Abbot at the other end of the line in the crime-scene unit. "That's right," he said. "It may be that you have to do a little historic research on everybody to either bring in or cancel out a connection to the present, and to the Carter family. Our town was named after them."

"Does this have to do with the Carolina Carter case?"

"Yeah, it does."

"Okay, I'll get back to you ASAP."

He hung up the phone, then rang his nephew who'd been working for him off the record. "Hey, you got anything for me?" Bud asked once he had his young relative on the line.

"Nothing much, Uncle Bud." He hesitated. "I did read in an old newspaper article that the reporter at the time claimed that the foundling, the baby who grew up to become Abby Carter's father, was born to the girl who died a couple of days after being in the same car accident that killed William Henry Robertson's son. The baby lived but was taken from the hospital a day after being born by an unknown person. It appears that no one followed up and the incident went into the cold-case files."

"Son of a bitch," Bud muttered. He'd been right. There was more to Abby's birthright on her father's side, and Carolina must have known or suspected. All he needed was proof, like a birth certificate for starters.

"What did you say?"

"Nothing important," Bud replied. "And thanks, George. I'll be contributing to your college fund."

"I'll tell Mom that when I get home."

He hung up, his mind fastening on the newest piece of information: Abby might be related to the Robertson family, and the old man suspected it, hence his encounters with Abby. That would explain why a man in his nineties would be motivated out of a reclusive lifestyle. He was hoping to find a legitimate heir to his bloodline so that it wouldn't die when he did.

"Shit!" he said. If that was the case, he'd want her alive, not dead. He paced his office, stopping in midstride when another possibility occurred to him. That's what the old man would want, but were there others who wouldn't—like whoever was in line to inherit the Robertson fortune.

He glanced out the window and realized that it would be dark soon. Damn, he'd promised Abby he'd be back before that.

The phone on his desk rang just as his cell phone went off in his pocket. He grabbed the landline first.

"Williams here."

"Bud Williams?"

"Yeah, who is this?" He was conscious of the persistent ring of his cellular phone and grabbed it, ready to talk as soon as he cleared the first call.

"The fire department. We're responding to a fire on your property. Your sister gave us your number."

"Shit!" he cried. "Hang on."

He flipped his cell phone open, which said that the calling number was Pam's.

"Bud, come quick," she said. "There's a huge fire right near your house. We think it's the woodpile."

"I'll be right there."

Switching phones, he spoke again to the fire department response unit and told them the same thing.

He grabbed his coat on the way out, ran down to his car, slapped his emergency light onto the roof, and, with siren blaring, headed out of town toward his house.

What in the hell next? he thought, driving as fast as he dared, grateful that the evening traffic was still light for a Saturday night.

He pulled out his cell phone and called Abby, to let her know that he'd be delayed. The phone rang and rang and no one answered. He'd try her cell phone next, but he had to wait until he stopped. He hadn't memorized that number and needed to check the little black book he kept in an inside pocket.

Damn it all to hell. Where was she? He just hoped she'd taken her cell phone with her.

Chapter 55

ABBY SAT IN THE YACHT-CLUB parking lot, watching distant boat traffic on the Hudson and the few yachts that had inched up the waterway to glide into their designated slip, guided by the skillful hands of the owners at the wheel. Behind her, a train rattled along on the tracks, slowing for the Carterville station to allow the city commuters to disembark. It had turned into a nice fall day, but Abby wasn't in an emotional place to appreciate nature. She was confused.

Night was approaching and she knew she should be inside her house before dark, but still she sat on, her thoughts spinning. The documents she'd just read lay in her lap, a bare-bones sad story that had affected the lives of a few generations. Had Carolina known the facts? Was it she who'd hidden the documents in Abby's little desk drawer? If so, why? What would have motivated her to do such a thing, to hide the truth from her niece?

Because it was dangerous. Had she been trying to protect Abby?

The realization came unbidden. There was no other explanation. She fingered the old papers. Were they the reason behind Carolina's murder?

Ridiculous, Abby told herself. Don't make assumptions. At least not yet. She needed to get home, show them to Bud, and let him sort it all out, find out whether they had anything to do with all that had happened, including the obvious search of the attic.

Had someone already looked through the rest of the house? she wondered. God in heaven, she prayed mentally. Don't allow me to jump to wrong conclusions, or any conclusions at all yet. The documents might not be connected to anything that happened on the Carter property. It could all be coincidence.

But something told her she wasn't wrong. She replaced the papers in her handbag and started to drive up the hill. On the way she called Bud, got his answering machine, and left a message to call her ASAP. "I've stumbled onto something that could be important," she told him.

As she drove into the barn-turned-garage and got out, she felt her neck prickle with apprehension. She made a run for the front door, glad that Bud would be driving up any minute now.

She needed him.

Damn, there were messages, she thought, coming down the stairs a short time later, her handbag still over her arm, as though she needed it. Upon coming into the house she hadn't noticed the red light blinking on the answering machine, her thoughts on replacing the documents in the secret drawer, the place where they'd been safe up until now. But once in her room she'd hesitated, conscious that her sense of not being alone was still prickling a warning on the back of her neck. Conceding to primal instinct, warranted or not, she left the documents in her purse.

Pressing the button, Bud's message soared into the silence.

"Hey, Abby, this is Bud. I'm going to be a little late because of an emergency at my house. I'll keep you informed. Stay inside, keep the doors locked and your cell phone in your pocket." His voice continued after a brief pause. "Stay safe until I get there, sweetheart."

The next two messages were from reporters, one from the local newspaper and the other from a national tabloid, both requesting interviews. "You've got a gift," one of them said. "We'd like to talk to you about it."

Abby sighed, knowing that Bud was right as she took her cell phone from her purse and slipped it into the pocket of her jeans. The word was out. She figured there would be more requests. Tomorrow could be a hectic day and she wasn't looking forward to it. When the Sells left she might not have more guests. After another round of cancellations she'd have to seriously consider an alternate course of action to keep things going. No one had to tell her that her aunt's bed-and-breakfast as a viable business was probably becoming a thing of the past.

And maybe it was time to close the doors for another reason, one she hadn't allowed herself to seriously consider: her own safety. Her aunt had been murdered and she'd felt threatened on a daily basis since coming home. Worst of all was the fact that she felt scared all the time while in the house: hearing strange sounds, seeing flashes of movement, and imagining that she was being watched.

She went on to the office and sat down at the desk, placing her handbag at her feet, her thoughts still on possible options for her future. That she had been living with a sense of impending doom didn't help her decision-making process.

The sudden ring of the phone startled her. She stared at it, wondering if she should answer. Then she grabbed it. It could be Bud and not a reporter.

"Hello?"

"Hi, Abby," Sam said. "I've been worried about you and felt I should call. Is everything okay?"

"As good as can be expected under the circumstances," she replied, at the moment relieved to hear even his voice.

"Are you referring to your latest fame as a forensic artist?" He sounded annoyed. "I heard about it on the news and couldn't believe that you would sketch another criminal, Abby."

"Yeah, I know. I did it for the fee, and because I was promised anonymity."

"Jeez, you need to get the hell out of that town," he said, sounding impatient. "Can't you rent the place out, sell it . . . something?"

"I've been thinking about my options, Sam, whether I want to or not. My reservations are canceling and I don't think the B and B can make it much longer."

"I'm sorry about that. I know how much the property means to you."

"Thanks, Sam. I appreciate your concern."

A silence stretched across the line between them.

"Do you need me to come up there and help you with the decision-making process?"

"No, that's not necessary. But it was nice of you to

offer." She switched the receiver to the other ear as she glanced through the doorway to the hall, where she'd thought she heard something. "As I said, I'll be making a decision soon."

"Okay then, I'll check back in a day or so, see how you're doing."

"I'll look forward to that," she said before hanging up. Then she sat staring at the phone, wondering why her life had taken such a drastic turn for the worst.

Too unsettled to dwell on her finances, Abby realized she needed to turn on the interior lamps. She kicked her handbag into the corner under the desk well, then headed toward the entry, intending to check the front porch first, wondering if what she'd heard was Bud's car. She'd taken only a couple of steps when someone stepped from the darkness of the parlor into the entry and faced her.

Her shock was so intense that she couldn't catch her breath. She screamed and started breathing again, grabbing the hall table for support when her legs threatened to fold under her.

"Oh my dear," Velma Sell said, rushing forward to steady her. "I didn't mean to frighten you."

"Mrs. Sell," Abby said, managing to whisper. "When did you get back? I wasn't expecting you."

"You weren't here, Abby. I used the key and came in." She shook her head. "I became ill with a migraine headache and my son brought me back so I could rest. I was asleep upstairs and didn't hear you come in."

Abby took deep breaths and her heart rate settled back into a normal range. "Are you feeling better now?"

"Much. The nap helped, but now I'm bothered by something else entirely."

"What is that?"

"The noise I heard upstairs." Her expression creased into worry lines. "I thought it must be you, went to tell you I'd returned early, but you weren't there. Instead I find you downstairs."

"What kind of a sound did you hear? Could you tell where it came from?"

"It was down at your end of the hall but across from your bedroom."

"That would be my aunt's room." Abby felt immediate alarm. "Are you sure?"

"Uh-huh, I'm positive. And the reason is because I heard it a second time once I was in the hall."

"I'll go up to make sure something didn't fall over." Abby smiled reassuringly at the older woman as she stepped around her. "We're the only people here."

"I'll go with you, dear, just in case."

"In case of what? This house may be old but it doesn't have a resident bogeyman," Abby said, lying.

"I'm sure you're right," Velma said. "It just helps morale for the two of us to go together."

Abby smiled. Velma and Jacob were such considerate people. She was glad to have them staying the night. But as they reached the upper hall and were approaching Carolina's room, she found that her apprehension had returned. She forced herself to remain calm as she turned the knob, pushed open the door, and stepped inside, pausing to glance around before she switched on the light. Everything was as she'd left it. Nothing was out of place. And there was no one ready to pounce on them.

Abby left out her breath, relieved.

"Over there," Velma whispered, having come up behind her. "Something moved in that slight alcove by the fireplace. Maybe it was only a shadow from outside the window but—but I don't know for sure."

Abby saw nothing as she crept closer to the indentation on the side of the fireplace where the window seat ended at the brick wall. Again, Velma was right behind her.

"See, it's just fine," Abby began. "No one is here."

A moment later Abby knew she'd spoken too soon. The wall moved, and a black-clad figure jumped out of the darkness behind it and grabbed her in one fast motion.

The last sound she heard was the brick wall snapping back into place.

Chapter 56

BUD TURNED OFF THE MAIN road onto his lane and saw the flames blooming like a bouquet of huge poppies against the darkening sky. From the bottom of the hill it looked as though one of his outbuildings was burning, that the brilliant red-orange conflagration might not have spread to the back of his house. Son of a bitch! He prayed that it hadn't.

Somewhere behind him he could hear the wail of a siren, heralding more emergency vehicles from the local fire department. He stepped on the gas, driving up the slope as fast as he dared, his heart racing in his chest, hoping he wouldn't see total destruction when he reached the top. Skidding to a stop well away from the house and detached garage, Bud jumped out and ran to Pam and Bill, who were already there spaying water on the flames with his garden hose. The first fire truck had arrived before him and the firemen were pulling out their big hoses to fight the blaze. They'd obviously called for more help.

The air whistled out of his lungs in relief. It was his shed where he kept his tools and garden equipment that was totally engulfed, its walls and roof quivering like red tissue paper, about to collapse. His winter supply of wood, several cords that he'd chopped and stacked into a neat pile over a month ago, was also burning. The back deck to his house, which was only twenty feet away, hadn't ignited yet, thanks to his sister's family, who fought to keep that from happening before the firemen arrived on the scene.

"For God's sake, Bud, how did your shed catch fire?" his sister called.

"I thought I smelled burning gasoline," Bill, her husband, shouted above the roaring and crackling of the flames as he sprayed the fire. "We're just damned lucky we were home and George saw the flames as he came up the driveway."

"I owe you guys." Bud had already yanked off his jacket to help his nephews, who were running between another outside faucet and the deck to dump buckets of water on the wooden surface.

The emergency vehicles turned off their sirens as they came up the hill and stopped in the yard. Immediately, those firemen went to work with the first responders, dousing the flames with water. It didn't take long for the experts to get the fire under control. A short time later it had been reduced to glowing embers that were sprinkled with Bud's destroyed equipment. The woodpile had become ashes.

"I'm happy we got here in time to prevent even more damage," the tall, blond captain told Bud as he took off his helmet and gloves. "The house could easily have been engulfed within a very short time." He shook his head. "We haven't made a final determination about the cause but all indications point to arson.

One of my men reported smelling an accelerant, which would explain how the fire got started."

Bud walked around with the captain as they examined the fire scene, discussing how it would be investigated. "I'll leave one of the men until we know it's completely out and won't flare up again."

"I'd appreciate that," Bud replied, his mind going over the possibilities of why he'd been targeted, who might have that strong a grudge against him.

A short time later the firemen left, although one man stayed behind to keep watch for several hours longer. When Bud finally went inside after thanking Pam and Bill and the boys yet again, he felt grimy and headed for the shower. He hurried, eager to get back into town and the bed-and-breakfast. Abby would be waiting.

He dressed in a navy turtleneck sweater and blue jeans, then went back to the kitchen and checked his messages. When he heard Abby's he felt vague alarm. Something about the stilted sound of her voice told him that whatever she'd discovered was too important to leave on his answering service. He needed to get over there . . . fast. There was another request from the crime-scene unit to call and he punched in their number immediately.

"Hey, Detective Williams here," he said. "Who am I talking to?"

"Stella," the woman replied. "What can I do for you?"

"I had Jeff Abbot check out some information for me earlier. Is he around?"

"Yeah, you caught him just before he left. Just a minute and I'll put him on."

"Abbot speaking."

"Jeff, it's Bud Williams. How you doing on that little project I gave you?"

"Piece of cake, Bud. Velma and Jacob Sell are clean. She's related to that old, rich recluse, William Henry Robertson. As you said, their son, Raymond, is a struggling musician, and he lives in a cheap apartment in town."

"How is Velma related to Robertson? I thought he was the last in a long line of important ancestors."

"That's right, he is. Velma is the granddaughter of his second wife. His first wife died shortly after their only son was born, and a year later the old guy remarried a woman with a small child, Velma's mother. Robertson's boy was killed at age eighteen in a car wreck. The second wife never produced another heir, and the step-daughter's child, Velma, is reported to be the person who'll get everything when the old man dies."

A silence went by as Bud digested the information. Jeez, he thought, the plot was thickening.

"Thanks, Jeff. Now I'd like you to look into another aspect of the family, the son who was fatally injured in the accident. I understand he was with a girl who also died a few days later, after giving birth. That baby was abducted from the hospital. I'd like to know names and dates on that incident."

"Okay, that sounds easy enough."

"And one last thing. Once you substantiate the dates, check out the orphanages in this and surrounding counties for the admittance of an infant around that same time. I'll want that name and date, too."

"I'll see what I can come up with," Jeff replied. "It'll be tomorrow before I can get to it."

"That'll be fine."

They disconnected and Bud immediately called the department for a man to be put on night surveillance—at his house. Then he strapped on his shoulder holster, grabbed his jacket, and ran out to his car. After informing the fireman that a police officer was on the way to stake out his property, he started the engine and headed down the driveway. Once on the highway, he slapped his emergency light on the roof, turned on the siren, and floorboarded it.

His fire was no accident, he suddenly realized. It was a ploy to get him out of the way.

For what?

He didn't dare think about that. He just needed to get to Abby, in case he'd used the correct building blocks to finally come up with the motive for Carolina's murder. If so, the woman he had fallen in love with was in great danger.

Chapter 57

SLOWLY, AS THOUGH SHE were awakening from a bad dream, Abby opened her eyes—to the darkness of a narrow, rickety staircase where the phantom figure in black was holding her upright, even as he was dragging her deeper into an abyss, her shoes bouncing down each wooden step. Oh my God, Abby thought, fighting panic. There was no chance to escape; her body would not obey her mental commands. She was a rag doll. She must have been drugged by whatever was in the hand that had come down over her face—chloroform?

Her thoughts began to race. The man's penlight hardly penetrated the blackness but she knew they were in a passageway under her house. Realization hit her. Her sense of being watched had been valid, as had been her glimpse of moving shadows and the strange sounds that had startled her.

Someone had really been in those rooms at those times when she'd dismissed the unexplainable incidents as imagination.

For a minute her mind stalled. There really were secret passageways that went back to the years of the

Underground Railroad, just as the rumors said. She and her aunt had never found any evidence of them over the years. Therefore, they had dismissed the stories that their house had once been a hiding place for escaping slaves, that it had secret entrances and hiding places. Carolina had called the old gossip an urban legend. They'd laughed off the questions from the few people who still bought into the rumors of unexplained phenomena. "Rubbish," her aunt had said whenever the subject came up. "The Carter family has a long history but not a scary one."

But it did. Momentarily, Abby's thoughts boggled again. She swallowed back an urge to scream, fearful that she'd be murdered then and there.

A draft of putrid, dead air assailed her nostrils and her skin felt damp and clammy. As they descended farther down the dilapidated steps, Abby concentrated on keeping herself limp, on not alerting her captor to her growing awareness, that her limbs were regaining strength.

Keep your wits, she told herself over and over. Pretend you're still unconscious. It might be your only way to survive.

What had happened to Velma Sell? she wondered. Let her be okay, she prayed. She wouldn't allow her mind to run wild, to envision what had happened to her aunt.

A few seconds later she knew that Velma was safe. They'd come to the bottom of the stairs where the pathway through the tunneling leveled out for a short way before it veered downward. Her captor still held her firmly against him, keeping her upright, dragging her along over the packed dirt floor.

"Raymond! Stop!" It was Velma's voice from some-where behind her, and Abby almost cried out in shock. Her trusted friend *knew* her attacker?

Realization hit her like an electric shock and she couldn't have run at that moment if she had been free.

How could this be so? Wasn't Velma on her side, the sympathetic mother figure who'd been there for her after she'd been attacked in her apartment? She'd believed that Velma cared about her feelings, had hated that she had to move, and had been instrumental in returning her computer.

But she knew Raymond, Abby's captor.

Oh dear God. Why was Velma involved?

She set you up, encouraged you to go to Carolina's bedroom. Why? Because Raymond was waiting for me?

Abby could no longer disregard the evidence.

Whatever was happening, Velma and Jacob Sell were involved; maybe they were even the ones orchestrating Raymond's actions.

"Leave her here, Raymond. She's out cold. We're safe for the few minutes it'll take for me to get down to the car and you to get back to her." She hesitated. "Your dad is waiting and we can't have anyone remember seeing him being parked there. A witness would destroy our alibi."

"What if she wakes up while we're gone?" the man asked in a husky whisper that was vaguely familiar to Abby. "You know we can't afford to have her escape now either."

"I know that, Raymond, far better than you can imagine. But right now I need to get down to the road so your father and I can get back before we're missed. If we need an alibi, I need to be where that can happen."

"I don't know," Raymond said. "I say she stays with me."

"Don't be stupid," Velma snapped, and gone was her sweet, caring tone. "You'll have her soon enough. Besides, even if she wakes up, there is nowhere she can go. The only way out of this hellish hole is where we'd be going and she wouldn't get past us. If she went back up the stairs and into the passageways, she wouldn't know how to open the various panels to the house or barn."

"Okay," Raymond said, and Abby suddenly remembered where she'd heard his voice before. *He was the man who'd been in her apartment.*

He was the musician in the park, the son who'd driven his parents to the bed-and-breakfast several hours ago. Was he also the killer who'd murdered her aunt? The shadowy person who'd stalked her, watching her day and night from those secret hiding places, the threatening voice on the phone? Why had he waited so long to pounce? Because he'd been searching the house for something—the documents that Carolina had hidden in Abby's little desk that were now—oh God—in her purse?

Abby's spinning thoughts ended abruptly as he let go of her and she fell onto the hard dirt. She remembered just in time that she must not break her fall or they would become aware that she was awake.

"We never did find those fuckin' documents," Raymond said as they stepped away from Abby. "You okay with that?" he asked Velma. "What if they turn up later?"

"They won't. We know the old bitch hid them somewhere on the property. After the buildings burn up they'll be ashes, too," Velma retorted. "And of course this bitch will be dead as well and there'll be no one left to make trouble. And this time it will look like an accident."

They planned to kill her and burn down the house.

Horrified, Abby watched as they moved away and their voices became inaudible. She waited another minute after their tiny light had been swallowed into the darkness, until she felt it was safe to move. Then she stood up on shaky legs and took deep breaths to steady herself, knowing she needed to get out of there fast. Raymond, the sick monster, would be right back. He'd tried to rape her once but had been stopped by his own father—because they were still looking for the documents? Tonight he meant to complete what he'd started back in her apartment.

Don't think of that now, she instructed herself. Get going.

But which way should she go? She knew the wooden steps were behind her and Velma and Raymond blocked the other direction, which must lead to an opening somewhere on the wooded hill below her house. It was obviously the old route from the river that the escaping slaves had taken so long ago.

Narrowing her eyes, she peered into the absolute-black space surrounding her and tried to get her bearings, fighting back her terror. It was hopeless: She couldn't see her own hand in front of her, let alone anything else. Abby realized that she would have to feel her way as if she were blind.

Then she remembered the cell phone she'd slipped into her pocket. Pulling it out, she flipped it open and it lit up the keypad. There was no service so deep in the tunnel, but if she could get to ground level maybe she'd be able to call for help.

Using the tiny cell-phone light, she found the stairs and started up, stepping carefully to avoid making noise. She kept the phone in her hand but used the light sparingly. If the battery died, she would, too. It was only a matter of time before Raymond found her. The dirt walls didn't offer even a crevice or an alcove large enough in which she could hide.

At a landing she flipped the phone open again . . . and almost panicked. Across the small platform the stairs continued up, but there were also stairs that went up from both ends. Which of the three choices led to Carolina's bedroom, the place where she'd have the best chance of getting back into the house?

She had no idea because she hadn't been conscious on the way down. It was a crapshoot. All she knew for sure was that time was running out. She crossed to the steps that were straight ahead of her. Even if they weren't the right ones, she needed to reach the top, which might enable her to use her phone.

"Hey, bitch, you can't hide!" Raymond called from far below her. "And there's no way out!" His crazy, high-pitched laugh filled the tunnel. "I'm coming for you. You've made this game even more exciting than I ever imagined." The laughing was closer. "I'm gonna give you a great send-off to them Pearly Gates."

She was climbing as fast as she could, still trying not to make a sound. If she didn't give herself away before Raymond reached the landing, he'd have to choose which of the three stairs to take. The odds were in her favor that he'd make a wrong guess. That would give her a bit more time for her call at the top. She dared not think about what would happen after he found her.

With one hand outstretched, she finally reached the wall that ended her climb. Abby figured there was a lever somewhere close that would open the panel but she couldn't find it. Quickly, she flipped open the phone to have a look from the tiny light—and saw nothing but the tunnel walls and the wood barrier in front of her. Feeling around would have to wait. She had to be above ground now because her service was back.

Abby punched in Bud's number and got his answering service. "Shit!" she muttered under her breath. She had no option but to leave a message.

"I'm in the mythical tunnels under the house. One of the entrances is the side of the fireplace in Carolina's bedroom."

Her heart almost stopped when she felt a slight sway on the staircase beneath her feet and heard the labored breathing of a person who was running. It was Raymond and he was only seconds away from where she stood.

"Velma and Jacob Sell are behind everything and their son, Raymond, killed Carolina," she went on, speaking so fast that her words ran together. "I don't know why. They plan to kill me and burn the property. I found documents that my aunt hid in a secret drawer of my bedroom desk. They're in my purse, which is under the desk in the office."

She hesitated, hearing Raymond come closer and seeing the point of light from his penlight.

"Raymond is closing in on me and I can't find the lever to open the panel and escape into the house."

Tears of frustration, fear, and a profound sense of loss poured from her eyes and ran down her face.

"Bud, I'm about to die and I need you to know something important, something I might not have told you yet because we haven't known each other long. I fell in love with you. I've never felt this way about any other man. Thank you for that."

"I see you up there, bitch," Raymond shouted from twenty or thirty steps below her. "You're going to wish you were dead long before you actually die."

Abby flipped the lid over her phone, ending the connection, and slipped it back into her pocket. That slimy piece of shit who was bearing down on her didn't need to know that she'd made a call, that she'd ratted him out. If he knew that, he'd kill her where she stood, then run. She wanted Bud to catch him—and his evil parents.

Then he was on top of her, his eyes glinting with anger in the glow from his penlight. "You're gonna pay for the trouble you've caused," he said between clenched teeth. "No woman does this to me."

His fist came from out of the darkness, striking Abby high on her cheekbone. She didn't even see stars before everything went black.

Chapter 58

BUD WAS ALMOST TO TOWN, another five minutes more and he'd arrive at the bed-and-breakfast. He'd returned Abby's call after hearing her message that she'd found something, but she hadn't answered. Nor had she picked up when he'd tried her cell phone. He'd kept checking back with his answering service, hoping to hear from her, but there'd been no other response.

And that wasn't like her. Something was terribly wrong; he knew it in his gut.

Damn but he'd screwed up, fallen prey to the oldest ruse in the world: the diversion tactic. Someone had torched his place to lure him away so that the person had a clear run at his prey: Abby.

The cars on the highway moved over when they saw his flashing red light and heard the siren, and Bud flew down the middle of traffic going in both directions. Somehow he knew there was a life-or-death situation about to happen.

Briefly in the clear of vehicles, he again checked his answering service at the department—and heard Abby's message that had come in only a few minutes earlier. Raymond's taunting threats came over loud and clear just before the call was terminated.

"Shit!" Bud cried into the empty car, his gut reeling first from Abby's revelation and then from the threat of what was about to happen. He pressed down on the accelerator to go faster, but the pedal was already floor-boarded under his foot. "The fucking son of a bitch!" he shouted, pounding the wheel in frustration. He'd kill the bastard if he harmed Abby. "Jesus!—God in heaven, don't allow that pervert to harm her."

Reason reasserted itself and he radioed the department with a series of orders. Get out to the Carter Bed-and-Breakfast and bring a SWAT team to get into the tunnels under the property. One entrance is in the side of a fireplace of an end bedroom. Also alert the fire department of an arson threat, make sure the house is searched, that Abby's handbag in the office off the kitchen is found under the desk and brought into evidence.

"I have a confession on my answering service by a Raymond Sell that pertains to the Carter case," he told the officer. "Make sure that Abby Carter's messages to me are also secured. We may get a voice match to the threat that was left on the Carter answering machine."

"Will do, sir. Officers are already en route to the location."

"Also, I want officers sent out to the William Henry Robertson estate to bring Velma and Jacob Sell in for questioning. They're the parents of Raymond and possibly behind everything that's happened in this case. I have information that Abby Carter is the rightful heir of the Robertson estate, not the Sells." He paused. "Just bring them in, okay?"

"What is the probable cause to do that, sir?"

"Jeez, man, haven't you heard a word I just said? Listen to my recorded messages and fill in the blanks yourself," Bud retorted. "It has to do with the Carolina Carter murder case, and the threats to Abby Carter and her property." He expelled a sharp breath. "I hope we can stop this guy before he kills again and torches the property. Just make sure you bring them in. I'll take responsibility for my order."

"Yes, sir."

Bud disconnected, realized that he was close to his destination, and slowed the car. He was the first one on the property. He could hear sirens approaching in the distance.

He unsnapped his holster and took out his gun. Then he moved forward to the house.

Raymond Sell was a dead man if he'd harmed Abby. Nothing would matter if she died. Except to get his hands on the killer.

Chapter 59

ABBY WAS OUT FOR ONLY a minute or two and regained her awareness just as Raymond was dragging her through the opening into Carolina's bedroom. She began to struggle and he twisted her arms behind her, until she cried out in pain, not allowing her to move even though her legs were still free and kicking at him.

"Stop it, Abby, or I'll kill you right now. Don't get me so mad that I think you're not worth fucking." His smile was a grimace, his face only inches from hers, his breath smelling of alcohol. "I've wanted to do that since I first started following you in New York City with a throbbing dick."

His burst of manic laughter chilled her to the bone. Any pleas or protests wouldn't help her at all. She was at his mercy.

"That's why I was in your apartment that night. I couldn't control my urge to fuck." His expression hardened. "My parents stopped me, said your death at their place could shine a bad light on them since I'd just killed the old lady the day before." His crazy laugh seemed automatic. There was no humor in the fixed stare of his eyes. "They didn't want anyone investigating them and connecting the dots back to you and your aunt."

Horrified by his calmly stated words about murdering Carolina, and by his candid explanation that told her he felt safe because she would never live to tell, Abby realized that he was a complete sociopath who killed with no remorse or compassion for his victim. He was motivated totally by his twisted sexual needs. There was no doubt in her mind that he wanted sex with her, but she would not survive the encounter. His climax would result from her death.

Her slim chance to live depended on whether she could get away from him. Abby decided to play his game—and hope for a chance to escape if he lowered his guard.

"Why would you want to murder an old lady who didn't even interest you in a sexual way?" she asked, and then marveled at her own calmness. Shock? she wondered. Or just an animal survival instinct that had superceded every other emotion to beat him at his own game, even if that meant killing him in the process?

"For the inheritance, you dumb bitch."

"My aunt Carolina was leaving you her debt?" she asked, her manner innocent.

"Shit, you are stupid. No, I killed her because she'd found out about you."

His reply took her by surprise. "Me? I have nothing to hide."

"No, you don't," he said, agreeing. "You've had a pretty bland sex life up until lately when you've engaged in—uh—activities with our esteemed detective."

Her anger was instant. "How dare you talk about my private life!"

He yanked her against his chest. "I'll dare to say anything I feel like, and if you object too hard, well, then I'll just have to start killing you now."

He drawled the rebuff and waited, watching as she regained her control, relishing the process of his power over her. His smile was a twisted leer, an expression she was getting used to. "But your grandfather who died at age eighteen did have something to hide, Abby. He had a girlfriend from the wrong side of the tracks who was pregnant with his baby. Their union was out of the question, your great-grandfather saw to that."

"What in the hell are you talking about, Raymond? Is this some part of your deviant sexual foreplay?"

He raised his sparse brows into a pimply forehead. "I don't think so, my sweet. Believe me, my foreplay, when we get to it, will leave you gasping for breath and wishing for a quick death."

Momentarily, Abby ignored his statements about what awaited her and asked more questions. If she was to die, she needed to know why. "My mother comes from a long lineage of Carters, my father was an orphan who grew up without a family until he married my mother, so what are you saying, Raymond? It's ridiculous to imply that my family is hiding something. If they are, for God's sake tell me what that is."

His grimace broadened. He was enjoying her upset, and in some strange way Abby knew that his power trip over her excited him sexually, delaying her fate.

Regardless of his motives, she had her own, and that meant learning why she had been targeted by his parents and by him, who carried out their wishes.

"Do you know William Henry Robertson?" he asked, feigning interest in her answer.

She shook her head. "I believe I spoke to him at the school carnival."

"Yeah, that's right."

She didn't question his knowing. He'd obviously been stalking her. "He was interested in my art."

"That's because you're an artist, as was his first wife, the woman he was married to before my great-grandmother, the mother of his only biological child, the kid who died in that car wreck."

"So what does this have to do with me?"

He slowly shook his narrow head. "You really don't know, do you?"

Despite her fear of him she couldn't contain her annoyance. "If I knew, would I be asking you, a person who is about to kill me?"

"Alas, the reason I have to kill you. Briefly then, in a nutshell," he said, breathing faster, as though he was aroused by stretching out his fantasy. "Old man Robertson is your great-grandfather; his wife the artist was your great-grandmother. Their son who died was your grandfather, and the baby he had with the unacceptable bitch, who also died a few days later after giving birth, was your father."

He poked a finger in her chest. "So you, my dear Abby, are the final descendant in the Carter family and in the Robertson family. The latter distinction sealed your fate. My mother, whose grandmother was the second wife, stands to inherit everything so long as there are no other living descendants to give DNA and upset the plan."

She was struck dumb, could only stare at his pock-marked face in disbelief.

"Are you saying that William Henry Robertson is related to me?"

"Yeah, kid, that's what I'm telling you, so you know why you must die. Without you, my mother will inherit a fortune, and she's promised to put money behind my music career. Not to mention helping Sam."

"Sam?"

"Uh-huh, my cousin on my mother's side, the person who directed you to the apartment building in the city."

Stunned, she could only stare at him.

"Close your mouth, Abby. Sam isn't in on any of this, and doesn't know about your connection to the family. He has no idea that we manipulated him into suggesting our apartment house for you to rent—because we needed to keep track of your whereabouts." Again he grinned, like something out of a horror flick. "We even arranged the opportunity for the two of you to meet."

For a moment she was speechless.

"Your parents kept my computer so they could see if I knew anything about my background, didn't they? The taxi driver didn't overlook it because it had already been removed from the hall."

"Hallelujah, the girl is getting smarter."

"Too late smart. Isn't that an old European saying?"

He shrugged. "Whatever. The lesson is over. Any more questions before we, uh, get on with things?"

She shook her head. "You wouldn't have the capability of understanding my sadness that I'll never know Mr. Robertson." She hesitated. "Did he suspect that I was related to him, was that why he came to the carnival, and to the park where I was sketching?"

"Yup, he'd been watching you for years, but he doesn't know for sure if you are his son's grandchild. Over the years my mother, her mother, and grandmother made sure that all documentation was destroyed or kept out of his reach. Then we heard about the copies that came to your aunt after your parents died, documents your father had been gathering to understand who had abandoned him, and why." His laughter soared again as he watched her emotional pain. "Did you ever wonder if their deaths were really accidental?"

Abby swung her fist at his face but he caught it before contact. "You sick bastards killed my parents?"

"I ain't saying yes or no. I'm gonna leave that in your head to think about while I fuck your brains out." His hysterical laugh was brief. "It's time for my ritual to begin—on your bed. My fucking will cancel out your tender feelings for the detective."

"Nothing will do that, you creep bastard. You may kill me, but you'll never see me lower myself to your level." She twisted out of his grasp. "The likes of you—and your evil parents—will never possess someone like me. You're all beneath my contempt!"

The instant rage that twisted his features was frightening, but now she was on her own turf and momentarily free. She whirled around, yanked open Carolina's door, and almost leaped into the hall. He was right behind her, and grabbed her just as he came out through the doorway.

Everything happened at once after that. Bud jumped from the side of the door and gave Raymond a fierce chop to the back of his neck, and the killer dropped to the floor without a whimper. Two police officers were instantly on top of him, cuffing his hands behind his back, forcing him to his feet, and then taking him away.

Abby collapsed against Bud's chest, and the tears she'd been controlling suddenly burst forth in a torrent, a steady stream that flowed silently down her cheeks. "I thought I'd never see you again," she whispered.

"There was never even a small chance of that happening, sweetheart. I protect my loved ones."

"Loved ones?" She lifted her face so that she could look into his eyes. "Does that mean me?"

"It especially means you, Abby." His eyelids lowered over his pale wolf eyes. "And it always will. I love you," he said simply.

"I love you, Detective Bud. And I always will, too."

He pulled her to him and held her close for a very long time. They could talk of what had happened later. Right now all Abby needed to know was that she was safe within the arms of the man she loved and who loved her.

A while later Bud took her down to the parlor, where an old man was waiting. He stood as they came into the room, walking slowly toward Abby. They both paused, then as if by a silent mutual agreement she was in his arms and he was holding her close, as if he couldn't believe that she was real.

"You are so like my beloved Melly, my first wife and love of my life," he told Abby with a quaver in his voice. "You look like her, you draw like she did, and even your hands look like hers. When I saw you I knew you were my great-granddaughter even though I couldn't prove it. The documents that were found in your purse substantiate what I've known for many years."

More tears streamed from her eyes. "I want to know about your Melly, and about your son who died so young, and I'll tell you what I remember about my father. My Aunt Carolina always said he was a good man even though he had no roots."

And then they both cried together.

Much later still, after everyone had gone and the Sells were in jail, Abby locked up and left with Bud for his place. She could never spend another night in her aunt Carolina's house. After everything that had happened in those black tunnels, and discovering that the old stories and myths about the property were true, she would never again feel safe there.

But the property that had once been a station stop on the Underground Railroad needed to be kept just as it was for future generations to better understand those brave souls who'd endured terrible hardship to escape slavery. She meant to talk to the County Historical Society and set up some type of foundation that would safeguard the property and its history and allow people to know the price of freedom. She knew her aunt Carolina would agree.

Bud took the next day off and they discussed everything that had happened, including his fire and her nightmare in the underground tunnel. He proposed and she accepted, and they agreed that their wedding should take place at his house.

"This will be our home," he told her. "You'll paint here, our kids will grow up here, and we'll be together in our rocking chairs on the front porch when we're your great-grandfather's age." She nodded agreement, her happiness reflected in her eyes. He kissed her, sealing their personal vows.

When they visited the Robertson estate—another place where Abby could never take up residence—her great-grand-father asked a favor of them.

"May I be the one who gives you away?" he asked Abby with tears in his eyes. "In all of the years of my life I've never had that honor."

She nodded agreement, too choked up to speak. In recent days she'd learned how the old man's second wife had orchestrated taking the grandbaby he didn't know about from the hospital, and then given the tiny boy, who was Abby's dad, to the orphanage. Velma and Jacob were willing to kill to keep the secret and inherit the estate.

Now she, her husband, and their son would stand trial for murder and an assortment of other charges. The police had also taken DNA samples from Raymond, hoping to connect him to other murders.

A month later, Abby and Bud were married, she given away by a beaming great-grandfather.

"Hey, how much do you love me?" Bud asked as they began their honeymoon down on the Jersey Shore.

"More than I can express," she answered, snuggling up to his lean body that had just made love to her.

"I feel the same," he replied, nibbling at her ear.

They were beginning a life together, one that was now enriched with family, his and hers. And, sometime in the future when they were blessed with children, theirs.